FIRST CROSSING

W·W·NORTON & COMPANY NEW YORK·LONDON

FIRST CROSSING

A PERSONAL LOG

MALCOLM AND
CAROL McCONNELL

Published simultaneously in Canada by George J. McLeod Limited, Toronto.
Printed in the United States of America.
The text of this book is composed in Janson,
with display type set in Ampurias. Composition and manufacturing
by The Haddon Craftsmen.
Book design by Elissa Ichiyasu.

Library of Congress Cataloging in Publication Data
McConnell, Malcolm.
First crossing.
1. McConnell, Malcolm.
2. *Matata* (boat)
3. Voyages and travels—1951–
I. McConnell, Carol.
II. Title.
G470.M39 1983 910.4'5 82-22327
ISBN 0-393-03282-5

W. W. Norton & Company, Inc., 500 Fifth Avenue, New York, N. Y. 10110
W. W. Norton & Company Ltd., 37 Great Russell Street, London WC1B 3NU

IN GRATITUDE TO LAVERNE EMERY

AND IN MEMORY OF ROD EMERY

CONTENTS

PART II

PART III

TECHNICAL APPENDIX

Before we began our long passage from New York to Greece, we decided to record our thoughts in separate, private journals, or logs. We are both writers, and we were aware that the voyage would offer us an opportunity to examine and record our emotions and our personal interactions under unique circumstances. We were also aware that the passage would affect us deeply and possibly change us in unforeseen ways both as individuals and as a couple.

Transcriptions of unedited logbook entries, however, make dull reading. We therefore agreed to meld the events, insights, and emotions recorded in our separate logs into one narrative. That this narrative is written in the first person from the point of view of Malcolm does not alter the fact that the scenes recreated in dramatic form are true and accurate renderings of the actual events, as seen and recorded by us separately.

As many sailors, and writers who sail, have learned before our passage, it is the internal, private voyage that one remembers long after the memories of dark wind and sunny wave crests have faded.

Malcolm McConnell
Carol McConnell
Lindos, Rhodes

PROLOGUE

Log Entry
July 20, 1979: 0400
DR: 38°45′ North, 52°35′ West
Wind: North force 6–7 (30–38 knots)
Sea: Rough (swell 8–10′)
Sky: No moon, 4/10 cu (cir-strat to NW)
Barometer: 30.94↓, dropping slowly
Sails: Double-reefed main and storm jib
Taffrail log: 978 miles from Ambrose Light

A cold, lonely night. I don't like the feel of the wind or the way the swell is getting up again. Hope we don't have another gale on our hands. We don't need that *right now.*

Problems:

1. Masthead and compass light keep popping circuit breakers. There's probably a short someplace.

2. The rudder is making this odd clanking sound: either we've picked up a piece of fish net with a float and that's banging, or the rudder itself is coming adrift on its shaft. Don't even want to think about that.

3. Can't get the WWV short-wave frequencies for a storm warning. Just static. Crummy Sears radio. Wish we could have afforded something better.

I've got a headache, too, my own fault for drinking three glasses of wine with dinner. The boat's beginning to pound again. We're pinching up too high on the wind, and the gusts are overpowering the wind vane. Must be hard for Carol to sleep. It certainly was for me. In fact, I haven't really slept since yesterday morning. Been awake all night, first reefing the main, then changing headsails down to the storm jib. Should have done it all at one time, could have slept then. Got *to get some sleep after this watch, if we're going to have another bad blow. I'm irritable again—jumpy. Got to check myself and not lash out at Carol. But I wish she was more interested in doing some of the navigation, so I could sleep in the morning. What's she afraid of? Failure, I suppose. Navigation's supposed to be a male prerogative. . . . Getting too hard to write now, we're pounding too bad, can hardly read this. Put the vest and harness back on, and go up to adjust the damn vane. Story of my life. Hope it's not going . . .*

The boat heeled especially hard to starboard and banged down off a wave. I closed the steno pad of my personal log, secured it with a rubber band, and stuck the pad back under the shock cord that held the navigation books in place on the chart table. Even with the hatch closed and the storm boards in place against spray, I could feel the gusts overpowering the wind-vane steering system. We were sailing too high, losing a lot of speed by smacking the steep swell rather than riding it.

Reluctantly, I braced myself between the chart table and the galley sink and pulled on the flotation vest over my oilskin jacket. They were both greasy with half-dry spray. The white nylon webbing of the safety harness was stiff. It would be nice if we'd get some rain to wash off the salt we've taken on deck in the past twenty-four hours.

For some reason, I hated going back up to the cockpit. I looked at the swaying accordion door separating the chart table and galley from the forward half of the cabin. Carol was sleeping in there, wedged into the low-side bunk, with the canvas lee cloth up to prevent her falling out when we rolled. It would have been nice to put the other cushion down on the cabin sole and curl up in my sleeping bag, braced against the bottom of her bunk. I had gotten drowsy at the chart table, secure in the bright cone of light from the lamp, warm and dry. Down here, the wind didn't sound so menacing, so lonely.

Hell. Nerves, that was all—just strung-out, overtired nerves. It was *my* watch. Carol had been up in the cockpit from midnight to three, resetting the vane every five minutes as the wind increased. She'd been soaked with spray and chilled when she'd called me. Now it was my turn to hassle the vane. I'd get some sleep in the morning. No sense stalling any longer.

Gathering up the loops of the safety-harness lines, I pulled myself up to the hatch, clumsy in my full set of oilskins and my sea boots. The boat was really moving around now. Bulkheads were beginning to make that nasty, snapping sound when we rolled back from a bad heel, as if the hull itself were starting to break apart under the strain. It wasn't, of course, but the noise was worrisome, especially because I was overtired.

Paused on the companionway step, one boot on the engine box as I crouched under the closed hatch, I could suddenly *see* the stressful gyrations the boat was undergoing: the forty-foot alloy mast formed the shaft of a giant clock pendulum, the end of which was the two-ton iron bullet of the keel base. The masthead and the keel were whipping back and forth every thirty seconds with speed and violence sufficient to produce incredible torque on the fiber glass of the hull, the keel bolts, chain plates, and swaged ends of the rigging shrouds. Crouched there under the hatch, listening to the brittle, metallic sounds, I knew I shouldn't worry about the hull integrity, but it was difficult to purge the pictures of terminal metal fatigue from my mind.

And I *was* concerned about the unexplained noise from the rudder, and about the problem with the lights. Of course, everything would seem much less threatening when the sun came up, but right now, in the darkest hours of a moonless night, the boat seemed almost flimsy.

I knew this feeling well. In the past two weeks, there'd been times, usually if I'd been trying too hard to fall asleep in bumpy weather, when the boat seemed a fragile toy, thirty feet of cheap plastic, weighing only six tons, hopelessly outclassed by the elemental forces of the Atlantic. At times like those, I'd lie in my sleeping bag and feel the delicate shell of the hull being drawn irrevocably east by the mindless flow of the Gulf Stream, out into the empty mid reaches of the ocean, where the big storms could breed and grow in force from the convergence of the Stream's warm waters with the cold countercurrents to the north. We were going to be hit by one gale after another until, finally, we'd lose something major—the mast, the rudder . . . maybe a hatch would be stove in by a crashing sea. I licked brine from my lips. Cheery bedtime thoughts. I hadn't had that particular spookiness for a few days, but tonight I was edgy. I was once again questioning the rationality of this trip.

We were almost a thousand miles out in the north Atlantic, five times farther than either Carol or I had ever been offshore before, and we hadn't had time to give the boat a proper shakedown before setting out on this crossing. The day sails we'd taken out of New York harbor had been made in relatively calm weather, certainly nothing like the gales we'd ridden out south of Nova Scotia, or this cold and nasty northern blow in midocean.

At that moment, still crouched, anxious, under the hatch, I didn't even bother to reassure myself with the comforting fact that we had sailed an Arpege sloop identical to this boat for five years in Greece, through screaming Meltemi gales with their short, crashing seas, out among the unlighted islands and rocks of the Aegean. Paused there under the hatch, wrestling with my nerves, it also did not matter that this boat had passed a thorough professional survey in New York. I was feeling the *weirdness* of the undertaking, the sense of isolation from the mundane normality of land civilization. There was nothing I could do right then to dispel this mood; I just had to get on with my watch chores.

The hatch was sluggish with dried spray as I slid it open. Some decidedly wet spray hit me in the face. Yes indeed . . . your 4:00 A.M. Atlantic Ocean with a near-gale blowing. The vane was way off again; I'd have to reset it and back up the tiller lines with more elastic shock cord. But first I had to get out of the companionway without taking too much spray onto the chart table. This involved standing on the engine box, removing the top section of storm board, then managing a kind of gymnast's scissors jump and spin into the cockpit while quickly replacing the board and sliding the hatch closed behind me—all in one extended motion, also taking care not to slam the hatch too loudly, thus waking Carol. She was no doubt as overtired as I, but she always tried to keep her fatigue and discomfort to herself through an unobtrusive kind of stoicism.

Getting out of the hatch under these conditions was not without actual or imagined risk. The real nightmare of a shorthanded offshore passage is the fear of one person going overboard while the other is in the deeply oblivious sleep of physical exhaustion. Naturally, having read the novel *Overboard* and several nonfiction accounts of this tragic occurrence, each of us was nervous about being alone at night in the cockpit in rough weather while the other person slept. I gripped the slippery wet fiber glass of the hatchway and carried out my gymastics as best I could, suppressing any florid pictures of going overboard.

After managing this maneuver with reasonable efficiency, I snapped the longest tether of the safety harness into the portside lifeline. If the boat took a real bounce now, I would not end up in the water. Sitting, I looked around, instinctively to windward first. The sea was certainly impressive, if not a little frightening. This was the first night since leaving New York without moonlight on the long watch after midnight. The darkness of the sky, matched by the heavier darkness of the northern swell, undoubtedly accounted for a good part of my jumpiness. I'd gotten used to having that chunk of moon overhead; it gave sense and form to the void of the nighttime sea. Now, there were only the dark, rushing clouds and the steady progress of the northern swell. The wind, of course, was invisible. I could feel its chill, and hear it in the rigging, but I had no visual stimuli with which to judge its true strength. I was anxious for dawn.

But that was a good two hours away, and I had work to do before then. Shifting on the wet cockpit bench, I forced myself to examine the advancing seas more closely. The waves were high and close together, the crests creamy white but not yet ragged. There was spray, but nothing too serious yet. Okay, force six, steady from the north. Our course toward the Azores was supposed to be 110 degrees magnetic, which, figuring magnetic compass variation, equalled 90 degrees true, due east. I turned and looked into the flickering red light of the bulkhead compass. We were averaging between 80 and 90 degrees magnetic, 30 degrees too high. While I'd been goofing off down at the chart table, the wind force had increased to the point where the vane was being continually overpowered. The first thing I had to do was reset the vane, bringing the tiller further to windward before securing the two lines in their jam cleats. That would help compensate for the weather helm and bring the bow back down where it belonged. Easier said than done.

After ten minutes of frustrating work, punctuated by soft curses at my own clumsiness, the gusts, and the Rube Goldberg complexity of the wind vane's lines and pulleys, I had the boat back on a reasonable eastward course. With the vane reset and the sails eased slightly, we took less spray in the cockpit and were riding the steep waves more smoothly. I untangled my harness lines and settled down facing aft in the shelter of the starboard cockpit corner. I could not see the compass from where I sat, but there was a bright star or planet to the west, just above the rocking plywood blade of the vane. If the star remained in that relative position, we were still steering east. I wasn't going to get too picky about a few degrees here or there, not with this kind of sea.

Carol and I had learned to use stars as steering points, celestial landmarks, ten years ago, sailing with Greeks when we had crewed on charter boats, the first couple of summers after we had gone to live in Greece so I could spend most of my time writing fiction. The summer sky in the Aegean is invariably cloudless, and, given the absence of city glow, the night skies are crowded with brilliant stars. Most Greek yacht crew began as fishermen, and one of them, Stelios, taught us the trick of steering on bright stars like Sirius, Rigel, or Altair. Given the short, choppy swell in the Aegean, keeping a bright star hanging on the port spreader during a long night watch proved to be more relaxing, and more accurate, than trying to steer a close compass course. Out here on the summer Atlantic, most of the nights had so far been clear enough to do the same.

From the low side of the cockpit, the rolling swell looked less wild, more manageable in height and the distance between crests. Also, for the first time since coming back to the cockpit, I noticed how much phosphorescence there was in the water. As we rose with each wave, the crest would spread into a flashing sheet of foam, branching into thick rivulets that raced past the stern. The boat would hang for a moment, heeled on the crest, then slide down the face of the wave into the dark trough. It was on the slide down that the phosphorescence was most visible: tumbling spirals of cold light exploding beneath the smooth wave face from the rudder skeg and the keel. At the bottom of the troughs I could look over my left shoulder at the retreating wave and witness a display of swirling greenish light, like a computer-graphic simulation of colliding galaxies.

Normally, the sight of so much phosphorescence would have provided a diversion, something to enliven the boredom of the chilly predawn watch. Tonight, though, the icy fire in the waves made the sea appear alien and hostile.

For the first time on the crossing, I *felt* the great distances around us. This cold sea seemed to be driven straight down from the Arctic, from the glaciers of Greenland, twelve hundred miles due north. For the past ten days we had been in the embrace of the Gulf Stream, with prevailing southwestern breezes between warm southeast storms. Despite the heavy weather, the sea and the wind had somehow felt less primitive, less atavistically threatening than with this cold northerly. I had been able to trick myself into imagining the boat on the edge of the Caribbean, not actually in the empty longitudes of the North Atlantic. At sunset, with the two of us sitting in the cockpit over a glass of wine before dinner, we had been able to look south and west at the gilded cumulus clouds and feel we were on a relatively tame body of water, that the southern breeze was somehow a mild extension of the trade winds. I could often sense the curvature of the planet, leading gradually down the gentle blue sea to the West Indies, and the tropical beaches of South America, eight hundred miles distant. That had been a comforting illusion.

Now I was acutely aware of our isolation. We were on a thirty-foot sailboat approaching the center of the north Atlantic Ocean. The nearest land was the coast of Newfoundland, 940 miles to the northwest. Out ahead of us to the east, the Azores, our first landfall, lay over a thousand miles away. Two days before, we had passed below the northern European shipping track. The New York-Gibraltar track lay over two hundred miles farther south. I sat with my back to the wet cabin bulkhead and tried to recall if we had ever been so far away from human civilization.

Maybe once or twice in Africa, when we were in the Foreign Service, I thought, then quickly corrected myself. Even in the Western Sahara, there had always been oasis villages or refugee settlements within three hundred miles of the routes we had traveled. In the Congo and in East Africa, the empty stretches of forest or savanna had seemed immense but had been, in reality, rather narrow. I was coming to realize that the truly lonely places of the world are not the deserts or the rain forests but the rolling gray oceans that made up three-fifths of the planet's surface. We were on one of the smallest of these oceans, yet it seemed impossibly big. We had been at sea for two weeks but had only logged one-third of the distance across. Crouched in the cold wind and occasional spray, while the boat creaked and rattled through the swell, I tried not to think about the prospect of another month of these dark and lonely nights.

Just then the rudder started clanking loudly, as the gusty wind heeled us into a series of high swells. The noise was muted through the hull, but I found it unreasonably frightening. I pulled the tie strings of my hood tighter and thrust my hands into the warm jacket pockets, wishing that the night were over. I also wished that Carol would wake up and come to see what the noise was: I would then assume a calm façade and reassure her that we had only picked up some fish net, that there was nothing wrong with the rudder. She would intuitively sense the poorly hidden anxiety in my voice and manner. Then she would want to stay awake and would make some coffee. And we could sit side by side in the shelter of the spray dodgers, the wet shoulders of our oilskins touching as if for physical warmth. We would chat about little things until I found a way to put my fear into words. In so doing, of course, the fear would dissolve. But Carol had earned her sleep, and I didn't break down and call her.

The dark, sparkling swells continued to roll toward us from the north. The boat rose noisily to meet each wave. The rudder clanked, and the bulkheads creaked. To the west, clouds had covered the bright signpost of my reciprocal steering star. I untangled my arms and legs, bulky in the salt-stiff oilskins, and leaned over to check the compass. The binnacle glass was dark; again, the circuit breaker had tripped. Automatically, I craned my neck to look up toward the bright masthead light. It, too, was dark. Above, there were only fast-moving dark clouds, and banks of coldly distant stars. I clearly pictured the boat beginning to break down. I could see a relentless series of gear failures . . . the rudder, the lights, the swaged ends of the rigging. Soon there would be leaks. Then, another gale, and a stove-in hatch. Behind us, a thousand miles to New York. Twelve hundred to the Azores out in front. The shipping lanes were a long way to the north and south. We were alone out here on the empty ocean, in a boat that had given all it could but was eventually unsuited for the task assigned it.

At no time in the years I had spent dreaming about an ocean crossing, or during the months actually planning it, had I anticipated a bout of nerves as bad as this. My pessimism was unreasonable, but it was all-pervasive. In the rational quarters of my mind I knew that my mood was a product of fatigue and a combination of small but annoying problems. I told myself again that the lighting problem was caused by salt spray in the circuit breaker box, that a cleaning in the daylight would solve the problem. The clanking from the rudder *had* to be some tangled flotsam—fishing net or floating trash from a ship. As for the snapping noises from the bulkheads, they were half-inch mahogany plywood; they didn't just *cave in* when the boat underwent these sudden rolls and heels. The bulkheads moved; they were supposed to do that. A well-built ocean keelboat like an Arpege was designed to be elastic. It was built like an airplane and could take the pounding of a full hurricane if it had to.

This rational litany had become a kind of catechism for me. If I repeated these comforting facts enough, I usually ended up feeling better. And, after a while, I was able to relax. It would be light in a couple of hours, and I could open up the circuit breaker box and clean all the contact points with silicon spray. Clearing the flotsam from the rudder would be a little more difficult with this sea running. But, maybe if we tacked and jibed the boat a couple times, whatever was wrapped around the rudder skeg would drift free. If that maneuver didn't work, I could always drop the sails and lie ahull while I used the boat hook to clear the skeg. As for the snapping noises from the bulkheads, it was really only the bulkheads framing the two quarter berths that made the worst noise. There were probably some loose bolts.

I hunkered down lower under the shelter of the cabin bulkhead. There was still warmth trapped between my wool turtleneck and the hood of my sweatshirt, and I wanted to protect and husband it. Repairs need tools, I thought, special tools, and supplies. We'd spent a lot of money on these things for the crossing. We had five different types of epoxy glue and putty, including some that would dry in five minutes, *under water.* There was a plastic tackle box containing an amazing collection of stainless steel and bronze bolts, washers, and screws. Under the portside quarter berth there was a plastic milk crate full of engine parts, spare filters, and belts. Up in the forepeak I'd stowed a sheet of one-half-inch marine plywood already cut up into pieces to reinforce each hatch and plexiglass window. And beneath the chart table sat a Tupperware container full of spare wire, solderless connectors, and electrical fittings. I'd measured the main-cabin dining table and found it perfect for adaptation to a jury rudder if we ever needed one. All this careful planning had been fun ashore; Carol and I working through checklists and long equipment inventories. There'd been an aura of honest-to-God adventure in trying to cover every possible repair job we might encounter out here, and in trying to procure the correct tools and materials to insure true autonomy, independence from the land.

I had felt definitely smug when I'd assured friends and relatives that we had the right gear on board to cope with any emergency. An ocean crossing, I'd told everyone who'd listen, was the big league of sailing, and a person shouldn't undertake a crossing unless he felt confident to face *any* potential emergency—from a compound fracture to a dismasting—and still bring his vessel and crew safely ashore. Brave words, easy to utter over beers and foolscap equipment lists while the driving winter snow of upstate New York clicked against the thermopanes. A thousand miles out at sea, however, strung-out from lack of sleep, huddled in the cold spray on the darkest night of the passage, the prospect of facing *any* emergency seemed too grim to contemplate. As for the repairs, I'd think about them in the morning, when it was light.

But before I attempted any of those repairs, I was going to get a few hours of uninterrupted sleep. Earlier in this watch I had heard the bubbling whisper from the cockpit scuppers metamorphose into a human voice mumbling vicious gossip, just below the level of comprehension. This auditory hallucination had occurred to both of us before, always when we had gone short of sleep in bad weather, when spent adrenaline and fatigue poisoned the system and the brain became oversensitive to threatening stimuli. Other sailors we'd known had experienced similar paranoid hallucinations: unlighted rocks in the path of the vessel, phantom waterspouts, or bizarre lights on the horizon. Carol and I had discussed this problem and had agreed that "the scuppers talking" was only a symptom of fatigue and should not be taken too seriously. The vicious little whisperer who lived like a troll down inside the plumbing of the cockpit scuppers was not a serious threat. But he was an unwanted stowaway, like rats or cockroaches. Unfortunately, there wasn't any easy way to trap or poison the little bastard.

The swell rolled down on us with the chilly gusts. I crouched in the sheltered corner, listening to the dark wind and the clanking rudder. Occasionally, the troll in the scuppers hissed slander and taunting insults. Around me, the phosphorescence in the waves grew less vivid as the sky began to lighten with false dawn. If I had been feeling energetic enough then, I could have prepared myself to take some sextant sights of the early morning stars. But it would have been foolish even to try with that amount of wind and swell. I'd be lucky if there'd be a flat enough horizon for sun sights later in the day. It would have been a waste of time to try for stars.

In reality, I had not yet mastered star sights. I'd tried for an early morning star fix several times at calmer dawns, but the lines of position that resulted had been so far off as to indicate obvious sextant errors. To get a good three-star fix from a pitching and rolling six-ton sailboat obviously required skill and experience that I lacked. So far, however, there'd been ample, clearly visible sun during the day to give me several morning LOPs, a meridian pass at local noon, and two or three afternoon shots most days. Also, our Walker taffrail log appeared to be quite accurate, if we managed to keep the trailing impeller free of sargasso weed. Screwing around down at the chart table laying out azimuths of three stars would just be an excuse for getting out of the cockpit, a weakness I'd already given in to twice during that watch, and one I did not intend to encourage in myself. I had boasted enough about wanting badly to sail the deep ocean sea; well, by God, the least I could do was stick out my watch.

So, I sat there in my corner, waiting for the sun to rise on our fifteenth day at sea, feeling more confident and less anxious in direct proportion to the swelling volume of light in the sky.

The wind seemed to have finally steadied off, a solid force six. We were making over 5 knots with these storm sails. And we were on course; every hour drew us five nautical miles closer to our landfall in the Azores. At last the vane was correctly adjusted to wind and sail. I could relax. Reaching under the damp rubber of my oilskin jacket, I adjusted my wool hat and the hood of my sweatshirt, finally snugging the oilskin hood back in place with its salty drawstrings. The boat was minding itself nicely. I could doze off now for a while.

Leaks and rips and splits, the nasty little scupper troll hissed as I closed my eyes. I rolled over to push my shoulder deeper into the sodden flotation cushion we used for a backrest. There were times when all of this became quite funny.

"Hey," I whispered, over my shoulder, "you down there . . . Hey, you little shit. You hear me?"

Splits and cracks and rips, the scupper troll answered.

"I'm going to catch you with the fish net," I said with a slow and menacing cadence. "Then I'm going to put you in the *pressure* cooker. That'll give you something to whisper about."

Keel rips . . . rudder rips, the scuppers hissed.

I rubbed my eyes. They were sore and crusty. The hell with the troll. Time for a few minutes' sleep. The wet cushion felt soft and warm through my double hoods. The boat was going to be okay; I'd just finish this watch then go down to my sleeping bag for a little while. Later, I'd get my fancy tools out and fix all these problems. Later . . .

I dreamed that we were back in Greece, in the village of Lindos, where we had lived off and on for almost six years after I'd quit the Foreign Service to write. In the relentless illogic of the dream, Carol and I were trying to move a house, which was really some kind of boat, up the narrow central lane of the village, using an impossible collection of hydraulic jacks and winches to accomplish this task. The cobbled lane was blocked by yelling, gesticulating villagers, each trying to advance his personal theory on how the difficult move could be best accomplished. The boathouse was fiber glass; its fragile skeg rudder was being crushed up against a massive gray rock that had somehow appeared in the center of the lane. The villagers hauled on their ancient winch capstans; the house jammed hard against its rudder. I was trying to shout, to warn the workmen. But I had forgotten all my Greek. I was shouting in meaningless English. The workmen smiled indulgently at my incompetence while they leaned harder on their capstans. The rudder was about to snap.

I woke, opening my gummy eyes to see the edge of my oilskin hood and the salty cockpit coaming, five inches from my face. I could hear the wind and feel the snapping pendulum roll of the boat. It was dawn. For several long moments, I was still back within the dream. Then the reality of the morning took force. I was on the boat. The anxious night was finally over. I listened for the whisper, but the scupper troll had gone to sleep with sunrise, like a little vampire. I sat up and looked to windward.

The swell was unchanged: high and white-crested, rank after rank of steep, gray waves. Yawning, I checked the vane and compass. We were holding our easterly course. From the high side of the cockpit, I could look forward past the taut storm jib. To the east, the sky was cloudless; the sun was about to rise above the heaving lavender horizon. Back to the west, where the weather came from, the cirrus clouds were less pronounced. Maybe we were going to be spared another bad blow. That was a nice thought.

I braced myself on the cockpit bench and watched with growing pleasure as the eastern horizon became clearer, acquiring the color of ripe apples. Always, the sight of the sun again after a long night was unreasonably pleasing.

My stomach rumbled for breakfast. I decided on using the last of the Brick Oven wholewheat bread from New York to make a thick strawberry jam sandwich. Then a mug of instant coffee with a lot of canned milk in it. Then maybe a whole can of fruit salad. No, a can of chocolate pudding *and* the fruit salad.

A junk-food breakfast, Carol would rightly call it. But I had a sweet tooth this morning. Probably my stupid anxiety all night had something to do with low blood sugar . . . as plausible an explanation as any other. Shaking my head, I felt a rush of embarrassment at the fears of the night. Broken rudder and crumbling bulkheads—goddamn ridiculous. A crummy eight-foot swell and I had started imagining us being broken up and sunk. This was just the way the Atlantic was sometimes.

I unsnapped my oilskin jacket and the bib of my chest-high trousers to adjust the multiple layers of clothing underneath. After putting on the kettle for coffee water, I decided, I'd make my sandwich and come back up here to eat it. It was going to be a beautiful morning; I'd let Carol sleep in and just doze up here myself until it was time to do the first sun sight. Whistling, I sat back to fasten the various buttons and zippers of my oilskins. Then I glanced to windward for no particular reason and saw the *thing* in the water.

I sat there, immobile, on the low-side cockpit bench. The thing hung near the crest of an advancing wave, windward of the boat. It appeared to be a collection of half-submerged plastic trash bags, probably garbage dumped off a merchant vessel. I thought I was witnessing a tangible explanation for the clanking rudder, and was actually relieved to see this greasy-brown mass in the water. The wave hung there, perhaps thirty-five yards from the boat. I looked closer then at the strange shape near the swell crest.

This was *not* a sausage-link string of plastic bags. The reddish-brown color was rust. Those objects were metal, rusting metal drums, maybe three feet in diameter. I found myself on the high side, kneeling into the wind with my oilskin jacket still unbuttoned. The wave rolled closer, appearing to gain height as it approached. Now I could clearly see the object in the water. It was some kind of flotation device, a section of dock or the work float from a dredge or salvage barge, maybe something off an oil rig. There were four rusting drums, secured in line with steel strapping top and bottom. Three of the drums were more or less intact, but the fourth was full of water from a triangular rip in its side. The wave drew itself up above the port beam. Stupidly, I knelt there, still a little sleepy, staring at the rusty drums as they bore down on the boat. They were only twenty yards away. As the wave crested more steeply, so that the drums began slowly to tumble, I saw the sharp metal grid bolted to the underside of the assembly.

My mouth went dry; a sour knot formed below my throat. There were three sheared-off girders attached to the steel strapping with long, weedy U-bolts. The girders had been twisted off, so that their ends formed a kind of jagged trident. The whole mess was sliding down the wave face now, gaining speed as the crest began to tumble. I could see the yellow clumps of sargasso weed caught on the metal. The object was now ten yards away and turning quickly as the swell steepened. This sharp fork of girders was on the forward end, three feet above the water, cutting a ripply wake on the swell face. My jacket flapped and the boat heeled to starboard. In a few seconds we were going to be struck by this debris. It was heavy and sharp enough to puncture the hull in several places.

As so often happens in emergencies, the flow of time took on a drowsy, elastic quality, not quite the slow-motion of a film but a definitely retarded speed of sequence. I thought that I must yell down a warning to Carol, so that she wouldn't be thrown from her bunk on the low side when I tacked the boat trying to avoid the collision. I also realized that the tiller would be hard to free because of the square knot I had tied in the wet lines from the wind vane, and the double web of shock cord I'd secured on the windward side. But before I could free the tiller, I was strangely preoccupied with the flapping tails of my jacket and the loops of the safety-harness line. I think some nonverbal part of my brain sent out a survival signal to avoid, at all costs, bringing together the tangle of jacket tails and harness with the web of tackle on the tiller. Obviously, my mind was working on the assumption that the boat would be quickly sunk, and that I must not allow myself to become entangled or I, too, would sink.

While I knelt, dull with indecision, the boat heeled over into a very strong gust, and the self-steering vane was once again overpowered, so that the bow swung to windward. We were climbing the steep swell at an oblique angle, and I was tossed off-balance, against the companionway. I clung there for a moment, thinking that the violent gust was heaven-sent, as it would sharply reduce the angle of impact with the girders, giving them much less of a hull surface to puncture. In effect, the boat had almost tacked itself; an "Australian tack," we used to call that maneuver during races in Greece, kidding Aussie helmsmen who insisted on sailing as high as they could. By pinching up like this with the vane overpowered, our speed was reduced and we presented a smaller target. I crouched down, gripping the port sheet winch in both hands, waiting for the sound of the boat being hit.

The wave finally crested to a foamy ridge. We hung there on top, heeled in the cold wind with the sail tops just catching the first direct sunlight. I was aware of the moaning wind and the taste of salt on my dry lips. Foam rivulets swirled past the stern, and we were sliding down the following face of the wave. We had not been hit.

Still, I crouched, staring at the flowery pattern of brine on the dirty white fiber glass of the cabin. The steep angle of heel lessened as we left the crest, and the boat clawed ahead again, the elastic cord on the tiller forcing the rudder down. I pulled myself up against the hatch. The thing was in the water, maybe five feet away, on the starboard side now, just below the retreating wave crest.

I was close enough to see the rusted double nuts and washers on the U-bolts holding the girders, and to differentiate between the dull orange of rust and the lighter patches of old red-lead paint. Turning, I watched the debris as it swept past the stern, ten yards behind us now, then twenty. I stood there at the hatch, my mind hollow and my gut muscle beginning to relax, staring after the brown jumble in the water.

We were in the trough again, lying almost straight on the keel. On either side of the boat there were blue crests. The next sea advanced and we climbed the swell. I saw the top of the alloy mast glow yellow in the sunlight. Next came the head of the reefed mainsail. We were cresting another swell, sailing well on course, almost directly into the hot golden eye of the rising sun. I looked behind us again. The thing was gone, invisible, as if it had never been there.

There was moisture in my mouth again. Sitting down, I buttoned my jacket and located a reasonably dry cigarette in the pocket of my oilskins. I sat for quite a while as the boat sailed along. I can remember lighting a second cigarette. I can also remember noting that the wind had backed slightly to the northwest with the sunrise.

The swell was opening up now, with the wind getting behind the east-going flow of the Stream. The sun climbed well free of the horizon. It was a bright, windy-blue morning, and the spray was drying fast on my jacket and on the skin of my face. From the wave crests, I halfheartedly searched the surrounding sea for signs of additional flotsam. There was nothing, only the steady ranks of waves. Whatever that thing had been, it was gone now, and there did not seem to be dangerous debris floating near it. The sun was higher. I was dull and sleepy.

Once more, I stood and braced myself against the roll while I carefully searched the waves for any solid object. Nothing. My stomach made noises for breakfast. My eyes were sore. In two or three hours I would have to take the morning sun sight. Then I'd have to check the bulkheads, circuit breakers, and clanking rudder. Nothing had changed. We were still in the middle of the Atlantic Ocean, two weeks outbound from New York, en route to the Azores and the Mediterranean.

Torpidly, I pondered the quirks of physics that control our lives. Of all the possible combinations of wind, sail, rudder setting and swell that influenced the speed and direction of this boat and of that piece of floating debris, the unheeding rules of physical motion had come together in just such a way as to propel that fork of girders to within inches of our hull, then slide it harmlessly away again. This near-miss could easily have happened in the dark an hour earlier, and I would not have witnessed it. Or, just as easily, the debris could have passed fifty yards away and been outside my immediate vision. Instead, we had come very close to being struck and holed, only to be drawn out of danger by a random gust of wind.

Puffing on my cigarette, gazing dully off at the blue void, I could muster no ironic insights on the rules of fortune. I did not feel graced by divine protection, although probably I should have. I felt only the arbitrary nature of the watery planet. Boats floated; oil drums also floated. The ocean had brought us close, but we had not touched. I could find in this encounter no lesson or pattern. On the scale of planetary dimensions, we were practically invisible, like microscopic spores on the roiled surface of a lake. The water of the Atlantic would continue to roll whichever way it would; our presence was neither felt nor acknowledged. The wind blew cold from the north, and the sparkling ranks of waves moved steadily south. The boat sailed itself east.

I sagged back against the bulkhead, smearing some new brine flowers. Breakfast and my chores could wait a little longer; I felt the need to take stock, to figure out what the hell I'd just gone through. Closing my eyes against the new day, I saw only a tangle of orange, backlit capillaries. I should eat; I should sleep and try to forget the crazy night. I opened my eyes and studied the endless, empty blue around us once again. Maybe I had hallucinated the thing in the water, just like the nasty voice of the little scupper troll. Getting up on one knee, I stared off to starboard, to the rolling void of the southern horizon. The sea was almost featureless downwind; certainly it was free of menace.

When I sat back down, I saw the accordion door jerk open. Carol was on her bunk, one naked leg braced against the portside bunk frame to keep her balance while she brushed out her long hair.

"Good morning," she called up cheerfully. "How's the wind?" The spontaneous first morning question of an offshore sailor, *How's the wind?*

I stared down into the shadowy cabin, watching her braced there like an agile teen-ager, a woman almost forty who once wore elbow-length white gloves at an embassy garden party in Morocco as she handed a cup of tea to the Duke of Edinburgh. For the previous two weeks she had washed in a bucket of salt water that had heated in the sun. She had reefed sail in a moaning 45-knot gale as the boat rolled and pounded through truly frightening Gulf Stream seas; she had wedged herself in front of a swinging, gimbaled stove and produced delightfully inventive meals from our canned provisions. And last night she had managed to sleep while the groaning hull slapped and pendulumed through the black wind.

I watched her brush down hard on the sun-lightened length of her hair. She had let it grow long when we'd left the Foreign Service and moved to Greece eleven years earlier. Nineteen sixty-nine, I mused, ten years ago already. She pulled on a pair of jeans, deftly alternating bracing legs as if she'd been dressing herself in a thirty-foot sloop, snap-rolling through a gale, her whole life.

"Am I going to need my oilskins?" she called up.

"Just your jacket." I tried to hear my own voice, curious if the tensions of the night tainted my tone. "I'll stay up here a while if you'll make breakfast."

"Okey-dokey," she said in the same cheerful voice.

I was amazed how a few hours sleep could transform her. When she'd come off watch at three, she'd been chilled pale and silent, squinting against the glare of the chart lamp as if in pain. Now she was as buoyant and happy as on a bright weekend morning somewhere back on predictable land. Watching her bend to pump water into the tea kettle, I decided not to mention the jumble of metal that had almost hit us. What good would it do to worry her? We were out here now, almost a thousand miles from land. Any direction we turned, the sea would be the same, so we might just as well keep sailing east, toward the Azores and Europe.

"How about some French toast?" Carol said, holding up the Brick Oven bread. "We'd better eat this before it gets moldy."

"Great," I said, "but we're moving around a lot. Are you going to be okay cooking?"

She was already breaking eggs into a yellow plastic bowl wedged into the galley sink in front of her. "I'll be fine. I'm hungry."

I sat watching my wife of almost twenty years cook breakfast on an alcohol stove that seemed to swing through a seventy-degree arc every forty seconds. In fact, the gimbaled burner plate of the stove was stationary, held by the gravity of the solid planet, the rocky crust of which began fourteen thousand feet beneath our feet. We were the ones who were barrel-rolling through the morning like a team of acrobatic circus clowns on some eastern European TV special.

As the pulsing globe of water turned silently toward its parent star, the boat was steering itself through the morning of windy sunshine.

I sat in this bright wind, my body responding now in simple, predictable ways to the scent of hot food and freshly brewed coffee. Five feet away, Carol breathed air from her dry nest below the water line. Bread and eggs turned golden on the stove. I squinted into the flooding sunlight where there had only been atavistic night an hour before. I felt the brine tighten my face, acutely aware of being in a strange environment, a passenger on a strange contrivance, in the middle of a very strange endeavor. I wondered what bizarre compulsion had brought us out to these rolling gray longitudes.

PART I

CHAPTER ONE

ADIRONDACK MOUNTAINS
MAY 1979

The winter was slow to release the mountains that spring. As we chugged up the long incline out of Tupper Lake, heading south toward the New York Thruway at Warrensburg, I could see banks of old crusted snow beneath the new green in the brushy hollows. Our red Chevette was trying hard, but she wasn't designed to carry a load like this on a steep grade. I downshifted into second and pushed the accelerator to the floor. We crawled up the hill, bouncing roughly over the winter potholes on our flattened springs. In the side mirror, I could see a big orange semitrailer coming up fast behind us, impatient to pass. There was nothing I could do to help him short of pulling off onto the muddy shoulder, and I didn't want to risk getting stuck in a quagmire, not with this load.

With the rear seat down to form a cargo bay, and with the roof rack holding the bulky, lightweight bundles, we looked like some kind of incarnation of the Joad Family in *The Grapes of Wrath.*

Behind the two bucket seats were jammed seven suitcases, two typewriter cases, a sail bag with a working jib, a neatly folded mainsail, two small duffle bags, several assorted briefcases bulging with manuscripts, and a twenty-five-pound CQR plow anchor. Up on the roof, there were three more bright yellow sail bags and a couple of old Army duffles. On the sloping surface of the hatchback, two rolled foam mattresses jerked in the slip stream, their garbage-bag covers already shredded by the wind, giving the entire vehicle a shoddy, refugee quality. I gripped the wheel, thrusting unconsciously ahead in my seat, as if to encourage the car up the mountainside.

Carol sat quietly beside me, working with her crochet hook to ravel up the cuff of her best Greek sweater. As we climbed the hill I glanced at her, trying to gauge her mood. We were a couple of hours into a ten-hour trek from Canton, near the Canadian border, to Brooklyn. The car was jammed so full of bags and boxes that there was no room to stretch out comfortably, and each pothole jolted us. But I was less concerned about her comfort than with her frame of mind.

Our destination in Brooklyn was Danny Dimeglio's boatyard, a spur of weedy landfill in Mill Basin where our boat was waiting for us. If everything went according to our improbable plan, we would sail that thirty-foot Arpege sloop 7,600 nautical miles, across the north Atlantic Ocean and the Mediterranean Sea, from New York to Greece. That was the plan, at least—in actuality, much more of an implausible wish projection on my part than a sober decision mutually agreed upon by two adults. In four months I would be forty years old, and I had vowed that I would sail a small boat across a deep ocean before that birthday. That vow had been easy enough to believe in lying under an electric blanket late at night while the leafless elms creaked outside the bedroom window deep in a frozen North Country night.

Winter was over now, however, and I had to face some decidedly valid facts, some reality that had been fully stripped of any vestigial romance. Carol and I now "owned" a very mortgaged boat; I had told everyone I knew that we planned to sail that boat to Greece; and now we were actually on our way to do it. This was no longer a dream for the future; the future had begun today.

The previous two weeks had been a frantic marathon of preparation: finishing up the teaching year, trying with only partial success to jury rig some kind of financial structure that presented at least a strong possibility of our being able to sail before the end of June, and, finally, the mundane but exhausting task of sorting clothing and personal effects, some for storage, some for the trip.

Throughout all of this, Carol seemingly had been as committed to the crossing as I, but also considerably less voluble. In the past week of hectic preparation, she'd become increasingly silent, and I knew she was worried . . . anxious about money, about the time needed to prepare the boat, and, ultimately, about our ability to sail that boat safely across the Atlantic.

Worse than her unspoken anxiety was my own reluctance to face up to my growing suspicions that this whole elaborate and flamboyant exercise was the result of a rather standard midlife crisis, and that I had unfairly snared Carol into my unworkable delusions.

The big orange semi passed us, mercifully without the blast of an air horn, and we had the isolated mountain highway to ourselves again. I was able to return to my musing speculation, which the truck had interrupted. It's funny, I thought, how juvenile moods can come creeping back into your adult mind when you least expect them. Here I was, about to begin the most mature, most serious project of my thirty-nine years, and I was feeling almost exactly as I had twenty-two years earlier, when, as a seventeen-year-old army volunteer, I had ridden the sooty old Northwestern Railroad south from Wisconsin to Fort Leonard Wood in the Ozark foothills, to face the rigors of basic training. I knew then that I was facing an experience completely alien to anything I'd previously known; I also realized that I would be irrevocably changed by that experience, and that I would return home a different person from the skinny boy with a crew cut who stared back at me from the smeared day-coach window. That experience and those changes, as well as the chance to save money for college, were things I had wanted badly.

But I had also been gripped by a diffuse yet pervasive reluctance, a kind of emotional inertia, which I would later recognize as ambivalence. At the time, however, I was not that sophisticated: I only knew that somehow I was uneasy. Sitting on that cracked leather train seat with my overnight bag held snugly between the toes of my desert boots, I stared down at the creases in my chinos, which my mother had pressed for me that morning. The next time I wore khaki trousers, I knew, they would be washed and pressed by my own hands. I wanted that semblance of adult responsibility, the duties of a peacetime soldier, but, inside, I was afraid, and saddened at relinquishing the carefree dependence of the adolescent. The cumulative effect of this emotional conflict was a sense of powerlessness in the face of the direction my life seemed to be taking. I may not have liked being there, but I didn't want to get off the train either.

In less than a month, I knew, watching out of the dirty train window as Chicago's northern suburbs came into view, I would be running through some muddy training course, clutching a rifle, screaming "Kill! Kill! Kill!" while I bayoneted gunny-sack dummies. That odd speculation was compounded by the fact that I myself had volunteered for this and had known full well what I was getting into.

Six years later, in 1963, as a very young and brand-new U.S. Foreign Service officer undergoing training in Washington prior to overseas assignment, I'd felt a similar kind of vaguely paralytic ambivalence when I filled out the form expressing the area preferences for my first overseas assignment. "Africa, Far East, Middle East," I'd written in, as calmly as I could, knowing perfectly well that any junior officer requesting duty in one of the new embassies the Department was setting up all over the boondocks of recently independent Africa was bound to get his wish. As I sat at that long table with my classmates in the Foreign Service Institute, gazing out the frosted window at the ice floating in the Potomac, I realized that by writing that one word, "Africa," on the top line of the printed form, I was shunting my life in exotic and unpredictable directions. Out there ahead of me waited the heat, isolation, and diseases of black Africa, not to mention the political confusion and civil wars we all knew were inevitably going to follow in the wake of independence. Unlike volunteering for the army at age seventeen, however, my requesting embassy duty in

Africa as a young FSO directly affected another person.

Carol and I had married when we were both still in college, each working to pay our own way through the University of Wisconsin. We'd known each other since high school in Milwaukee, and when we met again at Madison we formed a kind of natural hometown "unit." Both our families had tried without much success to delay our marriage until after graduation: the sensible course of action. But I was single-minded to the point of stubborness. And, to my surprise, Carol showed herself to be just as determined. We got married when I was a junior and she was still a sophomore.

After eighteen months of what they called married bliss we faced our first real crisis together. I had been selected as a Foreign Service officer and had to begin language training and area studies in Washington prior to overseas assignment. Carol still had at least one semester to go before completing her degree. But my superiors at the Foreign Service Institute stressed the importance of wives joining their husbands for as much of the training as possible. In those days, it was assumed that the officer in the family was always the husband and the wife the dependent who dutifully joined him.

I'm sure the psychologists on lucrative consultancies to the State Department had warned of the grave moral dangers unattached young FSO husbands faced in the flesh-pots of Georgetown, not to mention the unspeakable degeneracy that might threaten young wives suddenly left unguarded back in the lusty Midwest. Whatever the reason, my bosses encouraged Carol to sacrifice her degree and come with me to Washington.

It is indicative of the prevailing mentality that I simply assumed Carol would come with me. I never once considered delaying my appointment until she finished her degree. After all, I was the man; I would have a brilliant career and Carol would assist me, an attractive complement to an intelligent and ambitious young officer.

When I sat filling out my area preference form at the institute, I did have a couple of twinges of conscience. It was one thing for Carol to sacrifice her professional ambitions with the promise of embassy assignments in London or Rome, but had she considered Abidjan or Leopoldville when she'd made her decision? I recognized that I was dragging her off on an odyssey the outcome of which neither of us could predict. Not for the first or last time in my life, I pondered why I felt this compulsion for unique experience, why I wasn't satisfied with the normal; why, for example, I wasn't writing "Western Europe" on my form like most of my young colleagues.

I asked the same question six and a half years after that cold February morning in Foggy Bottom. As a United States consul in Tangier, Morocco, aged twenty-nine, I was about to face another risky watershed: submitting my resignation letter to Washington. As I sealed the brown envelope, I was assailed by the same sense of emotional isolation I'd felt at seventeen on the train and again at age twenty-three in Washington. Although I was one of the youngest people to be granted consular rank in the history of the Foreign Service, I was chucking in this promising career to go off to a Greek island and actually attempt to make a living as a fiction writer. I carried the important letter slowly down the consulate corridor to the vault door of the pouch room, realizing that a lot of people would think I was crazy.

Our living conditions in Tangier were luxurious, a three-story suburban villa with swimming pool and a lovely terraced garden. My duties as consul and director of the American Cultural Center were not very stressful. And Carol had an interesting job directing the American English Teaching program and expanding its operations, bringing together AID funding and Peace Corps English teachers: a position that made good use of her organizational and administrative talents. Our life in Tangier was a peaceful and rewarding refuge after five years of hectic work in the Congo and Rwanda, three of those years spent upcountry in small, isolated posts during the protracted turmoil of the Simba rebellion. One would have expected me to be satisfied with what I had.

Further, one would have expected such an urbane and patently reasonable young man to have consulted his wife before he decided to walk away from such a comfortable life and promising career. But I did not. I came home one day from my office, made a rather larger-than-normal pitcher of martinis—unconscious at the time to the fact that I was using $2.43 PX Beefeaters—and announced to Carol that I was going to quit, to resign my commission as a Foreign Service officer, and that *we* would move someplace cheap, peaceful, and beautiful so that *I* could write the great goddamn American novel, or at least an approximation thereof.

Carol sat on the leather couch in our tiled parlor, staring into the sputtering coals in the fireplace. The martini pitcher was empty. I prattled on, glibly explaining that there was no real "risk" involved in this decision; if my book didn't work out, I could always come back in the Foreign Service—as long as I didn't wait too long. She remained silent for quite a while, then looked up and asked if she could have some time to think about my decision. I was already in the door of the long hallway leading to the kitchen pantry, where we kept our well-stocked liquor cabinet.

"Sure," I said, my mind already on such important questions as whether I should grow a fashionable counterculture mustache to fit my new role of novelist, and whether I could somehow order a new IBM typewriter with a 220-volt motor while I still had APO mail privileges. Say what they will about the sixties being a time for general consciousness raising, I somehow missed the boat. I remained a vintage American macho husband: I made the important decisions; my wife naturally came along with me. That was her job—never mind what her profession was.

As I mixed the second pitcher of martinis that night, I smiled out the leaded-glass window of the pantry at the wet Levanter blowing through the Straits. Yippee for me; I was about to taste some real freedom. Soon I'd be rich and famous. In the parlor, Carol sat very still on the couch, staring at the red embers.

We went to Greece, to a village called Lindos on the island of Rhodes. For the next five years Lindos was our home, and we learned to live a different kind of life, devoid of the glitter and protective but constraining bureaucratic cocoon that comes with a black diplomatic passport. The house we rented in the village had been built for a fifteenth-century merchant, cut into the granite of the acropolis close beside the Hellenistic amphitheater. The tower room, where the medieval merchant had stored his grain and cloth, became my studio. I could look out over the blue cove of St. Paul's Bay, and beyond it to the dark swell of the Aegean. It was a wonderful room in which to work. I wrote my first two novels in that tranquil, whitewashed tower.

For five years Carol and I had what can only be described as an "idyllic" life in Lindos. The village itself must be one of the most aesthetically pleasing towns in the Mediterranean: a white jumble of cubistic houses spread across a rocky saddle separating the shear granite acropolis from a spur of wooded coastal mountains. On either side of the acropolis promontory lay two circular bays of transparent blue.

When we got to Lindos in 1969, there were perhaps thirty foreign painters, craftsmen, and writers living there among five hundred Greek villagers. Neither the prosperity nor the inflation of northern Europe had yet reached the Greek islands, and life was both quiet and almost ludicrously cheap. We rented our first house for twenty dollars a month, a house that was later sold to a British rock star for over a hundred thousand. But at the time, we were not concerned with investing our savings in a village house; we felt we had entered a kind of timeless, immutable utopia where our hard-working clan of expatriate artists could coexist in mutually rewarding harmony with the community of villagers.

For several years, most of us never thought much about inflation or the ruthless juggernaut of mass, package tourism. While I worked each day, drafting and rewriting, Carol edited my earlier drafts and other writers' manuscripts. Again, her organizational skills found good use. By the end of our second year in Lindos, she had developed into a first-rate professional editor and had also begun writing her own fiction.

Our life in Greece had settled down to a rewarding and stimulating simplicity. During the winter we wrote; during the summer we sailed. The first two years in Lindos, we crewed on a large charter yawl belonging to a German friend; the next three sailing seasons we ran a charter sloop ourselves, in partnership with a Frenchman. Those three summers of running a charter sailboat taught us a great deal about the sea and about ourselves as sailors. We cruised the entire Aegean, all the way from Mount Athos to the southern coast of Turkey, from the Dardanelles to Crete.

As an English skipper we knew once put it, running a charter sailboat business is the best merchant marine academy in the world. Because you have to do everything yourself, and because you also have to convince your paying guests that you're fully competent in all facets of seamanship, you quickly become expert in navigation, mechanics, sail and rigging repair, crew morale, weather forecasting, foreign languages, and maybe even maritime law. Although neither of us considered himself truly expert in these skills, we both learned an amazing amount about seamanship working five seasons on charter boats in Greece.

Almost unnoticed, our whitewashed village and the tranquil, productive life we led there began to be eroded by the twin problems of inflation and the mass tourism brought by the European prosperity that had engendered that inflation. Soon, the tourist season extended from May through September, then April through October. Prices rose. Discotheques and trendy boutiques began to choke the cobbled village lanes. The incongruous, amplified dissonance of the Bee Gees and Kiss echoed off the medieval walls until dawn each summer night. Mass-produced "Greek" blankets and shirts—imported by the bale-load from Taiwan—fluttered from almost every courtyard doorway facing the tourist stream up to the acropolis. The two bays became noisy with water ski boats and gaudy pink *pedalos.* It was time to leave.

When Carol and I moved back to the States, we fell into a disruptive pattern of one-year and even one-semester university assignments, with me teaching as writer-in-residence at various universities in the flat monotony of the Midwest. Soon it was 1979; swelling inflation and a rapidly diminishing market for serious fiction had us living on the shakiest financial ground of our adult life together. There was a relentless, spiraling quality to our dilemma: in order to keep writing decent fiction, I needed plenty of free time, and to achieve this, I had to accept part-time, temporary appointments. What little extra we were able to save was soon eaten up with moving expenses and the need to rent short-lease, furnished apartments.

Separately and together, we found ourselves increasingly gripped by nostalgia for the halcyon days in Lindos, for a simple, quiet life, with candlelit dinners in the vine-covered courtyard, and long afternoons swimming in deserted bays rimmed by clean white sand. But each of us eventually had to admit that such nostalgia was escapist delusion. If we were ever going to find a tranquil island life again in the Aegean, it would not be in Lindos. After rejecting this romantic longing for the irretrievable past, I found that I needed another sustaining dream to help me make it through the hectic drudgery of working on my own books each morning, teaching all afternoon, and red-penciling Freshman Composition papers and student short stories late into each night.

Unannounced to Carol, I made the firm, private resolution that we would somehow blast out of this cage of mediocrity if only we could get our finances squared away. If, for example, I were able to land a decent advance on a new novel, and if that advance coincided with a good royalty payment from an earlier book, then we would buy a sailboat and sail it all the way from the States to Greece. In that way, we would have our own boat to live aboard and to cruise among the unspoiled islands of the Greek archipelago during the long academic vacations each summer.

The relevance of the fact that I had acquired this ambition shortly after my thirty-ninth birthday did not register for several months. Midlife crises, like a softening waistline and gray hair, always had seemed to me to be unfortunate afflictions that struck other people. However, once I had embraced this new dream, I became fully and unreasonably committed to it.

My obsession to sail a small boat across an ocean did in part go beyond the normal restlessness we all feel approaching middle age. I knew that if we didn't take the first real opportunity we had to buy a boat and make the crossing, we might not get the chance again. The world was changing rapidly, becoming more violent, less predictable. I had lived and traveled professionally on four continents and had chalked up almost ten years in the Third World. From this experience, I'd absorbed a pessimistic view of the planet's immediate future. I did not give in to the utter despair of accepting a nuclear holocaust as inevitable, but I had to agree with leading contemporary thinkers who predicted that the coming twenty to fifty years would be a cataclysmic period of unpredictable change for mankind and for the planetary ecosystem over which we arrogantly claim sovereignty.

Deep down, I was afraid that any life I might be able to live for the thirty or forty years I had remaining would be a shoddy parody of those stolen years we had in Lindos before the inevitable bludgeon of twentieth-century progress fell on the village. The easy, installment-plan prosperity and unrestrained social tolerance of the sixties and early seventies had been smothered by more permanent realities. All over the world, package tourism was invading even the most isolated corners of tranquillity. The chemical and radioactive poisoning of the biosphere that had begun in the industrial North was becoming evident on a staggering scale all over the Third World. I also recognized that, should I choose to remain a writer and a writing teacher, I'd have to put up with the economic incongruities and dislocations that America was bound to undergo in the next thirty years.

I really did not envision any old-fashioned stability during the remainder of my life. There were bound to be hard times ahead: credit squeezes for us middle-class strivers, shrinking funds for universities, a mushy publishing industry, and violent squabbles over tight resources on a planetary scale. It didn't take the insight of a pundit to see this coming. But I wasn't a survivalist who mortgaged his trilevel to buy contraband Armalites and freeze-dried potatoes to hoard in some secret bunker in the mountains. I just wanted the chance to experience the freedom on the sea we had first known in Greece. I did not consider myself unrealistic or especially hedonistic. Most of us who'd lived and worked as writers and journalists during the sixties and seventies accepted this pessimistic assessment.

I knew that Carol shared many of these views, but I also knew that she hoped a certain kind of stability was still possible in our lives. Her pessimism was tempered by the dream that one of my books would one day catch on, that there would be a movie sale, and a main selection by a book club, probably even half an hour on the Dick

Cavett Show, with me wearing a new tweed sports coat—in one inside pocket there'd no doubt be the deed to a house on an unspoiled Greek island and in the other a glowing letter from our stockbroker. But I was not so sanguine, not by a long shot.

It was funny: Carol did not want a suburban-house-two-point-three-kids-a-dog-and-a-cat stability, but she did dream about getting out of debt and finding a quiet place near the sea where we could both write and live a productive life among interesting, like-minded people. I was not at all sure how investing in a small boat to sail seven thousand miles to Greece would fit into those plans. But I did know one thing: any chunk of advance money or royalties that came in, sufficient to buy an ocean-going sailboat, could also be used to get us free of debt and would go a long way toward establishing that life she envisioned.

We each had to hold our private dreams in abeyance for several years after we came back to the States in the late seventies. We knocked around from college to college and managed somehow to afford charter flights back to Greece each summer. There we sailed a friend's Arpege sloop and each nurtured a private dream: for me, an ocean crossing; for Carol, a renovated house in a secluded bay on an untouched island like Khálki.

In the bitter-cold month of February 1979, events coincided in such a way as to make my dormant ambition spring to life. I was on a one-year visiting professorship at St. Lawrence University, way up in Canton, in New York's North Country, close by the Seaway and the Canadian border, an area on the slope of the Adirondacks where, I'd been told, there was nothing between us and the North Pole but two medium-sized hills and three pine trees. When the temperature sank to thirty below and stayed there, day and night, for six straight days, I believed the business about the pole's proximity. We were a long way from the Aegean sun and the stark brown grace of the islands, from the blue coves and clean, uncrowded anchorages of the southern Dodecanese. Outside our cramped apartment, the steep banks of crusted snow, crisscrossed by ski tracks and stained with dog piss, seemed permanent features of the landscape, like summer glaciers in the Ice Age. It seemed as if we'd never get back to Greece, that this long winter would never end.

I was teaching three classes each afternoon and working hard each morning, trying to complete the second draft of a new novel, a serious political thriller entitled *Just Causes,* in which Viking Press had expressed some definite interest. But we were in debt, and the drab, confining indoor life in the quaint backwater of Canton only increased our pessimism.

Then, one chill Tuesday morning, a letter arrived from Pocket Books containing a royalty statement on my second novel and an entirely unexpected check for five thousand dollars. That afternoon I called my editor at Viking and frankly discussed the chances for the new novel. He told me things looked promising, judging from the chapters he'd seen up to that time.

In the evening, Carol and I conferred in our sparsely furnished living room. It was a classic Carol-and-Malcolm situation: I was ebullient, pacing around the room, flourishing in one hand a legal pad on which I'd scrawled optimistic financial projections, and gripping a large glass of wine in the other; Carol was poised on the edge of an old wing chair we'd borrowed from somebody, hunched quietly over her ledger books and file folders of accounts on the coffee table.

"So, you see, Honey," I said, continuing my impressive argument, "we really won't have anything to lose, buying a boat now . . . in the winter when prices are low. If the rest of the money doesn't come through by June, we just won't make the crossing." I gulped some wine. "We can cruise down to the Caribbean instead. How does that sound?"

I was high on more than Lake Country chablis. The Pocket Books royalty check represented only the book's first six months on the market; there was bound to be a check for three times that much after the second royalty period, in August; hell, they'd printed over two hundred thousand copies. Actually, I assured Carol, I was being conservative; I'd applied the same sober conservatism to my estimate of the money that was "bound" to come rolling in when Viking bought the as yet incomplete novel, *Just Causes.* All we had to do was put a down payment on a boat now, and we'd have plenty of money later that spring to outfit it for an ocean crossing and probably even to pay off the boat mortgage.

Carol rearranged some of her neatly printed account sheets, then opened the manila folder of outstanding bills. "You know," she began softly, "we *could* use this check to pay off Master Charge, Sears, and Penney's . . ."—she flipped a beige computerized invoice—"maybe even what we owe on the car." Looking down again, she tapped out some quick figures on the pocket calculator. "Yes . . . look, we could pay off all these accounts and save about four hundred a month in payments . . . then, in June, we'd actually have . . ."

"Sixteen hundred dollars saved," I muttered coldly. "You're missing the point, Carol. Sixteen hundred bucks won't do us a bit of good for a down payment on a decent boat. We've got a good block of money now, so we have to act now . . . not, well, piss it away on monthly bills." I was a little surprised by the vehemence and the anger of my tone.

Carol was obviously taken aback. "Malcolm,"—her voice had taken on a clipped precision, which told me she was losing patience—"if we're going to get a twelve- or fifteen-thousand-dollar advance from Viking in May or June, why can't we wait to buy the boat then?" She waved her hand at the toppling pile of sailing magazines next to the coffee table. "God knows there are hundreds . . . *thousands* of boats for sale. The more we can pay up front, the better deal we can get."

Her argument was rational, obviously reasoned and fair. But I was in no mood to accept reason or fairness. "Look, Honey, I'm sorry I yelled at you . . ." My mind clicked ahead, searching out new and plausible arguments. "But we really can't wait until June to start looking for a boat, not if we want to sail this year." I walked slowly to the window, pulled back the drape, and stared at the truck headlights on the ridges of dirty snow. "It will take us at least a month to outfit a boat for a crossing. The hurricane season begins in June, and we certainly cannot wait much longer than the middle of June to sail." I turned back toward her with what I hoped was a convincing expression on my face. "I *know* it would be more logical to wait until we have all the money in the bank, but we'll never get our own boat to Greece that way, not this year at least. Don't you want to be out in the Aegean in the good weather this fall . . . in Patmos, in Bodrum?"

A car with chains clanked by on the rutted ice outside. Carol bent over her figures once again, perhaps swayed now by the force of my argument. It was time to strike again.

"We'll get the second half of the Viking advance and the next royalty check once we're in Greece. We'll have all next year just to write and sail. Won't that be great? Isn't that what you want?"

Carol looked up again, her blue-gray eyes wary and tired. I could see that she was on the verge of calling my bluff, that the years of my irrational *adventurous* decisions had finally had their predictable effect, that she was going to say no, that she did not want to play this game any more.

"Malcolm," she began again, "we aren't sure that there'll *be* an advance from Viking." She closed the file before her on the table. "You haven't sold them the book yet. I think we should . . ."

"Listen," I interrupted, "how are you going to feel when we find ourselves with twenty, thirty thousand dollars in the bank this summer, with a whole year free to just write and no boat? Wouldn't you rather be halfway to Greece when that happens?"

"Of course," she said sitting back in her chair. "But . . ."

I held up my legal pad, again interrupting her. "Just trust me on this one. I've got this really strong feeling that everything's going to work out just the way we want it."

Outside a snowplow blade was scraping on bare pavement or maybe on solid ice. Carol stared at me across the narrow apartment living room, compressing her lips as if in reaction to the external cacophony. I stood a few feet from her, clutching my grandiose financial projection scribbled on the yellow pad, holding it now in two clenched fists as one grips a sacred text at times of solemn self-dedication. We had reached one of those pivotal moments in a marriage when it suddenly becomes clear just how frustrating and difficult it is for two individual adults to function as a single social and economic organism. I had always felt a deep compassion for Siamese twins, traveling through their lives in an unbreakable lockstep of flesh, of common arteries and shared cartilage. Now I felt a similar kind of empathy for Carol; she was like a Siamese twin who enjoyed the soft music of strings while the other insisted on blaring horns.

If we chose it, of course, the ultimate breaking of our bond would be easier than surgery. Divorce these days no longer carried much stigma; indeed, some people we knew looked at us with condescending suspicion because we had somehow managed to compromise and adjust to each other over a period of twenty years. Surely, our friends implied, each of us must have been forced to give up some precious and irreplaceable part of his individual identity in maintaining our identity as a couple.

There was no denying that. But we *had* survived those twenty years together, many of them under stressful circumstances. The sixties and seventies were a confusing time of flux, and like everybody else, we'd seen many of our married friends drift apart and most of our single friends flinch from the commitment of marriage. We ourselves had experienced a couple of shaky periods, times when we'd tried living apart, times during which we had also tried—in tentative, groping ways—to find other partners. But, eventually, we'd come back together and struck that way, as the saying goes, for better or for worse.

I think that we had learned a fundamental lesson from all the confusion and self-examination of the previous fifteen years: anything worth experiencing, any important event in one's life, was intensified by sharing it with another person. We each had learned this truistic lesson well; each recognized that the other knew it. I was banking on this recognition when I tried to badger Carol into accepting my plans. But I also felt, no matter how remotely, the fear that she could only be cajoled so far, that there was only a certain amount of brassy, kinetic horn music this Siamese twin who loved melodious balance would accept.

Eventually, I looked away from Carol's gaze. She gathered up her papers and rose from the chair. "It's late," she said with quiet resignation. "I'll go start dinner."

I gurgled more chablis over the melting ice cubes in my glass. Through the window, I watched the headlights splinter on the banks of black ice. Carol had left the choice to me. No doubt she saw something in my tone, in my desperate manner, with which she felt she should not argue. I swallowed lukewarm wine and leaned closer to the cold glass. It was a black night in February. In four months, it would be green spring, and we would have our boat ready to cross an ocean. I swallowed more wine. In the morning I would call our banker.

We coasted down the long access ramp and onto the Northway Interstate, connecting Montreal and New York City. On this flatter ground, the overburdened Chevette was holding her own better with the trucks and other cars. But, as drivers passed us, I could see them glance back, trying to get a look at us: some kind of domestic refugees, an interesting diversion to break the blandness of interstate driving. I knew their curiosity was natural; we did look pretty weird with that load. But I still felt hot anger at those smug people, speeding arrogantly along in their big Chryslers or Pontiacs, probably on their way down to Florida for a late spring vacation now that the summer rates were in effect. I had a prejudice against people who drove big, gaudy cars and went to Florida to play golf. Such people ran the country, of course, but I still found them silly, inconsequential.

My feelings of anger and distaste were at least partially engendered by the swelling uncertainty that had been working on me all day. In the middle of Dimeglio's boatyard, a couple hundred miles to the south, suspended above the weedy mud by steel oil drums, sat our boat, a white Dufour Arpege sloop, six years old. The boat had been named, rather coyly, *Body et Soul* by the original owner in 1973. It was rechristened *Kimberely III* by the subsequent owners. But for the past forty days she had been known as *Matata.* She was now ours, and we were going to sail her the seven-thousand-plus miles from Danny's yard to Greece . . . God, Viking Press, and Pocket Books willing, of course.

Carol had dozed off beside me in her seat, and I stretched back as far as I could in the cramped little car, keeping the accelerator all the way down to maintain, barely, our fifty-five miles an hour. It was the third week of May. In about four weeks we were supposed to have the boat ready, equipped to sail across the Atlantic. That took money, a lot of money.

I drove steadily south in the Friday traffic, trying not to dwell on our financial situation. Viking had received my manuscript three weeks earlier, but they were reading very slowly and had cautioned me not to expect a decision for another four weeks. After paying off local bills in Canton and putting our household effects into storage, we had about six hundred dollars to see us through until the Viking advance was issued. And we owed three hundred dollars to the boatyard before we'd be able to slip the boat back in the water. There was a minimum of six or seven hundred dollars worth of equipment I wanted to install while the boat was still on land. The impact of this reality had hit us both in the frantic last week in Canton, packing up our things.

Carol had become rather quiet, preoccupied with the mundane details of separating clothes and wrapping books and fragile trinkets we'd collected here and there in Africa and the Middle East. I busied myself with closing up my office at the university and getting my students' grades in—mindless but absorbing enough work that kept me away from the apartment most of each day. The nights were bad, what with the borrowed furniture already gone and most of the rooms now crowded with half-filled cartons that only intensified the transience and uncertainty of our situation. At least we had a house in which to stay in New York. Carol's cousin Judy and her husband lived in Brooklyn; Dave was a Lutheran minister, and the parsonage had several spare bedrooms and a big backyard, plenty of room for us to stretch out sails and tackle. We'd been lucky in that part of our preparation.

By our last day in Canton it was clear to both of us that the next few weeks, waiting to hear from Viking, were going to be frustrating and anxious. We couldn't equip or provision the boat until we got the advance, and there was only so much work we could do on the engine, hull, and rigging without using up our ridiculously small cash reserve. And always, we were gripped by the somber possibility that Viking would either turn down the book cold or ask for extensive revisions before offering a contract. There was, of course, a very easy and direct way to end this worrisome uncertainty: I could simply tell Carol that I'd decided to cancel the trip, at least for this year: that I had finally seen the logic of her original position. I felt that she would agree to this change of plans, that her preoccupied silence was a signal to me that she was awaiting my imminent return to sanity. But I couldn't yet give in to the unyielding pressure of reality.

Behind my seat, the bags and suitcases clumped and squeaked as we crossed rough pavement. The shank of the plow anchor, resting on the floor behind me, clanked as we bumped over a pothole, the overloaded car almost touching bottom. Carol stirred beside me and then sat upright to rub the sleep from her face. A pearl-gray Mercedes sedan hummed by us, driven by an attractive woman in her late thirties. For a moment, I recognized a wistful expression in Carol's eyes as she watched the silver car speed smoothly away. Carol was thirty-eight years old. She had been a dutiful partner to me all our adult life together; she'd worked selflessly in Africa, helping me establish my offices in those remote towns and branch posts. In Greece, she had delayed her own writing projects to edit and type my long manuscripts. Now she sat confined in a muddy little Chevette, surrounded by most of her worldly goods, with ten fifty-dollar bills and a few twenties in the purse at her feet representing our savings after almost twenty years of married life. She might well look wistfully at the stylish woman in her humming gray sedan.

I sighed and gripped the wheel more tightly.

"What's wrong, Malcolm?" Carol asked, her voice soft with concern. "You look . . . well, worried."

I wanted to let all my pent-up anxiety and doubt come rushing out, but I clamped my mouth shut and stared out at the greening hills around the freeway. Finally, I spoke. "I hope this next couple of weeks isn't going to be too hard . . . I mean, too, well, confusing, too much of a hassle."

She reached over and stroked the tense muscles of my neck with her cool fingers. "Do you still want to go on with it . . . with the crossing?" There was traffic around us, and I couldn't see her face to judge her feelings as she spoke.

"Of course," I said too quickly, then added in a milder tone, "Yes, I want to go on with it all. That is, if *you* agree."

Now I was able to turn and look at her. Her face was calm, smooth, completely devoid of anxiety. "Let's just take things as they come this next month. We've certainly been through worse than this, and I'm sure there'll be some pretty bad times out on the Atlantic." She smiled now in the thin afternoon sunlight. "Let's not make things any harder now than they actually are by worrying."

I nodded, silently accepting her words. On either side of the car, our fellow citizens sped by at blatantly illegal speeds. She had taken up her sweater and was again patiently working with her crochet hook. I was glad suddenly that she was no longer looking in my direction, because I was afraid she would somehow see beneath my fashionably long hair and graying sideburns, beneath the lined veneer of my face, and recognize that this car was being driven by an unlikely throwback to the 1950s, by a skinny, smooth-cheeked boy with a crew cut.

CHAPTER TWO

MILL BASIN
MAY 1979

It was drizzling when we bounced through the gates of the cyclone fence and onto the rutted mud of Danny Dimeglio's boatyard. Through the open car window, I could smell the ripe iodine scent of Jamaica Bay at low tide. This Monday morning was the start of our first full day in Brooklyn, outfitting the boat. Across the gray water of Mill Basin, the Belt Parkway rose on its embankment above the salt marsh and landfills. The rush-hour traffic hummed in the distance like a huge machine. In the overcast above, big jets growled and whined into their final approaches to Kennedy Airport, five miles to the north. The city of New York was going about its normal, rational business this bleak spring morning. And Carol and I were going about our own tasks, which, perhaps, were not quite so normal or obviously rational.

There was still a week until Memorial Day, and the yard was crowded with sail- and powerboats resting on rickety-looking slat-

and-barrel cradles. Between the boats, the ground was green with new stands of weeds growing around clumps of last year's paint cans and clots of soggy, curlicue wood shavings. I drove halfway down the central lane between the boats and turned to the left. Setting the hand brake, I let the windshield wipers thump away at slow speed as we stared out through the drizzle at our boat. From where we sat, it didn't look like the kind of vessel two sane people would contemplate sailing across the North Atlantic Ocean.

On the heart shape of the small, reversed-shear transom, the boat's previous name, *Kimberely III*, presented a forlorn picture, with several of the glue-on letters missing or hanging, half-peeled, off the stained white fiber glass. Untidiness, dirtiness, actual *shoddiness* was in fact the overriding impression I had, and I'm sure Carol was also having, as we gazed into the soft rain. When Michel Dufour designed the Arpege sloop in the late 1960s, he obviously envisioned that her lines would be revealed as the boat floated in water, not as she squatted in a littered boatyard, ignobly supported by four rusty and paint-splotched oil drums and some battered two-by-fours. Staring through the rain at the boat, I was overcome by a sense of stupidity, of having been badly tricked, cheated.

When we had first seen the boat, on a raw, sleety day in early April, she'd looked exactly right, an ocean-going fiber glass sloop, well within our buying budget: the $25,000 loan ceiling that our bank had given us. Maybe we were slightly blinded by our success at having the loan approved, but *everything* about the boat had seemed perfect then, even the minor flaws and defects that had helped lower the asking price.

She was thirty feet, length overall, with a nine-foot beam, and the shorter keel option, giving her a draft of only five feet. I was most impressed by the strength of the hull in relation to her light, six-ton displacement. The solid iron keel was hung by a double row of thick, oblique stainless keel bolts; the sturdy rudder was supported by its own steel-armatured skeg, and the one-piece interior liner was stiffened by five thick marine-plywood bulkheads. The hatches were by Goïot, heavy armored plexiglass. When you threw in the reliable Volvo Penta diesel engine and the large, sit-down chart table, you had a package of premium offshore features we simply hadn't found in any American-made boat selling for less than $40,000. In addition to all this, we knew the Arpege design well, having sailed one in Greece for the previous four years. *Kimberely III* had looked very good to us that nasty April day. Standing in the frozen mud of the boatyard, we'd decided then and there to make a bid on the boat.

Two weeks later, on another windy, cold April day, Carol and I had sat in a store front yacht broker's office on the waterfront of Huntington, Long Island and calmly affixed our signatures to numerous copies of a multipage boat mortgage document that committed us *and* Carol's mother, LaVerne, as cosigner, to paying $241 a month for the next *ten* years. That Sunday had represented the culmination of a hectic spring's negotiation, convincing the bank that we were not only currently solvent but that our financial future—dependent on *me* as a writer—made us the kind of financial risk the bank was willing to accept. Eventually, I'm sure it was the fact that Carol's mother was willing to cosign for us that swung the deal. Be that as it may, the day we closed the deal on the boat, I felt near the zenith of one of my periodic upswings of unbridled optimism.

We'd been fantastically lucky to find an Arpege, I'd thought, a *good* one that hadn't been sailed too hard, that was going for a reasonable price due to a few minor cosmetic problems. Over the years, we had come to feel unlimited confidence in the boat's strength, design, and handling characteristics. The previous winter I'd taken a student sailing group to the Caribbean and met a colorful English charter skipper, Paul Adamthwaite, in St. Thomas. Paul showed me his own private boat, a 1971 Arpege called *Cassiopeia*, anchored in Red Hook Harbor. In a very British, practiced casual manner, he let it be known that he'd sailed his little Arpege eleven times across the Atlantic, usually alone, and once around the world. I sat there in his cockpit, my hand playing across the teak trim on the coaming. Any boat that could be sailed around the world, not to mention eleven times across the Atlantic, would be good enough for us.

But now, staring out through the streaming windshield at the Arpege, at *our* boat, my unlimited confidence was badly eroded. Suddenly the minor cosmetic problems that had lowered the boat's price seemed decidedly major. Looking from the foreshortened perspective of the stern, I could see serious pits and corrosion in the propeller blades. The previous owner had not been careful enough using a sacrificial zinc to prevent electrolytic reaction below the water line. Maybe the bronze shaft tube and cutlass bearing were also badly corroded. Even though the boat had passed a thorough professional survey before we bought it, I could now see that she needed a lot more work than I'd previously allowed myself to believe, before she'd be fully ready for an ocean crossing. On the port topsides, the decorative gold-tape stripe dangled down in ugly broken strips at several places along the length of the hull, giving the chalky, unpolished white of the fiber glass a feeling of neglect. Along the starboard rail, two stanchions were so badly bent that I now saw they'd have to be replaced, and that to fit the replacements I'd have to cut into and then resplice the swaged ends of the double lifelines. All the teak: rails, mainsheet traveler support, grab rails, and cockpit coamings had been heavily and sloppily covered with thick, bulging polyurethane varnish. All this would have to be stripped away and the wood carefully sanded before decent teak oil could be applied. Along the topsides, the gelcoat was badly chipped and marred by thin fractures in several places, especially at the beam ends. The mast was down, unstepped, lying fore to aft and overhanging the bow and stern pulpits on each end. Around the alloy spar the thick wires of the shrouds were twisted in a nasty-looking snarl.

I gripped the soft plastic of the steering wheel cover, somberly assessing the problems I could *see.* They were only minor symptoms, I now realized, giving in to a wave of pessimism, of the work that faced us of preparing the boat for sea.

Besides this obvious external work, there was a long list of other less obvious but essential repairs, additions, and modifications I had to complete before the boat would be ready for the crossing. In fact, that work list sat wedged in next to my bucket seat. The drizzle spattered into heavier rain against the roof of the car. We waited, the wiper blades thumping dully. I was trying hard not to think about hurricanes and that the "official" season began on June 1. By the first of July, the probability of encountering a tropical storm would increase threefold, by July 15, sixfold. That was why we had to have the boat ready to sail by June 25 at the very latest.

The rain tapped harder on the car roof. Picking up my clipboard, I scanned the work list I'd typed the night before at Judy and David's house:

Engine: *pull water pump, inspect shaft, replace impeller and gasket;* exhaust system: *drain silencer box, clean, inspect for corrosion, change gaskets;* starter/generator: *dismantle, change brushes, inspect shaft and coil, clean and remount;* fuel filters: *dismantle and clean, check for leaks;* injectors: *check spray pattern, clean and remount . . .*

The list for the engine and prop shaft *alone* went on for two typewritten pages.

I had prepared similar detailed work-list pages for the rigging, running tackle, ground tackle, electrical system, lights, pumps, through-hull fittings, rudder and tiller assembly, bulkheads, and hatches. In actual, real-world fact, I held in my lap a work list requiring the dedicated and skillful work of an expert for at least five weeks: a week for the hull, a week for the tackle and rigging, a week on the engine, a week to provision, and a week for the shakedown cruise. We were hoping to accomplish all this in just over three, plus mount all the new gear, such as the life raft and VHF radio. If we absolutely couldn't get all this done in four weeks, by June 17, then we could allow ourselves a not-a-minute-later deadline of June 25.

Wonderful; I scowled out at the rain. In the next five weeks, a number of complicated and uncertain elements would *all* have to fall into place. Viking would have to agree not only to buy the new book but to expedite writing a contract, which would then have to be read by my agent and signed. Then, Viking would have to rush through the delivery of my advance, so that we could pay for the specialized and terribly expensive equipment (life raft, EPIRB mayday beacon, VHF radio, radio compass, and so forth), which, we sincerely hoped and prayed, some kindly marine supplier would let us order soon with no money down. We then had to install all this on board before it got too late to take a real shakedown cruise to test the boat in rough weather, so that we could check for leaks, bad stowage, weak rigging, and all the other important items on a shakedown checklist.

I snapped the clipboard hard against the leg of my jeans. The rain popped on the car roof, louder than before. Sure, right, absolutely . . . now that we were actually down here, in the yard, looking at the boat, I had to stop kidding myself. It wouldn't be humanly possible to accomplish all that work in five weeks. No marine supplier would take equipment orders without some kind of down payment, and no New York City bank would lend me seven or eight thousand dollars to outfit a boat for an ocean crossing, buy insurance, and clear short-term debts using the *possibility* that I was about to sell a novel as collateral. Two days earlier, on the highway down from Canton, I'd been close to admitting defeat. But now I knew that I couldn't delay that admission any longer.

Carol obviously sensed my mood. Turning to face me, she spoke with quiet determination. "I *know* that there's a lot to do." She nodded toward the boat to emphasize what she said. "But we've outfitted boats before. If we work hard on this one, we'll get her ready."

I smoothed the pages of the work list. "It's not the work, Carol," I said as calmly as I could. "It's the money." I sighed loudly. "We're never going to get enough money in time to buy all the new gear and get it installed on board. I've just been kidding myself . . . ever since February."

She stared out into the rainy weeds. "Sometimes you make it sound like you're in this all by yourself, that I'm just a child you've brought along for the ride. Don't you realize I've thought about the money and about the hurricane season, too? I read all the same books you did . . . I know the chance we're taking."

I spun in my seat to face her, but she continued to gaze out at the rain. What could I say? She was right; I had been treating her badly, underestimating her determination to make the crossing and her ability to assess the problems we were facing. I bit down on my lower lip and nodded wordlessly. "Okay," I said after a while. "All right. We'll take things as they come. Who knows? Maybe we'll get lucky. Anyway, we've got plenty of work to keep us busy while we're waiting to hear from Viking." I opened the door to get out, but Carol reached over and touched my arm.

"Whatever happens in the next month, we're in this together." Her voice was even, reasoned. "Don't think that you're all alone and that I'm some kind of innocent bystander. If I didn't want to be here . . . "—she twirled her fingers to take in the boat and the overgrown yard—"if I didn't think we were going to make it, I'd tell you."

She smiled then, and I found myself grinning back at her. "Okay," I repeated, "if that's the way you feel, let's get started."

I went around the back of the car and dragged out the first sail bag. The rain fell cool on my face and neck. Out in the misty bay, a barge hooted twice, turning to starboard. Carol was next to me now, reaching into the car for the next bundle. I felt a welling sense of purpose, of determination. We were a long way from the winter mountains. This was the edge of the sea. That was our boat. We were going to work together to prepare her to cross that ocean. The money would either come in time or it would not. Right now, that wasn't important.

Carol had the big genoa jib in its yellow sail bag, hoisted over her shoulder; she strode through the wet weeds toward the boat, not looking back to see if I would follow.

CHAPTER THREE

BROOKLYN
JUNE 1979

By June 10, Carol and I had completed all the major items on our work list. We'd practically rebuilt the Volvo diesel, spending a good chunk of our precious cash reserve for new parts in the process. Everything for the imported engine was hellishly expensive—flywheel belts, gaskets, generator brushes . . . you name it. The same was true for odds and ends from Dufour, U.S.A., in Stamford. Twice we had driven up the New England Turnpike to Connecticut to buy parts, coming back each time with the needed item but considerably poorer. We were learning the underlying truth to the old adage that a boat is a hole in the water into which the owner throws money. At twelve dollars for a three-inch ring of sacrificial zinc, and thirty dollars for a stanchion, the boat was rapidly developing into a submarine canyon, not just a hole.

But we were making progress. The expenditure of hard work and money had produced some tangible results. There was a remarkable improvement in the appearance of the boat, which still sat on the yellow and blue oil drums in the middle of the boatyard. One of the most obvious changes we'd made was to paint on the new name. *Kimberely III* had officially become *Matata.* That was the title of my first novel . . . a Swahili word meaning *trouble:* all boats are trouble, and this one was no exception.

On the inside, we'd taken out practically everything movable—the cabin soles, battery boxes, water tanks, bunk tops and cushions, and all the accumulated paraphernalia that had come with the boat. Then, we'd cleaned the interior surfaces, Carol using Fantastik spray cleaner on the fiber glass liner and bulkheads while I scrubbed the filthy bilges with paint thinner, dissolving about five years' grease and oil. When the bilges were back to the original white finish, we carefully inspected the fiber glass for cracks or any evidence of hull strain. Finding none, we went on to the sea cocks and through-hull openings, dismounting, cleaning, and repacking each of the nine fittings, then testing them with a fresh-water hose so that we were satisfied each was perfectly sealed. When we finished with the sea cocks, I doubled off the stainless hose clamps on all of them, a recommendation that Al Cramer, the surveyor, had made in his report.

Twice during my work on the through-hull fittings we came upon bronze bolts so badly electrolysized that they crumbled into greasy fragments under the pressure of a ring wrench. One was in the three-inch-diameter toilet exhaust vent, the other in the echo sounder-transducer mounting. It took me most of a day to drill out these broken stubs, retap the holes, and fit new bolts. But the work was absolutely necessary, as difficult and time-consuming as it was.

Bending around the toilet commode in the small head area, one hand stuck out of sight behind the bronze vent housing while the other carefully worked the ratchet handle of the tap back and forth, I swore a bitter string of vindictiveness at *Matata*'s previous owners who had let the sea cocks get into this condition. The toilet exhaust vent housed a cone swing valve that was secured by a bronze "bow-tie" plate, itself secured by two bolts, one the corroded stub I was now replacing. As I delicately worked the handle, scared of breaking off the tap inside the hole, Carol hunched over me in the cramped space to spray silicon penetrating oil around the hot tap shaft. This job was taking up most of the morning. Outside it was warm and sunny, a perfect time to patch and sand the bad spots in the topside gelcoat. But here I was, stuck in this stuffy hole, wasting hours to replace a crummy little bolt.

But then I stopped swearing and closed my eyes. That crummy little bolt giving me so much trouble secured the plate that held the cone swing-valve in place. If that swing-valve should come popping back into the hull under a couple of hundred pounds of pressure as the boat fell off a wave crest and pounded down into the trough of a deep swell . . . and this happened on a dark night a thousand miles offshore, when we were both asleep . . . *then* what the hell would we do? Curled up there, my shoulder muscles contracting painfully, I could clearly see the gout of black water shooting into the boat from the ruptured valve, like a severed jugular . . . just as traumatic, just as life threatening. I stopped my juvenile cursing and worked the ratchet handle slowly back, then slowly forward. Before we took this boat out onto the deep sea, we would be sure that no amount of pounding would threaten the hull's integrity.

After almost two weeks working down below on the interior fittings and the engine, we turned our full attention to the hull and the rigging. There was plenty to do, and I was glad to have the straightforward tasks so obviously arrayed before me. Splicing new end fittings into the lifelines on the starboard side might not have been everyone's idea of a relaxing job, but, sitting up in the breezy sunshine, working with vice-grip pliers and marlin spike on the finicky but direct problem of the wire splice, I was able to forget my other problems. It was already the second week of June, only seven days from our original departure deadline, and we still had received no definite word from Viking Press.

I spent two days absorbed with the rigging, spraying then scrubbing down each swaged end fitting and testing every inch of the shrouds and stays for kinks and wear. When I was satisfied, I moved on to the prop shaft, cutlass bearing, and finally the rudder shaft.

Working on this gear, the guts of any sailing vessel, gave me a definite feeling of solidity, as if my ability to dismantle, clean, and reassemble the fundamental parts of the boat was proof of my own value and my ability to pull off this complicated undertaking. I needed that kind of reassurance right then.

Around us in the yard, there were far fewer boats now. Owners had come down to work each weekend and almost every weekday evening, sanding and antifouling bottoms, fixing the odd bit of rigging or brightwork, using the long black hose to wash away the winter grit accumulated on their decks. One by one, Danny and his crew maneuvered the boats in the web slings of the huge blue travel lift across the dusty yard to the launching slip. One by one, the boats that had sat in their cradles around us were launched and sailed away. We began to feel lonely up in the yard. Meanwhile, we worked away, filling cracks in the gelcoat, sanding and painting the keel, mounting the refurbished prop, and sealing the corroded bronze cap of the cutlass bearing.

It was Tuesday, another flawless June morning, a perfect sailing day. I was reinforcing the rudder's trailing edge with a four-inch-wide strip of finely woven glass fabric and several coats of epoxy resin. I'd heard stories of people losing their rudders out at sea after hitting flotsam, cracking open the hollow rudder blade, which would then flood and rupture. By carefully reinforcing the leading and trailing rudder edges, I hoped to prevent this. Perhaps it was make-work, but the job was exacting and took my mind off money worries. Over my shoulder, I heard Carol driving across the rutted yard, the tires crunching old paint cans and scraps of wood. She was returning from Judy and Dave's, where she'd been sewing bunk cushions, and she seemed to be driving faster than usual.

I turned to face her, keeping pressure on my putty knife to hold down the bottom corner of the reinforcement strip. My fingers were sticky with glass resin, and I wanted Carol to take the tool while I cleaned my hands. But before I could speak, she burst out with her news.

"Alden called." She was coming toward me, her face flushed and animated. She'd forgotten to close the car door and the ignition-key warning buzzer was making its annoying racket. I knew there was news from Viking. "You're supposed to call her back right away."

In one extended movement I wiped the putty knife down the gummy strip of cloth, grabbed a cleaning rag, and started jogging toward the phone booth next to the launching slip. Halfway across the yard, I dug into the pockets of my jeans for change. A couple of quarters and a dime stuck to the resin on my fingers as I jumped across the mud ruts. Overhead, tan and gray gulls were sailing between the puffy, fair-weather clouds. My mouth was dry and my chest tight under the splattered T-shirt. There was news from Viking on *Just Causes.* We were going to make it after all. We were actually going to win our crazy race against all the odds and the hurricane season. *Or maybe it's bad news,* a rasping voice said inside my head.

I pulled open the door of the phone booth, my fingers sticking to the handle. Carol was two steps behind me.

"Fifteen thousand," I said. My chest was fluttering so badly that I had to stop speaking for a moment. "Fifteen thousand total advance . . . eight now, the other seven on acceptance of revisions." I leaned against the cool aluminum side of the phone booth, unconsciously clenching my fingers until I felt the tacky epoxy resin on my skin.

Carol closed her eyes in relief and expended a long, pent-up breath. After breathing deeply several times, she opened her eyes. "Eight thousand will just about do it," she said evenly, as much to herself as to me. "I think my last total came to seventy-six hundred, *if* we can get that Winslow life raft at the discount price. I'll have to check my figures."

From nowhere, a sudden bolt of anger shot through me. *Goddamn it.* I spun away to face the docks below the embankment. *After all these weeks of sweating it out, all she can do is nitpick about how little it is.*

But then my rigid shoulders sagged. Carol was only being practical, and I had simply been giving in to unrealistic optimism, *again.*

Her expense list was detailed and accurate; it would take all of seventy-six hundred dollars before we would be prepared to leave on the long voyage to Greece. Getting mad at Carol for reminding me of that hard fact would not change its immutable reality. If we were going to sail a boat safely across the Atlantic and the Mediterranean, we needed almost four thousand dollars worth of new gear . . . a life raft, an emergency radio beacon, strobe lights, safety harnesses, deck boots, oilskins, hundreds of feet of new line, blocks, cleats, more engine parts . . . the single-spaced typewritten list went on for three pages. There was also the inevitable large outlay for Lloyd's insurance. And above all this, we would still have our monthly payments to make while we were away: the car, the various charge accounts, the boat mortgage itself. Middle-class life clanked on in its predictable, unromantic manner, even if we were out there in mid-Atlantic being heroic.

I kicked a crushed beer can at my feet. Wouldn't it be nice to just sail away from all this, the monthly payments and the terse, word-processed overdue notices from Sears and Master Charge? Wouldn't it be wonderful if we really could escape the skein of money and contractual responsibility that shrouds us all the months and years of our adult lives? I kicked again, and the flattened beer can rolled down the bank to splash into the coagulated oil at the tide line.

Turning back, I faced Carol. She was staring at a small yellow sloop out past the boatyard point. The boat was heading up Mill Basin to the open bay with two couples on board. The sloop appeared new, and the guy at the tiller looked nervous. I could see concern in Carol's face. It was obvious that she was feeling sudden empathy for anyone going to sea in a small boat, even these two couples out for the day in Jamaica Bay. The young man stood stiffly in the narrow cockpit, gripping the tiller awkwardly with both hands, straining to see over the top of his cabin. It was Tuesday, June 12. If all went well, we'd be sailing down that channel ourselves in less than two weeks. But we wouldn't simply be heading out for a day sail to the Verrazano-Narrows Bridge. We would be starting a voyage one-third of the way around the planet earth.

Since that raw night in February, such a possibility had seemed to both of us more fantasy than plausibility. Now we both knew that we were actually going to sail, that in less than twenty days we would be hundreds of miles farther from land than either of us had ever been before on a small boat. There were bound to be gales; surely there would also be accidents—minor ones, we hoped. Our celestial navigation was basically untested on the open sea. What if one of us were injured? What if one of us went overboard on a dark night of violent weather?

I watched Carol. She gazed at the little yellow sloop as it breasted the tide and the wash from the barges, steering bravely east toward the bay.

I rubbed my clotted fingers on my work jeans. "Okay, Honey," I said. "Let's finish up on the rudder. We've got a lot of work to do today . . . and later I guess we should sort of, well, celebrate."

Carol seemed to snap back to the present from whatever grim picture had been gripping her. She nodded. "Yes, let's finish the rudder. Let's do it right."

It was a stifling Wednesday afternoon, two weeks later. I sat in the car, hemmed in by the rush-hour traffic on Ocean Avenue, about five blocks from Sheepshead Bay. The normal afternoon congestion was compounded by construction work, road gangs filling winter potholes, and by the incredibly long gas lines snaking out from the service stations. Some of these lines extended back for several blocks, then looped around a corner to continue on down a side street and eventually out of sight. Carol had said earlier that the spectacle of the gasoline lines made her think of some improbable science fiction movie about an ecological collapse. But the shortages and the lines were two weeks old now. Neither of us was laughing anymore.

The temperature was in the high eighties, and the car radio informed me that the humidity and air pollutants had combined to give the city its first day that summer of *unhealthful* air quality. My eyes stung. My throat felt like I'd smoked a couple of packs of Camels that day. Around me on the potholed street, cars jerked ahead, then braked hard to stop. In a minute or so somebody was going to start blowing his horn. Then others would join in, and soon there'd be a cacophony of horns, blasting out frustration, discomfort, and anger.

It was already quarter after four, and I was late. I'd been doing some of the final equipment buying: fishing gear from a bait shop in Sheepshead Bay; now I was headed up Ocean Avenue to a discount lumber supply house to buy a sheet of half-inch plywood to use as emergency hatch and window covers—"strong boys" they called them in the cruising books we'd read. But I was running behind schedule, just as I'd been doing every day this past frantic week. If I didn't get to the lumber store before four-thirty, they wouldn't rough-cut my sheet of ply for me, and I'd have to come back in the morning.

But I had other plans for the morning. The Viking check had finally been issued, and we had an appointment at nine with the manager of the Defender Industries marine discount house out in New Rochelle. We were going to pick up our specialized gear for the crossing—the life raft, EPIRB mayday beacon, oilskins, strobe lights, and all the rest of the items on our long shopping list.

We hoped somehow to get the provisions and new gear stowed on board by Friday night, carry out our three-day shakedown cruise over the weekend, and actually set sail for the Azores on Monday, July 2. If we were going to hold to that schedule, we had to complete every item on our final checklists, on time and in the correct sequence.

I gripped the steering wheel in my sweating hands, swearing under my breath then out loud as a guy in a big Buick edged over from the right lane to cut me off. He slid forward, his face straight ahead so as to avoid looking at me. His big, moss-green car was closed tightly. The son of a bitch was breathing sweet, filtered, conditioned air while I sat there in the polluted sunlight, choking on his exhaust. I raised my hand to pound on the horn, then caught myself and lowered my fist. The hell with it. The poor bastard had to drive these streets every day of his life. In less than a week, I'd be someplace much different from this. Let it be. Besides, not three blocks from this spot, only a week before, a similar incident had occurred in a gas line, one man cutting off another from the right. A horn was pounded, words were exchanged. Then one driver reached through the other's window and slashed the man's throat with a long-bladed knife. The man who died had three children. The killer had no previous criminal record. Crazy times. Let it be. In six days, I'd be on my way east, away from this continent.

The big green car shot forward, stopped sharply, then seemed to rear up and blast ahead once more, leaving behind a dense cloud of exhaust. In the rearview mirror I saw that the left lane was momentarily open. I jammed my turn signal down and hit the accelerator. I was free and moving at twenty and then thirty miles an hour down the center lane of the wide street. Far behind, the Buick was embedded in a solid, unmoving lane of cars and trucks. I found myself howling with childish, unreasonable delight, pounding the steering wheel with vindictive pleasure.

Shit, I suddenly thought, getting a grip on my emotions, what a crummy way to live. And people think I'm crazy to want to sail away from all this.

In the lumber store, the warehouse stockboy seemed bored but also reluctant to fill my order. He was an Italian kid, successfully pulling off a good John Travolta impersonation.

Taking my pink cash receipt, he scanned the racks of plywood, then sauntered down the row to select my sheet. He stopped, hunched his shoulders, and turned slowly to face me. "Sorry, Mistah," he began in pure Brooklynese, "no cuts aftah four-tirty."

I strode toward him, giving in now to the pent-up frustrations of the long day. "Come on, for Christ's . . ." I said between my teeth. I caught myself; getting into a brawl with some stockboy was no way to sail any earlier. "Wait a second," I continued in a softer tone, pointing inside to the sales floor. "Mr. Francolucci in there just told me that any order *paid for* by four-thirty gets a custom cut. Look at the slip . . . it says four twenty-six."

The kid glared at me, rocking on his platform heels. Finally, he deigned to lower his gaze to the receipt, then shook his head with practiced scorn. "Yeah," he muttered, "Wondaful . . . ya want *six* cuts in one sheet of ply, huh? Whataya buildin', a doghouse for ya little poodle?" He smirked at me, flicking back his head to flop his long, styled hair into place.

The fatigue and frustration of the previous weeks came to an unexpected, immediate head. "None of your goddamn business what I'm building." I was five feet from him, closing fast. The physical catharsis of a fight was now mindlessly appealing. I only hoped the kid hadn't been through one of the karate academies that were mushrooming all over Brooklyn.

To my great surprise, the boy jerked away from me to seek the protection of a palletful of wallboard. "Okay, Mistah, okay. Yur right. Yur abso-fuckin-lutely right . . . da customah's always right . . . *right?*"

He had my sheet of plywood out and was dragging it toward the wide metal table of the band saw.

I stood there, fluttering inside with spent anger and sudden embarrassment. Looking away, out the door of the warehouse to the blocked traffic on the street, I forced myself to relax. All week I'd been snapping at Carol as we worked together, but she understood my frustration and anxiety. When I turned back to the stockboy, he was using a T-square to mark the cut lines on the sheet. I went over to the saw to help him.

"Sorry about that," I muttered. "It's been a pisser of a day."

The kid was ready to start his first cut. "Yeah," he said with quiet sarcasm, "tell me about it, huh? People been ridin' my back since fuckin' seven-tirty. . . . Everyone wants dere stuff done like *yesterday*. . . ."

The screech of the saw blade cut any further awkward attempts at conversation. I was glad. What could I tell this kid? He had his life, I had mine. There wasn't much common ground between the two. For a moment, I resisted the urge to clear up the bad feelings, to tell him about the boat, about the trip, and Carol and my dream to sail across an ocean.

Then I looked more closely at the young man. His fingernails were gnawed to bloody crescents; there was a crudely stained street-gang tattoo on his left forearm. He wore a cheap gold wedding ring. Someplace in the polluted mediocrity of Brooklyn, he probably had a teen-age wife and a baby. He didn't want to hear about anyone else's dreams, broken or intact. Standing there in the flying chips and noise, I was overcome by the stagnation of this city, by the worn-out streets, the burnt-out neighborhoods, the mean and hopeless lives I'd observed in the previous month. For five weeks I'd dealt with people like this kid: stockboys in marine hardware stores, engine-parts men and clerks in fancy Manhattan chandleries. They had not wanted to hear my spiel about the crossing. When I'd attempted to explain my plans, they'd made it quite clear they weren't interested. And now, after seeing first-hand the life of working people here, I couldn't blame them. What I was doing represented escape, and they didn't want to hear about it. There wasn't a hell of a lot of romantic escape in their own lives; why should they stand there listening to some "rich bastard" who didn't have to ride the rush-hour subway every day or try to make ends meet on the minimum wage?

There was nothing I could tell this kid. He spun the last section of plywood on the steel table. The saw howled and was silent. The job was completed. Without thinking what I was doing, I slipped a folded dollar bill out of my workshirt pocket and passed it across the table to the boy.

"Buy yourself a beer," I said, piling the ply slices on the table in front of me.

"Tanks," the kid muttered, "tanks a lot."

I had my arms full of cut plywood now and was halfway out the warehouse doors.

"Have a nice day," the kid called.

You, too, buddy, I thought, *you, too.*

Once the wood was stacked in the rear of the car, I stood at the open hatchback, staring down the wide, pothole-lined avenue. It was still choked with vehicles, almost all of them enormous cars carrying a single occupant. The cars surged ahead then halted hard, rocking on their springs as the traffic stalled. Engine fumes shimmered up from the acres of hot metal toward a bile-colored sky. The gasoline lines were several blocks long, stretching back around side streets from the two service stations I could see. It was hot. The air stank. In the nearest line, at a Standard Oil station with a huge NO GAS TIL SIX placard, there'd been a minor fender-scraper and several people were yelling at each other. Across the street, a fried-chicken store presented a boarded-up window, the result of recent vandalism. SPICS EAT SHIT!! had been spray-painted on the wood.

I watched the expressions of the drivers and the occasional pedestrian shopper. I saw what I had seen inside the warehouse on the pinched face of the stockboy: tense and angry boredom. That kid at the band saw, who'd been sweating over nasty customers' orders since seven-*tirty* that morning, did not want to hear about our planned route to the Azores or how we had stored our supply of emergency water. He wanted to finish his shift, fight his way home through the rush hour, then blank out on dope, or booze, or TV. If I had tried to convince him or any of the people out around me in the caustic afternoon that Carol and I were about to sail a thirty-foot sloop across the Atlantic Ocean, leaving from a dock in Brooklyn less than six blocks away, they would have taken my words as some kind of crazy, elaborate put-down.

I slammed the hatchback and drove off the loading dock into the river of cars. For half a block I was able to move freely, then the lane stopped, and I waited, sweating in the shimmering engine gas. What a goddamn shame, I thought, again remembering the stockboy. His own recent ancestors, like mine, and those of most people making up Brooklyn's ethnic mosaic, had probably crossed the Atlantic Ocean on sailing vessels a lot less seaworthy than *Matata.* Crossing oceans by sail power was a natural American endeavor. Yet nine people out of ten we had met here in Brooklyn would have told us we were crazy to attempt the voyage. The few who we'd actually told about the trip had made it clear they thought we were definitely *weird* not to choose a normal life as they had.

What a shame. People forgot their own heritage in just one or two generations; they often got trapped in the monotonous present, and some I'd met resented examinations of the past or dreams of a more exciting future. I had lived away from this glum urban mentality most of my life, and I wasn't about to start conforming to the narrow normality I saw around me on that Brooklyn street.

In the previous busy week, Carol had found a way to tell me that she, too, had firmly committed herself to our unorthodox venture. We had finally slipped the boat at the end of a hectic Thursday, half of it wasted chasing up to Queens for a new engine water-pump shaft and back to the Bay Ridge section of Brooklyn for some missing stainless rigging pins. Danny and his yard crew had waited until we had the boat ready to go in the water, on the high tide well after their normal 5:00 P.M. quitting time.

It was dark by the time we had the mast up and the rigging adjusted and were tied snuggly alongside Danny's beat-up floating dock. I sat in the cockpit, taking in the clean lines of the deck in the last of the twilight.

Carol came up from down below, automatically ducking to avoid the phantom mast and rigging that had always blocked the companionway when the boat was up in the yard. She smiled, slapping herself lightly on her paint-spattered forehead. There was more blue antifouling paint on her bare arms, and brown grease from the boat slings on her chin. She gripped two cold bottles of beer from the ice chest.

"Well," she said, handing me a beer, "here's to *Matata.*" She stroked the gleaming, waxed fiber glass of the cabin bulkhead. "She's beautiful, Malcolm. I never would have thought we'd get her to look so good, or that we'd ever actually have her in the water and almost ready for the trip."

I sipped some icy beer, letting the chill bitterness linger in my dry mouth. "Honest?" I said. "Didn't you really think we'd pull it off?"

"Well, there were times it all seemed so . . . *impossible.* But now . . . " Again she stroked the smooth gelcoat, as if petting a beloved animal who could not respond to words alone. "Now I *know* we're going to sail, and that it's going to be better, much better and more important to us both than either of us can guess right now."

She lowered her face, as if embarrassed by the strong emotions she had just revealed.

Overhead, the setting sun caught the tops of some cumulus domes. Out to the east, over the Atlantic, stars were blinking on. I drank more beer, my throat tight with happiness.

Inching forward in the traffic, I squinted in the hot chemical sunlight. People might call us crazy; so be it. The hell with them. In a few days, we would be sailing.

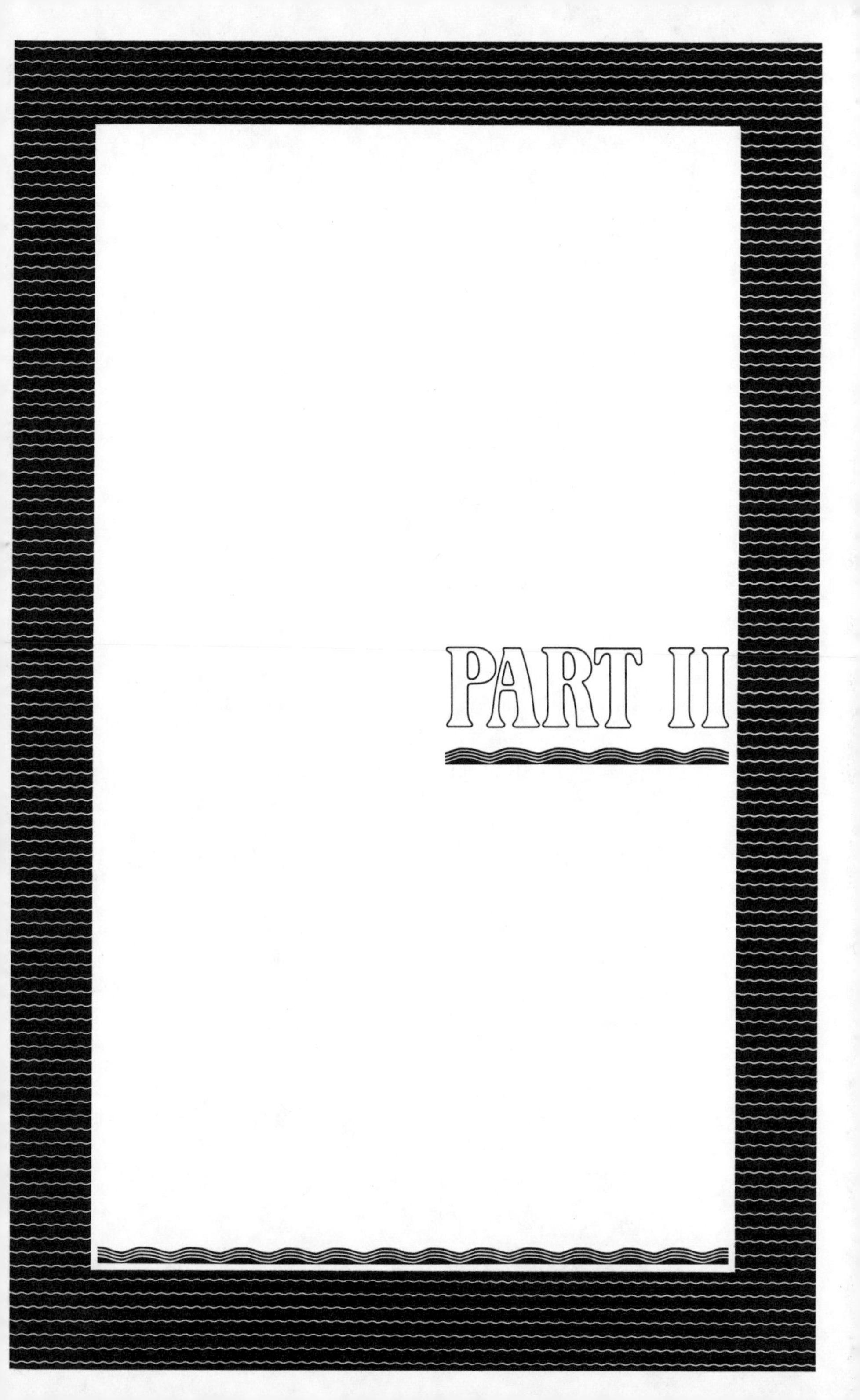

PART II

CHAPTER FOUR

JAMAICA BAY
JULY 6, 1979

I stood on the rough wooden dock of Dimeglio's boatyard, holding a braided Dacron line in my hand. The other end of that line was secured to the portside sheet winch of *Matata.* This smooth polyester cord was our last tangible link to land; I had already cast off bow and stern, and paused now for a moment with my bare feet on the sun-warm planks, gripping the spring line while the ebb tide swung the bow clear of the pilings. Carol was in the cockpit, ready at the engine controls and tiller. I had perhaps thirty seconds to wait, to look at our boat, and to examine the person with whom I was going to share that small vessel on a voyage one-third of the way around the world.

The water swirled past the pilings, making greasy rainbows on the surface. Across the narrow channel, a white egret picked among the yard trash on the mud exposed by the tide. The grass and weeds of the channel bank were vivid green, the comforting color of land.

Above us, the sky was deep blue, cloudless. Five minutes before, I'd been up in the phone booth near the slip, calling the local maritime weather service. A ridge of high pressure was forecast for all the east coast, wind west northwest, 10 to 18 knots; sea 2 to 3 feet: a perfect day to be borne away from this continent and out onto the Atlantic.

Carol waited patiently in the cockpit, dressed in old jeans and a clean T-shirt; her long hair was carefully done up in a blue scarf. She looked tired but determined, ready to leave. She had been working late at the chart table writing checks for various bills that would fall due in the next few months, addressing envelopes in her even, oblique handwriting . . . quiet, purposeful, checking off each item on her long, final list. I swallowed a yawn. We hadn't gotten to sleep the night before until almost three, and we'd been up at six-thirty, a bad way to be starting a trip like this, overtired. But we really did have to sail this morning; already we were seven days past our *final* departure deadline.

At least we didn't have to worry unduly about hurricanes. The previous afternoon I'd stacked up several rows of quarters and dimes on the shelf of the phone booth and made two important phone calls, the first to the National Hurricane Center in Florida, the second to NOAA in Washington. Through some cajoling and a bit of blarney about Congressional connections, I'd actually managed to speak to two senior meteorologists, questioning them both about the probability of a north Atlantic hurricane in the next ten to twelve days, the time we'd need to get out into the Azores High. Both men were adamant; there was currently no south Atlantic storm nor tropical low-pressure wave in the Canary Islands breeding ground. Even if a wave began today, they said, it would take longer than twelve days to mature into a hurricane and travel north to the latitudes 38°–40°, the area of our intended track to the Azores. With that assurance, I felt free of one major anxiety.

It was almost eleven o'clock; the full ebb tide was just beginning to swing. We'd pick up at least 1 knot going down Jamaica Bay and out around Rockaway point. I watched the bow catch the tide stream, wondering how I looked to Carol. A moment like this was certainly a time for introspection and for assessing your partner in such an enterprise. She looked calm. From out of nowhere, I had a sudden, vivid memory of Carol climbing into the front seat of a bush pilot's battered Piper Apache in Central Africa years before. That day, too, she had looked serene. An hour later, we had almost crashed into Lake Victoria, fleeing from a massive equatorial squall line with a faltering engine.

I swallowed and looked away. Behind me, across the flat monotony of Brooklyn, the city rumbled, going about its hectic business this workaday Friday morning. For a moment, I remembered the angry, anxious people in the gas lines. That wasn't my problem today. I was about to step onto six tons of plastic, steel and wood and steer it out into the deep ocean. By tonight we'd be fifty miles below the eastern horizon; by this time tomorrow, a hundred. I swallowed again and looked more closely at the boat.

The white topsides, with their gelcoat, shone brightly under two coats of silicon wax. The teak was smoothly oiled and the sails and tackle well washed with fresh water. On the cabin top, the new life raft box was reassuringly lashed down beside the bright red canister of emergency water. The telltales fluttered cheery orange plastic from the taut shrouds. *Matata* looked a salty little boat, brave with her new canvas spray dodgers and strong mahogany wind vane on her transom. The radar reflector spun on its swivel, gold foil gaudy in the morning sun. Up on the double backstays, the crimson man-overboard strobe hung above the horseshoe life ring. We did indeed appear ready for a long ocean passage. I looked again; suddenly the boat seemed very small, almost puny, definitely fragile . . . the hell with that: last-minute nerves, brought on by lack of sleep.

I was jangly inside with the pent-up fatigue and uncertainty of the frantic previous month. All the on-again, off-again craziness about money and deadlines had taken its toll. Even though we'd delayed our departure well past Monday and had managed to get in four fruitful days of shakedown sailing, the cumulative lack of sleep had made me jumpy and irritable. I was oversensitive to small problems. Despite the fact that we'd tuned the rigging perfectly after a day of beating and running in a choppy, 25-knot blow outside New York harbor, I was worried about the tension on the backstays. My eye went from the taped turnbuckles to the toe rail. I could see that a screw in the bracket of the new taffrail log was not fully driven into the teak. I suppressed a wild urge to pull in on the spring line, to tie up again and tighten that screw. It was as if the integrity of the entire boat depended on that one screw. Nerves . . .

The bow swung away from the dock. It was time to go; I'd fix the bracket when we got under way.

Since dawn, I'd been thinking of hearty and clever things to say at this moment, brave parodies of "One small step for man . . . " But now my mind was devoid of wit.

"When I shove off," I managed, "give her a little shot astern."

Carol nodded; obviously she, too, was not feeling especially lighthearted. I pushed hard on the shrouds. Then I was on the deck, and Carol was going smoothly astern. Up in the yard, Danny and his crew were busy maneuvering a red power boat under the travel lift. We were finally under way, and there was no one there to wave goodbye.

Out in the main channel of Jamaica Bay, reaching along under main and genoa toward Rockaway point, my oscillating emotions curved upward once again. Jesus, Carol and I were really *doing* it; we were on our way across an ocean in our own boat. This was real, this was actually happening, no longer just an improbable fantasy. I thought for a moment of the thousands of other sailors living on that broad continent off to starboard who had also dreamed of an ocean crossing. Most of them, hell, 99 percent of them or more, would never realize that ambition. The unpleasant realities of the daily world would intervene to prevent them from even seriously considering such an endeavor.

The sun lay heavy on my bare shoulders. I thought of the dark snow and freezing winds in Canton, of the pessimism of the winter. I remembered the hectic strain of the past few weeks, the gas lines, the confrontations with certain rude clerks and nasty marine suppliers. All of that was back on the *land.* None of those worries could touch us now. The strain of the past month evaporated with the steady breeze and the good sounds of the boat working well under full sail.

I found myself smiling, then singing sea chanteys . . . "Greenland Fishery," "Away You Ri-oh." It was a perfect day, offering a rare, smogless view of the city moving slowly past our starboard side. The blowing rain of the previous week had been swept aside by this high; the air was temporarily free of pollution, and the Manhattan skyline sparkled like a Big Apple tourist poster.

Carol was down below, finishing some last-minute stowing: the bane of everyone who has ever attempted a long passage in a small boat. I was glad she'd volunteered for that chore, as it gave me the opportunity to survey my own small ship from the privacy of my own tiny quarter deck. It hardly looked like the same boat we'd seen that drizzly morning only six weeks earlier. The white gelcoat shone brightly. Every line and halyard was clean, and the ends were all properly whipped. The turnbuckles and spreader tips were neatly covered with waterproof duct tape to prevent sail chafe. There seemed to be nothing out of place or missing. Again, my eye went to the squat fiber glass raft container lashed to the cabin top.

I stopped singing. The big north Atlantic Ocean chart rose in my mind: 2,550 nautical miles from Ambrose Light to Faial in the Azores, twenty-five days, minimum, away from land. The longest overnight passage we'd ever had in the Med was three hundred miles, two nights. Our shakedown cruises out of New York had all been day sails. Were we really ready for this? I knew sure as hell that I wasn't any Francis Chichester or Alex Rose. Competency sailing a boat under most conditions was one thing, thirst for dangerous adventure quite another.

Well, I thought, sitting down to set the tiller lines to the rocking plywood panel of the wind vane, in the next few weeks you're going to find out just who you really are. But not today; I was too tired for continued philosophical speculation. As soon as we cleared Ambrose Light, I'd get in a good afternoon nap, preparing for our first full night at sea out there in the converging shipping lanes. Ships were going to be our biggest problem until we were at least three days offshore. One of the difficulties with shipping was that we couldn't talk to them; we finally had not had enough money to afford a VHF radio.

There were people, of course, who thought that we were crazy, absolutely bananas, to be sailing without a proper radio. To them, that fragile, complicated piece of modern technology was a vital link to civilization, a tangible connection to the world of men and machines. The fact that we were sailing without this link many others considered reckless. Well, I would certainly have liked to install a new solid-state Horizon six-channel VHF, and that item had been number one on our shopping list, right before the life raft. But Defender Industries had sold out their supply of the excellent little transceivers, and the next comparable set cost more than $500., plus antenna. We deferred that purchase on the day we bought our big order, hoping we'd have the extra cash before we sailed and would be able to find another bargain price elsewhere. But things hadn't worked out that way.

As for extra cash, there was none. The eight thousand dollars Viking paid us as the first half of the advance had quickly dissipated. First, 10 percent went off the top as agent's commission. Then, we had a short-term bank loan that we had to repay before sailing. Carol wisely suggested, and I agreed, that we should prepare predated checks for all the monthly payments we'd have to make between sailing time and the end of the year. That way, if we got delayed en route to Greece, we wouldn't have to worry about a late payment on the boat or car or to the credit union. Doing this left us with less than four thousand dollars. After we'd placed the huge equipment order with Defender Industries, we had less than two thousand and still no insurance.

By June 28, it had looked as though we were stymied. No American underwriter we'd been able to locate would give us coverage for the actual crossing. Several offered to insure the boat out to the longitude of Bermuda, and again after the Azores, but none would cover the two thousand miles of deep ocean. Finally, only three days before our original departure date, a sailing friend from Maryland had put me in contact with a Dutch Lloyd's agent in Rotterdam. A couple of expensive trans-Atlantic phone calls and a telegraphic bank transfer later and we had Lloyd's cruising insurance coverage from New York all the way to Greece. The annual premium was expensive—almost $1,500.—but securing insurance coverage was our last obstacle, and having overcome it, we were able to sail.

If insurance was the final problem to overcome, we did have one last *worry:* money. After sending off $1,500. to Holland and completing the final provisioning, we were left with a grand total of $310. in cash. And we were about to embark on a voyage scheduled to last three months. As Carol had pointed out, however, there was no Safeway out in the Gulf Stream or McDonald's stand on the Grand Banks. Whatever food or drink we'd need en route to Faial we'd already bought. Once we got to the Azores, our three hundred dollars would have to suffice until Alden was able to telegram us our share of the August Pocket Books royalties. That there would actually be a sizable second royalty check had become an article of unshakable faith for both of us.

So, moving smoothly down Jamaica Bay on a beam reach, the boat hitting almost 7 knots through the water and 8 across the ground, I was intensely relieved to be leaving behind the complicated problems of land. And I also felt a strange sense of comfort that we had not been able to afford a VHF transceiver. We were on our own, literally out of contact with the anxious, speedy civilization of the land. For the next month no one could reach us.

We did have a good mayday beacon, however, a brand-new Narco EPIRB, which I'd had tested at a marine electronics shop in Sheepshead Bay and then sealed in double layers of plastic and foil. To complement the beacon, we had *two* extra new batteries, also well sealed in our survival kit. With this set of emergency radio equipment, we could send out a mayday signal on two VHF frequencies for over twenty days nonstop. Given the route we'd be sailing, there had to be plenty of aircraft flying overhead, big transcontinental jets that are obligated to monitor constantly the two VHF mayday frequencies: 121.5 and 243 MHz.

I eased the main sheet and the jib, then watched the buoys to judge the strength of the tide. We were doing fine and would catch the full ebb right where we wanted it, in the Ambrose channel. Sheepshead Bay opened up to starboard, revealing the modern university campus and the yacht basin. I thought of my former colleagues at the various universities at which I'd taught.

I smiled. It was funny sometimes how political conservatives categorize all academics as dangerous radicals. In fact, my former colleagues were exemplars of middle-class caution. They almost all thought Carol and I were exotics to be attempting this trip. For most of the teachers I knew, physical adventure was somehow déclassé; for them, true excitement lay in constructing a well-crafted critical paper and having it accepted in an academic journal. One mustn't attempt anything too big or too original, however. Above all, restraint was the watchword: a predictable, fixed class schedule of familiar subjects, which brought in a modest but regular salary. That was the limit of the ambition I'd seen around me. So be it; they could have any life they wanted. I just simply didn't feel obliged to follow suit.

In the Sheepshead Bay yacht basin, I could now see a clutch of small sloops and cutters riding their moorings in the puffy breeze. Most of these boats were solidly built, seagoing vessels capable of ocean crossings or at least of cruising as far as Bermuda and the Caribbean. But few of them would ever leave the confines of New York harbor or Long Island Sound. I fingered the lashing on the new canvas spray dodgers. Suddenly I was filled with a sense of haughty contempt for the academics I'd known and for the owners of those pretty little boats in the yacht basin. People put up such constricting barriers around their lives. They were so afraid to take risks. I eased the main sheet a bit more and looked up to see the set of the sail. For a moment, I considered calling Carol up to the cockpit to share with her my marvelous, original discovery about others' craven fears.

Then I caught myself. Here I sat, in the cockpit of a mortgaged boat, literally up to my ass in debt, about to begin a voyage the true nature of which I could only guess, aboard a vessel that had not been fully tested or adequately equipped for the sea. And I had the tasteless gall to condemn as spineless cowards all those who didn't share my recklessness. This certainly was not a very appropriate way to be thinking. It was probably downright unlucky—bad karma or something like that. In any event, it was stupid. Many of the people onshore this morning would have risked very much indeed to be where I was.

And it was not simply a question of taking risks. Luck and random circumstances played a very big part in all our lives. My profession, as precarious as it was at times, allowed me the time and the periodic hunks of advance money to undertake this trip. In these circumstances, no doubt many would do just as I was doing. But most people simply did not have the chance. They owned houses, and mortgages simply did not take vacations; they had kids, and kids needed not only shoes and corduroy pants but braces on their teeth and ten-speed bikes. Most everyone living in that sprawling city off my starboard beam had a job, too, a regular, day-in, day-out job that was vital to his physical and social survival and that of his family. People simply did not have time to take off on an adventure like this. Their lives had not been shaped that way.

I reached back to ease the shock cord on the vane's tiller lines, letting the boat swing a bit to windward to fill the sails better. Maybe I was a freak; perhaps my life had been so far out of the mainstream as to render me some kind of an outcast. Whatever the circumstances or blind, random luck that had shaped my life for almost forty years, events had allowed me to be in this cockpit, on this boat, with my wife, on this day, about to begin this long sailing trip. I knew then that I should be thankful instead of arrogantly scornful.

I pondered that thought a few moments. Sheepshead Bay was gone, and we were coming up fast on the lower bay, with Coney Island already slipping past the beam. Carol stuck her head up through the companionway.

"Almost finished stowing the vegetables," she called. "You think we ought to drink a beer or something . . . you know, as a toast?"

I looked out at the sunlight on the sharply defined New York skyline, then along the blue contours of the bay to the dunes of Rockaway point. There were several ships and a couple of barges in the Ambrose channel but, amazingly, no other sailboats. It was as if we were the only people who had ever thought of connecting a cloth airfoil to an upright pole and using that force to drive a vessel through the water. What a strange thought. I really was lightheaded from lack of sleep. A beer would probably knock me out, but we were leaving the confines of Jamaica Bay and the Ambrose channel was relatively uncrowded. A drowsy beer in the sunshine, then a nap on the cockpit cushion would be a good idea.

Carol climbed up, blinking at the cloudless sky. She clutched two bottles of Piels Light, frosted from having been in the bottom of the ice chest. I watched as she instinctively ducked under the taut main sheet and thrust out her bare right foot to grip the smooth fiber glass of the cockpit well with her toes the way a large primate effortlessly makes himself comfortable on some precarious perch in his zoo cage. I took a beer, then realized what wierd thoughts were bouncing around my head. Christ, Carol would *not* be happy if she knew I was comparing her to an orangutan or gorilla.

I sat down, suppressing a childish giggle. Actually, she loved large animals, especially apes. When we lived in Rwanda, we had climbed up to Diane Fossey's first camp in the Virunga Volcanos and Carol had tracked several bands of mountain gorillas with Diane, through the tangles of stinging nettles and the surrealistic vegetation of the equatorial alpine tundra.

Carol had always said that she admired any creature that had reached a harmonious balance with its environment. Now, watching her sip her beer from the brown bottle, legs apart, hips and torso swaying perfectly with the motion of the boat as we bucked through some wash from a power boat, I couldn't help but see her as such a creature.

"What's funny?" She lifted her sunglasses to squint at me.

"I was remembering going up Mount Mikeno to see Diane Fossey. Remember the elephant tracks in the snow?"

She sat down beside me, her graceful sun-brown leg touching mine, and gazed out at the city. The visibility was flawless; even from this distance we could see details on the Statute of Liberty and on the buildings of lower Manhattan, five miles away. "What made you think of Mount Mikeno and the gorillas?"

My head was beginning to spiral from the first swallows of beer on an empty stomach. "I'm not sure," I answered. "It's just that . . . well, we *have* done some pretty strange things together. And . . . " I swept my arm horizontally to encompass the boat and sails. "Well, here we are one more time."

Carol laughed warmly. "You want to turn around and go back?"

I shook my head. The boat chopped through more wake; a small buoy tender was cutting across our bow, outbound for Rockaway point and Long Island's south shore. When I closed my eyes against the glare, I saw a narrow laterite track through the rain forest on the mountainous eastern shore of Lake Kivu, the plum-blue body of water that separates the Congo from Rwanda.

October 1966: Carol and I were bounding along the dried mud ruts in our Volkswagen bug. It was almost dark, and the colobus monkeys were sailing through the pink sky above the road cut, returning to their nesting trees. All day, we had been on this narrow, washboard road, stopping every few hours to warn American missionaries that the *Inyenzi* rebels had infiltrated the country again from Burundi and the Congo and that the embassy wanted all American citizens evacuated to the relative safety of Kigali, the capital. Now, we were trying to make the Congo border crossing at Kamembe, twenty-five kilometers to the south, so that we could seek refuge for the night in the American Consulate compound in Bukavu. We should have stayed the night at the last mission station, but we'd misjudged the distance to the border and the slow driving conditions.

On the back seat of the Volkswagen were wedged an M-16 automatic rifle with a curved 30-round magazine and a pump shotgun loaded with heavy buckshot. Carol cradled our .38 pistol on her lap as we jolted along. These impressive weapons were supposed to make us feel confident, superior to the ragtag *Inyenzi,* who usually carried vintage Mausers and a few stolen FN rifles. As the sky got darker to the east and the flat water of the lake took on the metallic luster that marked sunset, however, I felt anything but confident. At the Adventist mission where we'd stopped an hour earlier, we'd gotten reports of armed rebels moving through the banana shambas ahead of us.

I was scared, the laterite dust drying on my sweaty face and my mouth gummy-tasting. Carol gingerly laid the big pistol at her feet and sloshed water onto a handkerchief from the green plastic canteen.

"Feel good?" she asked, smoothing the wet cloth over my forehead and down my cheeks.

"Yeah," I muttered, "thanks."

Carol washed the dust off her own face and, inexplicably, broke into a half-stifled laugh.

"What the *hell* do you find so amusing?" I took my eyes off the tree line bordering the road long enough to glare at her.

She squared her shoulders as if to gain composure, then laughed again. "You know . . . all of a sudden the subtotals and line-item balances in the third-quarter budget projections just don't seem as important as they did yesterday at this time."

Now I, too, joined in her laughter. The Regional Budget and Fiscal Office in Nairobi had been bombarding us with breathless telegrams about some minor arithmetic errors in my office budget, and Carol and I had been diligently going through the complicated document line by line to find the errors.

I picked up the canteen and took a swig of water. She was right, of course. The day before, I'd been as anxious as only a young bureaucrat fearing a reprimand can be, but this late afternoon, just twenty-four hours later, I couldn't have given the smallest damn about RBFO's stupid subtotals. There were problems much more worrisome than budget line-items hiding out in those hardwood trees. And Carol had seen through to the heart of the matter, as she always did.

I opened my eyes. The boat heeled to port as we neared the open water of the lower bay and the wind found its true direction and strength. There were ships ahead of us, freighters of all sizes and container vessels, seeking berths or outbound for the whole world. In about thirty minutes, we would jibe over, enter the outbound lane in the Ambrose channel, and join that line of vessels. We'd steer a course of 95 degrees true and try to hold as near as possible to that rhumb-line course for the next twenty-five days. I shook my head and rubbed my eyes, willing away any lingering memories of that dark African road of twelve years ago.

Carol cupped her beer bottle and turned to gaze back at the angular brown city growing smaller astern. She smiled, obviously absorbed by the fullness of the day and the throbbing intensity of the moment. We were taking our small boat across an ocean; the problems of contracts and money on land could not affect us now.

I stretched out my legs and lay flat on the cockpit cushion. Carol slid away to give me room. "How you doing?" she asked.

"I'm just a little tired after the running around and . . . all the excitement." I craned my neck to take in the set of the sails. "I think I'll try to doze off a little before we get in the channel."

"Fine," she said, turning again to watch the city sliding away behind us.

When I closed my eyes, she was still silhouetted against the bright sky and the darker land of the continent.

July 6, 1979. Sunset.

I threw the plastic bucket plunking over the side and pulled up hard on the lanyard. The braided cord dug into my hand. We were still making over 6 knots with the main and genoa filled and drawing well on this broad reach. The boat slid through the flat water with a distinctive audible hiss. It was as if some type of pneumatic device were driving the hull from hidden apertures below the water line. I pulled the bucket of dish-washing water up gingerly into the cockpit, careful not to splash salt water on my clean Levis. These pants would get wet soon enough, with spray or waves, and I wanted to keep them dry as long as I could. Behind us, dead astern, the huge neon peach of the sun flattened out to slide beneath the sea horizon. Already the serrated edge of the North American continent had glided back below the curvature of the earth. There were two smudy vertical shapes directly behind us though, the tops of the twin World Trade Center towers. When the sun lost its glow, those two towers would still provide distinct beacons with their red aircraft warning lights.

I sat down in the cockpit, the sloshing bucket of sea water between my bare feet. The water was cool, but nowhere near as cold as I'd expected. Carol passed up the supper dishes and the plastic bottle of detergent, and I began what was to become our nightly ritual: dish washing in the cockpit before dark, then a cigarette and a cup of coffee for me, the first watchkeeper, while Carol prepared for sleep. Before she actually turned in, however, she'd mind the cockpit while I went forward to check the decks for loose gear and the sails for set and chafing.

After my nap that afternoon, we'd rigged a continuous jack line from the two stern cleats, up the length of the deck outside the cockpit and cabin and through the bow cleats. With these lines, we could snap on our safety-harness tethers before leaving the protection of the cockpit and work all the way foward or aft without having to unsnap.

We had decided on a definite set of rules governing safety at night. Whoever was on watch wore a yellow foam flotation vest and a safety harness on top of it, no matter how calm the weather. Attached to the vest and harness were a stainless steel police whistle, a waterproof life-jacket light, and a small plastic Honeywell strobe light. Further, the person on watch always carried a sharp bosun's knife, secured with a neck lanyard. We both felt strongly about observing these safety-equipment rules. Also, we had one cardinal commandment about leaving the cockpit at night. The person on watch alone would not go further forward than the shrouds. That is, if there were any sail changing or work at the mast to be done, the watchkeeper had to call the other person. This, of course, would be a bother, especially if the person off watch had just settled down to sleep after changing out of wet and salty watchkeeping clothes. But, being bothered was the least of our worries.

We didn't burden ourselves with many other rigid watchkeeping formalities or schedules, but night safety was important to us both. I guess this concern reflected our unconscious recognition—our awe, if you like—of the empty region we were about to enter. In our excited imaginations, a person falling off the boat at night, far out on the Atlantic, would be just as irrevocably lost as a science-fiction space voyager drifting away from his ship into the eternal void.

It didn't matter that part of the trip would be spent near regular shipping lanes. We both felt the *emptiness* rising to meet us as we sailed toward the dark eastern horizon that first night out of New York. I sat there, washing our plastic dinner plates in the feeble salt-water suds, thinking about the incredible courage of sailors who actually set out alone on long ocean passages. Single-handing, I decided, took a very strong character.

By 2130, it was dark enough to put on the running and masthead lights. The breeze was holding steady, and we were still hissing along at over 5 knots, dead on our true compass course of 95 degrees, the

2,550-mile rhumb line to Faial in the Azores. Even with the dry, steady breeze, though, there was a lot of dew on the sails and deck.

I went down to the chart table and pulled on a lightweight nylon rain suit, then put a time/dead reckoning tick on the chart and turned to go back up above. I caught myself, my face burning hot with sudden embarrassment. The flotation vest and safety harness lay crumpled in a heap on the starboard quarter berth. Next to me, the accordion door to the forward half of the cabin swayed shut on its latch cord; Carol was in there sleeping, and here I was, on the very first watch of our first night at sea, inadvertently about to break our *firm* rule about safety equipment. A dumb mistake, stupid and careless. The fiber glass decks were slick with salt dew. I was barefoot still, and my night vision was temporarily ruined by the bright chart-table light. How easy it would have been to go hopping up to the cockpit, stub my bare toe on a cleat or the tiller lines, and tumble ass-over-tea-kettle off the boat. My palms were sweating as I pulled on the vest and harness; I could picture the billowing legs of the rain suit filling with sea water, dragging me down. What a *silly* way to die, twenty-six miles east of Ambrose Light, on the first night of our voyage.

Up in the cockpit, I sponged the dew off the cushions, checked the course and tiller lines, then settled down to wait for my eyes to readjust to the darkness. Slowly the stars began to stand out again, and the orange glow of the compass light gave definition to the cockpit. Out ahead of us, maybe five miles off the starboard bow, I could see two bright range lights of a large vessel approaching in the westbound separation lane. We were still on a good course, out of harm's way in the empty water between the two lanes. To the north, off the port beam, I could distinguish the white stern lamp and green running light of a smaller eastbound vessel, probably a fishing trawler on his way to the Grand Banks. There were a couple of northbound range lights back aft, but these ships were hull-down below the horizon, obviously nothing for us to be worried about.

I got up gingerly, my bare feet on the wet gelcoat of the cockpit well, and scanned once again. Already, there was another set of bright westbound range lights, these at a sharper angle than the first set: a big, fast freighter or tanker approaching us. The compass held quite steady around 105 degrees magnetic: 95 true. *We* were right where we were supposed to be. What the hell was this new guy doing? I knelt on the cockpit bench to peer ahead. Damn; the new range lights had already slipped behind the blocking white expanse of the genoa. Reluctantly, I lay over the cockpit coaming and ducked my head through the lifelines so that I could see beneath the head sail. To do this, I had to stretch right out over the hissing quarter wave, about ten inches beneath my chin, and hold myself suspended there awkwardly with my arm twisted uncomfortably behind me, my hand gripping the lifeline. We weren't heeled very much at all, and I was happy for that. If we had been, I wouldn't have been able to see forward this way but would have had to leave the cockpit, walking up to the portside shrouds or even further forward to see past the sail.

But to do *that*, I would have had to call Carol up to the cockpit: to comply with our firm night-safety rule number two: no one went forward of the shrouds at night without the other person in the cockpit. But I didn't have that particular worry right then. The new set of lights was going to pass at least a couple of miles to starboard. Even if he was slightly north of the regular separation lane, that guy was no danger to us.

I crawled out from under the lifelines and back into the cockpit proper, awkward from the foam vest and harness, the dangling flashlight and strobe, and the looping bosun-knife lanyard. My impulse right then was to get rid of all this crap, simply to take it off and put it all away in lockers down below. The breeze was steady from the northwest, about ten to twelve knots. On this broad reach, the boat was hardly heeled at all, and there certainly wasn't any sea to worry about. What the hell was I doing in the Sir Francis Chichester-Cape Horn rig?

But then I looked back at the glass face of the taffrail log, weakly reflecting the orange glow of the compass light. The log now read something like thirty nautical miles. It would keep turning, day and night for almost the next month, two *thousand* five hundred more miles, minimum, before we would again see solid land. This trip was not an overnight crossing between Rhodes and Marmaris or a two-day cruise down Chesapeake Bay; this was the real thing, what William Buckley called "the Big One." If ever there was a time for disciplined rules, it was now. There were undoubtedly lots of tasks I would have to perform on this trip that I wouldn't like doing but would have to do nevertheless. As I had realized that afternoon, I no longer had to worry about checks arriving or checks bouncing or homicidal citizens in gas lines. Now I would have different preoccupations, now I must make an effort to shift my outlook. The place where comfort and convenience were primary considerations was on that continent of land that had slipped some thirty miles below the dark line of the horizon astern of us.

The spreading, mucous-yellow glow above the western horizon was the diffuse light of metropolitan New York. If I were seriously attracted to undisciplined comfort, I should never have left the city. It was late on a Friday summer night, a good night to hang out in the air-conditioned bars and discos. Nobody back there was worried about the converging lights of freighters or bothered by the inconvenience of a safety harness and stiff life vest. The people back in that mustard glow wore loose, sexy clothes; they drank and snorted this and that, letting the chaotic, numbing waves of music wash away conscious thought and unconscious worry.

I fingered the damp nylon web of the safety harness. Did I want to be here or back there? Did I want to be a sailor or some suburbanite in a sheltered marina or yacht club bar waxing brave over the third gin and tonic, talking about how *some day* he'd throw it all in and sail across the goddamn Atlantic?

I leaned across the cockpit to check the compass. From now on, I vowed, no more bitching. You wanted to be out here, right now, right in this place at this time. And you're here, so make the most of it. We were on course. The wind held steady and the creaking plywood wind vane worked with its lead counterweight to pull the tiller lines, holding the bow firmly to that imaginary pencil line across the sloping ocean bottom three hundred feet beneath our iron keel.

I was sleeping so deeply that when Carol called me I had absolutely no idea where I was. Instinctively, I reached out to cuff the electric alarm clock on the bedside table. Something was wrong; there was no alarm clock, no bedside table. There was no bed. Sitting up in the silky folds of my sleeping bag, I was fully awake and aware of my surroundings. My eyes felt sticky and my head ached. The cabin was dark, but the light of the newly risen moon illuminated the webbed scratches of the plexiglass center hatch above me, like weak winter sunlight on cracked ice.

"Mal . . ." Carol called again. Her voice sounded thin and anxious. "Mal, did you hear me? There's a ship. Can you come up here?"

I was out of the sleeping bag and pulling on my Levis. "What's wrong?" I yelled, too loudly. "Where's the ship?"

The damn accordion door would not slide open. I struggled with it, tugging hard. Then I remembered that I'd tied it closed with a piece of braided line. After more clumsiness, I stumbled up into the cockpit, dragging on my damp nylon jacket over my bare chest. I wasn't prepared for the scene I saw around me.

The moon was well clear of the eastern horizon and almost full, gilding the surrounding sea with wide paths of painfully bright light. We'd been in the city for two months and had forgotten what a real moon looked like, free of the omnipresent dome of pollution. There were other lights out there in the night, too—the bright, fast-moving range lights of ships, lots of ships.

Standing there, still thick with sleep, I had a hard time getting my bearings. All of this looked suddenly foreign, as if I'd never been on a boat at night before. I remembered once when Carol and I had ridden as passengers on an Air Force C-130 transport in Europe, a night flight between Torrejón in Spain and Évreux, near Paris. Ten minutes before landing, the pilot had invited us up to the flight deck to sit behind the crew on the bunk at the rear of the greenhouse cockpit. When we'd climbed the three stairs up to the flight deck, the scene that had confronted us was similar to what I now saw around me, a confusing, alien array of strange lights, moving at ungaugeable speeds and at bizarre angles. Watching from the flight deck of the plane, I'd been fascinated and had overcome my temporary vertigo, knowing the crew was fully competent. Paris was tilted out before us at a shallow angle: sparkling strings and loops of colored lights, miniature galaxies, winking beacons. Aircraft sailed by above and below us, friendly neighbors, their pinprick navigation lights carrying no hint of menacing collision.

It had been one thing to watch a professional air crew navigate their vessel through the crowded night sky; it was quite another matter to undergo a rude awakening and find myself faced with several large, fast ships converging on my own small vessel from different directions. Beyond the problems of the approaching ships, we had another; the wind had backed further to the north and dropped to a fluky three or four knots. On the starboard side, the big, ghostly white genoa popped softly as the breeze filled it, then collapsed to drag in the slow wake, rattling the sheet blocks on their track. The main was slatting now, too, the triple coil of its sheet and blocks dragging across the coach roof.

I stood there, shivering now from the damp chill and my own fatigue. The first thing we had to do was stop these sails from slatting. Reaching down to uncleat the jib sheet, I turned my head toward Carol. "Bring it up a little, for Christ's sake," I heard myself bark in a nasty, gratuitous manner. The digital watch hanging above the chart table said 0210, which meant that I'd had less than two hours' sleep.

Carol bent to disconnect the lines from the wind vane, then pushed the tiller hard to starboard. The bow did not swing, and she thrust the helm over again. "We don't have enough speed."

"No kidding," I answered in the same gruff tone. About to speak again, I caught myself. Where was all this sudden anger at Carol coming from? It sure as hell wasn't *her* fault that the wind had dropped. I raised my eyes to look at her, and she stared back with an expression of concerned understanding. My back ached and my mouth tasted like scorched rubber. "I'll start the engine," I said in a smoother voice. "We're going to need some steerage way with all these goddamn . . . with all this shipping." I reached down to sheet in the useless sails. "Maybe we'll get lucky and the wind'll come back."

Carol sat silently at the helm. Once more, she was in her stoic mood while I was kinetic, running off at the mouth about what might or might not happen. For a moment, I had a flash of irrationally pessimistic insight that we were entirely unsuited to be on this trip together, that our emotions and intellects were badly mismatched, that there would be some disastrous confrontation between us far out on the empty ocean.

I shook my head violently. “I’ll start the engine, Honey,” I repeated.

“Fine,” she said. “I’ll be okay up here once I have some steerage.”

I went down and hit the priming lever on the diesel’s injector pump, leaning over the greasy-warm bilge stench of the engine compartment in the process. Shit, I thought, I’m feeling a little *seasick*, and there’s not even any sea.

With the engine running at half revs and the sails in tight, the motion steadied. I stood back in the companionway and looked all around the horizon. Behind us, the moon had washed out the New York city glow, but the faint red points of the World Trade Center were still visible above the horizon. Off to port, maybe three or four miles away, two big, rumbling tankers seemed to be engaged in some kind of crazy race, the trailing ship pulling dangerously close alongside the bigger vessel. Then I realized from the angle of their range lights that the leading ship was headed due east while the second was steering something like 60 degrees true, bound for Cape Cod and points northeast. Reluctantly, I left the companionway and stretched out over the cockpit coaming and under the starboard lifelines to see forward beneath the bottom of the Genoa. This big sail, I thought, is going to be a real pain in the ass in these shipping lanes.

Carol was sitting bundled up in her blue, thigh-length rain jacket in the rear of the cockpit. She was still quiet, obviously wary of my foul mood and not eager to get into a fight our first night out. I couldn’t blame her. I’d been definitely nasty but was now unable to find the words to apologize. Instead, I squinted silently ahead into the dark night, forcing my tired faculties to identify and analyze the patterns of moving lights I saw out there to starboard. One set of range lights was obviously moving northwest, more of less toward us. But, given their speed and apparent distance, the ship would pass well ahead of us. Another set of smaller lights was steering almost due west, the reciprocal of our own course. This ship, though, was a good four miles south of our track. Further south still, there were three or four vessels, all traveling southwest toward Jersey ports or the Chesapeake . . . no real problems; I could go back down and get some sleep.

Carol, of course, would have to steer the rest of her watch, another hour and a half. That, I thought rather uncharitably, was the way the cookie crumbled. I'd let her sleep a full four hours after dinner. Now *I* needed my sleep, and she'd just have to tough it out. I wasn't in the mood to recall that Carol had worked for several hours earlier rearranging the final provision stowing, shifting heavy plastic milk crates full of canned goods and the bulky five-gallon plastic Lug-a-Jugs of fresh water. She'd been doing that while I dozed in the afternoon sunlight. Then she'd prepared a wonderful meal of pork chops, mashed potatoes, and fresh carrots as a celebration dinner. If anything, she was more tired than I was, less able to judge the confusing array of ships' lights around her in the night of dazzling moonlight and colorless void.

But I didn't care about any of that. I was still conditioned to a landsman's concept of *needing*, absolutely requiring, sleep and dry comfort. I wanted only my silky-warm sleeping bag, a need as sensual as any hunger for food or sexual desire.

"Just keep her on this heading," I mumbled over my shoulder. "Call me in a couple of hours."

When I slid into my sleeping bag, I could actually feel the sleep rising inside my head, like a smoky billow.

The white blast of light cut into and splintered whatever weird dream was gripping me. Again when I sat up I reached instinctively to the right to cuff silent the bedside alarm clock. Instead, I banged my elbow painfully on the wooden edge of the upper berth. My legs were over the side of the bunk, still wrapped in the sleeping bag. I could feel the boat turning hard to port, the engine thudding loudly at high revs. What the hell was that light?

Again, the hot beam cut down into the cabin. Jesus, Carol was shining the nine-volt searchlight down here. I was suddenly at the companionway, the sleeping bag behind me on the cabin sole. Remembering that I was naked, I dashed back to grab my Levis from above my bunk. The engine seemed to be racing, revved much too high, as if the throttle were stuck and the machine was going to rip itself loose from its mounts.

Stumbling up to the dew-slick cockpit, I found an even stranger scene than earlier. Carol was standing, the tiller jammed between her knees, her two arms raised above her as if in prayer to some heathen idol, the beam-gun light blasting a hot shaft of light onto the mainsail. The engine was indeed running at high revs; behind us in the moonlight, I could see a curling, bubbling wake. I shook my head hard to clear away the clotted sleep. The big genoa was backed, twanging on the shrouds as we spun in our emergency-power circle.

"What the hell . . ." I began. But something in Carol's wide-eyed expression made me stop speaking and look forward.

There was a blue and white freighter out there, *right* out there off the bow, coming dead at us, maybe half a mile away. I could see both his green and red running lights and also the creamy white bow wave curling back from his stem.

Without further speculation, my brain took over my body and I leaned down to ease the throttle. Roughly, but without anger, I pushed the beam gun away from my face and grabbed the metal handle. Then I had the tiller in my other hand and Carol was sitting down in the companionway.

"The mast floodlight," I said, my voice surprisingly calm, hiding the confusion inside. "Start flashing the floodlight and don't stop till I tell you."

She was gone inside within three seconds. The seal-beam floodlight on the forward midmast flashed on and off, billowing the genoa with bright light. I closed my eyes for a second, then grabbed a look at the dim orange disc of the compass. The freighter was coming from about 105 degrees; we were swinging hard to port, moving up on due north. So be it. We'd steer 360 degrees and hope he'd pass astern of us. That left the ship hidden by the genny, but making another turn would waste too much time. I reached down with my big toe and advanced the throttle a few more revs. We might blow some oil past the rings and loosen the stern gland, but an extra half-knot was worth the risk. Like Carol, I gripped the tiller with my knees and used both hands to flash the beam gun's hot light on the mainsail.

The boat bounded ahead; the engine thudded and roared, and we careened north through the calm water, our sails spreading the light.

When I looked aft, the freighter was just behind us, thumping away at a course perpendicular to ours. I could clearly see the details of his hull, tall derricks and superstructure. There were white life-raft canisters stacked like supermarket fruit on his bridge deck. On his stack, a faint yellow light illuminated his company logo, some kind of squiggle inside a triangle. His engines twanged across the four hundred yards of water like monstrous rubber bands. I swallowed hard, then wiped my damp palms on the legs of my jeans. If we hadn't turned, he would have nailed us.

"Kill the light," I yelled down so that Carol could hear me over the roar of our diesel.

The hot floodlight went dead, and its afterglow blanketed the water out ahead of my eyes like moonlit gauze. Bending to ease the throttle, the stack gas of the freighter washed over me, stinking like a bus station. When I stood back up, Carol was sitting next to me, staring back at the freighter's stern.

"He never even saw us," she whispered.

I released a stale breath and sat down beside her, holding the tiller stiffly before me. "Where did he come from?" I tried to keep any trace of residual anger out of my voice. We'd just had a near miss, and there was no sense trying to blame anyone for it.

She pointed off to starboard. "All I know," she said in the same tired tone, "is that one minute there was a ship going west, south of us"—she twirled her fingers toward the darkness—" and the next minute the ship was right on top of us . . . " She shook her head. "That's when I called you."

I patted her leg. Beneath her jeans, her muscles were tense. Somehow, we'd slipped south of our chartered track and into the westbound shipping lane. Either that, or more than one freighter had strayed north of the lane. I eased the throttle even more and began a slow swing to starboard, back to our original course. As we turned, I suddenly realized what had happened. Current, of course . . . a south-going current had set in with the evening flood tide. With the northerly component of the breeze behind the current flow, we'd made perhaps three or four miles of southern leeway. It was obvious to me now, an elemental piloting problem I'd completely ignored in my hedonistic longing for uninterrupted sleep.

This sure as hell won't do, I thought bitterly. On our first night at sea I'd let the boat drift south right into one of the world's most crowded shipping lanes. Foolishness, inexcusable incompetence, compounded by a bad attitude. That certainly was not the way to make it safely across the Atlantic Ocean on a small boat. Now there was no sense giving in to crippling remorse. I must simply take corrective action.

First, I had to get that blinding blanket of the worthless genoa down and furled so that we could see what was out there. Then, I'd steer north for maybe forty-five minutes and snatch a couple of radio-compass bearings to figure out just exactly where we were. After that, I would steer the boat on a safe eastward course until dawn. That was a good four hours away, and what I proposed precluded any sleep. But my body was aching for sleep—silent, mindless oblivion in that warm sleeping bag down below. I rubbed my face violently. No.

I'd sleep in the morning; now I needed my wits. For a moment, I thought of going down below and washing my face with cold fresh water from the ice chest. Then I remembered that fresh water was too precious a commodity to waste washing one's face. There was a small supply of amphetamine tablets in the medicine box . . . maybe half a tablet now. No. Ridiculous. Speed was the last thing I needed; I was nervous and strung-out enough already. What I did need now was some resolve, some strength of character. Four hours was not a terribly long time to steer a boat. Besides, we could split it up, each taking the helm an hour at a time, while the other rested on the free cockpit cushion or just inside on the comfortable quarter berth.

Standing up to look ahead, I could see the line of westbound ships on the horizon. "Take the tiller," I said. "I'm going to put some clothes on and see if I can get an RDF fix."

Carol looked uncertainly around her at the white lights of the ships moving silently through the black water. "We should have waited to leave until just before dawn, like we planned to do," she said, "so that we'd have the worst of the shipping in daylight."

"We should have done a lot of things differently," I shot back, the submerged edge of exhausted anger just breaking the surface of my voice. I caught my tone and tried to relax. "We'll take turns steering, Honey. I'll make some coffee. It'll be light in a few hours."

Carol looked around again. The moon was getting high, and the water shimmered in patches like dirty ice on a winter highway. The robotlike displays of ships' lights moved along through the rippling darkness like esoteric training aids in some computerized navigation simulator. "I didn't think it would look like this," Carol finally said in a small, disappointed voice.

I nodded in silent agreement. "Yeah . . . I know." Before ducking down to the cabin, I turned to face her again. "Don't worry, by this time tomorrow we'll be on our own."

Again Carol glanced around her. "I sure hope so."

CHAPTER FIVE

DR: 39°10' NORTH, 69°50' WEST
JULY 9: 0800 LOCAL ZONE TIME

A beautiful clear morning, after a moonlit night of light westerly breezes. The taffrail log read 203 miles from New York harbor. Not much distance to show for seventy hours under way, but the light air and flat sea had given us both the chance to sleep long, to restore our physical and emotional energy after the rat race of the city and the first chaotic night in the shipping lanes. Now we were clear of the congested coastal area and were about to slide across the continental shelf and onto the truly deep soundings. Maybe it was my imagination, but I thought the early morning sea around us already looked a darker color.

Perhaps this feeling of distance from land was simply engendered by the clear beauty of the flawless morning. The only clouds we'd seen in three days had been some scattered fair-weather cumulus. The barometer had remained high and steady and the sea was a clear, almost Mediterranean blue.

I had been on watch since before dawn. Now the western breeze had fallen away completely, and I got up to furl the genoa, quietly, so I wouldn't disturb Carol, who slept down below with the accordion door tightly closed against the morning light. Indeed, in the previous two days, we'd gotten quite fond of shade, of the cool shadows of the closed cabin, when at midday up on deck there was only the glaring sky circle and the reflecting disc of water. The featureless scope of the sky and seascape was impressive; we were going to have to grow used to it gradually.

By eight that calm morning, I already needed my dark sunglasses. There were occasional cat's-paws, and the air was still cool from the night. I'd just eaten my second breakfast: canned peaches, salami, and wholewheat bread, washed down by a mug each of orange juice, the last of the fresh milk, and hot coffee. The boat rolled slightly in the vestigial swell, but not enough to make the mainsail slat. We were in the Gulf Stream now. Even if we were becalmed, the current was moving us steadily east at a little more than a knot.

I sat back in the cockpit and gazed around the blue rim of the horizon, yawning, content, not really tired. The sun was twirling scattered wisps of mist from the slowly pulsing mass of the sea. Above, the sky was porcelain blue, cloudless, but softer than the cobalt high-pressure sky of three days before. The morning was friendly, clean, incredibly silent. Sitting there, drowsy and musing, I slowly became conscious of a primitive, atavistic quality to the sea and sky around us, as if we had somehow traveled back in time, and not simply across distance, as if the gentle ocean belonged to an earlier geological epoch.

This calm spread of blue water was certainly not the North Atlantic I'd read about or pictured. For one thing, the only swell present was a pulsing ripple that might have raised and lowered the boat three inches every minute. It was as if the sea itself were basking, breathing slowly as it drowsed, like some docile, huge animal. There was a certain *thickness,* a coagulated texture to the water exaggerated by the scattered twirls of night mist and slow beat of the swell. Sitting there in the warm cockpit, my own breathing cycle unconsciously synchronized with the swell, I felt the ancient *shape* of the sea. My conscious, rational brain told me that water was a constantly changing, blending liquid; but now the sea seemed to have become a living jelly, like protoplasm, a vast creature that had occupied this part of the earth since primordial time. An immense, benign animal, so big that people had never been able to see its true dimensions and had thus been unable to identify its true nature.

The boat slid quietly through this thickening cellular plasma. A blue-gray fish splashed quite near the starboard shrouds, sending up a sparkle of definitely liquid droplets, and the drifting fantasy was shattered. I was on the liquid ocean once again, a couple of hundred miles outbound from New York. But, somehow, the primeval quality of the sea remained. Even though we were only a ten-minute jetliner ride from New York, I sensed that we had entered an untouched wilderness as primitive as anything in Alaska or the Amazon basin. Most of the world, I suddenly realized, was composed of water like this, living, moving salt water, untainted by land, which supported most of the world's microscopic and invertebrate life. The sea shone this soft aquamarine because of the chloroplastic algae living in its tissues. The fish that had just broken my daydream was as wild a creature as any impala or zebra I'd seen on the savanna of central Africa. We were crossing a plain far wider and far more fertile than the green plains of Parc Albert or the Serengeti Plain.

There had been dolphins in the night, on both our watches, large schools, splashing toward the boat across the calm, moonlit water, sounding from a distance like rain on canvas. Those little toothed whales had fished *this* water since before man first walked upright on the African veld. The prey they chased and the invertebrates and plankton those fish fed upon were indigenous to this sea. The collective evolution of these creatures—the ecosystem, as they now call this gigantic cooperative endeavor—was almost unchanged since Tertiary times. The ice ages, of course, had had some effect on water levels and salinity, but, out here, on the edge of the deep soundings, basic biological relationships had not changed much for an unthinkably long period.

Back astern, the land of the continent, as well as its rivers and lakes, had been irrevocably adulterated by human technology. We had set free in the biosphere polymeric chlorinated hydrocarbons—PCB, PBB, and all the rest of them—that could never have evolved in the natural universe and that had proved devastating to most life forms. In some parts of the Midwest, I'd read, the composition of the soil had been so altered by sixty years of chemical-interventionist agriculture that the production of any kind of food crop was no longer possible without man's annual bribe of synthetic fertilizers. But here, away from the continental influences of the shallow shelf water, the liquid three-fifths of the planet managed quite well on its own.

I looked above the masthead at the canopy of the sky. Around the boat there was only the blue expanse of the water. My reverie about crossing some kind of time frontier, I realized, had not been so farfetched. Carol and I had entered a region of temporal as well as physical isolation, an unchanged wilderness that only a few of the world's people had ever visited. This offshore water—enclosed, as it were, by the encircling river of the Gulf Stream—was more or less the way it had been since the earth's climate had "stabilized" in the past million years. Here, the existence of thinking, synthesizing humankind on the nearby continent so far had produced remarkably little environmental impact. This small fiber glass boat was actually a very efficient time machine: *Matata* had carried us back to an epoch in which man and his hissing, toxic vats of giant molecules did not exist.

We were now on that part of the earth's surface where the true nature of the planet becomes apparent. This was a world of water: Planet Ocean, as some ecologists have dubbed it. In our sun's planetary family there is no other world even remotely like this one. As seen in those wonderful photographs from the Apollo flights, the planet's disc is a blueberry-and-cream swirl of intercycling liquid water and water-droplet atmosphere. This staggering wealth of bonded oxygen and primordial hydrogen offers not only the logical explanation of why life exists here and not on our waterless neighbors but also a more fundamental reality: the ocean planet itself *is* alive, a vast, complex cauldron of self-replication, a molecular river stretching behind us four thousand million years to that cloudy, primitive sphere of gaseous methane and tentative, unstable nitrogenous compounds.

Reaching down from the teak rail, I touched my fingertips to the cool water. I smiled. We had become used to thinking of the earth as a solid ball—its dry crust coated by spongy brown soil and green vegetation—as an angular composite of vertical shapes: mountains, bluffs, gullies. Now I saw the chauvinistic error of this perception. The planet was more than three-fifths salty water in which the solids of the crust were dissolved as nutrient to support most of the world's biomass: the blue-green algae and the invertebrates that lived with them in silent partnership.

Earth was not solid land; it was a blue-and-white sphere of liquid water, and now Carol and I had the chance to observe—to live on—this normally unseen world, at least for a few summer weeks. The North Atlantic, of course, did not lend itself to close observation from a small boat during the six winter months; nor did the huge crown of water that occupied the southern one-third of the earth during any season. The Atlantic was certainly not the Southern Ocean or the gigantic void of the Pacific. This was a small, manageable sample of Planet Ocean's actual face.

The boat rolled slightly with the slowly passing swell, and the shackle of the topping lift creaked. An answering creak sounded from astern. In the night, we'd picked up a pair of black and white shearwaters, pretty little swallow-tailed birds that I had first thought, mistakenly, were land birds blown far out to sea. With the dawn, though, I'd been able to see them clearly. Carol had called them 'Bob and Betty' in her 0400 log entry, and that name was good enough for me. 'Bob,' if indeed the larger of the pair was the male, had two crooked tip feathers on his right wing, so it was easy to identify the pair as the same birds that had appeared in the night. There was something about the shackle of the topping lift that interested them, and twice during my late watch they had dive-bombed the end of the boom, swooping dangerously close to the sail and rigging.

The two birds were still out there astern, floating on the calm surface of the water, little friends, shepherding us out to sea. I shivered with contentment. The summer Atlantic was so much more peaceful than I had pictured it. Somehow, I'd imagined there would always be wind from some direction. Nothing I'd read about these latitudes had prepared me for this gentle calm. But, in a few hours, there was bound to be more breeze, and we would again be cranking out miles on our course toward the Azores. Now we had a respite, lazy and relaxing.

I sat more upright and glanced around the horizon for ships. Nothing: we'd already passed fifteen miles south of the main New York-Gibraltar shipping tract. Or at least I thought we had, if my navigation was anywhere near accurate. That wasn't really much of a worry, though. Yesterday's celestial navigation had coincided almost exactly with my dead reckoning and with the RDF fixes from Ambrose Light and Block Island.

The calm weather of the first few days had been a terrific piece of luck. Not only had we been able to catch up on our rest, we'd also been able to thoroughly test the new plastic sextants. So far, I was completely satisfied. That morning's first line of position put us right on the rhumb line, almost exactly on our DR position. After the sun's meridian pass, I'd have a fresh fix and could gauge the speed of the Stream's flow.

I glanced around the horizon again. Flat blue rim, no ships . . . booming empty sky. I thought I could feel the whispering start of a westerly breeze, but there were no tracks on the water. In fact, the boat's head had slipped south, so that we were *steering* about 170 degrees true. Actually, we were slipping beam-on to the current, almost due east. A free ride, relaxing and peaceful. Maybe, I thought with truly foolish optimism, the Azores High was beginning already.

I dozed for a while, a sailor's catnap that was becoming increasingly natural, then awoke to the chattering of the two shearwaters. The mainsail was slatting, and the creaking shackle excited the birds. Instinctively, I looked around the horizon. Jesus! There was a big red buoy, right out there, about a thousand yards off the port bow. Grabbing the binoculars, I quickly focused on the buoy. My fingers were sweaty on the focus knob and my breathing was erratic. Could my celestial navigation and RDF work have been *that* far off? Had some freak, unnoticed current pushed us north to the Nantucket shoals? For a panicky moment, lots of disastrous possibilities caromed around my head. My inexperience was taking charge; I wanted to start the engine, to steer away from the shoals that the buoy *must* be marking. I was actually sweating and breathing hard on this unmenacing morning of China-blue sky and water.

The buoy came into focus: dull red and rust-spotted, a fat metal tub float, supporting a girdered gong structure and light. "44004," I read through the glasses. Sitting back, I could now remember. There was no freak current; we were right on course. When I'd come off watch at two this morning, we'd switched to a new chart covering the longitudes from Montauk to the Grand Banks. Sleepily, I'd noticed there was a strange chart symbol exactly at the crossed coordinates of 39°00′ North latitude and 70°00′ West longitude.

Carol had been pulling her safety harness over the flotation vest, glancing over my shoulder as I wrote up the log entry and put a time tick on the rhumb line of the new chart. "Is that a *buoy* way out there?" She reached around me to tap the chart with her fingertip.

My eyes had been tired, and, just down from the cockpit, I'd found the bright chart light dazzling. I squinted at the symbol, and then at the soundings near it: 1,360 *fathoms*, over six thousand feet of water. Whatever that thing was, I thought, it sure as hell was *not* a buoy. "Some kind of loran symbol," I muttered, ". . . don't worry about it."

Carol finished getting into the watchkeeper's gear. Like me, she was not worried about buoys or shoals this far out at sea. "Okay," she said. "Have a nice sleep."

I pulled myself tiredly up from the chart table, the strange marking already forgotten. "I'll sure try."

So much for my piloting skills. There was indeed a lighted gong buoy anchored in over 6,000 feet of water, exactly at 39°00′ North and 70°00′ West. We were less than a mile from it, and I could now see what a boon it represented for us. We would wait at the buoy for the sun's meridian pass. Already knowing our exact position, we could verify our sextant work, judge the log's accuracy, the true force and direction of the current, and also check compass deviation. I focused more tightly on the rusty tub, seeing the swaying skirt of weed at the water line.

Thanks, NOAA, I thought. I'll never bitch about high taxes again.

We reached the buoy a little before noon on the chronometer watch and putted around, circling the metal tub, waiting for the sun's meridian pass. The earlier breeze had dropped away completely, and the sea was as still as polished turquoise. Only around the base of the buoy was there any indication that this immense, pale blue surface was a fluid. The skirt of weed at the rusty water line eddied and flowed with the Stream. Close alongside the tub, the sun thrust deep gold streamers into the abyss. It was hot and still. We motored slowly in a wide circle, waiting for the sun to crest out at its zenith, taking turns at the tiller while the other person had a cooling bucket bath.

While I was drying off, Carol slipped the gear lever into neutral and pointed astern. "Great big fish," she said in quiet astonishment. "Look . . . really *big* ones. They're following the boat . . . like puppies."

Moving slowly, so as not to alarm the fish, I knelt on the hot lazaret hatch. Just under our transom, no more than three feet beneath the calm surface, nine long yellow-fin tuna swam in echelons of three fish each. They were definitely following the boat, and their upturned saucer eyes did give them an aura of guileless, puppylike innocence. To the south the sun mounted toward its daily peak. I shut down the throbbing engine and we drifted in a slow ellipse. Around us, the sea and sky seemed to fuse into a single, booming, silent bowl, as if we had slipped into a shallow but incredibly wide *hollow* in the sea, the very center of which was marked by the buoy. Again, I had the strong sensation of the primordial, that we'd been drawn backward in time to a more innocent epoch. The faithful shearwaters paddling fifty yards behind us, and the juvenile trust on the cartoon faces of the fish suddenly combined to carry me into a kind of tableau, something akin to Edward Hicks's painting, *The Peaceful Kingdom,* in which the lion literally does lie down with the lamb.

The two birds rose from the water and flew over to the buoy, where they perched, preening their feathers. Beneath the stern, the squadron of big fish kept station just under the surface. I braced myself in the cockpit and took a preliminary sextant shot of the sun's altitude. Pulling the muted yellow disc down to the horizon, I was suddenly struck by the meshing geometric precision of the day. Here was this slowly swaying red buoy, floating directly above a dot on the ocean bottom that represented the crossed coordinates of the thirty-ninth parallel of north latitude with the seventieth meridian of west longitude. The sun was rising almost visibly past seventy-two degrees elevation above the horizon. It was 1240 local zone time; in a few minutes the sun would crest out at 73°13′, today's zenith altitude, and the time would be exactly 1244, plus three or four seconds. At that moment, the sun would bear exactly 180 degrees true or 195 degrees magnetic: due south. The nine fish swam in three weird, seemingly predetermined groups of three each. The birds flew in a uniform, symmetrical unit of two, just as Carol and I were voyaging across this spherical surface. I had never before seen nature reveal so clearly its internal, usually hidden, symmetry.

By carefully and frequently observing the sun's altitude, we could time the moment the meridian pass began and ended. This would give us our exact longitude. Knowing that, we could judge the accuracy of the Phasar digital watch we used as a chronometer, independent of any outside radio time signal. The combination of calm water, clear sky, and flat horizon and the precisely known location of this buoy offered a rare navigational experience. It was as if we were privileged observers at some epochal trigonometry experiment, as if this buoy had been transported all the way out here and located exactly on this spot so that some arcane mathematical theory could be demonstrated on a cosmic scale. I couldn't help but think of Stonehenge and other monolithic astronomical observatories in Europe.

Gripping the hot plastic handle of the sextant, I slowly turned the micrometer drum, rocking the bottom edge of the sun's brassy mirror disc on the geometrically flat horizon. Carol was keeping the time log in our navigational workbook.

"Mark," I said.

"Twelve hours," she intoned, writing the numerals in the notebook, "forty-four minutes . . . and two seconds."

"HS," I said, turning the sextant to read the scale, "seventy-two degrees, fifty-seven minutes. . . . that should be about it."

She was jotting down more figures. "Okay," she answered, looking up to smile. "With zero index error and dip minus three minutes . . . that renders an HO of seventy-three degrees, fourteen minutes, which . . . "—she nibbled quickly on the pencil eraser, then wrote some more quick figures—" . . . which gives us a calculated latitude of thirty-nine degrees one minute north latitude . . . pretty close."

I held the sextant away from my hip and squinted at the southern horizon. "Close enough for our game of horseshoes. What's the compass bearing on the sun?"

Carol leaned over the bulkhead compass and looked down the lubber line. "Just about one ninety-five . . . maybe a degree shy. One eighty true."

"Not bad . . . exactly right, as a matter of fact. HS . . . HO . . . latitude, time of pass, sun bearing and longitude, and there's the proof . . . " I pointed the sextant at the big red buoy, swaying slowly in the flow of the Stream sixty yards off the starboard beam.

Carol went over her figures again, then looked up. "Incredible," she said, almost whispering. "It's like . . . "

"Stonehenge," I said soberly.

Wordlessly, she nodded. Then, pointing to the west, she rose a little on the cockpit cushion. "There's our breeze."

She was right; there definitely was a soft westerly coming toward us out of the flat midday glare, as if our allotted time in this marine Arcadia was over, as if the geometrical clockwork of the spinning planet would now be discreetly hidden once again, as if we were being told to continue on our way.

For a long moment, we both sat there, watching the small wrinkles of the westerly approach us across the blue surface and the red metal buoy slowly draw away from us as the first of the breeze combined with the steady east-going flow of the Stream.

When I went down to the shady cabin to put away the sextant, I sat for a moment with the multicolored sheet of the pilot chart before me on the chart table. The July sheet predicted zero probability of gales at this latitude. And we were within two hundred eighty miles of being clear of the mean July hurricane tract. I looked back up through the open hatch at the empty sky. This was the way the entire trip would be, I assured myself; easy westerlies giving us daily runs of almost one hundred miles, then some calms, then more steady westerlies. The pretty red, blue, and green pilot chart was a wonderfully comforting document. It proclaimed us now well away from the coastal storm tracts. With the confirmation of our noon position, we had slipped over the edge of the continental shelf and hopefully away from the influence of continental depressions. Now we were in the warm clutch of the summer Stream. We had made it, out and away from the land, and into the benevolent stability of the Azores High.

I stretched and yawned. Time for one of the last cold beers, then a sandwich and a nap. Carol had the watch now, and I could sleep in the cool, shaded cabin.

After lunch, as Carol reset the genoa, poled-out wing-and-wing with the main, I lay in the cool shadows of the cabin, thinking how foolishly unfounded my earlier doubts had been. Crossing oceans, I decided as I hunkered down for sleep, was a lot easier than coastal cruising.

I remember that afternoon sleep as I recall the untroubled backyard naps of innocent childhood.

Early evening. I awoke wonderfully rested and lay on the cotton sheet covering my sleeping bag. For several minutes I enjoyed the luxury of being free to lie there with no duties or decisions to draw me up on deck. From the angle of heel and the faint strumming tone of the rigging, I knew we were on a starboard tack, a broad reach giving us about five knots; we rode the same fair westerly that had risen after the noon sight.

When I climbed up to the cockpit, I found Carol staring through the binoculars at a large ship crossing our bow from the north a couple of miles ahead.

"Toyota something or other," she said, lowering the glasses. "He's high on his marks . . . must be empty."

I took the glasses and scanned the long blue hull. There was plenty of ocher bottom paint showing. "Coming down empty from Canada," I said, pointing to the north. "Must have unloaded his cars somewhere on the Saint Lawrence."

Carol kneeled on the bench cushion to watch the vessel's rapid progress across our track. "They really don't look so scary in the daylight, do they?"

"They're so tall and fast that they don't even see us at night, even with our radar reflector." I sat down beside her. "We'll just have to remember that."

"They certainly are fast." Carol shifted slightly to see the merchant ship under the genoa. "He'll be through the Panama Canal, across the whole Pacific, and loading more Toyotas in Yokohama by the time we get to the Azores. It's like we're not even traveling the same ocean . . . like we're not basically the same kind of machine." She glanced up the bellying mainsail and the jib. "We're like a hang glider and he's like a Boeing 747."

"I prefer to think of us as a very small clipper ship," I said, smoothing my fingers down the fine grain of the teak cockpit coaming.

Carol laughed with full, unembarrassed mirth. "Okay then, Captain Bligh, how about the evening grog ration?"

I came back up from the galley with a jug of chablis beaded cold from the ice chest, two plastic glasses, and our cassette player. The tape was Savoupoulis singing Theodorakis. Carol filled the glasses while I checked the taffrail log reading and wrote up the deck log for 1800. Behind us to the west, the sun was still golden warm, beginning to swing down to the level horizon. The large Toyota car-carrier was gone to the south. We were alone again in the soft afternoon, the boat steering well on the rhumb line for the Azores.

"In New York," Carol said, nodding behind us toward the lowering sun, "people are lined up shoulder-to-shoulder in the bars, trying to get three gimlets down the hatch before it's time to leave the air conditioning and face those trains. I guess we can't complain too much."

"So, who's complaining?"

She adjusted the volume on the cassette player and sipped from her glass. "Wine, women, and song," she raised her eyes to meet mine. "Would you like to make love?"

It had been several confused and anxious months since she herself had asked that question.

I slid my hand beneath the edge of her cotton shirt, feeling the taut warmth of her flesh. "I thought you'd never ask."

The blade of the vane rocked slowly, the tiller drove the rudder to windward, and the sails filled. Above us, the sky went from blue to lavender.

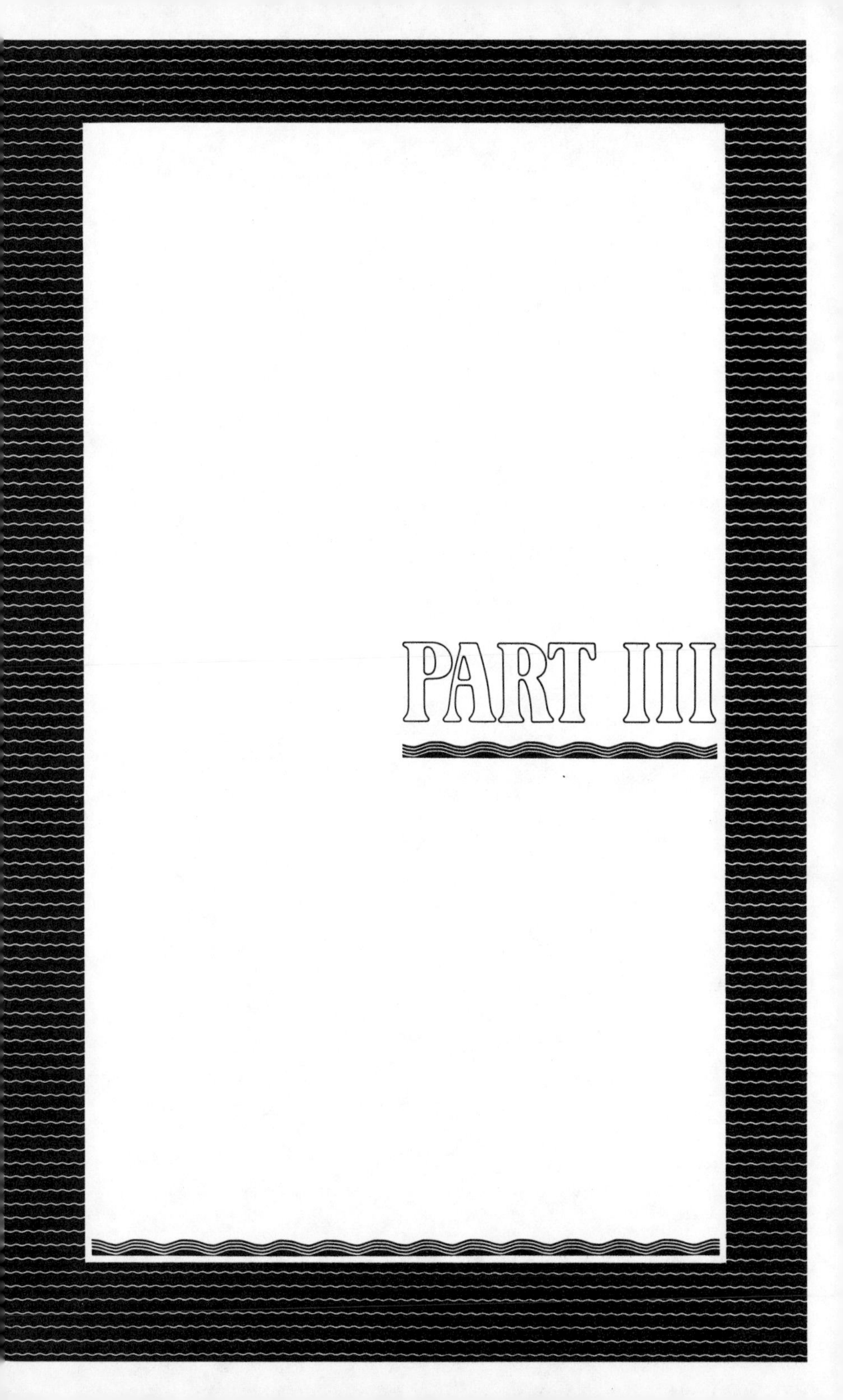

PART III

CHAPTER SIX

DR: 39°15' NORTH, 67°05' WEST
JULY 11: 1700 GMT

The barometer had been falling for twenty-six hours, slowly but without pause. Around us, the sea was a dirty gray, matching the greasy-dishwater color of the sky. Monday's flat sea and blue sky were an improbable memory. It was as if we were on an entirely different ocean now. The boat was beginning to pound with alarming violence as the rising wind headed us.

A little after noon, and after a futile attempt to find the sun for the meridian pass, we'd put one reef in the main and changed from the genny to the working jib. Soon, if this wind continued building, as it surely would, we'd have to think about another reef and the storm jib. I rubbed the scratchy brine on my face, licked my lips nervously, and looked forward, out around the protection of the cabin top. If anything, the waves were steeper than they'd been five minutes earlier.

It looked as if we had a goddamn *gale* on our hands. The previous day, all the classic signs of a big depression had appeared: sharp mares' tails high in the western sky, curving into milky cirro-stratus; a calm followed by a steadily rising wind and a slowly mounting swell from the east southeast. Several times that dark and bumpy night, I'd hunted for storm warnings on the WWV frequencies . . . nothing, too much lightning static, a bad sign in itself. I'd also tried to get WINS from New York on AM. Again, too much crackling lightning static. There was definitely a very active cold front between us and the East Coast.

By noon, we didn't need any forecast to tell us we had a storm on our hands. We had seen plenty of bad weather in the Aegean, working charter boats, especially during the spring and fall sirocco seasons. So we weren't exactly strangers to storms, and, as I watched this one build, I kept reminding myself that the only reason these conditions looked so menacing was that we were four hundred miles offshore. Nevertheless, the weather was definitely bad: low stratus clouds blowing beneath a solid overcast of nimbo-stratus, wave crests getting toward ten feet and mounting, and a sharply backing wind. The center of this depression was going to pass somewhere to the north, but I had no way of knowing how wide the trough was, how long it would take to pass, or how steep the pressure gradient was. Therefore, I had no way of knowing just how bad conditions might become, or how quickly. But I could now see that this rising wind and nasty swell were definitely going to hit us from the east southeast, and that put the full energy of the storm dead against the steady 1-knot flow of the Stream.

As any sailor who has raced the Florida circuit can tell you, a strong countercurrent gale in the Stream—with the typical steep, short seas—is not just another summer storm.

Reaching back around the web of lines and shock cord connected to the tiller, I readjusted the tension on the violently rocking wind vane, then looked out at the waves. They were building, close together, and crested with dingy white. The boat still rose to meet most crests, but every few minutes we'd get jammed in between a couple of waves converging from different directions and take solid water across the deck.

We banged into an especially steep one, and the closed companionway hatch slid half open.

"I'll get it," I called down to Carol.

I sprawled over the open hatch, staring down at her. She was in the galley, using a yellow plastic sponge to wipe spattered coffee from the bulkhead above the sink. She had already washed and put away the dishes from our soup-and-sandwich lunch, which she had bravely volunteered to prepare even though the boat was practically standing on its ear. Her insistence on maintaining the pleasant domestic ritual of a hot lunch on such a nasty gray day had been brought on by more than a housewife's pride. With this weather we might not be able to heat food on the stove again for a day, at least. The minestrone with salami chunks and extra noodles had provided enough palatable nutrient to see us both through a long period of physical labor out in the chill wind and soaking spray.

Beyond the physical comfort of a hot lunch, however, she had also recognized the psychological value of maintaining a kind of regular domestic pattern in the face of our first full gale so far offshore. This storm had not been predicted, as far as we could tell. We simply had no idea how bad conditions would become. To keep this gnawing uncertainty at bay, Carol was forcing herself to stay busy with mindless tasks like cleaning up the galley.

Earlier, she had volunteered to reef the mainsail because I had gotten banged around and soaked changing the headsail down from the genoa to the working jib. She was funny that way: a stranger seeing her there at the galley sink sponging off the white gelcoat of the bulkhead would envision a nervous helpmate, dragged out here to these stormy waters by her domineering, crack-pot husband. An hour before, the same observer would have seen her up on the exposed cabin top, the lines of her safety harness whipping in the gale, reefing pendant clenched in her teeth like a pirate's knife, her hair wild, salty streamers around her head as she subdued the rifle-cracking cloth of the main.

Carol had never learned to posture very well, to construct deceptive façades. Because of this, people often underestimated her.

A couple of weeks before we sailed, we had attended a garden party at the fashionable Village townhouse of a friend in the publishing industry. We had been sipping white wine and chit-chatting with all the attractive people when a well-known editor from one of the bigger publishing houses strode up to explain how "fantastic" he thought it was that I was going to sail a small boat across the Atlantic. I pointed out to him that I wasn't planning to sail alone, that Carol and I were doing it as a joint venture.

He deigned to glance in Carol's direction. "You must have had to learn a little about sailing to help him out," he said in kindly tones. He was serious.

I could see Carol grit her jaw, then she smiled. "Yes," she said evenly, "a little."

"I guess," the amiable editor continued, "you handle the galley and Malcolm does the sailing."

Carol sipped her wine tranquilly. "Something like that."

"Boy," the editor added, "I envy you two, I really do." He produced a troubled frown. "But . . . well, what do you do at night? When do you sleep?"

I was about to speak, but Carol cut in, speaking in the same untroubled, unassertive tone. "We always anchor at night." She beamed at the gray-haired gentleman.

"Oh," he said, smiling now himself. "I see . . . sure."

I felt a surge of embarrassed laughter rising for the man, and again Carol spoke. "The only problem with anchoring each night is pulling up the fourteen *thousand* feet of anchor chain each morning." Again she grinned benignly. "We take turns."

She strolled off into the elegant, candlelit garden. The editor drained his martini glass and rattled the little machine-made ice cubes. "Ummm," he mused, " . . . umm, well." He cleared his throat and I looked away. Fortunately, a mutual friend arrived, bearing a tray of fancy crab-meat hors d'oeuvres, and we could break the hot discomfort of the silence by commenting on the food.

Carol wiped down one last sponge stroke and looked up. She'd changed into a dry sweater and jeans and tied up her hair since being on deck. "How does it look . . . the swell, I mean?"

I raised my face from the dry warmth of the companionway, into the stinging wind. "She is definitely still blowing, Honey."

Carol reached over to the swaying stove and plucked off a plastic glass that was balanced on the gimbaled burner plate as if by conjuration. "Coffee," she said grinning self-conciously. "I made two cups of that nice Swiss mocha, but they spilled. I managed to save a couple of swallows."

I took the glass she held up to me and craned my neck to drink a mouthful of lukewarm coffee. It was sweet and smooth. Above my head, the wind was beginning to twang the rigging.

"*That* doesn't sound so good," Carol said.

"I know." Again, I raised my face into the stiff spray. "We're going to have to reef again if this keeps up."

"That bad?" She sat on the end of the starboard quarter berth. Her oilskins and sea boots lay in a dripping mass at her feet. "You look really, well, worried . . . What's wrong?"

Thrusting my head and shoulders down into the shelter of the cabin, I tried to assume a calm expression. But inside my head, the word "hurricane" banged around as if trying to punch a way out. This was ridiculous, of course; the sky signs associated with the approach of a tropical depression would have been much different from what we'd seen in the past two days. Rational reassurance, however, was not my strongest card just then. I'd been up on deck for the past hour and knew that this howling wind and crazy, mounting sea added up to something much more than a summer squall line. Finally, I found the right words. "The sea's getting pretty short . . . steep, too. I wish we had a VHF, so we could talk to some ship and get a decent weather forecast."

Carol nodded. "Well, we don't have one." She flicked dried salt flowers off the chart before her on the chart table. "A weather forecast won't *change* the weather, Malcolm."

I leaned deeper into the warmth, the top storm board in the hatchway digging into my chest. "Yeah," I sighed. "You're right, of course. I'm just sorry we've got this storm, Honey. I didn't think we'd have anything like this. I'm sorry . . ."

Carol smiled up at me in the sliding shadows. "Malcolm . . . the weather is something even *you* can't control."

I found myself joining her laughter. Jesus, it was nice having someone else along on a trip like this. How the *hell* did the singlehanders do it? I closed the hatch behind me and sat up to face the gale.

Carol's humor and thinking about those brave singlehanders had cheered me up. I needed cheering, as I now realized that I was feeling quite definitely up-chucking seasick for the first time in years. All I could do was sit here in the shelter of the canvas spray dodger and let the Bonine work while I watched the sea get crazier by the minute, while the sky lowered and the wind began to roar in the shrouds. Out of nowhere, I could clearly see the pretty colored lines of the pilot chart.

"You bastard," I muttered, giving vent to my sense of betrayal. Some friend and ally that chart had turned out to be. Less than two days after our idyllic episode at the offshore NOAA buoy and here the wind was rising past thirty-five knots, headed for a full gale. But the pilot chart said, right inside those little blue quadrant squares, that there weren't supposed to *be* any gales on these latitudes during the month of July.

A hard gust hit the boat, and we heeled off the crest of a big one and fell, smacking into the trough. I shook the drenching spray off my hood and wiped my face. Already the tender flesh under my chin was getting chafed by the salty hood working on the two-day beard stubble. The pilot chart, I now recalled, was a *statistical* compilation, not a weather forecast. Like most people, I liked to believe statistics were in my favor, that a low statistical murder rate in a certain town meant that I would never be murdered, not that my own murder would be the only one that happened in a given ten-year period. This damn gale, I now saw, wasn't statistically normal, but like a murder, it was painfully real.

The wind howled unusually loudly through the rigging, and we slammed way over. Carol stuck her head out of the hatch looking pale beneath her suntan.

"How are we doing?" she asked, obviously trying to keep her voice calm.

I leaned over the coaming to look forward. The sea was larger and noticeably more confused than it had been five minutes before. The size of the waves really didn't worry me so much, but their *shape* was nasty: short and steep and getting shorter and steeper as the wind direction steadied off a few points south of east.

"What's the barometer say?" I stalled, answering her query with a question.

She leaned over the chart table, was thrown back dangerously as we rolled, then braced herself more securely and tapped both barometers as they swayed above her on the bulkhead. "The big one says 30.58 and falling." Again, she tapped the older glass. "The little one says 30.60 and it's falling faster than the other."

They were both registering too high, I knew. The violent motion of the boat and the banging of the instruments against the plywood bulkhead was causing the needles to jump with the shock.

I put my head and shoulders through the open hatch again to see the instruments, just as we fell off a wave. Green water came sloshing along the high side, and a bucketful splashed down into the newly cleaned galley.

"Get your oilskins on," I said as kindly as I could, "and a harness. We've got to shorten sail right now."

It took me a long time on the foredeck to get the working jib down and loosely tied, so that I could try to bag it alone. Every simple task was made quite difficult up on this bucking-bronco deck. The wind, too, was a real problem. Every time I thought the billowing sail was secured, a huge pocket would blow out from the ties and snap into my face, flailing my wet skin painfully. During the past thirty minutes, the wind had risen to the point where fist-sized chunks of spray were being chopped off the wave crests. The seas themselves were beginning to pyramid as the swell jammed harder against the Stream's flow. I was sitting on the streaming wet deck, snapped into the jack lines with one tether, and onto the solid metal of the bow pulpit with the other, not taking any chances of being thrown out into that crazy sea. Working as carefully as I could, I tried to force the clew end of the jib into the ballooning sail bag.

The boat rose under me, sharply, then heeled very hard to port. My hood was jammed over my eyes by the wind, but I could *feel* the wave crest hanging over me the same way a driver feels the presence of a truck whipping from behind into his blind spot on a busy freeway. Surprisingly, the water was quite warm when the wave broke over me, lifting and turning my body so that I found myself facing aft when the wave had passed.

"Keep the goddamn boat downwind," I screamed, sputtering out my fear in senseless anger.

I don't think Carol heard me because another big one drew us up, exposed the single-reefed main to the full force of the wind, then dropped us off the crest. Another warm green sea flopped over me.

"Let the main go!" I yelled. "Start the engine!" I waved my free hand in the wind, my jacket cuff flapping loudly. "Bring the goddamn boat down!" All the good, salty words of command were there; my brain was obviously functioning, but I sure as hell wasn't making sense.

Finding some spare braided line in the flooded jacket pocket, I secured the jib to the lifelines, reattached the sheet to the clew, then dragged myself upright on the weatherside shrouds. Back in the cockpit I could see Carol, white-faced and grim, fighting the tiller.

"Christ," I hissed, "come *on* . . . ease the main." She seemed to behave like some green dope, keeping the boat pointed so high while I was up on the foredeck, busting my hump. If she ever changed head sails herself, she'd know how hard it was. "Hey . . . " I began yelling again."

But then, hanging on the shrouds, soaked, gasping, and not a little panicked, I could clearly see that the main was already well sheeted out. I also saw that the sea had become truly wild, the pyramids transformed into steep hummocks, their slopes plastered with ripply white, their ridges amazingly close together. Something was all *wrong* here, my rational, well-read mind told me. The Atlantic was not supposed to hit you with this dangerously short sea. But we had a gale against the Stream, a steady current, which was itself compressed by the shoals and countercurrent to the north. Maybe it was my imagination, but the seas to the southeast seemed to be backing up in higher, toppling *ranks* as the wind speed increased and the short swell jammed against the current. Bending down, I snapped into the shrouds and tried to plan a strategy.

Bearing off to the north, to take the wind and seas on the beam, was not going to do much good here. The waves were now well over fifteen feet and growing quickly. And they were so close and steep that running was not a viable option, either. Maybe we wouldn't broach in the troughs, but the main, even with another reef and secured by a preventer, would back violently, jibing the boat.

The wind cut into the chafed skin around my hood, drying the spray to an itching brine. My mouth tasted foul and I recalled that it had been about thirty hours since I'd brushed my teeth. Under my streaming yellow oilskin jacket, my hooded sweatshirt was wet, clammy against my neck and shoulders. It was not easy to think, soaked through in the moaning wind, still quite woozy from my abortive attempts at sail changing. I peeled back the jacket cuff to see my watch, shocked to learn it was three-thirty local time and to realize that I'd been hassling that stupid jib for half an hour. In the cockpit, Carol looked exhausted, trying to keep us off the wind, which kept shifting in the bad gusts. To windward, rank after rank of these short, crashing seas rolled down on us.

We fell off another crest, and I ended up hanging onto the lee shrouds with my safety harness lines tangled around the halyard winches. As I pulled myself up again, we went through a near jibe in the trough, then heeled over hard on the next crest. When the bow fell off this wave, I banged my face painfully against the mast, my boots skidding on the wet deck. An especially hard blast of wind struck us, heeling the boat right over and jerking the tiller out of Carol's double grip. The bow dug in and the boat seemed to stop in the water. When I looked up at the main, I saw the broken top batten sticking out of its ripped pocket like a fractured bone. Time to get that sail double-reefed.

I forced myself to think in a logical, sequential pattern; panic wasn't going to help us at all. But the wind was howling so loudly, like during the worst of an August line squall in coastal waters. No, I swore, don't think about the damn wind. Work with Carol. Think about what you each have to do to reef the main. That attempt at logical thought lasted about ten seconds, until I saw the new plastic-strip telltale on the weather-side shroud separate from its stiffener and fly away in the worst gust so far. The strip was quickly followed by the hard plastic split ring on the stainless steel cable.

The hell with another reef. It was time to get that sail *down* before it blew to pieces. Yelling back to Carol was useless in this wind. The spray was solid and almost horizontal now. I waved my free arm, signaling her to haul in on the sheet once I had the halyard free. The boat was heaving so rapidly that I needed one hand to grip the mast at all times and was forced to free the coil of the main halyard using my right fingers and my teeth. The line had to run freely; if it snagged aloft in this wind with the sail neither down nor up, we'd be in real trouble. Once the halyard was more or less in a smooth coil, I wedged the looped tackle between the luff and the sail track to keep it out of harm's way while I shortened off on the topping lift. Even working carefully and keeping one hand-hold constant, I was banged around badly.

Finally, the mainsail came down, me tugging at the billowing folds, careful to stay to windward of the flailing slabs of wet dacron. Carol had a coil of three-eighths braided line ready, and I lashed the sail tightly to the boom, then worked back up toward the mast, doubling off my original sail ties, which had already worked loose in the wind and spray. Whatever sail we'd now use, it certainly wouldn't be the main. Amazingly, the only damaged the sail had sustained was the ripped batten pocket. Our extra work getting each seam triple stitched had obviously just paid off.

With the sail lashed tightly to the boom, the boat rode the seas much more smoothly. We weren't heeling so wildly with each gust, either, and I had time to think clearly now. Under this heavy, lowering overcast, it would be too dark to see the waves in a couple of hours, and the wind was still rising. Therefore, trying to run off dead downwind under bare pole was not a very good idea. Why not lie ahull for a while, I thought, so that we could get some rest and plan our next course of action? One of the last books I'd read before sailing from New York had been Richard Henderson's *East to the Azores: A Guide to Offshore Passage-Making.* He and his family had experienced a similar "freak" gale just north of this tract a few years before and had had considerable success with these crazy pyramid seas, letting their boat lie ahull with the sails stripped off and the helm lashed down, rudder to windward.

I looked around the heaving horizon a moment. With our speed reduced, we weren't being hurled off the top of each wave as we had been, and we'd stopped taking dangerous solid water across the deck. In effect, we were almost lying ahull right now, and it seemed to be working. But we were going to do it right, lowering and securing the boom before lashing down the helm. Maybe it wasn't the best tactic, but right then it was certainly the easiest.

"Sheet the boom in when I lower it," I yelled.

Carol crouched at the tiller, gripping the free end of the main sheet while I bent to slack off the topping lift. Next crossing I make, I thought, whenever *that* is, I'm definitely going to lead the main halyard and topping lift back to the cockpit.

Once the boom was down on the cabin top, I used strong braided dacron line to lash it to the teak grab rail portside, then doubled off the lashing down to the genny track just for good measure. If the wind and sea continued to rise, I didn't want to have to come back up to this exposed position to do the job again. While I worked, Carol lashed the tiller hard to port, right up against the teak trim on the cockpit coaming, securing it with a length of shock cord. When I joined her in the cockpit, I backed up her lashing with a second thick shock cord, making it fast with slip-proof fisherman's knots.

Now we could survey our work. The boat wasn't pitching so erratically as it had been, but we heeled over with each gust, taking the swell on the starboard beam, riding up and down each steep wave face. There were plenty of spray baseballs sizzling through the shrouds, but we didn't take much heavy sea across the deck, and we certainly were not smacking the bow as we had been.

I snapped into the jack lines outside the cockpit on the lee side. There was some shelter here, and I thought I'd sit for a while, making sure the tiller lashing was secure. I wasn't worried about the jib on the foredeck, as I'd lashed it quite tightly when I was trying to bag it; the clew was still clipped to the leeward sheet, and *that* was cleated off back here. Moving back aft from the shrouds, I'd been able to doublecheck the life raft lashing and the web of shock cord securing the canister of emergency water. It looked as if we'd done just about all we could on deck. Stripped of sail, and with the helm secured hard down, *Matata* was riding the sea quite well now. I looked out, around the lowering horizon. Nothing but nasty gray sky and savage gray seas. The wind was still mounting and, with it, the ranks of steep waves. The crests had to be getting up toward twenty feet now, as high as I'd ever seen the sea. I wondered how all this would look at night.

Carol stared at me from under the wind-twisted brim of her oilskin hood. "Are we okay?"

That was a good question. Before answering, I knelt up on the cockpit bench and peered ahead into the full blast of the wind and spray. On the foredeck, the gusts and the solid sheets of spray had molded the jib into a neatly furled roll at the rail. No problem there. The boom and tightly lashed mainsail were well secured to the cabin top, as were the raft box and water canister. All the sheets and halyards were accounted for. Back here in the cockpit, our heavy shock cord lashing on the tiller was holding well. Carol had secured the plywood blade of the wind vane quite tightly against a cloth pad on the starboard side of the stern pulpit, so it wasn't going to flail about in the gusts and hurt itself. The lazaret hatch was closed and locked. The taffrail log line seemed to be minding itself quite well, as we had just barely enough way on to keep the impeller from hanging straight down and fouling the rudder and prop. All told, we were battened down pretty well.

"Okay," I said loudly enough to be heard over the wind. "We seem to be riding fine. Would you mind going down to check the bilge and the barometers?"

She seemed relieved to get out of the cockpit. The spray wasn't so bad anymore, but the deep wail of the wind was enervating.

I crouched again over the open gap in the hatchway while she sounded the bilge and tapped both glasses.

"Almost nothing in the bilge," she shouted up, "but both barometers are still dropping fast."

Nodding soberly, I pulled the hatch shut and slid back on the wet surface of the plastic cushion to give the tiller lashings a final check. Then I scanned the crazy, rolling, gray horizon one last time and slipped down through the hatch, slamming it hard behind me. It felt decidedly strange to be out of the solid pressure and howl of the wind. I undid my hood and jacket snaps and dropped the wet mass of oilskins on the portside quarter berth that Carol had already prepared, covering it with thick plastic garbage bags in anticipation of the gale.

In the dry warmth of the galley, it was hard to believe the wild force of the storm only a few feet above our heads. Even though the bulkheads were creaking badly, and the subway rumble of the approaching waves was scary, I could see that we were not in any immediate danger. Drying my face and neck with a wad of paper toweling that Carol handed me, I tried to think clearly. This storm was severe, probably 50, 55 knots of wind against the 1-knot flow of the Stream, resulting in seas well over 20 feet. But these conditions were not yet life-threatening, not with the boat behaving so well as it lay ahull. I'd talked with Al Cramer, the man who'd done our survey in April, about exactly this problem. His opinion was that given the Arpege's strong, double-bolted iron keel and solidly supported rudder skeg, lying ahull in anything but survival-storm conditions would be our best tactic. Since that survey, we'd overhauled each through-hull fitting and inspected every inch of rigging. The boat was ready for this storm, and for a lot worse.

Sitting on the engine step, I pulled off my flooded deck boots. In the main cabin, Carol squatted on the low-side bunk putting on a dry sweatshirt, her soaked oilskins heaped on the cabin sole beneath the bunk. That wasn't a bad idea; a rubdown with a towel and some dry clothes would definitely go a long way toward improving our morale. Another Bonine was going to help, too.

It took a while to get changed and back into my oilskins again: working at any task in an upright position while the boat heeled and snap-rolled with each passing wave was more difficult than I'd thought it would be. But half an hour later I was dressed in dry jeans, dry socks, dry turtleneck, and dry sweatshirt under my damp oilskins. Before taking a look back topside, I pulled on the flotation vest and harness. I was feeling a little dizzy from the Bonine and from the stuffy, sick-making atmosphere down below. If I had to go outside to adjust anything, I'd certainly need the harness. Reluctantly, I waited for the boat to sled down a wave crest, then jerked back the hatch.

The scene outside was spectacular. It was as if the parallel hummocks of the wave crests had been transformed into steep, gray and white sand dunes, tall smooth hills in some nightmare desert, stretching off to the lopsided horizon. I crouched in the half-open hatch, fascinated by this weird landscape around us. The distinct, unshakable impression I had was that the boat was passing through some science-fiction stage set of gelatinous hills; that perhaps the boat had grown wheels and was now rolling through this range of ocean dunes. I was gripped by the persuasive illogic of dreams in which these kind of occurrences happen to us several nights a week. But this was no dream. That wind moaning in the rigging and those chunks of spray whipped off the shaggy crests were definitely real. I think now that my distorted perceptions were a product of fatigue, seasickness, the Bonine tablets, and no small dose of just plain fear. Whatever it was, though, my memory of the five minutes I crouched there in the hatchway watching the storm carries with it the unmistakeable image of the liquid sea transformed into solid hills. When I look back on this first gale, I think of a range of sea hills somewhere out there on the Atlantic, four hundred miles south of Nova Scotia. Sometimes, when I'm thinking of the crossing, half-asleep in bed at night, I can clearly picture that rugged, wind-blasted country, and I somehow *know* the hills must still be out there.

I slid back down into the dry hollow of the cabin. Things were fine on deck; the boat was minding itself well. The relevant question this gloomy afternoon of wind and breaking sea was, How were *we* managing? Had we taken on more than we could handle? I rubbed my wet face. What if the entire crossing degenerated into an ongoing bout of these nasty depressions, sweeping out of the continent and feeding on the convergence of the warm Stream with the cold countercurrents of the north Atlantic? It was a bad prospect. But this type of pessimistic speculation was as fruitless and naïve as my earlier optimism at the NOAA buoy had been.

Wedged in behind the chart table as the hull rolled and groaned, I saw that I had to face certain facts about the sea. The Atlantic Ocean did not *know* we were out here. Despite the idyllic conditions of Monday and the unexpected savagery of this storm, there was neither a benign nor a malevolent personality to this body of water. It was neutral, totally unaware of the small machines of commerce and pleasure that crawled across its face. The sea was going to act the way it would, regardless of what we hoped or feared. We were like invisible bacteria, unthinkably small passengers on its huge skin.

Arrogantly, perhaps, Carol and I had decided to cross this sea and had done our best to prepare the boat. Now the two of us were alone out here, inside the boat's relatively strong hull, more or less dry, protected from the wild, liquid environment around us. This gale was a small storm, as Atlantic storms go. Every year, hurricanes are measured with sustained wind forces *three* times stronger than these gusts, with seas easily sixty feet in height.

But this summer gale in the Gulf Stream had overpowered our limited skills and strengths. Now the boat and the sea were working together without our help or interference, an intricate ballet of physical forces. We could only wait down here for this dance to end. We may not have liked being there, but there was nowhere to run and hide. Like most civilized people, we'd gotten used to the concept of ultimate protection: that there would always be firemen to put out fires, police to arrest dangerous criminals, doctors to treat us if we fell sick. Indeed, protection from menace was probably the fundamental purpose of any civilization, and the intricate technological society we'd been born into was a paradigm of this. Out here, however, civilization did not prevail. We couldn't pick up the telephone and *complain* to anyone about the storm. No friendly police officer was about to arrive and tell the boisterous neighbors to turn down their music. There was no Ralph Nader out here, dedicated to the protection of yacht sailors, an ombudsman who'd take our case to the courts.

In the morning, the sun would rise as it always did, and the storm would be blowing less, or more, or with the same force. That was not for us or any other person to decide. It was an alien idea to which I had to accustom myself. Neither Carol nor I nor anyone else had any *control* out here.

We had done all we could; the boat was stripped of sail, the hatches dogged down, and the helm secured. Now we could only watch the barometer, check the bilges regularly, and wait. I looked around the cabin; our careful stowing had held up to the violent motion. The bilge was dry, although thick sheets of water spattered across the plexiglass hatches. We waited, air-breathing land creatures who had come out to play with the ancient sea. Now the sea was teaching us the rules of the game.

I lay on the portside bunk, wedged in behind the canvas lee cloth, stiff in the semidarkness. A gust hit the boat and we heeled hard to port. I closed my eyes and waited for the boat to roll back to starboard. Earlier, I'd dozed off, lying here fully dressed in oilskins, deck boots, vest, and harness, ready to hurl myself up into the cockpit if needed. Carol had presented a pretty convincing show of sleeping on the opposite bunk, so I had actually managed to relax enough for a short nap. Now I was fully awake, acutely aware of the sounds outside the thin skin of fiber glass. My watch said 1834 local time, but already it was almost dark outside, the sun completely blanketed by the storm's thick overcast.

When I'd first lain down, two hours earlier, I'd been too exhausted to think much about being capsized. Now I could think of little else. Once again, my imagination, so important in my professional life as a writer, was a serious detriment to my avocational identity as a sailor. I had to purge my mind of the nightmarish pictures of the boat not recovering from a roll, of the fragile hull heeling too far to port, as a crashing wave lifted it, cresting to a thin wedge that could no longer support the weight of the boat. We would roll past the horizontal; the lockers would all bang open, spewing out their contents; the batteries would fly from their boxes, perhaps the engine from its mounts. The *mast* would be ripped from its shoe up on the cabin top. The hull would split . . .

I sat up and shook myself like a wet dog. This kind of self-defeating paranoia definitely wouldn't do. It was childish and stupid. Only a 45- or 50-foot sea could capsize a boat the size of *Matata*, ballasted with a keel like ours. This fear of capsizing in a storm was akin to someone's fear of the wing ripping off a modern jetliner. I rubbed my eyes and began to untie the cords of the lee cloth so that I could get out of the bunk. Stopping, with the nylon cord in my fingers, I could see the terrible press photo of the DC-10 in Chicago, rolling uncontrollably over to port in its fatal stall, moments before it impacted in a fireball. Beautiful. Even my attempts at self-assurance ended in paranoia.

I laughed out loud as I dragged my clumsy oilskin legs and attached boots over the edge of the lee cloth.

"What on earth is *funny?*" Carol was looking at me with understandable alarm.

"It's hard to explain . . ." I shrugged, feeling the salty edge of the oilskin hood cut into my cheek. "I think I'm just getting a little punchy. Maybe I'm hungry."

She looked wearily back toward the galley. "I'm sorry, I really don't feel up to cooking anything . . . and besides, wouldn't it be dangerous to light the stove?"

As if in answer, the boat threw itself hard over and snapped back quickly with equal violence. "Yep," I answered.

Leaning down, I dug in one of the lockers under her bunk. The first object to roll into my hand was a large can of franks and beans. So be it. From the second locker, two bottles of beer tumbled out, as if they'd been shot out of a cockeyed vending machine. "Thanks," I muttered. Once I'd wedged myself into my bunk, and tied the lee cloth up again, I reached around the bulkhead and grabbed the can opener and a spoon. Opening the beans required two hands and both knees to grip the can, so I stuck the two squat beer bottles under the web of my safety harness as a GI hangs his grenades—ready, but out of the way. Carol was watching me. Slowly, she lost her expression of exhausted anxiety and began to smile.

"Those cold beans actually smell good," she said, sitting up. The boat groaned and creaked as it rolled with each passing crest. It was almost too dark to see clearly now in the cabin.

I finished my share of franks and beans and passed the can across to her. "That," I said, wiping off my mouth with the back of my hand, "was the best meal I've had in years."

She tentatively tasted a small spoonful, then began shoveling the beans down in earnest. "Good," she muttered.

I opened a bottle of beer. It was warm, and fizzy from the shaking in the locker. It tasted delicious. Looking up at the darkening hatch, I watched the shotgun blasts of spray strike the plexiglass. On deck the storm was the only reality. Down here in the sealed compartment, about the size of a small camping trailer back on land, we were dry, protected from the wind and able to eat in relative comfort. In a few minutes, I would get up to check the bilge and log the barometer readings. I'd take one more look at the deck before it got completely dark, then put on the masthead light for the night. When those chores were completed, I'd come back down here, into this bunk, and probably manage to go back to sleep. Incredible: this was the worst weather I'd ever encountered in a boat, yet I was seriously planning to go to sleep. The human ability to adapt to strange circumstances is truly amazing, I thought.

Cradling one of the beer bottles in two hands as I eased myself lower on the bunk, I realized that we had often been in more dangerously bizarre circumstances without knowing it. Only nine months earlier, on an Olympic jumbo jet, we had flown nonstop the six thousand miles from Athens to New York. We'd cruised at 37,000 feet over this same Atlantic, sitting side by side in shirtsleeve comfort, separated by a couple of inches of glass and aluminum from a gale 540 knots stronger than the one that now blew over this boat, and from the near vacuum of the stratosphere in which our blood would boil out through our skins before it froze. We had sat there, eating our little filet steaks and sipping our wine, then watching a Paul Newman movie while the three hundred fifty-ton machine careened through the sky at eight-tenths the velocity of sound, only a few knots above its high-altitude stall speed. After the movie, we'd both dozed, seven miles above Greenland, as little kids played tag in the aisles and old Greek *ya-yas* chattered to each other about their grandchildren. *That* type of travel was supposed to be normal.

The hull creaked up through the climb to yet another slashing wave crest. *This* means of transportation was supposed to be suicidal adventurism. Okay; to each his own. This little ship was certainly as strong and seaworthy as it had to be. Carol and I were good, careful sailors. We had sailed out onto the deep ocean, and we'd met a storm. Tonight, we'd take turns peeking out from our dry shelter, keeping watch for ships. In the morning maybe the storm would be over and we could raise some sail and continue on our way east.

I awoke just before the wave hit us. The cabin was dark, with only a glow from the distant masthead lamp splintering through the plexiglass center hatch. Around us in the darkness, the bulkheads creaked and popped; above the cabin, the wind keened in the shrouds. It was well after midnight, and we'd both been sleeping. Now we were both awake, aware that the sustained angle of heel and the swelling rumble from windward meant an exceptionally large wave was rushing toward us. Rogue waves, they are called. Carol and I knew of their existence, knew all about their formation during freak interactions of ocean tide streams, barometric abnormalities, and colliding currents. We also had read enough nautical literature to realize such waves can kill small boats.

I tore back the lashing of my lee cloth. Carol was already sitting upright on her berth, facing me with her boots wedged against my bunk frame. In the shadowy light, I could see that she wore a flotation vest and safety harness. She had obviously been keeping periodic watch from the hatchway while I slept. Her face was tight and paper-white as she stared at me.

"Just hang on until it crests," I managed to say with reasonable clarity.

"Listen," she said. "Just listen to it."

I thrust out my legs with my boots on either side of her hips. If we turned turtle, we would at least cushion each other's fall and, I hoped, prevent broken bones. The boat heeled more in my direction. Carol's knees were bending as gravity thrust her forward. Her right hand shot up to seize the overhead grab rail. To windward, the moaning rumble grew louder.

My throat itched badly from salt chafe. I was aware of a piercing mildewed scent from our damp clothes and of an acrid intermingling of our fear sweat.

"If we go over," Carol said, her voice amazingly calm, "what should we do?"

Her words forced me out of the encroaching stupor of panic. "Okay . . . if we roll all the way over, protect your face and limbs." I locked my elbows at my sides. "We'll turn upright again. Then we'll have to check for flooding. We'll . . . ah, we *will* turn up okay again."

The hull heeled more steeply, so that Carol seemed to be poised above me in her gaudy yellow oilskins and carapacelike vest. I had a bizarre flash of a pornographic film made with rubber-clad robots. Then the wave crest struck the hull, and all articulate thought was banished.

The noise was like dozens of wooden clubs slamming the exposed round-beam section to starboard. A heavy wash of water swept across the cabin top, deadening sound and light with shocking suddenness. We lay there, heeled perhaps 45 degrees from the vertical, and then the keel bit in and we rolled back.

The next wave did not crest for at least a minute, as if the undistinguished twenty-footers were loath to crowd the domain of the rogue.

"I'll check the bilge," Carol said. She disengaged herself from our weird embrace and swung aft, hand over hand to sound the bilge.

I licked my lips and fussed with the collar of my sweatshirt. We crested a smaller swell, then another. We were back in the relative stability of the 50-knot gale and away from the huge craziness of rogue waves. When Carol swung back into the cabin, she had the brandy bottle in her free hand. She slid down next to me and we shared the bottle through several deep, burning swallows. Finally, Carol leaned close and kissed my stubbly, salt-blasted face. "I'm glad I'm doing this with you," she whispered.

I returned her kiss. "And me with you."

The storm rumbled above us, and in the cabin we sat like suited-up astronauts, impotently waiting out the timelessness of reentry.

Note on Atlantic gale, July 11–12, 1979:

When we eventually got back to the States, I contacted NOAA to find out all I could about the storm that bit us on July 11. The officials there kindly provided me with NOAA/NESS satellite images of the storm as well as the Mariners' Weather Log *for the period.*

The gale that caught Matata *at 39° North, 67° West was unusually strong because of its origin, an Arctic low drawn south by the jet streams associated with a tropic depression flowing over the Ohio Valley from the Gulf of Mexico. The Arctic low produced an extremely steep pressure gradient between its center (999 mb) and the Azores High (1034 mb), resulting in unusually high wind velocities.*

The Mariners' Weather Log *gives ship reports for this storm that include sustained 50-knot winds with much higher gusts, and seas in excess of 20 feet sixty miles north of our position.*

NOAA estimated that seas were higher at Matata's *position because the full force of the gale blew directly against the eastgoing flow of the Gulf Stream, itself compressed by the Labrador current to the north.*

CHAPTER SEVEN

DR: 38°43' NORTH, 56°18' WEST
JULY 18: 0120 LOCAL ZONE TIME
LOG: 748 MILES FROM AMBROSE LIGHT

The first storm had blown itself out five days ago. Since then we'd had two more gales, and in the previous thirty-six hours the weather had come at us from damn near every point of the compass. Much to our frustration, the conditions had ranged from a nasty 45-knot southerly on Monday, the sixteenth, to a misty calm with a sloppy leftover swell on Tuesday morning, to a chill force seven from the goddamn *northwest* by midnight Tuesday. Now the wind had veered all the way around to the south again and was beginning to keep in the rigging, telling me it was time for another reef and a smaller jib.

I lay in the low-side bunk, snuggly warm inside Carol's sleeping bag—mine had gotten wet from a poorly secured center hatch during my watch, leading to a nasty exchange of accusations and denials. The hatch was well dogged down now, and I stared at the dark plexiglass, listening to the clattering rain and spray. Since coming off watch at midnight, I'd lain here, overtired and nervous, much as I'd been that first night off Ambrose Light. But now I was truly exhausted, strung-out physically and, I admitted reluctantly, emotionally worn raw. It had been at least two days since I'd slept for more than three consecutive hours. On top of this I'd developed a cold, with a sore throat and aggravating nasal drip. In the twenty-four hours since my late watch the night before, I'd reefed the main twice, shaken out the reefs one at a time, put another back in, then changed headsails up and down from the working jib to the spitfire to the 120-percent genny to the drifter, and back to the worker. And it was obviously time for the spitfire again. Which meant, of course, leaving this warm nest, struggling against the roll down here in the cabin to get into my Star Wars rig of oilskins, deck boots, yellow foam vest, and safety harness, then clomping up there in the rain and spray and getting thrown all over the place hassling the goddamn "jiffy" reefing before taking another cold salt-water jacuzzi on the foredeck.

I let my hand move across the dry cloth of my sweatshirt and corduroy jeans, which represented the last set of clean clothes as yet untainted by salt water. The boat rolled and snapped back, creaking loudly, as it did when we had too much sail for a gusting wind and short, crashing sea. Below me on the cabin sole lay the yellow and blue jumble of my sodden oilskins. I could almost feel the greasy wetness of the half-dry brine. Closing my eyes, my visual field was captured by a mashing swirl of neon strings, as if my brain itself were fluorescing. The lack of sleep was not alone responsible for this glittering tension. In the past twenty-four hours, I now realized, I had accidentally overdosed on a contradictory batch of pills from the Tupperware medical box: a couple too many eight-hour Dristan capsules, two Dramamine when I was trying to write up the DR that morning and, later, when I attempted to grab a half-assed noon sight with too thick an overcast and too lumpy a horizon. I'd also been hitting the beer and wine a bit too hard, not to mention the coffee. There had been some aspirin for my two-degree fever and one codeine pill for my wrenched back somewhere in that jumble. On top of this pharmaceutical nightmare, I'd gotten chilled and soaked three times. In short, I was in no mood whatsoever to go back up on deck and handle sail.

Carol was undoubtedly none too eager to get me back up there, either. During my scheduled long "sleep" period that afternoon, the southeast blow had fallen to nothing, leaving us in a rotten, vestigial swell, reefed too short for the sails to give any stability. We'd rolled and clattered, the cabin shut up tight, the bilge stinking, and the cutlery banging around in the galley. I'd lain there, already jangly inside, getting increasingly irritable. Finally, I stormed up into the cockpit, swearing foully, berating Carol for not sheeting in the sails, for not keeping the boat from rolling, for God knows what-all. Savagely, I'd torn the reefs out of the main and run up the heavier of the two genoa jibs, made a great display of securing any clattering deck gear, and stormed back down to the cabin, not bothering to apologize for my outrageous behavior. Lying there in the damp and stuffy cabin, I'd felt terribly guilty, and also deeply surprised at the intensity of my anger. The close physical and emotional warmth we had felt for each other after the near-disaster with our rogue wave had been shredded and blown away by the exhausting beating we'd taken in the past two days. Abstractly, I still loved and valued Carol as a wife and a partner. I just had a hard time *feeling* that love at the moment. Maybe, I thought, I'll be better if I can just get a couple hours' sleep.

Less than one hour later the wind returned, from the south, and soon gusted up to well over twenty knots, too much for the genoa and unreefed main.

That had been ten hours earlier. In the intervening time, my mood had hardly mellowed. Closing my eyes tightly, trying to ignore the popping colors under my eyelids, I rolled in a fetal curl and actually said a brief prayer for five minutes' sleep as the boat banged and snap-rolled through the dark and rainy night.

"Mal . . . " I felt the probing flashlight beam under the folds of the accordion door. "Mal . . . sorry, but we're taking a lot of sea now."

I was out of the warm bag, sitting up, already pulling on the wet oilskin trousers. "Okay. Fine. I hear you . . . " I reached up to unsnap the door, then pulled it back to be blinded by the hot cone of light from the big beam gun. Inside my chest, the anger surged like magma. "I *heard* you, for Christ's sake. You don't have to *blind* me . . ."

Carol's answer was a loud slam of the hatch.

I don't clearly remember getting into my deck gear, but I do recall stopping at the chart table to check the barometers. The big one read 29.78 and falling, about as low a reading as we'd had, even during the first gale. Up in the cockpit, I was taken aback by what I saw just as I had been that first night with all the ships' range lights. We had *hills* again, a tumbling range of high, parallel hummocks, white-crested and creaming, coming at us from the south southeast. Overhead, the low overcast rumbled by, seemingly just above the snapping ellipsoidal smear of the masthead lamp. Rain stung, warm and mixed with spray. The water blew at us sideways; horizontal rain, which I'd always been told meant you had a gale blowing. Once more, the treacherous polychromatic squares of the pilot chart rose in my mind.

Carol crouched under the canvas dodger, steering by hand. She was soaked and obviously chilled, despite the apparently warm rain and spray. I could see that the towel she had wrapped under her oilskin hood to stop drips was itself sodden and bulged out under her chin buckle to act like a wick, attracting the wet. Wordlessly, I clipped into the starboard jack line and went forward on the tossing deck to douse the jib.

Forty minutes later, I was still lurching through my clumsy sail-changing drill, again soaked, sheet-whipped, my thinking dull and out of phase. The rain still blew parallel to the deck; the sea still rose like foamy sand dunes above the starboard beam. But now thunder echoed and yellow lightning flared in the scudding overcast. The wind was also backing to the east, making the sea bunch up more. I was finishing tying off the reefing points when Carol shouted something from the cockpit, pointing out ahead with her yellow glove.

About a quarter of a mile off the starboard bow, bouncing around out there in the jumbled ranks of waves, a dark-hulled freighter was coming right at us. I clung to the shrouds, squinting into the salty rain, trying to make my brain work. Of all the damned times and places to be on an obvious collision course. I looked more closely; the ship was moving fast. At this the adrenaline took charge and I was down in the cabin, priming the engine, then back at the helm, steering through a tack while Carol wordlessly handled the sheets. My hood was down and my hair streamed with rain. The boat was headed dead downwind, steering about 345 degrees true. Out behind us, the waves rolled into splashing foam blankets. The engine rattled under my boots. But the ship was gone in the black rain, almost as if it had been a joint hallucination.

Ten minutes later, I lay on the wet plastic cushion of the high-side quarter berth, feeling the heat of the engine box, my flickering visual field cleared of synapsing neon. I slept.

When Carol called me again, it was as if I were being stimulated out of anesthesia. I jerked up automatically, banging my head on the folded teak cabin table nestled into its storage rack above me in the narrow quarter berth. The table came clattering down, and I dragged myself backwards out of the berth, my mouth tasting like old bandages and my mood even fouler. "*Jesus fucking Christ,*" I muttered, "just when I was finally getting some real sleep." The clock next to the radio read 0355.

Slamming back the hatch, I dragged myself up in the companionway. Once more I was assaulted by a strange seascape. The wind had dropped; the overcast had torn apart, and a waning moon sped among the furrows of gray and black clouds to the west. The waves were still large and running fast, with frothing crests still above ten feet. But there were weirdly bright bands of stars, some wide, some narrow, spreading north and south overhead, and the moon, I now saw, was a solid quarter crescent, bright enough to give the puffy edges of the clouds metallic definition and to glaze the slopes of the swell. Standing among the ragged silver cloud streamers were more solid islands of high-piled cumulo-nimbus, thunderheads that flickered with silent golden lightning.

I slouched there in the hatchway, dazzled by this weirdness. Never before had I seen the sea like this. The sky and the sea itself looked to be composed of separate, incongruous elements, as in some giant, animated collage; there were strips of storm and strips of cloudless, starry sky; between the sloppy swell of the spent gale warm ponds of calmer water seemed to be spreading. Way out ahead, where the retreating warm front blew away to the east, the thunderheads were more active, trailing below them dirty black skirts of squall rain. There were some scattered rain clouds behind us to the west as well, but they were not linked up to form a dangerous line squall. Tinting all this strangeness, the rising moon brought blue color back to the sea and plated the piled clouds.

I shook myself hard and automatically gazed up at the masthead wind arrow. "What do you want?" I muttered, looking down again. The wind was still vaguely south, about 10 knots.

Carol turned, squelching in her soaked oilskins. She pointed aft. "Those squalls are coming closer." She rose to peer forward. "There's more out ahead, too . . . "

As she spoke, I felt my limbs begin to soften and sag inside the briny plates of my oilskins. Only once before had I felt this exhausted: upcountry in the Congo on some ill-conceived field survey when I ended up in a river town called Lisala, a guest of the Six Commando mercenaries during a hit-and-run rebel mortar attack. That time, the combination of fear, fever, and exhaustion had done strange things to my emotions, too. Now, as Carol seemed to rattle on and on about "squall lines," I grew rigid again inside, her words taking on a nagging, nasty quality.

"Look," I finally blurted out. "Just steer the goddamn boat." I pointed to the sparkling sky. "The storm's over. Just steer like this for an hour and let me get a *little* sleep."

As I turned to descend the companionway, I noticed the jib-sheet winch handle on the port cockpit bench, carelessly left there for one of us to trip on, to get knocked overboard when we heeled again. Reaching down, I grasped the cool stainless steel shank. Carol still seemed to be nagging.

" . . . There's a lot of wind in them. Can't you see the *rain*, too? I think we should . . . "

I rose again to stand menacingly above her, the chill weight of the winch handle in my right fist. There were little popping spots of green and pink about a foot from my unfocused eyes. I wiped my hand hard across my face and stared aft at the drifting thunderheads and rain squalls outlined in the moonlight. "There's no real wind in those squalls. Don't worry. Just steer the boat. I . . ."

"How do you know there's no wind?"

Again, I sensed the smooth weight of the winch handle. "I've seen squalls like that before . . . Shit, the bad ones are up ahead. I . . . "

"*Where* have you seen clouds like that?" Carol's voice was biting with anger. "When?"

All of a sudden, I was out of the hatchway, my legs spread as my boots gripped the cockpit sole. "Don't you goddamn *interrogate* me. I'm telling you . . . "

My eye followed Carol's stricken gaze up the chest of my oilskins, up my cocked arm to the gleaming shaft of the handle. Inside my head, a faint pinging had begun, like faraway dinner knives on the rims of glasses. I swayed there in the breeze, watching the thunderheads pulse lightning against the gun-metal sky. On either side of the cockpit, alternating meadows of calm and foaming ridges decorated the base swell. The moon slid free of a cloud tendril, and I could see Carol's face more clearly, her skin sallow with fatigue, her blue-gray eyes brittle with outraged fear.

Silently, I lowered the winch handle into its place in the port cockpit locker. Then, still not speaking, I slid down the open hatch and crumpled into the waiting quarter berth. When I closed my eyes, I had a nightmare memory flash of the Congo, of renegade African troops smashing the fragile skulls of suspected rebel prisoners in the littered mud of a ravaged river town called Bumba. I closed my eyes more tightly, and the picture swirled into the abstract jumble of colors. A long way above me I heard Carol slide the hatch shut.

In the morning, a calm voice proclaimed behind my clenched eyes, you will turn this boat around. You will sail west, toward home.

My autonomous hands were unsnapping straps and buckles on my oilskins. In the morning, we *would* turn around. The north Atlantic was just too much for a couple like us, alone in this small boat. The weather would *not* get better; it could only get worse, one depression after another sucking out onto the Gulf Stream. I rolled onto my side again, letting my face nuzzle the warm gelcoat of the engine box. This ocean, I realized with ponderous sobriety, was not at all what they said it was. This ocean was a dangerous and malevolent animal, and if we stayed on it, we would die.

Again, I could feel the weight of the handle in my fingers and see the shock in Carol's eyes. Nineteen years of marriage, through all the normal twentieth-century hassles and calamities in seven countries, and never, never once before, had I raised my hand to her in violence. And the idea of having menaced her with a deadly weapon actually made my stomach cramp. In the morning, I repeated, a suddenly familiar litany, we'll go home. The Atlantic had beaten us. I didn't come out here to threaten my wife with a winch handle. I did not come out here to go crazy.

I pulled a damp pillow closer under my chin. Why, then, *did* you come to this place? The calm voice inside my skull was active again. I came . . . my mental answer faltered. I came because I wanted . . . something I could not find on the shore, in the cities, in the curving regularity of a subdivision street, in the fluorescent monotony of a classroom. I came because I wanted to feel that I had truly engaged the planet, that I could exist even briefly without the stifling shroud of technology, without the sober predictability of commerce, careers, inevitable retirement, and eternal, victorious death. I came because just once in my life I wanted to feel truly in control of my own time, suspended, isolated from the tyrannical umbilical of modern life. I came to this bizarre place for the same reason people go to Alaska, or to the high snow fields of the Himalayas, or to the tall blue glaciers of Antarctica: to exist for a short time as a thinking animal, free of restraint, free to ponder my connection to this spinning ball of rock and water; free to study the person with whom I had chosen to spend my months and years. I had come for a renewal that most of us never even guess exists.

Pulling the crusty edges of the oilskins away from my throat, I felt the sadness of encroaching defeat. In ten days we would be back in the world of numbers and flashing lights, of rutted streets and deeply unhappy people thrashing their years away in some immense, interlocking, but invisible ergotic frenzy we choose to call postindustrial civilization. I had attempted to escape, but the umbilical noose ran too long. In the morning, my schizoid inner companion reassured me, we'll sail home to all that.

When I opened my eyes again, plum sky filled the rectangle of the open hatch. Carol stood, freed of her oilskins, holding a cup of steaming tea close to the chest of her damp sweatshirt. From our angle of heel, I knew we were sailing well in a light northerly, east on a port tack, a smooth beam reach.

"How do you feel?" Her voice was concerned, devoid of residual anger or resentment.

That was an interesting question. I closed my eyes again; the dancing neon worms were banished. My limbs felt solid, intact. But I did not want to sit up just yet.

"What time is it?" I stalled.

She bent down to check the clock on the chart table. "Ten past six." She smiled now. "I let you sleep."

"What kind of course we holding?" I hadn't yet found a way to tell her of my decision in the crazy night.

She thrust her head and shoulders out the open hatch, and the breeze billowed her drying hair, spreading it in an arc in the first direct sunlight. "One-fifteen magnetic. . . . That's right on the rhumb line for Faial." Again she craned her neck to see the sails. "I shook out the reefs and put up the genoa. We're making about 6 knots."

I rolled over to stare up into the porcelain-blue sky. The boat hissed east through the calm ocean, purposeful and composed. I knew then, suddenly and unalterably, the true reason I had come out here on the deep ocean. I had come here to find out who I was. And now I had begun to discover. The boat and the breeze and my wife were telling me. I was the person who had wanted to sail across a wide ocean, and I was going to do this, despite weather, despite the dark lights and the echoes in my head. We would work together, the two of us, with this boat. The weather would be bad or good or in-between. That was not truly important. Our life, like all lives, was a voyage from one place and time to another. Now we had a chance to strip away the confusing and deceptive wrapping that had disguised the real nature of this voyage. Now there would be no more thoughts of return to *home.* We were already home.

"Please make me a cup of tea," I said, sliding feet first out of the narrow berth. "It's my watch."

CHAPTER EIGHT

DR: 39°06' NORTH, 48°32' WEST
JULY 23: 0200 LOCAL ZONE TIME

It had been twelve days since the first gale, three nights since our near-collision with that floating oil-drum junk. Our life had compressed itself to a series of night watches, daytime sleep periods, navigation, maintenance, and sail handling. We listened to the radio, read a bit, sometimes actually had conversations about the "current events" brought to us by the BBC or Armed Forces Radio. But our main preoccupations were sleep, food, and keeping the bow of the boat headed east. Since passing Ambrose Light on July 6, our taffrail log had measured off 1,144 nautical miles.

I took the watch at 0200. We had a fluky easterly breeze, puffing up to about 15 knots at times but holding fairly steady at around 9 knots out of 90 degrees true: a slow, dead beat to windward. After dinner we'd steered northeast for five hours, and Carol had helped me tack back southeast when I'd taken the watch. It was another dark, moonless night, but the absence of the moon no longer spooked me as it had with that chill northerly blowing three days earlier. Sitting in the cockpit, lazily smoking a cigarette while I watched the passing phosphorescence in the slight chop, I thought about the near-collision of Friday morning. No matter how I reconstructed the event in my mind, I was unable to accept it as an occurrence in *my* life, as part of my personal history. I've heard that accident victims often feel as if the injury has happened to someone else. I felt the same way about that dangerous flotsam; it had almost hit a boat, but not our boat. Anyway, it was gone now, and I didn't want to think about it.

I reached back instinctively and adjusted the shock cord reinforcing the tiller lines. We were holding about 150 degrees magnetic, 120 degrees true. For the past twenty-four hours we'd been beating like this, zigzagging our way toward the Azores, close-hauled on either side of the rhumb line. Once again the optimistic predictions of the pilot chart had proved false. Easterlies out here in July were as statistically rare as gales were supposed to have been. So much for statistics. The log reading was off, too; sargasso weed fouling the impeller was causing the instrument to read at least 10 percent short.

There'd been good sun and horizon that day, though, and I'd gotten solid fixes. Sometime in the morning or early afternoon, if the breeze continued, we would cross the halfway point to Faial Island. We'd been at sea for just about seventeen days. To me, sitting there each night in the familiar hollow of the cockpit, watching the dark sea and the starry sky above, it often seemed like I'd been born and raised out here. I wasn't *bored;* it was just that I could not remember what solid land actually looked like. The dynamic, fluid nature of our world had become so familiar, and compensating for the constant rolling motion of the boat so instinctual, that I no longer felt myself out at sea on a boat engaged in an ocean crossing. For many hours each day and night we went about our work of handling sails or gear, using the sextant and charts, just as if we had been behaving this way our whole lives. In short, we had adapted fully to our new environment.

I threw the cigarette butt into the slowly passing swell and hunkered down to doze a bit. In the past ten days I'd acquired the ability to doze for almost exactly twenty minutes, wake up, scan the horizon for shipping, then lie down and sleep for twenty more minutes. We really were becoming ocean sailors. Pulling the hood of my nylon windbreaker tight, I closed my eyes.

"Mal . . . " Carol's voice was small and sleepy in the cabin. I opened my eyes, not sure if I'd actually heard her, or only imagined the sound. "Mal . . . " she called again, "did you put on a red *light* down here?"

I shook the sleep from my face, vaguely annoyed at myself. I'd probably dropped the damn flashlight behind my bunk when I'd gotten dressed for watch. Now the beam was casting a red glow through the damp sweaters and shirts I'd spread out to dry. I was lazy and didn't want to clomp all the way down to the cabin, then back up here, snap in again, and finally settle back down for my twenty-minute nap. Carol was already in the cabin; why couldn't she do it?

"It's the yellow flashlight, I think," I called. "Just reach across and turn it off, okay?"

No answer. Obviously, she was as reluctant as I was to leave her resting place. We'd become as covetous of sleep as starving people were of limited food rations. I closed my eyes again, snuggling the hood close to my stubbly cheeks. Just a little nap, then . . .

"*Malcolm!*" Carol's voice was loud and frightened. "There's a *fire* or something . . . "

I was upright, feet first into the open hatchway. The harness tether snagged and I had to spin back to unsnap from the jack line.

"Mal!" she cried again. "It's . . . there's something burning down here."

When my boots struck the cabin sole, I could smell the unmistakeable odor of burning epoxy resins, a sour, chemistry-class stench that had the hair on the back of my neck literally standing erect. I snatched the fire extinguisher off its bracket above the chart table and dragged open the accordion door. Carol was sitting upright on her bunk, her legs still in her sleeping bag as she pulled at the zipper. The choking smoke was now visible in the cabin, illuminated in broken layers by the chart-table light. Her arm shot out, pointing directly at the opposite side of the cabin, at the white fiber glass liner just below the forward end of the tear-shaped starboard window.

I stood fascinated by the malignant oval of molten gelcoat. In the half-light, the brick-red glow was plainly visible. The thick bridle of lighting wires was under the liner at that level. Obviously, there'd been a bad short circuit.

My first reaction was to squirt the entire side of the cabin with the extinguisher. But then, leaning closer, I could see that the red glow was actually fading as I watched, that the circuit breakers in the panel beside the chart table had finally tripped to cut the juice. Or at least I hoped they had. Pulling open the thick blade of the bosun's knife, I called over my shoulder to Carol, who had finally freed herself of the sleeping bag.

"Hit the two big circuit breakers under the chart table . . . both of them . . . *quick.*"

The tone of my voice cut any urge she must have felt to ask questions.

I knelt on the starboard bunk, my face close to the stinking molten spot in the liner. The chart-table light went out as Carol cut the two main circuit breakers. In front of my face the blackened, warped patch of gelcoat had lost its menacing glow. The fire was dead, deprived of electrical heat. At least I *hoped* it was out. Digging the blade tip into the fragile, burnt center of the meltdown, I flinched back from a puff of choking chemical fumes.

"Get me the big flashlight," I called. "I can't see a thing in here."

Carol obediently answered my gruffness. She had obviously become used to me losing my temper when I was frightened.

The bright beam gun dazzled me as she held it over my right shoulder, playing the light on the burnt gelcoat. "What on earth happened?" Her voice was wide-awake now, normal.

I dug more with my knife blade, breaking away carbonized resin and brittle, blackened glass cloth. "Goddamn short," I muttered. "The wires shorted out and burned the plastic . . . " My knife blade finally hit hard, unmelted resin. In the dazzling light, I could see the fused wires of the lighting bridle, a crumbly mess, like burnt spaghetti. "Jesus," I said softly, "I'm glad you saw that glow, Honey. . . . we could've really caught on fire."

The light beam shivered, and I knew Carol had just shuddered. I felt the same way. A runaway resin fire was not what we needed twelve hundred miles out in the Atlantic.

The blade had peeled away all the obviously melted plastic, leaving an oval cavity maybe three by two inches. Inside this hole, the burnt insulation broke away like the black fragments of a badly decayed tooth. I rocked back, resting my elbows on my knees, balancing on the tilted bunk. "Can't see well enough in the dark," I said, letting frustration slide back into my voice. ". . . have to finish this in the morning." Tentatively, I reached my right index finger up into the black cavity to touch the broken ends of the seven lighting wires in the ruined bridle. They were still warm, but no longer dangerously so. "The juice is definitely off . . . at least the breakers are working."

Carol leaned closer toward me, peering into the light beam to see the damage. "Is it bad?"

"No, hell no . . . of course not," I said with needless sarcasm, then caught myself. "Sorry. Yeah, Honey, it's very bad. I'll have to open all that up tomorrow and then splice each wire back together if we're going to have any lights."

She sat back down on the opposite bunk, still holding the light. "Okay." There was calm determination in her voice. "That's what we'll do then. What more should we do tonight?"

I slid off the bunk and stood in the cabin entrance, swaying with the slight roll of the boat. "We'd better get the battery leads off and insulated with cloth or something, just to be on the safe side. I don't know what the hell caused that short," I pointed toward the black hole next to me, "but I don't want to take the chance of another fire."

Carol got up to join me. "Neither do I," she said tiredly.

By full daylight a little after seven o'clock, we had already eaten breakfast and were ready to start the repair. Unfortunately, the weather was not cooperating with our resolve to get the job done fast and well. The wind had veered around to the southeast and piped up to about eighteen or twenty knots, not enough to make trouble but sure as hell enough to make working down below uncomfortable. It was overcast, too, ten-tenths stratus, which gave the lumpy day an even more sinister look. This was the first solid cloud cover we'd had since the early gales south of Nova Scotia. I'd hoped that we were already well into the clear weather of the Azores High, but the southerly blow and the clouds reminded me just how far we still had to sail before landfall. And this, in turn, made the urgency of getting the boat repaired even more pronounced.

But doing a proper job on the wires was not going to be easy with the boat close-hauled, smacking and snap-rolling to windward under single-reefed main and working jib. I spent about twenty minutes kneeling uncomfortably on the starboard bunk, cutting away at the edges of the burn hole with a wide-bladed chisel. We were rolling around far too much, however, for me to do a decent job. Reluctantly, I went back up on deck and lowered the jib. Then, working with Carol, I put the boat into a modified heave-to position under reefed main alone. It took us another twenty minutes, but we finally had the boat steering east northeast, on the starboard tack, creeping ahead slowly and riding the chop with a relatively easy motion.

Down below, though, conditions were not much better. On this tack, the starboard side was high, and I had to work leaning forward against the angle of heel. Even though the motion was less violent than it had been, I found it almost impossible to do accurate work. Finally, Carol came around behind me and, bracing herself against the opposite bunk, steadied my torso with her two outstretched arms as I chiseled and sawed away at the edges of the burn hole, cleaning out the crumbly resin ruined by the heat of the short circuit. By the time I finished this, we were left with an elongated oval cavity, about six inches by three. I was sick at the sight of it. To me the enlarged hole appeared to be a near-mortal wound in the very guts of the boat. The fact that I had clumsily hacked most of the hole myself, searching for unmelted material and sound wires, made the wound even more repulsive. Just how deeply connected I now felt to the actual fabric of this boat was brought painfully home to me. I knew this vessel, its insides and outs, all its working parts, infinitely better than I knew the parts of my own body. Unlike our own anatomy, which we cannot completely fathom or explore, I had been over practically every inch of this boat from keel to masthead, from stem to the cramped interior of the lazaret. Now I swayed there on my knees, pounding a sharp chisel into the very flesh of the boat. This was like a doctor trying to perform surgery on one of his own children. To make things worse, the impossible position and the uneven motion of the boat made me brutally clumsy.

"That's going to have to be it," I said, sliding down to rest my back. I handed Carol the chisel and hammer, making me feel even more like an incompetent surgeon. I'd always known that sailors grew to love their boats, but this was ridiculous. Just get on with it, I thought. When we reach the Azores, I can buy some gelcoat and do a really pretty repair job.

Getting on with it, though, was even harder than the initial part of the repair. To splice each wire, I had to cut a six-inch connecting piece to be joined first to the aft and then to the forward end of each of the seven lighting wires, which ran in a bridle from the circuit breaker next to the chart table, forward to the cabin and exterior lights. Luckily, the wires were color-coded, making the problem of splicing in the connecting piece much easier. Unluckily, the wires had been burned off at different places by the intense heat of the short, and the twisted, plastic-strip conduit holding the lighting bridle was so distorted that there was no play in any of the individual wires.

It took me two-and-a-half hours of steady, back-cramping work to clean up and even off the fourteen stubs of the wires, separating each piece and carefully peeling back the insulation to expose enough copper-wire core to make a splice. By the time I finished that job, we were both woozy, so we took a break up in the cockpit.

The wind and the sea were about the same. It was a gloomy day after ten days of sunshine, and the weather seemed to reflect our mood. After a sandwich and a bottle of warm beer, plus about ten minutes' quick nap in the fresh air, I went back down to the stuffy, rolling cabin to start the actual splicing. It was just before eleven in the morning.

Seven hours later, I came back up to the cockpit. The job was finally done, and I was exhausted; my shoulder muscles felt like some sadist had taken multiple pairs of vice-grip pliers to them. My fingertips were cut and pierced by the needlelike ends of the wires, and I had burning particles of acid resin in my eyes. But the job was done; we had lights again, running lights and cabin lamps, and the bright twenty-five-watt lamp up on the masthead. That job had had to be done in the morning, and it was duly accomplished. My aching back and bleeding fingers were irrelevant. We needed lights and we had them. Personal feelings were secondary to the harsh but simple requirements of a boat at sea.

I lay back tiredly, smoking a slow cigarette, watching the southern swell. Overhead, the clouds were clearing as if in celebration of the hard day's work. Carol had volunteered to put away all the tools and clean up the mess. When I'd finished the splices and checked all the circuits, she'd carefully taped up the sagging bulge of spliced wires, using waterproof duct tape cut into an oval, then covering this patch with white surgical tape cut in the same pattern. The finished patch was not as ugly or crippled in appearance as I had feared it would be. All told, the long struggle had given me a pretty good feeling of confidence in myself and in the boat.

I now understood what had caused the short and the fire. The severe pounding the boat had taken when we'd lain ahull in the first gale then sailed under storm sails in the next two blows had *torqued* the boat, putting the hull under enormous strain. The plastic hull being flexible by design, parts of it moved. Undoubtedly there'd been some slippage between the hull and the liner, and this had chafed the wires, eventually producing the short. If I'd taken the time to investigate the problem three days before, when the compass and masthead lights had first started popping the circuit breakers on the panel, I might have found the trouble before the damage. Small annoyances can become big, and out here you don't want big ones. Therefore, a careful sailor takes the extra time to investigate every problem when it arises. Fatigue or hunger or general disinclination were valid excuses back on land. Out here, however, those rules did not apply; the requirements of the boat were paramount. The boat was our protector and provider, our master and our servant. I had not fully understood this fact before setting sail. It was a valuable lesson to have learned from the sea.

I lay back and watched the gilded ball of the sun slip below the western clouds. I'd gone a whole day with only one quick sun sight, producing a questionable LOP. Never mind, I would make up for it in the morning.

Over my shoulder, I heard Carol working down below, squaring things away in the galley before starting dinner. I was too tired even to think about helping her. The boat sailed east northeast, smacking a little now with the jib and unreefed mainsail close-hauled. Closing my eyes, I heard Carol grunt as she pumped out the bilge. Automatically, part of my mind counted the pump strokes, a habit that had become so ingrained in both of us that I'm sure we heard the other person pumping the bilge even as we slept—twelve, thirteen, sixteen . . . *twenty*—What the hell was going on?

I pulled myself over to peer into the hatchway. "Look at the log book there," I said, pointing to the open steno pad on the chart table. "Didn't I pump out around five o'clock, before I finished the splices?"

Carol nodded but didn't answer. She continued pumping, heaving the short metal handle back and forth as she braced herself against the engine box. "Thirty-three . . . " she muttered, "thirty-four . . . thirty-five strokes . . . " She stood up and wiped her forehead with the sleeve of her shirt. "It was really full . . . I . . . "

Not listening carefully, I dropped down and grabbed the log book. One of the rules we followed was to log every session on the bilge pump, noting the number of strokes needed to clear the bilges. Here was the hard, undeniable truth. At 1710 local time, I'd pumped twenty-six times; earlier, at 1103, I'd had to pump eighteen strokes. Now, at 1815, Carol had just pumped thirty-five times. There could be no question about what was happening: we had a leak, a bad leak that was clearly getting worse. I logged Carol's pumping and snapped shut the notebook. She slid in behind the chart table to sit, staring up at me with an expression of mixed weariness and apprehension. We were both wiped out from the long day working on the wires; this leak was the last damn thing we needed.

"What do you think?" Her voice was steady.

"It's probably the stern gland . . . " I blew out a clenched-up breath, then rolled my head on my aching shoulders. "That's the only place I can think of where that much water could come in . . .

where the leak would get slowly worse like this."

I'm sure I sounded neither convincing in my diagnosis nor enthusiastic about trying to verify the problem right then. I'd already worked for over twelve hours that day, almost nonstop down there in the stuffy, rolling cabin. I didn't savor the idea of ripping apart the quarter berths and engine box to crawl back into the claustrophobic hole behind the engine and tackle the delicate job of tightening the stern gland. But that's what we both knew we were going to have to do.

"You want a glass of wine before you start?" she asked, coming out from behind the chart table.

In answer, I reached down stiffly to fetch a bottle from the locker. "Yeah," I said wearily. "At least we've got lights to work with now."

Carol managed a halfhearted grin in answer.

It was sometime after midnight and I was twisted up in an uncomfortable ball, feeling around in the back of the toilet commode for a possible seepage from the head pump. We had been chasing the mysterious leak for almost six hours straight, and now I was so tired that I was functioning with a kind of mindless, robot inertia. Searching out a strange source of salt water inside the hull of the boat had become my obsessive *raison d'etre.* I could not really remember why I was doing it; I just knew that this was what I had to do.

We'd started with the stern gland, first opening up the aft area by removing the tops of the quarter berths on both sides and taking away the engine box. I'd lain on my stomach back there, protecting my chest and legs with cockpit cushions while I inspected and then tightened the clamps on the flexible rubber tube of the stern gland. This was always an awkward, taxing job, but trying to complete the work so that each of the triple hose clamps on the gland was adjusted with equal tension was especially hard with the boat pitching and rolling about on its windward course. The warm miasma of oily bilge just beneath my face didn't help matters much, either. When I got the clamps tightened so that there was just an occasional drop of salt water falling into the boat as the shaft freewheeled in neutral, I crawled backwards out of the stifling, smelly hole, shaking with fatigue.

I had pumped the bilge dry before going back there to work on the shaft gland. Now Carol pumped again to see if we'd located and stopped the leak . . . thirty-four strokes to clear the bilge. Wherever that leak was, it certainly was *not* the stern gland.

So, we grimly set to work opening up and unpacking lockers and storage spaces under the bunks, working slowly forward as we shifted awkward piles of cans and boxes, cartons of spares, coils of line and rigging wire, jiggling plastic Lug-a-Jugs of precious fresh water . . . all the ton and a half of assorted equipment and provisions we'd so carefully stowed before sailing. We had to move it all, a little at a time, to expose for inspection each of the nine seacocks and through-hull fittings. We were both convinced that the steadily increasing leak had to be from a seacock that had somehow worked loose or shaken free its hose. Working methodically forward, we got all the way to the head area just after midnight.

By half past twelve, I had checked not only the entire head area but also the echo-sounder transducer and the two seacocks just inside the jam-packed forepeak. Each fitting was as sound and dry as it had been when I'd overhauled it in Danny's boatyard. Yet still the water mounted in the bilge.

Beside me, Carol leaned against the mast support, looking pale and defeated. I pried up all the cabin-sole boards and tried at least to locate the direction from which the water was coming. By this time I was so punchy that it took me several minutes to see the obvious, that the steady trickle of clear sea water was flowing down the incline of the hull from the limber holes of the forepeak bulkhead. But I'd just checked the seacocks there, and they'd been dry! Then I saw the probable answer . . . we were leaking from the hull itself, from a fracture or a crack. Jesus . . . everyone's pet nightmare . . . the hull itself was coming apart below the waterline.

Without speaking to Carol, I scrambed ahead on my knees and began pulling sail bags and bundled equipment out of the crowded forepeak. My face was sweating now with panic, and my breath came fast and shallow. Maybe that thing in the water the other morning had actually hit us in the bow, and I simply had not heard or seen the collision. Maybe we were about to rip apart, the bow opening like a milk carton. What I ought to be doing, I knew, was dousing sail right now, to take the pressure off the bow. Hell, I ought to be getting out the life raft and survival kit.

Seizing the thick coil of three-quarter-inch anchor warp, I twisted and manhandled it aft over my shoulder. Carol was behind me, taking the gear as I furiously pulled it out of the forepeak. I stopped, then held my hands up to the light. They were dripping wet with cool sea water. The coiled line was soaking, so was the sail bag on which it had rested, so were the cut sheets of plywood strong boys stored around the bag . . . so was everything else on this side of the forepeak.

"Gimme the big light," I called.

Carol passed me the large seal beam. In the hot shaft of light, I could now clearly see the source of our mysterious flooding. The Arpege has a recessed anchor locker in its foredeck, and this locker is drained by two strong, three-inch scupper pipes, which exit from both lower aft corners of the molded box. Lying on my belly on a wet sail bag, I reached up to touch the fiber glass tube of the portside drain scupper. Cold sea water ran down my fingers and palm and under the cuff of my sweatshirt. The drain pipe was neatly broken, completely fractured about two inches from the point at which it joined the hull, maybe a foot and a half above the waterline. Heeled as we were on this tack, the bow wave sloshed back up and into the drain pipe, then right into the boat through the fracture. Wiggling the two halves of the scupper pipe with my hands, I was able to alternately stop and greatly increase the flow of water.

I lay down and rested on the pile of wet gear under me. The hull was still sound; there was nothing wrong with the boat's fundamental integrity. But the terrible weather we'd ridden out had twisted the hull badly enough to not only short out that lighting-wire bridle under the liner but also to fracture this scupper pipe, way up there. The pipe, of course, would have to be repaired, but that was a job that could reasonably wait until the morning. Now that we'd located the leak, we could rest, content to pump out every half-hour or so if need be.

I slid back out of the forepeak, so weary that I literally saw bright little spots before my face if I moved my head too quickly. Carol was putting on the vest and safety harness to take the watch above. I pulled off my dripping sweatshirt and lay down on my bunk.

"I'll put us on the other tack," she said, "so that the water won't splash in so badly."

I nodded without speaking. I meant to tell her to ease off on the course, just to steer a comfortable beam reach toward the south until we could repair the scupper. But before I could say any of that, my eyes fell shut and I was asleep.

I relaxed in the cockpit, sipping a tepid beer while Carol prepared dinner. It had been another long day, but I felt satisfied with the work I had done. Since early morning, I'd been cooped up down below again, working in the forepeak. After examining the whole anchor locker, inside and out, I'd discovered that the starboard scupper pipe was also damaged, ripped partially away from the rectangular fiber glass box of the locker. Because we were still sailing, and because the splintered glass fibers were soaking wet from the salt water that had already come in, I had to find some way of making a solid, watertight seal on soaking wet components. Ordinary fiber glass resin was out; so was ordinary tape or glue. Luckily, one of the last items I'd bought at Defender Industries was a one-quart batch of underwater epoxy. At the time, I thought I could use this to seal a hatch or window damaged in heavy weather. Now it was vital in repairing the damage done by the twisting stress on the anchor well. The torque we'd suffered lying ahull followed by the pounding we'd undergone reaching under storm sails had been greater than I'd realized. But, even so, the damage had been relatively minor, albeit frightening, when first discovered. Now though, we had put the boat right again; we had taken weather about as bad—short of a hurricane—as the summer Atlantic could throw at us, and we were still sailing. We were back in business, a viable little ship making its slow way across a large ocean.

Having read the right books beforehand, and talked to the right specialists, we'd used this knowledge to prepare a good inventory of emergency repair supplies and tools. With waterproof tape and the underwater epoxy, I'd been able to make watertight, durable "bandages" for the two splintered scuppers, a repair job that would last until we reached the Azores and I could dry out the anchor locker, then seal it properly with glass cloth and resin.

I watched the sun setting behind some piled cumulus. My neck and shoulders ached from the cumulative hours of awkward work. Tonight, however, we'd have compass and masthead lights. Tonight, we wouldn't have to pump the bilge every thirty minutes. The wind was steady from the south southwest, at about 15 knots. We were sailing well on main and working jib, clocking 5.5 knots, and the motion was easy enough to allow Carol to cook a special meal without danger of hot spills. I could smell the food now, Danish canned ham steamed in its own juices with fresh potatoes, carrots, and onions. I was hungry, and the aroma made my stomach growl.

To the west, the sky was clearing; out ahead to the east, the horizon was now cloudless. We were a long way indeed from the clotted traffic, angry gas lines, and chronic, frustrated tension of the city. This clearing sky and steady barometer indicated that maybe we were finally escaping the track of the continental depressions and entering the settled weather of the Azores High.

Taking the weed-fouling of the log impeller into consideration, as we did plotting the noon position each day, we were almost exactly halfway to Horta. We had gone through some rough weather, but that was to be expected on the Atlantic, and the resulting damage had not been disabling. In fact, we were in damn good shape, both physically and emotionally. I thought of the exciting phrase "point of no return," which had enlivened my childhood reading of nautical and aviation adventures. Words like that didn't mean much out here. We had learned how to sail our boat on the deep sea, and now we were just going to keep on sailing until we reached our destination.

I went down to the chart table and did some quick arithmetic on my clipboard, then turned to Carol, who was jammed into the aft end of the small galley, reading Gunter Grass's *The Flounder* in the failing light while the pressure cooker wheezed on the alcohol stove. It was strange; she could have been a suburban housewife, sitting in her kitchen, waiting for the timer of the microwave oven to ping, telling her the frozen quiche was ready. Instead, she was half the crew of a small plastic ship sailing alone some 7,000 feet above the wrinkled sea bed, halfway across the Atlantic.

"If we tacked now," I said, breaking the sunset tranquillity, "and steered about 275 degrees true, we could probably be back in New York a day or two before our present ETA in Horta." I had tried to keep a straight face when I said this, but I don't think I pulled it off.

Carol put down her book and leaned across, making a show of consulting the Atlantic Ocean sheet taped to the chart table. She fingered her sweatshirt and faded jeans.

"But I sent all my sequined jumpsuits on ahead to St. Tropez," she deadpanned. "They'd never let us into Studio 54 dressed like *this.*"

"Okay," I answered. "I guess we'll just have to keep sailing east then."

She looked through the open hatch at the darkening mauve sky, then pointed out the first star, a bright point hanging between the double backstays. "You make the wish," she said. "You're the one who worked so hard today. I'm going to open a bottle of that Valpolicella to celebrate halfway."

I studied the star a moment, wondering what would be an appropriate wish to punctuate the midpoint in the first long leg of the crossing. The star brightened as the sky went from mauve to soft black. Wishing for money was clearly irrelevant; we had only a little over three hundred dollars cash, but there certainly was no place to spend it out here. Wishing for good weather seemed risky, a kind of arrogant assumption that the ocean planet would rearrange its vast weather dynamics to suit our small needs. Besides, we were well past the July hurricane tract, and from now on, the Atlantic summer weather simply couldn't be any worse than we'd already had. Finally, I realized that I would return the wish, unused. Maybe somebody else had need of it.

Carol was opening the long-necked green bottle. "Well, you make a wish . . . movie rights on the new book . . . the Nobel Prize?"

I waved my open palm toward the hatchway, taking in the cockpit, the sunset's afterglow, and the bright first star. "I can't think of anything to wish for," I said, suddenly quite serious. "I've got everything I want right here."

The neck of the bottle clunked on the plastic glass as Carol poured my wine. "It's almost cool," she said, hefting the wine bottle. "We can pretend that it's iced."

Reaching up from my place behind the chart table, I encircled her waist with my free arm. "That's small change," I said. "I've gotten used to drinking wine warm." I leaned up to kiss her hand. "Anyway, there're a lot of rich young stockbrokers and corporate VPs in the Westport Yacht Club who'd pay a *hell* of a lot of money to drink a warm bottle of Valpolicella aboard a boat they'd sailed halfway across the Atlantic."

Carol sipped her wine thoughtfully. "They and their wives sailed, you mean."

I dropped my arm from her waist. "Yeah . . . sure. You know what I mean. I'm not pretending I've done this alone."

She picked up my arm and drew it around her once again. "Yes, I do understand. I was just being . . . I don't know. There were some times at the beginning of the trip, and then . . . well, that terrible night back there." She nodded to the west, to the faint gray horizon line. "Sometimes I thought you were really angry at me for some good reason, that I'd done something stupid or selfish, that I'd wrecked the boat somehow . . . that you knew things about the sails or rigging that I'd never learned, and that I was sabotaging the trip out of pure ignorance."

I lowered my hot face toward the chart. She was absolutely right. I had behaved horribly at times, out of exhaustion, but most of all out of fear, which preyed on my overtired brain.

"I was afraid those nights, Honey . . . worn out and just scared. That's how little kids act when they're tired and scared, they yell at the people close to them. Well, I'm no different. Nobody is. We've all got a scared a little kid inside us."

She sat down on the engine step and drank another sip of wine. "Malcolm, I don't believe that. It's not so simple. I've seen you do things without batting an eye that would frighten a trapeze artist from Barnum and Bailey. You weren't really scared when you got so nasty, you were *worried.*" She shrugged, struggling for the right words. "There's a big difference. The reason you were worried was that you felt responsible for . . ." She swept her hand around, indicating the boat, the sky, and the surrounding sea. ". . . for everything. The whole trip, the weather, for *me.* All *that* was supposed to be your responsibility. As if I had no say in any of it, as if I was some sort of dumb bystander who kept getting in the way. Like you were this brain surgeon who was the only one who could possibly save the patient and this ignorant *cleaning lady* kept sticking her hands in the way."

Carol drank down her wine in a loud gulp and poured herself another glass. "Why do reasonable, self-aware adult men turn into such macho adolescents when they sail boats with their wives?"

Her question was rhetorical. I could only nod my silent agreement.

"Who do you think does the afternoon LOP," she went on, "and changes sail, and pumps the bilge, and writes up the log book when you're sleeping?" She shook her head. "How on earth does any of that get done if you're the only person on this tub with enough seamanship to take any responsibility? Sometimes I . . ."

I raised my hands to silence her, palms open in a gesture of acceptance. "Okay. You're right. Henceforth, that crap is really behind us. I think maybe we've both learned some things we didn't expect to when we left New York."

She stared down at her bare feet on the cabin sole. "That was kind of a sermon, wasn't it?"

"Amen, Sister. And you've got a convert. You can do early morning star sights tomorrow if we've got a flat horizon."

"Great," she said, smiling warmly now. "I should have kept my mouth shut."

I put down my glass and took her hand. "No, Carol. You know you had to say those things. And I'm glad you did."

She stared at me for a moment, then nodded in silence. Through the open hatchway, the night sky was creamy with new stars.

CHAPTER NINE

DR: 38°13' NORTH, 34°33' WEST
JULY 31: 1310 LOCAL ZONE TIME

It was hot and still. The sea around the boat looked like flat blue stone. For the past thirty hours, we'd been becalmed, with absolutely no breeze for the past twelve. Since working up the meridian pass twenty minutes earlier, I'd been out in the stifling midday glare, trying to set the tiller lines to hold the bow east. I knew it was silly to worry about our compass heading when there was no steerage way, but fussing like this gave me something to do.

We had only two hundred sixty more miles to Faial, and I was becoming increasingly impatient to arrive. I was not temperamentally suited for these long calms; they got to me, driving me to frustrated activity, like fussing with these lines. Carol, however, didn't seem to have any problem with calms. She was down there in the cabin now, reading and dozing away the day in the hot shade, patiently waiting out this total absence of breeze.

But I needed something to occupy my hands, to keep me busy. With the breathless heat, neither of us was very hungry, so we didn't even have the formal activity of a meal to break the monotony. The sky, of course, was cloudless, achingly empty, as brassy as any sky I'd seen in the Sahara. Earlier that morning I had watched an airplane in the distance to the north, probably an Air Force Starlifter descending for a refueling stop at the base on Terceira, three hundred miles northeast of us. It was maddening; the Azores were right out there, just over the gentle blue curve of the horizon. Yet here we sat, as if stuck in this hot blue ice, drifting ever so slowly east in a dying branch of the main Gulf Stream.

I finally gave up trying combinations of tension and extra shock cord and cleated off the tiller dead amidships. The gentle pressure of the current coming from behind the rudder turned the boat inevitably abeam to the flow, so that we lay on an even keel, the bow pointing north, drifting along at maybe half a knot. The sun was heavy on my neck and shoulders. Beside me in the cockpit well were two plastic buckets of salt water that I was sun-heating for my daily bath and shave. But now I needed cool water, not hot. So I spilled one bucket sloshing across my bare feet and tossed it over to retrieve some cooler water to dump over my head.

As I heaved in on the lanyard, I saw that I'd inadvertently snared a spiral of golden sargasso weed in the bucket. My impulse was to throw it back. Then I thought it might break the hot boredom to see what little creatures were living in this particular clump of weed. We'd been fascinated the first time we'd pulled in the weed-fouled log-impeller line to discover tiny crabs scuttling among the yellow stalks and branches.

I gingerly set the overflowing bucket down in the cockpit well, then sat close above it, so that I could transfer pieces of the clump from this fresh bucket to the one already full beside it. Reaching into the cool water, I took a branch of the weed clump and spread it open. I stopped. Swimming slowly between my fingers was a tiny golden fish, oval in shape and no bigger than a dime. His softly gleaming yellow scales were almost exactly the same hue as the weed stalks and branches. I cupped my hand and rotated it, so that the small yellow fish nestled in my palm. He was a perfect miniature, a tiny adult fish, not a larva or a fingerling. The fish stared up at me with perfectly formed eyes, calm and unafraid. His fins and his tail fanned slowly; his gills opened and closed. He was living there in the transparent bowl of water formed by my cupped palm. When I opened my hand he was gone, back into the sheltering weed.

Pinching the pulpy stalk between my fingers, I lifted gently now, aware that the atavistically twisted knobs and limbs of the weed clump were home to a microcosm of life. As I brought the weed clear of the water, three or four small yellow shrimp jumped free and fluttered backwards into the refuge of the submerged weed. By dipping and raising the stalk several times with my cupped palm below the clump, I was able briefly to capture two of the miniature shrimp. Like the dime-sized fish, these little creatures were golden, an exact color duplication of the sargasso weed. They were also perfectly formed replicas of larger species, not immature juveniles. The tiny golden shrimp jerked about in my cupped hands, swimming on their backs, their minuscule legs kicking in rhythmic waves. I opened my hands to release them, and they scooted into the protective yellow jungle.

Probing further into the floating weed, I came across an exceedingly small crab. Just like the other creatures, he was bronze-gold in color and perfectly developed. I stuck my index finger parallel to his perch, and he crawled onto my hand, moving sideways like all crabs. Deeper in the weed, near the thick main trunk, I found a golden sea snail much smaller than the nail of my little finger. I nudged him gently and he moved with surprising speed along the stalk.

I was curious now to know if these small animals possessed chameleonlike color adaptation or if the weed clump itself exuded some kind of saffron dye that stained each creature it sheltered. Carefully cupping the little crab in my palm, I rubbed his shell gently with my fingertip. None of the yellow came off. Moving him into the shade of my body, I watched intently to see if he would change color, if he'd go duller out of the direct sunlight and away from the yellow weed. He crawled slowly in my hand, retaining the golden color. I repeated my experiment with the fish, snail, and one of the shrimp. The results were the same; these tiny animals' native pigment was the bronze-gold of their parent environment, the sargasso weed. The implications of my crude experiment were startling to me; they had not been stained but had taken on this specific color over millions of years of close association with the weed.

Salty sweat dripped off my nose and down into the bucket. The boat stood straight on its keel, barely forming a ripple, its bow pointing south now toward the near-vertical sun. There was no sound or perceptible motion in the day. Out to starboard, I saw two Portuguese men-of-war, their inflated purple sails drifting like obscene bubble gum. We were moving neither faster nor slower than these jellyfish. Indeed, we were all of us—the men-of-war, the inhabited clumps of sargasso weed, and the boat—just drifters in this current, children of Planet Ocean's matrix. Together, we had followed this ancient ocean river on its course, powered by the planet's thermal energy machine.

Squinting out at the yellow blurs that marked the drifting weed, I felt a powerful but unexpected sense of kinship. Those clumps of sargasso weed were self-sufficient, microcosmic planets, like this boat. We were all borne along our way by the same forces of sun, gravity, and rotation.

The shrimp, crabs, and fish had their own separate but related evolutionary heritage, astounding in its complex ramifications. Somehow, over immense wastelands of time, they had cast their lot with the sargasso weed and had linked their evolution so closely that they had all arrived at the same bronze-gold coloration, working from vastly diverse points of biochemical origin. A shrimp, crab, fish, and snail might *seem* much the same to a layman, but in many ways they were as different—from an evolutionary point of view—as, say, a human being from an oyster. That a vertebrate fish and a snail, a mollusk, had each evolved to mimic so exactly the saffron color of their protecting weed-planet, drifting together as cooperating species all these millions of years from the nursery of the Sargasso Sea up the Stream into the Atlantic, was to me a discovery of beautiful subtlety.

I touched the water in the bucket and felt a strange sense of peaceful union, a bond of parallel existence with the shrimp, fish, and snail, even with the "ugly" jellyfish in the still water to starboard. Their electric-lavender sails were, in many ways, as elegant an adaptation as my brain; the sails allowed them to cruise the entire circuit of the warm ocean currents, feeding in the shallow layer of photoplankton, perfectly in harmony with their environment. During storms, the jellyfish simply furled their sails by expelling buoyancy gas and sank to safety below the level of turbulent water. It would have been nice if fancy, expensive sailboats could do the same.

In any event, we were all out here this hot, still afternoon, drifters in the ocean stream, the little clumps of weed strangely mirroring their parent planet, which was, in turn, a spinning matrix of life, drifting in a regular course about its star, the sun.

And then I could envision the sun itself, moving relentlessly along a wider current: the galaxy's spiral arm, pinwheeling along through invisible currents of time and gravity, pulling with it a little menagerie of planets and moons just as the sargasso weed carried the fish, crabs, and snails. And the very galaxy, the Milky Way, was itself a drifter on vast currents, its three hundred billion stellar systems weirdly parallel to the hundreds of trillions of pulsing molecules of a little yellow snail. Indeed, the very spiral pattern of the snail's shell was duplicated on an unthinkably larger scale in the twirling limbs of the galaxy. The natural spiral of drifting rotation seemed to open up all around me. When seen with a satellite's television eye, I realized, a hurricane presented this same beautiful pinwheel as the storm drifted from warmer to cooler regions, redistributing the planet's heat.

I sat quiet and reflective in the silent heat, my mind drifting like the sargasso weed and the billions of galaxies out there in the currents of black eternity. Eventually I swirled my hand in the bucket. The water was getting too warm in the sun. If the animals sheltered by the weed were to survive, I would have to return them to the cooler water of the Gulf Stream. With great care, I lowered the bucket into the still ocean, balancing across the hot teak coaming on my knees, mindful not to dump the contents of the bucket too rapidly and rip apart the fleshy stalks of the weed clump. When the bucket was awash on its side, I slid it back, launching the yellow spiral of weed again on its course. The clump of bronze-gold stalks floated near the surface, turning very slowly from the turbulence left by the bucket. A minute later, the weed had drifted three or four feet from the boat but floated parallel to us, as if keeping station. I closed my eyes, absorbed with beautifully austere pictures of flowing time and gravity. I pondered the evolution of coin-small, gilded fish and the evolution of the human brain, which could recognize and almost understand both these astounding concepts.

After a while, I went down below and lay on my bunk, lazily watching the patterns of sun shimmer on the plexiglass hatches, no longer impatient or frustrated with our slow progress across the face of the drifting ocean planet.

CHAPTER TEN

DR: 38°56' NORTH, 28°41' WEST
AUGUST 4: 0200 AZORES TIME

We were very near our landfall. Out there, just ahead of us in the windy, overcast night, lay Faial Island, our first land since leaving Brooklyn twenty-eight days ago. The wind was force five from the southwest, blowing from dead astern, as we steered northeast on a rough radio compass bearing to the Faial Airport beacon. Around us in the darkness the sea was moderately high, with a rolling swell that clearly signified we were leaving the deep, obstacle-free reaches of the Atlantic and nearing the soundings of the Azores archipelago.

I sat tensely in the cockpit, chain smoking, the warm breeze lifting the boat with each passing swell. From the crests I would peer under the sails, trying to pick up the first glimmer of the lighthouse on the southwestern corner of the island. The south wind and the fast-moving dark overcast were combining to give the night an alien quality. For the past ten days we'd had absolutely clear weather, light northerlies, and flat seas. Now this following wind and sea made the proximity of land ahead of us seem a threat rather than the comforting reward after a long and difficult voyage that it should have been.

I didn't know it at the time, but landfalls, especially at night, are notorious for making long-distance sailors jumpy. The feeling of having land close out there—rocks, reefs, and beach—after so many weeks of knowing there was nothing solid ahead to worry about, was a hard concept to accept. But this hedged-in, claustrophobic sensation was as all-pervasive as it was diffuse; I couldn't quite give a name to the irritable nervousness gripping me. So I remained silent, smoking one cigarette after another, snapping my fingers, even starting to whistle off-key, until I realized the noise of my discordant attempt at musical relief would disturb Carol. Again, we were running up a sleep debt; she'd been on watch for over four hours and it was hard to sleep down below with this following weather producing an exaggerated roll.

As we crested the swells I leaned forward, my elbows on the coach top, my loose nylon windbreaker billowing forward in the soft, damp wind. I was accidentally scattering cigarette ash all over the cabin top, producing little black smudges. Normally, I wouldn't have worried; the next hard slog to windward would scrub the deck far better than either of us could. But there would be no beat to windward before port. We were actually going to sleep on solid land tomorrow night, probably in beds ashore, between real sheets. The idea seemed exotic. In less than twenty-four hours we would walk on an unmoving surface, on steady, unyielding concrete and stone. We'd stand in some strange white tile cubicle and turn a metal wheel . . . water—*hot*, fresh water—would fall down onto our bodies, and we could wash and then rinse our hair and skin as often as we wanted. Sometime tomorrow, in Horta, we'd eat ice cream and drink cold beer. Sometime before the next day was out, we'd sit at a steady, unrolling table and eat fresh meat off china plates rather than canned food from our deep plastic "dog" bowls.

I was well aware that our crossing of the 2,550 miles from New York harbor to Faial Island was hardly an epic voyage. This wasn't the great Southern Ocean and we had experienced relatively little hardship. But this was our *first* crossing. The reality of a month in a thirty-foot tube of plastic and steel, out on this empty, landless surface all that time, had psychologically affected both of us. For me, the habitual daily chores such as navigation, sail handling, and maintenance had become not only instinctual; they'd also worked in a strange way to reshape my self-perception, my sense of identity. For several weeks now, I had not thought of myself as a writer or a teacher, or even as a husband or a citizen of any particular country. I was simply one-half of this crew. Carol had become my shipmate; the boat had become our total existence. My responsibilities included the heavy sail work, the engine maintenance, and the navigation. I did these jobs and watched the sea and sky. Carol had her own set of responsibilities and habits. We slept in blue sleeping bags on rolling bunks, protected from falling by gray canvas lee cloths when the motion got too bad. For a month now, that had been who we were. There'd been no need to think about the problems of the civilized world, about war, peace, and personal wealth or poverty.

Now there was land out there, an island that we were going to visit, a port city, Horta, which was part of a wider civilization. There were letters waiting for us, probably telegrams as well. We were about to reenter the complicated, interlocking series of relationships and dependencies that wove together our adult lives, after having been absolutely free of this complexity for twenty-eight days. No wonder I felt this tension as the boat rose and fell with the dark swell and every hour we drew five nautical miles nearer to land. Our twenty-eight-day hiatus was almost over and I was jumpy.

But I still had to keep my head screwed on right. The land out there in the darkness was not only civilized, it was solid, the kind that can wreck a boat quickly in this type of wind and sea. In effect, the southwest blow and our northeast course had combined to make Faial a lee shore. And our landfall was definitely going to be at night. My last DR plotting had included pretty good RDF fixes from both the Faial and the Flores beacons. Also, the taffrail log was reading almost completely true now that we were free of the Stream's main axis and there wasn't so much sargasso weed in the water to foul the impeller line. The previous afternoon I'd combined the accurate log readings with a series of sun LOPs every ninety minutes, producing a group of running fixes that allowed me to judge the force of this southern current. If my sextant work and arithmetic were anywhere near accurate, we were due to pick up the Faial lighthouse at a range of ten miles at approximately 0245. Given that ETA, we'd close on the coast just about dawn and sail into Horta harbor on the eastern side of the island at about 0730.

I tossed yet another smouldering cigarette butt toward the quarter wave and stared ahead into the darkness. If only there were a moon and stars and not this warm, rushing overcast. I didn't like the feeling of being hemmed in by both the land ahead and the sky above. There was nothing out there to see, only the black horizon and the dully glinting wave crests; even my old friend, the phosphorescence, had temporarily abandoned me. For a few confused moments I experienced the navigational equivalent of vertigo; I was trying too hard to conjure up the chart in my head, and suddenly the compass directions and relative distances began moving about, so that I felt we were on some kind of a *curving* course, swinging up and around the dark end of the island to sail blindly onto an unlighted beach. I shook my head violently.

From the steady orange disc of the compass, I verified that we were steering 90 degrees magnetic, 78 true, our optimum course to raise the lighthouse at the maximum visible range, ten miles. Amazingly, despite the roll and the swell, we were holding a steady course. Just to dispel completely any remaining confusion, I went down to get the hand-held Sea Spot RDF from its bracket above the chart table. A strong, steady signal from the Faial radio beacon, only fifteen or sixteen miles out there in the darkness, would do a lot to reassure me.

But before I went below, I took yet another log reading, so that I could bring the DR up to date on the chart. I was down perhaps five minutes working out our position, then swung back up through the open companionway, careful to keep my harness lines free of the boxy RDF and dangling earphone wires. It took me a couple of seconds to get orientated in the cockpit, sorting out my harness lines and the radio compass. As always, I felt clumsy doing this because of the bulky life vest, the clodhopper sea boots, and the motion of the boat, exacerbated by the relative fragility of the Sea Spot.

Absorbed as I was with this maneuvering, I hadn't bothered to look ahead as we crested the swells. When I did look up, I thought I saw a pale white line of . . . *something* out ahead of us in the darkness. But my visual impression was so fleeting that I dismissed the image as an afterglow of ruined night vision, caused by the bright chart-table light. I should have used the red-lensed pen light, but I'd been too lazy to get it out. Spoiled night vision had not been a serious problem in the open midreaches of the Atlantic. So, not unduly alarmed, I closed my eyes to fully dilate the pupils and waited out a couple of passing waves. Maybe I'd only seen some phosphorescence, perhaps two white-crested waves lumping together.

Braced there in the cockpit, the Sea Spot RDF cradled in my arms and my eyes shut tightly, I was totally unprepared for what happened next. The boat rose on a slowly cresting swell, and just at the top I was assailed by a wash of warm, briny mist . . . a blanketing curtain of fine spray that carried with it the unmistakeable iodine, seaweed scent of a beach at low tide. The warm, fishy spray seemed to hang around me as I swung my head to see forward. Again, there was that strange ghost-flickering line of white, out there ahead of us at an indeterminate distance, yet somehow close.

As I gripped the Sea Spot tightly in my two hands, my sleepy brain finally made the proper connections. The flesh on my neck literally crawled; my stomach tightened in a sour knot. Jesus Christ, we were about to go on the beach! Somehow, victim of an unfelt current, we had obviously drifted east of the lighthouse cape and had bungled into the breaking surf on this unlighted side of the island, the lee shore I'd been so worried about earlier.

As I flung myself to the portside of the cockpit to uncleat the preventer that ran forward holding out the boom, I was assaulted by another threatening stimulus, this one a flopping, liquid rush of sound, the roar of the breakers just out there in the darkness. My mind was hot and yet also numb, as if I'd been badly slapped about the face. All the goddamned way from New York, through all that weather and through all those long calms, jut to lose the boat like *this* . . .

Finally, after a seeming lifetime, I had the preventer off and the tiller free of its web of wind-vane lines. I slammed the rudder hard over in an emergency jibe. The working jib backed violently; the main came slamming across with a vengeance, just as I knew it would, and we were around. . . . And, by some miracle, we weren't yet on the beach.

"Carol!" I yelled, desperately trying to sheet in the main with one hand and let the jib sheet fly with the other. "Carol . . . *emergency!* Start the engine . . . quick."

"Emergency" was a word we had both agreed to use in a life-threatening situation only. On a small boat, it's just as emotional a word as "fire" in a crowded theater.

In less than ten seconds she was out of her bunk and bent over the open engine box, priming the injector pump. In the reflected compass light, I caught a glimpse of her long hair hanging dangerously close to the flywheel belts. Too late to warn her; the boat was hobby-horsing at the top of a swell, the sails slatting loudly. We needed the engine to get clear. Beneath my boot soles, I felt the thumping rumble of the diesel catching, then the steady roar of it revving fast. I jammed the gear lever forward without throttling back, and the boat seemed to jump ahead. Carol was up in the companionway now, pulling an oilskin jacket on over her short nightdress.

"What . . . " she began, " . . . what's that . . . *smell?*"

"The beach . . . " I panted, "the goddamn beach. . . . Come *on*, get the jib sheeted in. We have to get out of this surf. . . . "

The wind was ahead of us now and I could feel its force. Frantically I sheeted the main in tight, then reached over the side of the cockpit to drag in the trailing end of the now useless preventer line. All we needed right then was to get the prop fouled and have to kill the engine.

Carol was stuffing her flailing length of hair under the hood of her jacket. "What's *wrong?*" she yelled, her voice now reflecting my wild tone. "What beach?"

Just then, even over the thudding engine, we both heard the whooshing resonance that I had heard earlier. Again, the iodine beach stink drifted down on us. But this time both the noise and the warm mist had come from well off the starboard beam, not from dead astern.

"Look," Carol said, pointing.

Off to the starboard the darkness was broken by a rippling line of white and gray and by some distant sparkles of phosphorescence.

The fine, redolent spray drifted onto us. Carol sat down. I sagged in my place at the tiller.

"Whale," she finally said. "A big whale."

"Yeah," I muttered. "A big damn sperm whale. . . . He must have been sleeping in the water . . . right in front of us."

Carol was peering out into the now dark swells to starboard. "He could use some mouthwash . . . what bad breath."

My legs and arms were trembling from spent adrenaline. My breathing was all rough. I eased off the throttle and peered to starboard. The whale was gone. He'd been sleeping on the surface when he'd felt our pressure wave, then had blown hard and sounded just before we would have struck him. He'd blown and dove once more out to starboard, but now he was definitely gone. We certainly had arrived in Azores water, I reflected, my shaky fingers digging in my windbreaker for a cigarette. When I had my emotions back under control, I stood up and looked around the dark rolling horizon. Nothing had changed.

"Let's put her back on course," I said tiredly. "We'll leave the engine on a while to let him know where we are."

By the time we had the boat back on its heading and the vane set, it was 0255. Carol came up from the galley, dressed now in a full set of oilskins and clutching two mugs of steaming, sweet coffee, each laced with some brandy for our jangled nerves. We laughed a little too readily and too long about the incident, both trying unsuccessfully to underplay our earlier panic. When we finished our coffee, Carol offered to take the watch for a bit, so that I could lie down in the quarter berth and rest my eyes. We both knew that sleep was impossible just then. She was standing balancing in the hatchway, holding the two empty plastic mugs, when she happened to look forward up the starboard side.

"How long has the light been there?" she asked quietly.

I knelt beside her, peering ahead. There it was, the bright flash-pause-flash of the Faial lighthouse, steady as it could be, a couple of degrees above the lumpy horizon, almost dead on the bow. It was 0314 local time on the morning of August 4, 1979. According to the taffrail log and the DR, we had sailed 3,104 miles from Danny's boatyard, about 400 more than the rhumb-line course. I had hoped to raise the light at 0230; instead we'd made it forty-four minutes late, not too bad an error when averaged over a twenty-eight-day span of time.

Carol leaned against me, still pointing, like a child at the zoo. "There it is," she said, "*there* it is."

"Jesus," I finally managed, "that's the *light* . . . that's Faial."

The boat rose and swooped with the warm following wind and sea. The bright group-flashing light held steady just above the horizon. In about two hours we'd be near the coast, and it would be dawn. We had just made our first landfall.

CHAPTER ELEVEN

FAIAL, AZORES
AUGUST 4: MORNING

Faial was many shades of pastel green, with darker tones where the rising sun cast shadows. Terraced fields rose from the black lava shore into a mantle of rain cloud on the caldera summit. Pico, the massive volcanic neighbor to the east, was still hidden by the gray line squall that had passed over us at dawn. After twenty-eight days, land looked wonderful. Pastures and fields were separated by hedges of blue hydrangea, with green blocks of pine trees on the steeper slopes. The farmhouses were whitewashed stone beneath orange tile roofs. Our following wind of the previous night had spent itself in the squall, and the gray shroud of rain was now lifting rapidly from Faial and Pico. Motoring along the south coast of the island, half a mile out from the breakers, the sun was warm on our faces.

For a long time, neither of us spoke. We were tired, of course, from the rough, sleepless night and the spooky encounter with the whale, but our silence was engendered by something more profound than fatigue. We were seeing land—pastures, fields, rock, flowers, and trees—as if for the first time, through eyes that had become absolutely accustomed to wide seascape and open sky. It had been almost a month since we had seen anything solid, any object that did not rise and fall with the sea. Now we could only gaze, captivated, at the subtlety of color and the incredible light patterns and textures produced by the interplay of sun and cloud on rock, soil, and trees.

Sitting at the tiller, I steered with my knees as I cupped yet another mug of coffee, staring like a child at a Christmas tree. I recalled once in the Congo flying upcountry on a small Cessna from a mission station and landing at a disused airstrip to clean the fuel filters. People had come shyly out of the surrounding bush after we'd landed. They were refugees from the fighting to the north, African villagers from the primitive region of Kibali-Ituri who had never before seen an airplane or, perhaps for the children, a white person. Watching the bright, guileless faces of those Africans, I thought of Caliban in *The Tempest;* I also regretted my own Western, mature sophistication, which prevented me from ever seeing the world with such innocence. Now, at least temporarily, I had regained a sense of childlike wonder.

"Look at the . . . the *trees,*" Carol said softly, obviously embarrassed at her own words, yet unable to remain silent any longer.

I set the binoculars down beside me. "Those are *cows* up there, past the wall . . . in that wide field . . . cows, black and white Holsteins . . . "

Carol had the glasses now. "The roofs are all tile . . . orange tile . . . they're beautiful."

We powered slowly up the coast, the night's swell smoothing out with the ebb tide. Ahead of us, the massive cone of Pico materialized from the gray cloud blanket. For the previous two days, the warm southern breeze had produced an evaporation haze that had kept us from seeing these two mountains. At the time I was annoyed; now I was glad.

At exactly 0900 local time, we rounded the lava-block sea wall of Horta harbor and powered into the anchorage, amazed at the variety of sailboats that swung on moorings or lay alongside the quay. All the way from New York we had seen only one other yacht. We'd gotten used to the idea that our adventure was unique, that we had the Atlantic to ourselves. Now we could see just how commonplace our crossing actually was. Maneuvering through the anchorage, we counted almost thirty sailboats, many bigger than us—forty-, fifty-footers—but just as many a good deal smaller than our thirty feet. These boats hadn't been delivered here on the decks of freighters; they'd been sailed across the open sea from North America or Europe, a number of them singlehanded.

Horta harbor in early August, we were to learn, was a gathering place of seagoing people, en route from America to the Med, Europe to the Caribbean—even some true world voyagers on their way from Capetown or the Pacific to Europe. It was one of these South African sailors, a lean, soft-spoken fellow named Peter, who hailed us from quay and indicated where we should tie up alongside.

As he took our bow line, he called out. "Good morning . . . New York?"

"Yeah," I called in answer, aware of how strange it felt to be talking to a human being other than Carol. "Yeah . . . New York, *direct* . . . we didn't stop in Bermuda." It seemed desperately important to make that clear.

Another man from one of the boats tied alongside, with his deep tan clearly marking him a sailor, took our stern line, while Peter stood by patiently above on the quay, waiting for the spring line.

"How many days?" the guy at the stern asked.

"Twenty-eight," Carol called up proudly.

As we made up our lines, other sailors wandered down the pier to say hello and chat about our crossing. The tide was dead low, and we had to crane our necks to watch the people's faces as they stood seven feet above us. But I could clearly see the famous Horta sea-wall paintings, the names and logos of all the many hundreds of yachts that had called here in the past forty years. There were names like *Wanderer III*, *Moonraker*, *Kochab*, and *Trekka*, plus hundreds of others painted in bright reds and yellows—some, elaborate cartoon renderings of the crew members; others, simple boat names with the number of days of their crossings to Horta. One caught my eye, the crudely painted name of a Dutch yacht with this explanation of their slow crossing: "Lost direction on the *rotten* Atlantic." I smiled; the Atlantic had been stern with us, but it certainly had not been *rotten.*

The group on the quay had swollen to perhaps fifteen, with the addition of five or six local kids, shy about their halting English but eager to speak to us. We bantered back and forth, putting the blue cover on the mainsail for the first time in a month and generally getting our deck tackle squared away for port. "How many days?" "What kind of weather?" they called down. We answered proudly, now conscious that most of these sailors were British or European, people who had *only* sailed a thousand miles or so to get here, that they saw us as worthy adventurers who had just braved twenty-eight long days on the open Atlantic. What a different feeling, after what we'd experienced in New York. Here we wouldn't have to explain ourselves to anyone. Here crossing oceans in small boats was a common occurrence.

Our new friends asked polite questions about the wind vane, about our rig, and about the problems we'd encountered en route. Naturally, we mentioned the storm, the fire, and the broken scuppers. As I spoke, I saw the tanned faces of these other sailors acquire expressions of concern and understanding. Bill down the line there, someone said, was a wizard on electrics; he'd have a look at the wiring, if we liked. Claude, the Frenchman out on that blue sloop, was good with fiber glass; he'd help us with the scuppers. It was a wonderful reception, like coming home to a family.

I looked out past the anchorage at the colorful town built into the green slope of the volcano. The buildings had an unmistakeable Iberian feel to them: whitewashed walls split by wrought-iron balconies, orange-tile roofs. Some houses were faced with cut black lava set into the white walls to form striking geometric patterns. There were tall umbrella pines, palm trees, and sculpted hydrangea hedges in the squares and parks. We were going to be here at least two weeks, while I completed numerous small revisions in the *Just Causes* manuscript. Standing on the deck of our boat, gazing off at the town of Horta in the bright sunshine of our first day ashore, I knew this was going to be a pleasant stay.

After clearing into customs and immigration, we headed for the harbor master's main office to pick up our mail. Unfortunately, it being Saturday, the office was closed. Although I was a little anxious to learn about the royalty payment we expected, we were just as happy to wait, to wander up the sloping, lava-block road to Peter Azevedo's well known Café Sport. *Wander* is not an accurate term to describe our progress, however. We staggered, we rolled, we tottered. In short, we had not yet gotten our land legs. All the old sailors' tales of the land moving beneath your feet after a long passage were not only true; they were understated. Luckily, the people of Horta are used to seeing the staggering, seemingly drunken gait of yacht sailors who step ashore for the first time. Climbing the crowded quay side, where fishermen pull up their dories on the sea wall and the ferryboats from Pico and Terceira load, smiling people stepped out of our paths as we tightly gripped each other's elbows and rolled and jolted up the slope. It wasn't even noon yet, but it looked like we'd both been on long benders. The damned pavement simply would *not* stay put. The straight, perpendicular edges of the shops and warehouses were definitely swaying—ever so slightly, but swaying nevertheless. So were the thick-trunked palms and even the dressed stone battlements of the sixteenth-century castle dominating the harbor.

Obviously, the only solution was to slip into the Café Sport to down the traditional first free drink Peter Azevedo gives to yachtsmen newly arrived. His place is an institution to visiting sailors. Traditionally, this is where they gather, where they meet each other and tell their sea stories, sitting around the solid, oak-framed, marble-topped tables, drinking iced bottles of Sagres lager or the lovely local *vinho verde,* a deceptively light-tasting white wine. It's cool inside, and the paneled walls are festooned with dozens of tattered yacht burgees and ensigns, pictures of well-known boats and scrimshaw done on whale ivory. Local fishermen, workers from the tuna plant at the base of the sea wall, and other islanders also frequent the bar, so it isn't an artificial foreigners' preserve. But in summer, most of the clientel are "yachties."

After we'd settled down with our wonderfully cold beers, we struck up a conversation with two young sailors seated beside us. They had that tanned, bleached-out, and grizzled look that marked them as professional crew; they were, in fact, delivery skippers, sailing a Canadian cutter, *Mango,* all the way from Vancouver to Spain, via Panama and Bermuda.

"How long you staying?" asked Willy, the bearded one of the pair.

"I'm not sure yet," Carol said.

"I've got some work to do on a book," I added, " . . . and there's stuff to be done on the boat, too."

Gordon, the smooth-shaven one, signaled Peter for another round of Sagres and grinned. "No one gets out of here on schedule," he muttered. "We planned on stopping one week, been here two, and now have to stay on for Sea Week." He got up and pointed down at the anchorage below us, where the boats on the moorings were being decked out with colorful bunting. "Sea Week starts tomorrow. Half the people here planned on staying four or five days, been here a week already, and won't get off till after the *Semana do Mar* . . . happens every year."

I looked at the dark green bulk of Pico across the channel, at the vineyards on its slopes, and, near the summit, the black lava flows. This place certainly did look good after a long time at sea.

Willy hoisted a fresh bottle of beer. "There's a lot worse places to stop a while . . . a lot worse."

Willy was right. Horta is one of the most pleasant, hospitable places we've ever visited. After a couple more beers and several rounds of sandwiches to soak up the alcohol, we set off unsteadily to find a room ashore. Our plan called for me to set up my typewriter on board and for Carol to install her portable electric machine in our room. That way, we could run a production line on the revisions of the manuscript, me working in the boat cabin and Carol retyping my efforts each day, keeping up with me. Even though we only had about $300. to our names, we were confident there'd be a letter from my agent for us when the harbor master opened on Monday. All we'd have to do for money once we knew how much the Pocket Books royalty payment had been would be to effect telegraphic transfer from our bank to an affiliate here . . . a bit complicated, but a procedure we'd often used when living overseas.

All that business could wait, however; our first day we were going to take care of priorities: fresh-water showers, plenty of fresh food, and plenty of cold drink. Surprisingly, we learned all the hotel rooms were taken; the Sea Week celebrations, started as a formal endeavor in 1975, had begun to attract a number of tourists from mainland Portugal. So, we had to "settle" for a room in a private house, the home of Senhor and Senhora Lima. The building was a typical Horta townhouse: three stories, whitewashed lava stone, with varnished hardwood paneling and floors inside, tall ceilings, cool rooms, and balconies on either end of our floor, one overlooking the harbor, the other the street of prosperous shops facing the cathedral square. The house was spotless and gleaming inside, with enough lace doilies, potted plants, and overstuffed velvet sofas to fill out the settings of several novels by Marcel Proust. Our room was right next to the bath, which was equipped with a butane-gas water heater that supplied a literally endless flow of hot water. To top all this off, Señora Lima was a professional pastry cook who provided the deserts for a local restaurant; there was always plenty of her work left over for home consumption. After I worked out the escudo-dollar exchange rate, I thought I'd made a mistake calculating the price of the room. I had not; it cost us the outrageous amount of three dollars and forty cents a night, *with* breakfast.

Later in our stay I learned that the Limas did not need to rent out rooms for financial gain; they did it during Sea Week as part of their civic duty. Indeed, when Sea Week began the next day with *morning* fireworks, a dinghy race in the harbor, and a procession of seamen to the cathedral, we learned just how seriously the people of Horta took the celebration. They obviously believed in it, and they went out of their way to make the week enjoyable for the foreign visitors. The reason for this, we learned from Senhor Lima, was that Faial had a longstanding maritime tradition. For hundreds of years, men from Horta had shipped out on Yankee whalers, Boston clippers, Portugese cod schooners, and, in this century, on a wide variety of merchantmen. Also, in the region of the Azores, the Atlantic was rich in marine life; the local people knew the sea intimately, respected it, and owed it their livelihood. When they banded together for one week each summer to celebrate their heritage, the resulting activities and the spirit shown truly reflected a maritime people's deep attachment to the sea.

They would undoubtedly celebrate the summer's calm weather informally, but the annual summer influx of foreign yachts gave them the impetus to channel the activities along more formal lines. For the next seven days, while I slogged away on my rewrites aboard the boat and Carol worked in the room retyping my pages, the activities of Sea Week unfolded. There were races every day in the harbor: for Vauriants and Optimists, which the kids of the local Club Navale built themselves from kits, and for model yachts and rubber dinghies. Every night there was a band concert in one of the parks, followed by a dance. Sandwiched into all this were excursions to neighboring islands for visiting yacht sailors, sports-fishing contests, open-air dinners at the Club Navale featuring the spicy local fish soup, and even a yacht name-painting contest on the sea wall. Meanwhile, of course, there were private parties on the sailboats and impromptu group dinners in the local restaurants, where we all stuffed ourselves on the gargantuan fish dinners, which averaged about two dollars a head, *with* several bottles of the *vinho verde.*

Looking back on those seven days, I remember them as one of the happiest, most productive periods in my life. Despite the ongoing party and the visits to other boats, I was able to get up at dawn each day and put in several hours' work, on the manuscript revisions in the morning and on the boat each afternoon. Every night, of course, there were cocktails aboard some neighbor's boat or at the Café Sport, followed by one of the group dinners ashore and the band concert and dance. The weather was perfect, with some late-night showers to keep everything green, and breezy, sunny days.

That first Monday we collected our mail at the harbor master's office and were a little disturbed to find no word from my agent about the Pocket Books royalty. However, I saw from the postmarks on our letters just how long mail took from the States. Apparently there was a slow-down wage protest in the Portuguese postal system. So, I sent my agent a telegram, asking her to cable back with the amount she'd deposited in our Washington bank account. Carol also cabled her mother that we'd arrived safely, and made arrangements for her to call us at the Lima's house. That week, everything seemed nicely under control.

Through Peter Azevedo, we met an American couple, Bob and Jane Silverman, who had settled on the island. Bob was a dentist who'd retired very young, having gotten truly hooked on sailing when he worked for the U.S. Health Service in the Virgin Islands. They'd sailed their British-built cutter *Açores* down from England the year before and were rebuilding a little stone farmhouse on the green slope of the volcano overlooking Horta and the harbor. Not only were Bob and Jane an interesting, pleasant couple, they were also both skilled sailmakers, equipped with the only zigzag sewing machine in the Azores. For about twenty dollars they took our mainsail in hand, remade the batten pocket ripped in the first storm, and reinforced all the main seams and reefing points. When we got the sail back, it was in better condition than when we had left New York.

So we passed the first week working on the manuscript revisions and on the boat and generally enjoying Horta during Sea Week. Some nights we'd walk back from dinner along the wide promenade overlooking the harbor, stopping to study the fine mosaics of black lava and white marble cubes arranged in motifs of schooners, whaling boats, and marine life. The town was impressive from this perspective, with floodlights on the battlements of the old fort and decorative colored lighting around the graceful umbrella pines and cypress trees in the park. Out in the anchorage, the yachts rode their moorings, kerosene anchor lights casting golden patterns on the water.

By the middle of the week, we'd also taken a free mooring near the ferry landing and rigged the boat out with sun awning and windsock in the forehatch, so that the cabin was shady and pleasant to work in, even in the midday heat. None of the days was too hot, though, as the northerly breeze held steady most of the time. Up on the green ridge above town, near the Silvermans' farmhouse, the Flemish windmills spun in the breeze, grinding corn to feed the large Holstein dairy herds, which provided the delicious local cheese. After the usual morning rain, the slopes of Faial stood out very clearly and the neighboring islands seemed to draw closer. While Faial was terraced green pastures hedged by blue hydrangea, Pico, across the channel, showed dark, primordial lava flows, its summit usually covered by cloud. São Jorge, north of both islands, was lower, with alternating bands of light cultivation and darker pine forests. Any number of times during our stay in Horta, I was struck by the idyllic nature of the islands. I'm sure any dry land with ample fresh water and a modicum of amenities would be pleasant after twenty-eight days in a small boat. But the Azores seemed truly blessed with a generous endowment of pleasant features: climate, rainfall, rich marine resources, and, of course, the hospitable local people.

The Azoreans are an interesting mixture of northern European stock, basically Flemish and Portuguese. Given their long association with other maritime nations, they are much more sophisticated and cosmopolitan than one would expect of people from an isolated archipelago. Almost everyone we met made an effort to speak English, and yet they were also helpful when we awkwardly tried out our skeletal Portuguese. Our first day in Horta, for example, a local fisherman gave us a Portuguese courtesy flag, then refused my offer to pay for it with, "Is okay Mister Captain." Peter Azevedo of the Café Sport is also a real friend to the cruising sailor. His visitors logbooks go back for over thirty years, and in them we found names like Hiscock, Chichester, Tabarly, and David Lewis. Any sailor's problem, be it a sick cat on board or a shredding forestay, Peter would happily point you in the right direction to get it solved. Like the others we met in Horta, Peter Azevedo (his real name is José, but all the sailors know him as Peter) is not fawning after tourist dollars; he has a true interest in and affection for the ocean sailor. He is fluent in five languages and equally friendly to the crews of homemade twenty-six-footers and of big-name boats like *Ondine.*

It would be easy to idealize the people of Horta completely, viewing them with a Pollyanna innocence that neglects the obvious shortcomings of the island culture. I'd seen this simplistic tendency to view all foreigners as quaint, childlike exotics among American yachtsmen in the Caribbean and the Med, and I was determined not to become overly sentimental about Horta. In fact, I was actively looking for defects in this apparent Eden. Naturally, I found a few.

There was a pronounced them-and-us class system, exacerbated by the social turmoil of mainland Portugal, which seemed to sour relations between working class people and the bourgeoisie. Yet we as foreign visitors never felt any of this animosity. In fact, I was constantly struck by the generosity of the fishermen on the quay and of the workers from the tuna plant, who were always calling me over to their café tables for a free cup of coffee or bottle of beer. They simply would not let me buy a round in return. And not once did these proud men bring up politics in our pidgin Portuguese-English discussions. The policemen on the street corners, I'd noticed, seemed to swagger and display their tommy guns with a bit too much enthusiasm, but these same cops would go out of their way, walking five blocks across town to show me a hardware store or chandler where I could buy brass screws or nylon line.

All during our stay in Horta, I was comparing how we were treated there with our experience in New York. Despite the fact that the island was undergoing the same political and social upheaval as the rest of Portugal, there was no street violence. Every day we were there, a long gas line would form at the small station near the yacht club and extend down the hill to the ferry landing. But the people in the line did not remain tense and isolated in the cars or on their scooters. They formed friendly groups, chatting and drinking little thimble cups of coffee in the sunny breeze, happy to have this excuse to socialize. Several times during our stay I noticed integrated married couples, either the husband or the wife a black from Angola or Mozambique. These couples were treated with the same courteous respect as everyone else. Once I inadvertently left my leather folder, with my wallet and passport in it, on the quay side after I'd gotten into the dinghy. Five minutes later a piratical old mackerel fisherman in a skiff was knocking on the hull. He was returning the folder and wouldn't think of taking a glass of wine as thanks. In fact, he was one of the men who formed the free coffee-and-beer gauntlet on the quay side through which I had to pass each evening.

One afternoon on my way back to the boat from some errand, I stopped on the corniche road and looked down at the anchorage. Suddenly, the bright harbor and the town seemed almost too perfect, a stage set constructed out here in the middle of the Atlantic and peopled by actors from Disney Studios. An old peasant lady was leading a flock of dairy goats up the cobbled road from the ferry landing. A brightly painted fishing smack cut through the calm water of the harbor, the helmsman steering with his bare foot while he sang. My mind went back to that hot afternoon in Brooklyn, to the polluted traffic jams, the restrained violence of the gas lines, the spray-can graffiti, SPICS EAT SHIT!! I decided then to stop probing beneath the smooth surface of what I'd found here and simply to enjoy this time while I could.

Seven days later, on a windy Monday morning, I didn't feel quite so fortunate. A telegram had finally arrived from my agent, and the news was bad. For some unknown reason, to be explained in "Letter follows," Pocket Books had decided not to pay *any* royalties this period on the paperback editions of my first two books. I stood on the edge of the lava-block sea wall, staring out at the anchorage. It was the nineteenth of August and there were many fewer boats in the harbor than there had been when we'd arrived two weeks earlier. The previous day, I'd completed the last of the revisions and Carol had finished typing the clean copies. As I stood there gripping the flapping sheet of the telegram, she was across town at the post office in the main square, mailing the packet of revisions off to New York.

The breeze blew fresh and cool from the northeast and the yachts swung nicely on their moorings. For a moment I had to fight down a swelling panic as bad as anything I'd felt on the open Atlantic. We were a long way from anyone who knew us. In my wallet I had two twenty-dollar bills and in the pocket of my shorts, about nine dollars in escudos: our entire cash reserve. But we owed the Limas fifty or sixty bucks for the room, and I'd estimated another couple hundred for diesel fuel and provisions would be needed before setting sail for the mainland. I gazed dumbly out at *Matata,* feeling a growing sense of isolation.

Several times in my Foreign Service career, I'd been involved with repatriating indigent Americans and "beached" U.S. seamen in Morocco. Unconsciously, I'd always felt a slight contempt for these people; they should have never gotten themselves in that position—penniless and in debt, cut off in a strange country. Now I was in that very position myself, and my feeling of self-contempt was more than slight. I kicked out angrily at a fly-blown mackerel head, half sun-baked on the black stone jetty. Suddenly Horta didn't seem colorful or hospitable but, rather, a shoddy, rundown backwater. I was working myself up to a proper stew when I decided to stop and take stock.

Out on the boat, I sat down at the chart table and totaled up a more realistic estimate of costs on the provisions and fuel we needed. I then added up our local bills, including the cost of a long telegram to my agent. A couple hundred dollars would get us out of here in decent shape. That figure seemed manageable. We could ask Carol's mother, when she called that evening from Wisconsin, to lend us the necessary amount and arrange for a telegraphic bank transfer. The money could arrive in a couple of days. In my cable, I would ask my agent to hound Pocket Books for the two or three thousand dollars they owed me on foreign translation rights already sold, and to forward that money to us in Gibraltar. I hated doing either; at age thirty-nine, it went against the grain to be borrowing money from relatives, and crying poor and desperate to a publisher was always bad strategy, prejudicing future negotiations. But we were up against it, and I didn't see any other options short of selling off spare equipment. We'd have to keep *that* unpleasant option in reserve.

I came back up to the cockpit and sat, waiting for Carol to come down the hill from the main square. Sipping a mug of coffee, I looked around the breezy anchorage and the sunlit town where the umbrella pines and palms were swaying so prettily against the whitewashed stone houses. No, Horta was much more than a shoddy backwater; it wasn't the town's fault we'd gotten ourselves into this financial bind; it was ours, Carol's and mine. We had made a conscious decision in New York, taking a calculated risk when we'd decided to sail with only three hundred dollars in our pockets. The alternative would have been to wait until August, but that, of course, would have been too late: only suicidal fools would have started across the Atlantic during the height of the hurricane season.

We could have decided to wait until next year, opting for the prudent approach, but prudent, cautious rationality would have dictated not sailing at all, ever. By definition, sailing the Atlantic Ocean in a thirty-foot sloop entailed risk. We had worked as hard as we could, choosing a boat and equipping it to minimize that risk. But, eventually, we'd had to let go and take our chances. There weren't any one-hundred-percent guarantees out on the ocean.

Thinking about it, sitting in the sunny breeze in the cockpit of the boat we'd sailed here from New York, I realized that there weren't any foolproof guarantees *anywhere,* even in the safest suburban tri-level, owned free and clear by the most successful young lawyer or corporate executive. People such as those were fooling themselves when they thought they could somehow insulate their lives from all risk. A drunken driver on an interstate highway or a microscopic clot of carcinogenic chemical doesn't know your bank balance or the names of your insurance companies. None of us likes to think about this, but life is a risky activity, and death is *always* the winner.

I got up, instinctively reaching out to steady myself by grabbing the end of the boom. I knew this little vessel better than most men ever knew their own houses. The sun was pleasantly hot on my bare shoulders. I flexed my arm. My muscle tone was good; I now felt rested and peaceful inside. Maybe I worried too much out at sea, but at least I'd taken the chance and actually set out on this voyage. Standing there in the warm cockpit, my bare feet on the clean white gelcoat, I could clearly picture the civilization I'd left back there under the steep blue curve of the ocean horizon.

It would be early morning on the East Coast, and men would be getting up to face another morning. I wondered how many of them who stood shaving before the steamy bathroom mirror dreamed of *one day* chucking it all in and setting sail across the ocean. Undoubtedly, there were quite a few.

The sun climbed the sky above Pico's green summit. It was noon in the Azores, almost seven o'clock on the eastern seaboard of America. I was here in the cockpit of my boat, about halfway through my journey from New York to Greece. Thousands of other men very similar to myself were about to face the crowded freeways during their anxious, resentful drive in to another day at the office. The breeze swung the boat smartly on its mooring. I sipped my coffee. Up on the promenade, I could see Carol's red kerchief among the straw hats of the farmers in town for the Monday market. Whatever risk it was we'd taken, I was glad now we had taken it.

August 25: 1600 GMT

We sailed out past the Horta sea wall on a clear and breezy Saturday afternoon, three weeks after we'd arrived. Once the main and jib were set, we both gazed back at the pretty jumble of parks, whitewashed buildings and orange tile roofs. Faial Island rose in green-terraced fields above the town. Up on the ridge, the line of windmills spun their sails, grinding corn and wheat. I thought I could see the Silvermans' farmhouse, but I couldn't be sure.

Just as when we left New York, we weren't rolling in extra cash, but we'd payed our bills ashore and had adequate fuel and provisions for this next leg of the trip: the thousand-mile shot to Cape St. Vincent. It would be our first landfall in Europe, technically the end of our Atlantic crossing. Carol bent to adjust the tension on the backstays, then stood up on the stern to look back at the town.

"I hope we can come back sometime," she said.

"So do I," I answered, knowing that some day we would.

In an hour the wind steadied off from the northwest to about eighteen knots. We were sailing very well on a broad reach, with the vane holding us smack on our course of 105 degrees true. Both of us were up in the cockpit reading in the late afternoon sunshine while the vane sailed the boat. Off to port, the rich green mass of Pico rose into its crown of rain cloud. This was enjoyably easy sailing.

At 1800, I took the log reading and went down to write up the DR. "Hey," I called to the cockpit, "you notice anything unusual this afternoon?"

Carol glanced around at the green island sliding by the portside. "I don't think so. Why?"

"Well," I said, coming up to stand in the companionway and to feel the breeze cool on my face and bare chest, "we just got ourselves squared away and set out on a thousand-mile sailing trip." I snapped my fingers. "Just like that . . . stow the ice and fresh provisions, raise some sail, set the vane, then sit down and start reading a book." I smiled broadly. "Like we did this kind of thing every day. Jesus, Honey, don't you remember how we were, leaving Danny's boatyard?"

Carol smiled back. "You're right," she said, leaning back on her cushion. "What should we do, *celebrate* or something?"

I shrugged my shoulders.

Carol shrugged back. "I suppose we *could* blow a whistle . . . or beat a drum, if we had one. I don't know what else to do. The decks are too small to dance a hornpipe."

I nodded in agreement. "Well . . . it just feels so different than when we left New York . . . " I waved my open hand slowly around at the rigging and the smooth sea in the lee of the massive green island. "It's a nice feeling."

Carol gazed up at the sails drawing well, then away toward the slopes of Pico. "It sure is," she said.

CHAPTER TWELVE

DR: 38°25' NORTH, 23°40' WEST
AUGUST 29: 0200 GMT

It was a beautiful, starry night of westerly breezes. The splendid southern blow we'd been riding for the previous three days was finally spent, but not before we'd made our record daily distance run, clocking one hundred sixty-eight miles for the twenty-four hours between local noon on the twenty-seventh and local noon on the twenty-eighth: a sustained speed of seven knots, not a bad showing for a thirty-foot boat with a crew of two. We had sailed that long, fast run under a single-reefed main and the sturdy working jib, bounding ahead through the open swells with the force five wind a little aft of the starboard beam. All the complicated elements of wind, sea, and sail trim had combined to help us; there'd been enough swell to offset the normal northerly current without causing a short, lumpy sea; the vane and sails had worked well under these steady conditions to hold us dead on course, so that there'd been no meandering or wasted time yawing too far off the optimum reach. For a full day of blustery sunshine and a bright, windy night, we had sped along like a strong white bird.

Now we drifted in the soft, star-spread darkness, the sea almost flat again, the present fluky wind barely enough to fill the drifter. But I didn't mind. A British weather forecast I'd finally managed to snare on shortwave indicated we'd have moderately fresh northerlies in these regions beginning the next day. Now there was a respite, allowing us to relax after our exhilarating roller-coaster ride.

At sunset, the conditions had calmed enough to permit some good sextant work, and we'd gotten a solid fix with accurate LOPs of the half-moon, Polaris, and Vega. This fix had coincided perfectly with the fix we'd made at the meridian pass, thus confirming the accuracy of the record distance run. To cap off such a satisfying day, we'd had the last of the beef roast from Horta, cooked up in a spicy, rich stew with fresh vegetables, the whole meal accompanied by an iced bottle of *vinho verde.* Carol had then taken the long first watch, and I'd slept peacefully in my sleeping bag, happy to be back at sea in our own boat, cranking out the miles of our second long passage.

When I took the watch I was fascinated to see how clear the sky was after the three-day blow. With the moon set, the stars stood out so brightly that I could actually see faint shadows as I moved about the cockpit. Working quietly in the galley, I made myself some coffee and a plate of sardine sandwiches. One of the luxuries of calm weather was the chance to eat in the cockpit without having the food ruined by spray. When I came back up, I automatically scanned the horizon in a full circle around the boat. Dead astern, there was a faint, slowly moving white light, way back there to the west. Probably the mast range light of a ship, a long way off and hull down. If he seemed to get closer, I'd turn on the running lights, but for the moment, the twenty-five watt lamp on the masthead was sufficient.

The sandwiches were tasty, with the pili-pili sardines mashed into the solid cornmeal bread we'd found in Sao Miguel during our brief fuel stop there three days earlier. I sipped my hot coffee, watching the wrinkling star patterns on the surface. We were three days outbound from the Azores, nearing the halfway point between the islands and the Portuguese mainland, the continent of Europe. The fact that I could be absolutely sure of our position by dint of celestial navigation alone was suddenly and irrationally pleasing. Before the crossing, we were apprehensive about our skills as navigators; also, I was worried that we hadn't been able to afford an expensive sextant or RDF. But our landfalls at both Faial and Sao Miguel had been perfect, so that I now had concrete experience upon which to place my confidence.

It felt damn good, but, sitting there smugly with my coffee, I had to admit that the accomplishment was in reality quite mundane. These days, a sailor equipped with the *Nautical Almanac*, a reasonably accurate sextant and time piece, and the sight reduction tables could perform his celestial navigation using nothing more than grammar-school arithmetic.

I realized that sailors today owed an incredible debt to generations of mariners, now long dead, whose names we would never know and to whom we could never give proper thanks. The *Almanac* alone was a wondrous and complex piece of human genius, full of cultural history that most people neither recognized nor acknowledged.

There were the star names, for example. Scanning the daily pages of the *Almanac* on the crossing, we had become enchanted with the exotic and melodious sounds of those star names . . . Aldebaran, Alnilam, Deneb, Enif, Mirfak, Nunki, Shaula. I remember sleepily thinking once, down in my bunk after a quiet, starry watch, that *somehow* these strangely beautiful names actually did have an otherworldly quality, that maybe they had slipped unperceived into human vernacular during ancient visits by extraterrestrials. Surely a name like Menkar or Rasalhague had its origins far away from this planet. But then, my romantic speculation was literally brought back down to earth by reading Chapman's *Small Boat Piloting* in Horta. I discovered that the *Almanac* star names have come into modern usage from the Arabic mariners of the seventh century, who used forgotten classical Greek star tables, which were themselves based on the work of Phoenician and Babylonian court astronomers, who, in turn, had been strongly influenced by the Sumerians. So, when we pronounced alien, melodic star names such as Diphda, Elnath, or Fomalhaut, we were, in effect, continuing a direct and unbroken human link with the earliest known civilized people of the earth.

I finished my sandwiches and leaned over to wash the plate in the cool wake. Just before my eyes, the faint, lime-colored star worms wriggled on the surface, meshing their pale glow with the bioluminescence in the water itself. I was charmed by the phenomenon and spent several extra minutes swishing my plastic plate back and forth, mixing the weak light that had taken hundreds or thousands of years to journey from the exotically named stars with the faint green glow of exactly the same hue and intensity being produced that very moment by the plankton living out their tiny lives in this sea water. To the cosmic currents of time and gravity I had "discovered" out in the calm of the Stream, I now had to add the ricocheting photons of weightless light.

When I looked up, the heavy, blinking stars seemed clearer in some way, less distant perhaps. I understood then why ancient people had been so familiar with the stars. Living in the clear desert atmosphere of Mesopotamia, at a time when artificial illumination was almost nonexistent and fuel for communal fires scarce, these people must have had excellent conditions for observation—what modern astronomers call "seeing"—almost every night of their lives. It's no wonder that they began naming individual stars. Certainly when people began living together in one place year-in, year-out, for continual generations, simply pointing to a star and saying, " . . . that one over there to the right . . . " or " . . . the one down below that bright one there . . . " became a rather inefficient way of communicating.

So, the ancient people of the Fertile Crescent invented names like Mirfak and Kochab and Vega . . . or, in fact, they invented hundreds or thousands of other names, which did *not* catch on or become incorporated into a common language. The naming of places on the land and stars in the sky and, then, more importantly, the mutual *agreement* to accept those names were some of the first completely civilized acts of mankind, most likely related to organized agriculture and market commerce, which replaced nomadism. When you live in only one place, and the night sky is clear, you quickly learn that the stars form a fixed, annual progression, that they remain the same from one winter or summer to the next . . . hence the zodiac, hence the concept that there is order, perhaps divine order, in the universe.

For the modern sailor, all this would be of little practical interest were it not for the fact that the people of the Middle East—starting with the Babylonians on their marsh-reed merchant vessels and continuing down to the present-day Omanis on their graceful dhows—were energetic and adventurous mariners. They made their long voyages around the littoral of the Indian Ocean, spreading civilization to the Indus Valley and the Horn of Africa along the way, all without the benefit of the compass. Their offshore navigation, therefore, had to depend on celestial guideposts: the sun, stars, and planets. But the use of these bodies was impractical without a commonly shared understanding of the annual relative positions of the stars. And this information depended on the prior existence of a stable, sedentary land civilization. There was, I realized, a direct link between the rough cuneiform on Sumerian clay star tablets and the spray-spotted orange volume entitled *The Nautical Almanac for the Year 1979,* compiled jointly by the Royal Greenwich Observatory and the U.S. Naval Observatory, a volume that normally stood, held by tight shock cord, just beside the chart table on *Matata.*

Civilized people agreed on common nomenclature; they produced works of mutually advantageous collected knowledge . . . Babylonian clay tablets listing the annual shift in the declination of stars named Nunki or Schedar . . . the Arabs' carved hardwood plaques offering this data and expanded information on planet zeniths and moon declinations . . . the first primitive celestial almanacs compiled at the navigation school of Prince Henry and printed on vellum . . . the heavy parchment logarithm tables of the British and the Dutch renaissance—all of this formed an unbroken chain of human invention, which culminated right down there on the chart table of this little fiber glass sloop. The Davis sextant, the Phasar 2000 digital watch, the *Sight Reduction Tables for Air Navigation,* Volumes I to III, and, of course, the orange-covered *Nautical Almanac* were gifts to us and other sailors from hundreds of thousands of mariners now dead, their bodies long ago dissolved in the salts of the ocean planet.

Out there ahead in the night, about four hundred and eighty miles eastward, stood Cape St. Vincent, with the old port of Sagres nearby. It was there that Prince Henry founded his school for navigators and that the ancient knowledge of the stars, including their Mesopotamian names, was compiled and first disseminated to the modern Europeans, so that the great voyages of exploration could begin. I sipped the last of my tepid, sweet coffee—itself a hybrid agricultural result of those voyages—and enjoyed the swelling sense of kinship with our nautical ancestors.

When I came back up after drying my dishes in the galley and noting the DR on the chart, I saw that the white light to the west was much closer now and that it was not the range light of a large ship but, rather, a single lamp from either a small fishing boat or a yacht. I ducked down quickly and flicked two switches on the circuit breaker panel, illuminating our running lights and stern lamp. A minute later, the vessel trailing us came alight with running lights and a bright masthead lamp. It was a yacht, and through the binoculars I could now see that it was white-hulled and single-masted, maybe a little bigger than us but very similar in design. As I watched through the glasses, the light southwest breeze freshened to ten knots and the other boat began to draw closer in the sparkling darkness.

Twenty minutes later it was only a quarter-mile behind us and gaining steadily. I was now positive that it was Chris Schultz, whom we'd first met in Horta, in *Tao Aloa,* a Dufour 35. He and his friends had left Faial the day before us, and we'd met them again two days later in Sao Miguel harbor where they, too, had stopped for fuel. I now felt a strong bond with the people on the other boat: Chris, June Marie Tzardzik, and Jeff and Karen O'Regan. This was their first crossing as well. They were using the same kind of navigation equipment as us, sailing almost the same kind of boat.

I had never been in a real offshore race, and all the way to the Azores we'd seen very little shipping. Now, four hundred miles out from São Miguel, in the middle of nowhere, *Tao Aloa* was going to come within fifty yards of us.

When they finally did overtake us, they passed perhaps sixty yards off the port beam, far enough so they wouldn't get blanketed by our sails. I flashed my pocket light a few times and their helmsman answered with a toot on their air horn. The breeze grew a bit stronger; their big genny pulled them ahead at about 7 knots, and soon I could no longer distinguish the shape of their white hull.

I sat with a little nip of brandy warming in a mug between my cupped hands. What a wonderful sense of comradship the encounter had given me. I knew that I'd never feel the same about the "empty" ocean again, nor about a long open passage offshore. The body of water lying along the rhumb line of 105 degrees true between São Miguel and Cape St. Vincent was not simply formless sea; it was a highway, a road of a special kind. Chris and I were traveling on the same road, at more or less the same speed, and it had been therefore probable that one boat should pass the other.

But what I found so interesting was that this road had no visible signposts or landmarks. The reason that *Tao Aloa* was moving through the same narrow tract of water was that to navigate, Chris and I were using the same invisible web of mathematical knowledge, painstakingly handed down to us from man's first civilization, more than seven thousand years ago. When the first Sumerian farmer pointed up into the dazzling night sky and said "Mirfak," he started a process that led inevitably to one beautiful white sloop flying an American ensign passing another midway between the Azores and Europe.

After checking the sail trim and the vane, I knocked down the warm brandy with one swallow, then lay back to nap on the dewy cockpit cushions. Overhead, the great dusty-white disc of the galaxy wheeled slowly through the night. Around us, on the dark water, the star glow melted into the phosphorescence. I curled into warm sleep, feeling peaceful and strangely at home.

I woke about an hour later and found Carol standing above me in the cockpit, a windbreaker over the shoulders of her nightdress, holding a cup of tea in both hands. Her face was tilted toward the starry sky, and her eyes were large and tranquil in the faint light. I reached out and touched her hip; she turned to smile down at me.

"The stars . . . " she said. "They were so bright through the hatch that I woke up." She spread the fingers of her right hand and waved them above the white gelcoat of the lazaret. "*Shadows* . . . you can see shadows from the starlight."

"How's the heading?" I asked, rising to one elbow on the dewy cushion.

She glanced at the orange compass disc. "Right on course. It's like the boat knows where she's going without us."

Now I sat up and checked my watch. "It'll be light in about ninety minutes. But I don't think we have to do early morning stars. The last DR will be good until the first morning LOP."

Again, she raised her face to see the pulsing white stars above us. "Let's do them anyway," she said quietly. "They're so perfect tonight that . . . I don't know, for some reason it just seems right to take a dawn star fix."

I rose and slipped my arm around her shoulder so that we leaned into each other as we gazed up at the bright sky. "I know exactly what you mean."

CHAPTER THIRTEEN

DR: 36°55' NORTH, 09°35' WEST
SEPTEMBER 4: 0230 GMT

The wind had been blowing hard from the north for three days, averaging between force five and seven. We were on a beam reach under reefed main and storm jib, heeled well over to starboard. In an hour or so, I estimated we would pick up the lighthouse on Cape St. Vincent, our first European landfall and technically the end of our first passage across the Atlantic Ocean. I crouched in the shelter of the canvas dodgers, spray-whipped and slightly woozy from the pounding ride. Around us the night was quite dramatic, with a bright, hide-and-seek moon above dark clouds, moving fast in the black wind. The sea was steep and short and carried with it a northern chill I hadn't felt since our close scrape with the floating debris in mid-Atlantic.

I felt the sea bunching up against the mass of Iberia out ahead in the night, and I also sensed the encroaching grip of claustrophobia as we drew near to land after a long passage on the sea. Since sunset, shipping had increased to the point where now I could continually see several sets of white range lights heading either north toward the Bay of Biscay or south toward Gibraltar and the African coast. Very soon we'd enter the separation lanes around the cape itself. Even with the violent motion, I'd managed to get in a couple of good RDF bearings on coastal radio beacons, so I felt pretty confident about our position; we would be traversing the lanes in the optimum place, just south of the cape, exposing ourselves to the heaviest volume of traffic for the shortest possible period. The alternative was to heave-to out here and drift south until daylight. But I was reasonably sure we'd have no problem. With the bright masthead light and the radar reflector mounted high on the spreaders, ships would be sure to see us, despite the annoyingly steep swell. As we rose and fell with the passing crests, however, our forward running lights and stern lamp would be obscured for thirty seconds at a time.

I made a mental note to buy a new tricolor masthead light in Gibraltar, then caught myself up short with the painful realization that we were still dead broke. If any fancy equipment exchanged hands in Gibraltar, it would be us selling off items like the spare compass, the various strobe lights, the second anchor, maybe even the EPIRB mayday radio and the life raft. These were items we wouldn't absolutely need in the Med, and the cash they'd raise might just do the trick of buying us enough fuel and provisions to complete the passage all the way to Greece. I had no real idea when Viking would pay the second half of the advance; certainly by Christmas, but we couldn't wait around in Gibraltar for money as the winter weather set in—bringing with the rainy gales some of the worst sailing conditions this side of the Southern Ocean—and expect to continue on to Greece.

As I crouched out of the cold spray, I suddenly remembered one rainy winter evening in Gibraltar. It was ten years earlier and I was serving as a U.S. consul in Tangier, just across the Strait of Gibraltar. I'd gone over to Gib to see our naval liaison officer there and, naturally, to do a little shopping in the duty-free stores. At age twenty-nine, I'd just been promoted to grade four officer, the equivalent of full commander in the navy or lieutenant colonel in the army. With the consulate paying our housing and expenses and with the travel per diem I'd been paid recently, I was in the best financial shape of my adult life. That wet evening, sitting in one of the Victorian pubs along the narrow cobbled length of Main Street, I met an Australian yacht sailor down on his luck.

The young man came into the warm, smokey pub clutching something under his dripping, rather threadbare oilskin jacket. It was a sextant, a beautiful prewar Plath micrometer-head instrument. He'd just lost his berth as the navigator of a big charter schooner moored down in the destroyer pens. Originally, the boat was scheduled to make the crossing to spend the winter working the Caribbean charter market. Now, financial trouble had caused the boat's owners to cancel the trip. The crew had been paid off short, and my new acquaintance found himself in Gib, a long way from a possible job in Antigua and down to his last quid. If he found a buyer for his sextant, he explained over a pint of bitter that I bought, he could hitch up to Madrid, where there would be a cheap student flight leaving for Puerto Rico.

I sat back on my comfortable bar stool and sipped my beer, sorry for this frank, open-faced young sailor but also feeling definitely superior. This guy was an exotic, one of those colorful types to whom one spoke in order to provide good party conversation later. I was perfectly willing to buy him a few beers—after all, the British pound had just been devalued and the dollar was almighty in Gibraltar—but I didn't want to get involved in his messy personal life. I was firmly convinced that responsible adults, especially those claiming impressive titles such as consul or navigator, had a duty to avoid, at all costs, any public indication of financial embarrassment. It was *bad form* in the British public-school sense, letting down one's team, the Establishment.

What I found especially troubling about this young sailor was that he was reduced to peddling his symbolic instrument of office, that lovely old sextant—going from pub to pub in the rainy night like some sneak thief trying to fence his loot. By the end of the evening, I had cashed one of his checks drawn on a Brisbane bank for fifty Australian dollars, as much out of impatience to be rid of him as from any sense of compassion. Riding up the narrow lanes in the clanking little Austin taxi to the Rock Hotel, I vowed that I would never make such a spectacle of myself, no matter how bad my problems might be.

So much for youthful arrogance. In Tangier I'd been narrow-minded, ignorant, and, worst of all, paralytically cautious. If I'd have stayed in the Foreign Service, I'd have been on my way to an ambassadorial appointment. Now I was almost forty years old, and what did I have to show for the intervening ten years between that rainy night in Gib and this windy night off the most eastern cape of Europe? Three novels, obscure books read by a handful of people. I'd already spent most of the money these books would ever earn. But in the decade since the sleek days of comfort in Tangier, I'd learned to sail boats with some skill; this crossing of a wide ocean was an obvious manifestation of that skill.

So what? Careful seamanship did not pay the rent; nor would it buy the provisions or diesel fuel we'd need to cross the length of the autumn Med. Ten years since that cozy pub on Main Street, and I was now in the same position as that smiling, ruddy-faced young Australian . . . "down a bit on my luck there, Mate."

It's fun sometimes to see events ironically, I now realized, sort of like having your own private flea circus.

I pulled the hood of my jacket tighter about my face, turning away from the spray. We'd sort out our money problems all in good time, once we got to Gib. Right now, I had plenty to occupy my mind. As Eric Hiscock has pointed out, the very last hours of an extended passage—the final landfall—call for the greatest diligence. The psychological letdown after a long crossing often causes laxness, lack of attention—just when the greatest care is required, especially during a night landfall. The need for a sharp lookout was compounded by shipping traffic around this cape, one of the busiest areas in the world. I forced myself to forget about our money problems and to concentrate on what lay out there in the dark, rolling night.

If a ship were on a converging course with us, I decided, I would turn on the bright floodlight on the midmast, illuminating both the reefed main and the jib with a hot cone of white light but also, unfortunately, ruining our night vision for several minutes. In the event of a definite collision course, I had the dazzling man-overboard strobe light ready to hang on the backstays, as well as the hand strobe from the life raft kit. This would be our first encounter with truly congested shipping lanes since New York, and tonight the steep swell made visibility much worse than it had been that smooth night of light westerlies east of Ambrose Light. I drew on my damp cigarette, feeling the familiar discomfort of the salt-crusted oilskin hood abrade my stubbly throat. It had been a long trip, but this first crossing would be over in just a few hours. By morning, we would have successfully sailed a wide and windy ocean.

I puffed my cigarette back to life again, near the lens of my watch, so that I could read the time. Almost 0300, time to call Carol. She'd only slept for two hours, but I needed her up here. We'd be in the Villamoura marina tomorrow and could sleep around the clock there. But tonight I wanted to have an extra set of eyes to make it safely through these separation lanes.

Carol made coffee before she came up, and the hot, sweet brew, rich with condensed milk, tasted wonderful as she joined me in the cold cockpit. I took another couple of RDF bearings and brought the DR up to date. Satisfied that we were still four or five miles from the western edge of the lanes and three miles from the maximum visible range of the Cape St. Vincent light, I lay down on the low-side cockpit bench and willed myself into a semblance of sleep. I had just dozed off when Carol called me. Struggling out of sleep, I sat up into the cold spray. Two sets of bright range lights were bearing down from the north, and there was another faint, shallow-angle set to the south, off the starboard beam. The boat rose and dropped swiftly away with the swell as I sat blinking off sleep, trying to judge the distance to the northern two sets of lights.

"They haven't changed bearing for about five minutes," Carol said, her voice calm and precise as it always was when she was worried.

"Okay," I muttered, rubbing my eyes. The lights were close, maybe two miles off, maybe a lot less. "Come down to 120 magnetic," I said, trying like Carol to sound calm and precise. "I'm going to put on the floodlight and start the engine."

To save her night vision, Carol sat up close to the bulkhead, staring at the compass while I lit the floodlight. When I returned to the cockpit I made the stupid mistake of gazing directly at the bright cone of light on the sails, then looked out on both sides searching for the ships. The two vessels to port were clearly visible: a big red and blue tanker, followed by a medium-sized freighter, both heading due south. They were definitely going to pass ahead of us. I glanced off to starboard from the crest of a high swell. Nothing. The faint lights we'd seen five minutes earlier must have veered off when I lit the floodlight.

"I'm going to go down and blink the flood a little," I called over my shoulder, " . . . just to make sure those guys see us."

I took this simple task too seriously. For several minutes after Carol called down that the two ships were well away from us, I remained seated at the chart table, reaching up to the circuit breaker to blink out long flashes on the floodlight. It was warm and dry down here, and I was lulled by the comforting throb of our diesel.

Coming back up, I didn't even bother to look to starboard but gazed ahead at the big tanker and its trailing freighter, a good fifteen hundred yards off. I lit a cigarette, further ruining my night vision with the flaring gas lighter. When I turned back to take the helm, I finally saw the lights of the big white ship rising above the starboard quarter as we crested a swell. He was less than five hundred yards from us, moving fast and apparently steering directly for our starboard beam.

"Jesus Christ . . . Hey!" I blurted out.

"Look . . . oh God," Carol shouted, equally shocked, "a ship!"

But there was no time for words. This was a nightmarish repetition of our first evening out of New York, the near-miss with the freighter in the Ambrose approach lanes. Frantically, I grabbed at the strobe light on the backstays, then seized the beam gun to shine it on the sails. Carol was already down at the circuit breaker, flashing the mast floodlight. The white freighter did not alter course. I could hear his engines now and see his high, creamy bow wave as he cut the swell. I kicked the engine into gear with my boot toe and tacked fast under power, wings of spray arching back in the glare of the floodlight, our own little diesel snarling like a hurt dog under the swelling rumble of the freighter's engines.

Carol was back up now, sheeting in the jib on the opposite tack. But the sheet snagged a moment and I reached over her back to free it from the block. When I looked aft again, I was stunned by the sight of the high white ship, sliding by our stern, less than seventy yards away. The superstructure looked clean, free of rust. There were a lot of radio antennas and several rotating radars up on his red-trimmed bridge deck. He appeared brand-new, a modern refrigerator ship maybe, carrying fresh produce from North Africa to Europe. Just like the freighter that first night, this guy's stack gas stank like a Greyhound station. His tall white hull went hissing by, and then his stern light seemed to get dim very quickly, as if he were in a hurry to depart from the scene of this near-collision.

My mouth tasted like I'd been sucking rusty metal. My limbs were trembling inside the salty oilskins. For the first time in weeks, the sea seemed alien and hostile.

"The bastard's making over 20 knots," I said, pointing at his fading stern light.

Carol sat down hard on the opposite seat. "Jesus," she whispered, shaking her head, "he didn't even slow down."

"He didn't even see us . . . " I sank down now, too, and throttled way back, so that the engine only gurgled faintly with the quarter wave slapping the exhaust pipe. "It's . . . well, it's just like that damn first night." I waved my hand vaguely. "You know, it's . . . " I didn't finish. I really had nothing to say, but my jangly nerves were making my mouth form words.

Carol looked out at the fast-moving white lights around us in the rolling darkness. "I wish it were morning," she said, rubbing wetness from her face.

Cautiously, we tacked back onto our original heading of 95 degrees true. More range lights passed ahead and astern of us, but nothing very close. Neither of us spoke. I smoked a couple of cigarettes and Carol set the vane, fussing with the tiller lines to get a steady course. When she was satisfied, she looked out ahead.

"Well . . . there's the light," she said, her voice drained and lifeless.

"Bring it down ten degrees," I answered, sitting up to see the bright flash of the light on the starboard bow. "I'll go log the cape."

When I came up, the light was more clearly visible from the crests, fine on the bow. We had just made a near-perfect landfall after a windy passage of a thousand miles, but neither of us was in the mood to appreciate it. A few minutes later, I saw we could come down ten more degrees, and while Carol set the new course, I made two of the big plastic mugs of strong coffee and poured a generous dollop of brandy into each. We drank it in the cold spray and watched the early dawn give definition to the hilly coast of Portugal.

"Europe," I said, pronouncing the word very clearly. "Europe . . . finally. We made it, Carol."

Her face was pinched and cold, hurt-looking, like a Hollywood version of a Dickensian street urchin. She stared back at the dark sea toward the northwest, squinting into the spray. "It's such a damn big ocean," she said, as much to herself as to me. "I wonder if we'd have gone if we'd known what it was really like. What do you think?"

Looking out past the swooping bow, I saw the gray-green headland sharpen in the new daylight. From that point, the sea must have looked wildly beautiful this morning, but also frightening. How many times had Prince Henry and his entourage stood on that headland, watching small flotillas of fragile caravelles pound and swoop out into the dark Atlantic, many to be swallowed up forever by this water? We were almost at the cape, the end of our crossing, but it would be several more days before the reality of this fact took effect, became personal truth. I held the tiller in my chapped hands, shaking occasional spray off my oilskin hood as I watched the approaching land and thought of the past seven weeks, about the storm and what I had felt in the mid-Atlantic when we'd overcome the weather and the damage and had learned to live with each other on the sea.

I remembered the sunny days in Horta, the people we'd met there. In the rising dawn, I stood in the cockpit to examine our boat. The white gelcoat had lost its gloss; the shrouds were bleeding rust and the teak was peeling and bleached in briny splotches. But the sails were in good shape, the rigging taut. I knew that the bilge was dry and that every piece of gear was in good working condition. We were ready to face the 2,600 miles of the Mediterranean between us and Lindos. Certainly, however, Carol and I had not *mastered* the Atlantic Ocean; only a fool or an ignorant novice would use such an expression when discussing the sea. But neither had the Atlantic defeated us.

Standing at the tiller, I looked back at the spinning hands of the faithful little taffrail log. Since Ambrose Light, we'd logged just over

4,150 miles of open water, the two of us in this small boat. Undoubtedly, the feat was minor when compared to crossing the Southern Ocean or the winter Atlantic; there had been no hurricanes, no week-long gales, or capsizings. We were just another cruising couple who had set off with faith in their boat and who had learned confidence in themselves as sailors, trust in each other as people, and understanding of the sea as an environment on which they could live. I had no idea if what we had learned would have any direct relevance to our life on land. Probably it would not. Living in a twentieth-century civilization was in many ways more risky and difficult than living on the open sea. Life on land was certainly more complex. Again, as I had at the NOAA buoy, I felt an odd yet peaceful sensation, as if we had slipped out of time's tyrannical lockstep and were now going to reenter it voluntarily.

I also knew, standing there with my boot soles on the half-dried spray, braced against the heel of the boat as I watched the Portuguese coast acquire color and shape with the dawn, that the interior voyage we each had made as a woman and a man had been much more important than the miles of salt water that had passed under the keel.

The voyage was not yet over; we still had our money problems as well as the autumn weather of the Med to contend with once we made Gibraltar. But those problems seemed manageable now. Somehow, I knew, things would work out. All we had to do was keep our faith in the boat and in each other. That combination had gotten us this far; it would carry us on to Greece.

Ahead of us, three gray dolphins broke free of the swell and hung for a moment, streaming pink jewels of water in the tenuous daylight. They glided back into a wave, only to arc free again. The wind was veering off the headland. I could smell the dry odor of rock and the olive groves, the primitive fragrance of the Mediterranean. Our first crossing was over. Standing there, my hood thrust back so I could catch the dry land wind full in the face, I realized that I hadn't answered Carol's question and that she might take offense at my silence. But before I could speak, she answered it herself.

"What a beautiful morning," she said in a clear, strong voice.

Tangier, Morocco
September 11, 1979

I thought I would be too exhausted to go ashore, but after we were tied up alongside in the fishing port, I could hardly wait for customs to be finished. Malcolm gave me a hand up the greasy dock and together we threaded the gauntlet of staring Moroccan fishermen. It was late morning and they were back from the night's trawling off Cape Spartel. Now they sat on the ground or on splintery fish crates, yellow nylon nets spread among three or four men who looked up from their mending as we passed. "*Sebah el sebrir,*" I tried in rusty Arabic; I wasn't sure if that was good morning or good night, but it elicited a few nods and smiles.

Ahead, past a crumbling stucco shed, we could just make out some masts in the shallow yacht basin. Rising behind the port, tiers of whitewashed buildings festooned with bougainvillaea presented a decorative backdrop to the low, peeling warehouses of the port itself. Vaguely I remembered that there was a yacht club here, and a good restaurant. We were hungry, but not at all as tired as we had a right to be after three days and nights tacking back and forth across the entrance to the Strait of Gibraltar. When we had left Vilamoura, we had expected to be in Gib within a day. But we had run into a 35-knot levanter that simply would not let up. We'd finally decided to wait it out in the relatively calm waters off the Moroccan coast to the south. And this morning the wind had dropped, the tide and currents were with us, and we had slipped around Cape Spartel into the port of Tangier. It hadn't been our plan originally to stop there, but we were close and needed a rest before continuing on to Gibraltar.

Malcolm was ahead of me, already pushing the door of the club restaurant open. I hesitated. I was so grubby, and, as usual, we were low on funds. We did have some money in our Washington bank now, deposited there by my mother as an emergency loan, and there might be more money waiting for us in Gib. But right now we had no local currency and only personal checks.

He stopped and turned back to me. "What's wrong?"

"I . . . how are we . . . I mean, we've got to go to the Consulate first, don't we, and get a check cashed or something?" I wanted a solid meal as much as Malcolm did, but we had to be sure we could get someone we used to know either at the Consulate or at the American School to cash a personal check, *before* we started spending the money. Malcolm's expression changed from one of annoyance to concern.

"We need the lift. Just let me ask the manager if we can start a bill."

I followed him inside.

The bartender had heard of our arrival, he said. In answer to Malcolm's request, he received a nonchalant "*Bien sur.*"

As so often in the past, I felt relief, but also a twinge of guilt for not having had enough faith in Malcolm's judgment. I *had* to let him handle these matters without always challenging him. Besides, for the time being, our financial worries were behind us, as, according to his agent, the second half of the Viking advance would be waiting for us in Greece.

I smiled at Malcolm as we tapped our beer glasses together. "To Tangier."

There was no menu and we didn't know the prices of any of the dishes the waiter mentioned. "*Filet,*" I said, and Malcolm followed my lead. "We might as well do this right and eat steak," I said. "You order the wine."

While we waited for our steaks and fries we sat quietly, leaning back in comfortable chairs and looking out at the activity in the busy port. A hydrofoil came planing in from Gibraltar or Algeciras. There were large cargo ships anchored in the bay, and a Yugoslav passenger ship was alongside the quay now. We couldn't see any other obviously foreign sailboats. The ones in the yacht basin were small, day sailers mostly.

Two hours later, we were climbing the steep, winding Boulevard Pasteur, which leads up to the center of the modern city. The Consulate, however, is in the eastern suburbs, an awfully long way to walk. But we were beginning to enjoy our unplanned return to a city we had liked very much. Naturally, we couldn't help but compare our present circumstances to those of ten years earlier. Then we had official titles, a villa and servants to look after it, even our own pool. I had a white sports car and a chauffeur picked up Malcolm each morning to drive him to his office. But it had all been a façade. Neither of us had much enjoyed the work we did, nor even the people with whom we socialized. Our conversation, I now knew, had been brittle and contrived. It had been boring. At first, when Malcolm said he was going to resign from the Foreign Service, I had been shocked. Then an odd, new emotion had overtaken me: I was actually relieved.

I know that in many people's eyes the way we live now is simply considered hedonistic. But often I hear a wistful tone in someone's voice. Then I point out that it's a trade-off. Not everyone can live with the financial and career insecurity.

"Hey, wait up," I called. I was falling behind on the last hill.

Malcolm was grinning back at me. "This is so exciting, being back. Thank God we had that Levanter and had to put in here." He held out his hand to me.

"That's not what you were saying yesterday." From where we stood, arm in arm, we could look down on the port. Just barely visible, *Matata*'s yellow alloy mast poked up behind a long, concrete warehouse. On the other side of the Strait, we could see the Spanish city of Tarifa, but further east, Gibraltar was lost in the haze. Malcolm pointed west, toward the deep blue Atlantic.

"We've come a long way, Honey," he said.

"A long way to end up where we started ten years ago," I responded. Then, "It seems more like fifty years, we're so different."

Malcolm just nodded. I thought he looked a little tearful. Some of those ten years had been difficult, and we had had our share of anxious times.

"You're not sorry, are you?" I had to ask, even though I knew the answer.

"No, but sometimes I thought that you were." Malcolm waved his hand toward the city behidn us. Up there, on one of those mountain roads of whitewashed villas, was our old house.

I thought about the last few days; then, looking west, about the whole crossing and what it had entailed: the original decision to take a chance, to do it even without a big bank balance; the hard work of preparing the boat; and the often dangerous storms at sea. If I had really ever had any serious doubts about giving up *that* life, I knew that I never would again. What Malcolm and I had experienced added up to a sum much greater than the parts. I sensed that the quality of our life together had changed.

Around us, Berber women cloaked in dark *djellabahs* brushed past, their eyes flashing curiosity at this *nasrani* couple who were so obviously happy with each other. "Come on," Malcolm said, squeezing my arm.

"Wait," I said, stopping. "I've got two singles hidden in my wallet for an emergency. Let's get them changed at that bank and take a taxi the rest of the way." I had completely forgotten about those dollar bills, but now was the time to use them.

About an hour later we had accomplished our mission at the Consulate and with cash in hand took a taxi back to the Place de la France, where we used to meet each other late in the day so many years ago. Little had changed. The Café de Paris, where we had spent long, happy afternoons, was just as crowded as ever, and with what looked to be the same people. Even the waiters appeared to be the same, and perhaps they were. We sat outside, at a small, round, marble table set on the sidewalk.

A shoeshine boy spied us immediately and approached, only to shake his head disappointedly after a glance at our sandals. Malcolm called him over anyway—"*Agie, Mohammed. Tfadel*"—and handed him a shiny one-dirham coin. The boy bowed and mumbled an ostentatious blessing in Arabic. I felt good, happy to be the partner of a kind person like Malcolm.

Glancing up, I noticed a smug look of disapproval on the face of the woman at the table next to us. American, I thought. Then I was sure. "Did you see that?" she whispered to her tan, safari-suited husband. There was no mistaking the accent. Or that attitude. For years I had had the opportunity to observe my compatriots overseas, often when they thought no one could understand what they were saying. That censorious and *fearful* attitude that this lady exemplified always embarrassed me.

The man raised his glass of Pernod, glaring over the rim at us. The two of them obviously thought we were Europeans, not Americans. The expression of disdain on their faces was identical. We were not dressed properly, in their eyes; we should not be encouraging the beggars on the streets; probably, they thought that we shouldn't be drinking these glasses of septic mint tea.

Malcolm met my glance, and we nodded in automatic agreement. That sleek couple could have been us. I tried to imagine Malcolm wearing that tailored safari costume, with a gold chain around his neck. The lady's short, blow-dried hair and saffron pants outfit would never have suited me. "Do you see that?" I said, leaning close to Malcolm so the couple couldn't hear me. There was a copy of *Paris Match* prominently displayed on their table. "Do you think they can actually *read* that?"

Malcolm smiled at me.

A vintage black Chrysler pulled up at the curb just then, and a tall Moroccan chauffeur jumped lithely out. It was the car from the Hotel Minzah, the big sedan reserved for wealthy day-trippers flown down by American Express-Madrid for twelve breathtaking hours on the

African continent. Obviously, this couple's "free time" had expired. The car blocked traffic while the white hunter placed some bills on the table. As he climbed into the car, the waiter, Abdelatif—Malcolm remembered his name from ten years earlier—approached the car waving the two bills, two ten-dirham notes.

"That's plenty," the man grumbled, spinning around to confront Abdelatif. "*C'est as-see . . .*"

But Abdelatif insisted, bowing slightly. "*C'est trop, Monsieur.*" Then, when the man obviously couldn't understand him—"It is too much, Sir"—Abdelatif repeated, still extending his hand with the two bills dangling from his fingertips.

The man stared, then saw us watching and grabbed the bills, turning away in stiff embarrassment.

I sighed. Their one-day visit to "Africa" would forever be tainted by the scene we had just witnessed. But I couldn't really feel sorry for them; they were hardly participants, only voyeurs—part-time, twelve-hour-special voyeurs at that.

Later that evening, after putting our boat in order and taking hot showers at the yacht club, we rode a taxi back up to town, to a pleasant English restaurant—the Parade—where we had a very civilized meal in the garden. Halfway through the meal the electricity went out, leaving us to finish in flickering yellow candlelight. At midnight, it didn't look as if the town were going to have the electricity restored, so we set out for the port anyway, walking, feeling our way in the darkness through the narrow Medina lanes.

"You're not afraid?" Malcolm asked when we entered a particularly dark alleyway.

"Of course not," I answered. With my left hand I guided myself along the rough sandstone walls of the buildings. The blackness gave up strong odors of spices, of charcoal burners and sputtering lamb-filled spits. A dark figure entered a doorway ahead of us and we slowed our pace on the steep hill. Suddenly, from a narrow lane a pushcart rumbled toward us, steel-rimmed wheels clanking on the stone pavement. Two bright, sputtering acetylene lamps swung from the handles lighting up the figure behind it. Beside me I felt Malcolm jump, and we both stopped.

The confrontation had been startling, but not of the same quality as a storm or a ship bearing down on us in the night.

Malcolm pressed his arm around me. "Well, if you're not afraid, then I'm not either," he said.

It was an exhilarating walk through the medieval darkness down to the port.

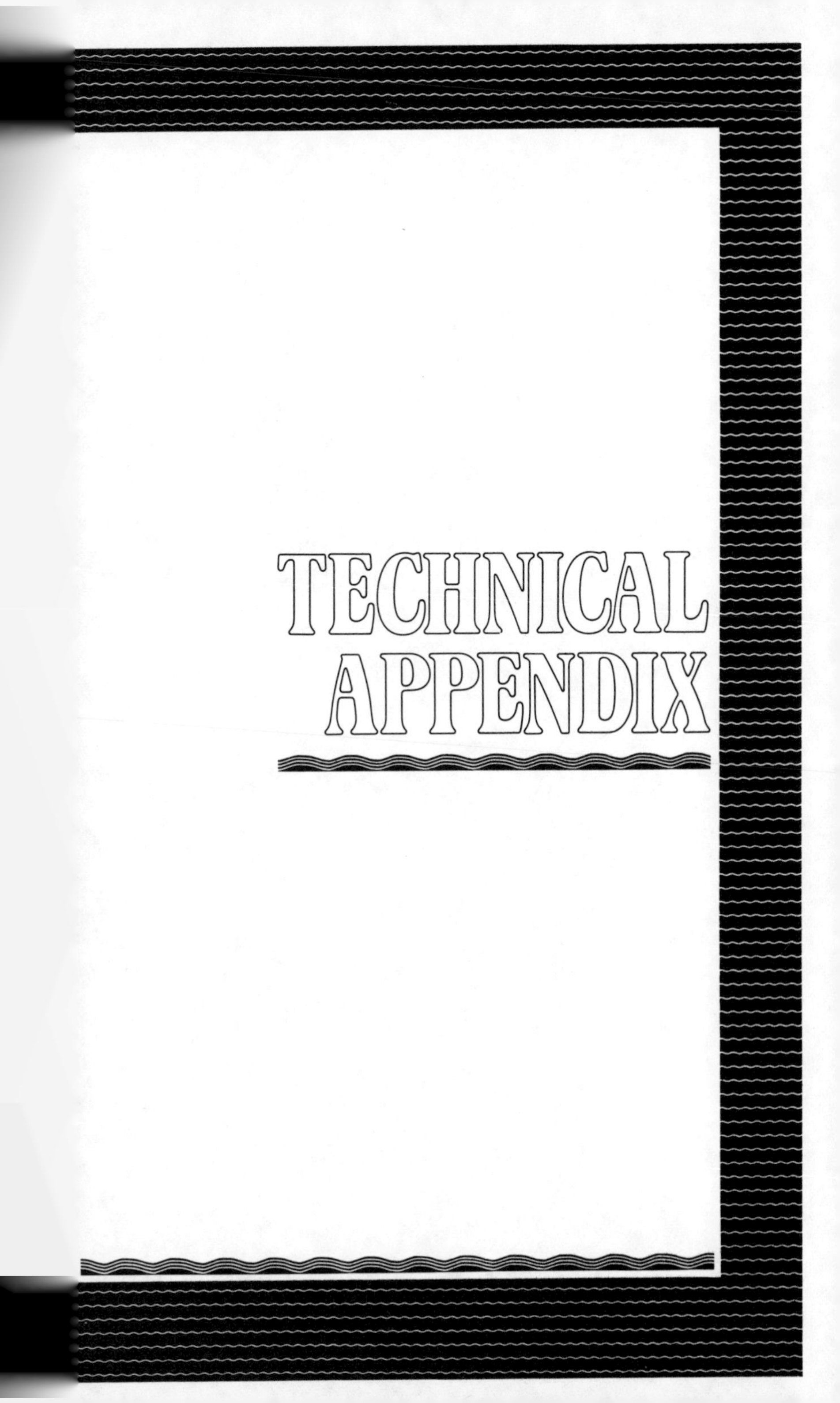

TECHNICAL APPENDIX

1. THE OFFSHORE SURVIVAL KIT: WHAT TO INCLUDE IN THE BAG YOU HOPE YOU NEVER HAVE TO OPEN

The morning we arrived in Horta, Faial, after a twenty-eight-day passage from New York to the Azores, I stood on the rough lava sea wall, staring down at our thirty-foot sloop, *Matata.* The boat looked very small to have carried Carol and me across almost 3,000 miles of open Atlantic. Then I glanced around the harbor. There were boats from all over Europe and the United States, as well as two from South Africa and the inevitable few from Australia and New Zealand. Passages made from as far away as Sydney or Wellington truly impressed me, for the first leg of our Atlantic crossing had taught me just how big and empty the ocean can feel, especially from the cockpit of a thirty-footer.

We'd also had one close call. Six days west of the Azores, at dawn on a windy day, we were rolling along under reefed main and storm jib, taking a northerly blow on the beam. I had the watch and was bundled up in the cockpit in oilskins, flotation vest, and safety har-

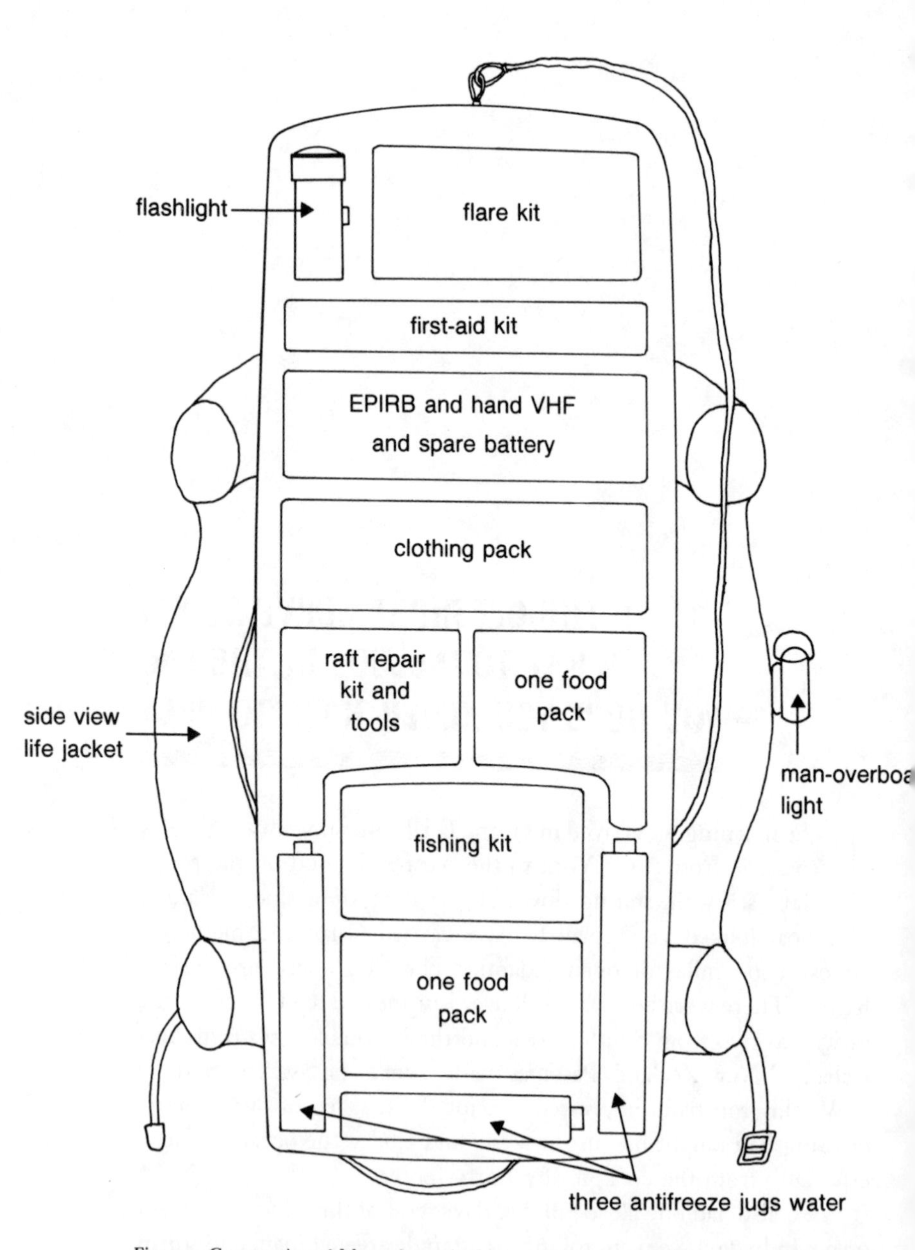

Figure 1: Cross-section of Matata's *survival kit, a 40-inch by 18-inch heavy-duty rubberized sailing duffle bag with attached life jacket, small man-overboard light, and 30-foot parachute line tether to life raft painter. A U.S. Army duffle bag, lined with three layers of heavy plastic trash bags and with same flotation and tethering as this sailing duffle, is kept below and carries balance of provisions.*

ness. Just as the sun cleared the heaving gray horizon, a creamy, ten-foot swell rolled down toward the portside shrouds, bearing at its crest a nasty piece of metal flotsam: three steel drums, bolted to a twisted frame of sheared-off steel "I" beams.

The floating junk missed us by only about a foot. I jumped up in a hurry and scanned the surrounding waves for more debris. There was none, but whatever that thing had been—probably something off a work barge or oil rig—it had come very close to holing and probably sinking us over 600 miles from the nearest land.

Looking down from the Horta sea wall at *Matata*, I was satisfied that the time it had taken us to put together the best life raft/survival-kit combination we could afford was well spent. Our new four-man canopy raft was secured in its sturdy fiber glass box just forward of the companionway. Next to it to starboard was lashed a rugged 2 ½-gallon emergency water dispenser tethered to an inflated fender for flotation and linked to the raft painter with a lanyard. To port of the raft was lashed our primary survival kit, a 40-inch by 18-inch rubberized sailing duffle. It also had independent flotation—a life jacket tied securely around the duffle—as well as a tether to the raft painter. If we did have to get into the raft in a hurry, we wouldn't have to worry about gathering together our distress signaling and survival gear (Fig. 1).

Later on that week word of the Fastnet Race disaster began coming in over the radio news. Before we left the Azores for Portugal and the Med, a number of our new cruising friends had paid a visit to *Matata* to have a look at our survival gear. All found our arrangements practical, relatively inexpensive, and worthwhile.

We had a rationale for designing the kit the way we did. First, you must assume conditions violent and disastrous enough to force a crew to abandon a strong, ocean-going sailboat: radical hull failure, fire, or stranding on a reef. Any of these conditions *could* occur with great suddenness. It doesn't matter that the chances of these events happening are very slim indeed. What does matter is if you have to get into your raft in a muddled hurry—say in the middle of the night with a high sea running—you don't want to rummage through lockers to locate and gather up your flares, EPIRB, survival food, and so on.

The way our survival kit is designed, the main bag and emergency water container go over the side with the raft. They have their own flotation, and they stay tethered to the inflated raft until they can be pulled inside. We have a second duffle bag handy to the companionway, and it also has its own flotation. After a couple of practice runs, I've estimated we could launch the raft and be inside it, with the two survival duffles, in ninety seconds if sea conditions were not too violent.

Obviously, you cannot duplicate all the security and comfort of an offshore yacht in a small life raft and survival kit. But you do want to provide a small part of the essentials and pack them in duffle bags and a floating water container. What should you carry?

Signal equipment: We've provided for a total of sixteen days of continuous EPIRB (Emergency Position Indicating Radio Beacon) distress signals on both 121.5 and 243 MHz; we also have a radio with two-way voice capability on 121.5 MHz and marine VHF channel 16 (156.8 MHz). The voice radio is new to our kit this year. It's a 5-watt hand-held VHF to which a radio technician has added the 121.5 MHz international aviation crystal. With this little set we can talk either to passing aircraft or to ships on marine channel 16. We can give them our position or tell them we are about to release orange smoke or red flares, which aids their search. The nickel-cadmium batteries for the EPIRB should be as new as possible and should be changed well before the expiration of their recommended shelf life. They are the guts of your EPIRB, so don't cut a corner here. Naturally, your EPIRB should be well packed to protect it from impact damage and sea water corrosion.

One interesting signaling device we've made up is a balloon display we can fly over the raft (Fig. 2). This display is centered around an international orange balloon, a self-inflating device that comes packed in its own small canister. The mayday marker balloon has a strong 100-foot tether, and to it we have rigged a lightweight radar reflector and a small hand-held strobe whose clear plastic lense has been tinted red with fingernail enamel. The visual effect is quite good. The strobe reflects off the gold foil of the radar reflector and the shiny orange skin of the balloon. Both the radar reflector and small strobe light hang on short tethers and swivels so they won't tangle on the balloon line, and there is plenty of movement to catch the eye of a potential rescue crew.

We also carry a Very pistol (25-mm) along with the larger hand-held flares. We have a total burn time of three hours from the hand-helds, and we've rigged one of the life-raft paddles with a bracket to elevate the flare and keep its sparks well clear of the raft. We also have spare batteries and bulbs (sealed in foil and plastic bags) for all the electric lights in the kit.

Food and water: A 5-gallon supply of water in three separate dispensers gives the two of us a quart per person per day for ten days. Beyond this supply, we have a 3-gallon can located on the portside quarterberth ready to put into the inflated raft.

Our food supply has been chosen to offer low-to-medium protein content, some bulk, and a certain amount of flavor appeal for morale purposes. Most sailors I spoke to in the Azores didn't know that protein digestion also requires high water intake, and they had unwisely set aside canned meat (high in protein and salt) for their basic survival food. Items like Carnation breakfast bars and Pillsbury food sticks are low in protein and salt and high in carbohydrates. They're also low-volume and lightweight. The sixteen small cans of fruit we have do weigh four pounds, but most of that weight is easily digestible liquid. Including a date-and-nut brown bread in our package is Carol's idea. She points out that stomach-filling bulk and chewable texture are important considerations in preventing seriously debilitating hunger spasms.

Malted milk tablets and milk chocolate candies provide easily digestible protein—in small doses, so as not to increase water need—and they take up only a fraction of the volume and weight of canned milk.

I include two plastic squeeze bottles of lemon juice to use as a marinade for fish. I'm not being epicurean here. Large deep-sea fish are often tough, and their flesh can be difficult to chew.

Finally, we carry a case of C-rations that is stored with the extra water can on the unused portside quarterberth. Should we ever have to abandon the boat, and we have time to take more than the two

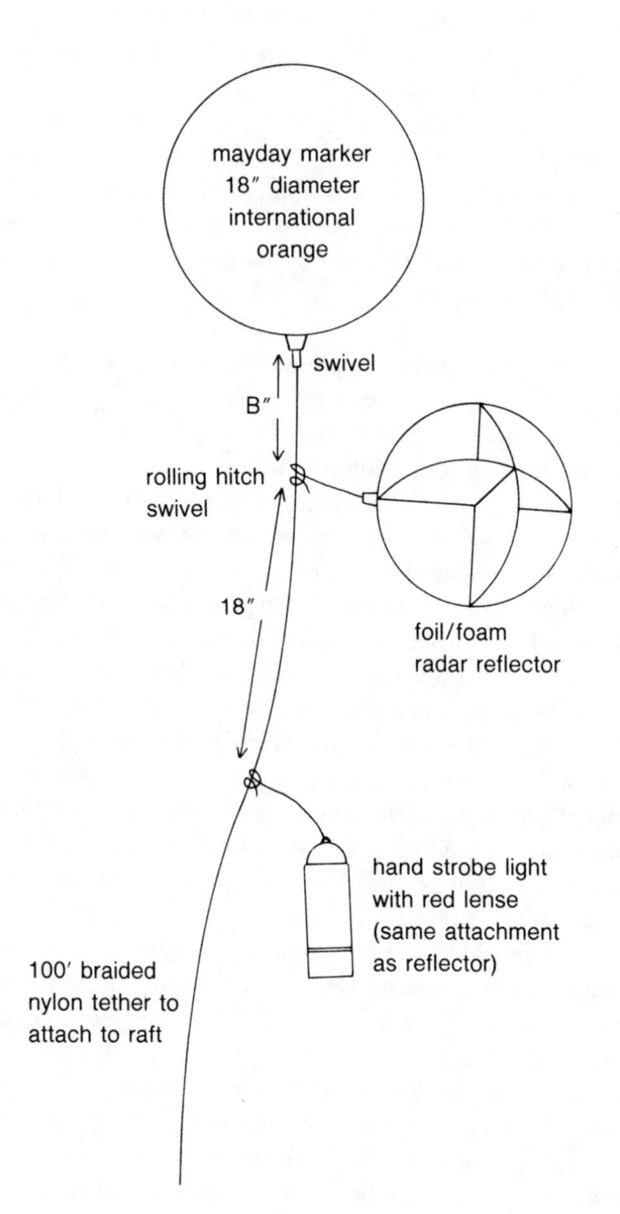

Figure 2: Mayday marker system uses lightweight foil radar reflector and hand strobe light with red lens.

basic survival duffles, we'd grab the case of C-rations. There are twelve individual meals in the strong waterproof cardboard case, and the meals include such "luxury" items as coffee, cocoa, and fruit cake. You can order C-rations directly from a regional United States government property agent or through a friend who has military commissary privileges. We also carry twenty mixed-size Ziploc plastic storage bags in the kit. These can be used for storing food from open packages, marinating fish, and so forth.

Tools and fishing gear: These items are more or less self-explanatory (see list). However, the cutting board for butchering fish is special, as are the large roll of waterproof duct tape and the heavy rubber work gloves. If you are trying to land a forty-pound tuna from a rolling and vulnerable inflated raft, you might expect some damage to the raft, not to mention your hands. That is why we have the rubber gloves (to protect hands) and the duct tape (to help patch the raft floor or canopy).

In the fishing kit, I include a number of steel-leader, large-hook lures. Offshore fish are the big ones, but they represent your ultimate survival food resource, and perhaps the difference between life and death. Fishing for them should be a well-considered matter, which is why I include 100 mixed-size hooks and plenty of spare leader and sinkers.

Your own style of sailing and the area you will be sailing in may modify what you finally put into your own survival kit. The important thing, however, is that you recognize the fact that you may have to get off your boat quickly and go into a raft. And you may have to do so in conditions that will be far more vigorous than your normal sailing situation. If you can accept those facts and plan a system that will work under those conditions, you will be adequately prepared to deal with an emergency if one should develop. After all, once you are involved with an extreme situation, usually it is far too late to spend much time thinking about what you might have done if you only had the time.

Survival equipment inventory

EMERGENCY SIGNAL EQUIPMENT

- EPIRB, new, plus two new batteries. (This device, with two batteries, will give a continuous mayday signal on 121.5 and 243 MHz for almost sixteen days at normal summer temperatures)
- hand-held VHF transceiver, 5-watt, 6-channel, including 121.5 (international aviation mayday) and 156.8 (marine channel 16) MHz
- 12 red hand flares (15-minute burn time each)
- 25-mm Very pistol with 24 red meteor flares
- 6 25-mm red parachute flares
- 2 hand strobe lights, one with red lens, and 2 sets spare batteries for each
- mayday marker balloon kit with 100-foot parachute line tether
- lightweight radar reflector
- 2 camper's signal mirrors
- 2 waterproof flashlights
- 3 throw-away plastic pen lights
- 6-volt spotlight
- man-overboard strobe light
- 3 small jars orange dye marker
- 2 small orange smoke floats
- 3 Teflon police whistles
- 2 international orange signal panels

EMERGENCY NAVIGATION KIT

- small plastic sextant
- almanac
- waterproof watch
- 2 scout-type compasses
- pilot chart of the North Atlantic with world ocean currents on overleaf
- 2 plastic triangles, plastic school dividers, pencils, ruled yellow pad
- *Noon Sight Navigation*, by A. Birney (Cornell Maritime Press)

PROTECTIVE CLOTHING

- 2 pair floating plastic sunglasses
- 2 pair cotton-wool long johns
- 2 lightweight white tennis hats
- 1 set featherweight plastic oilskins
- 1 red plastic/foil "space" blanket

MEDICAL KIT

- USAF surplus crew first-aid kit (plastic box)
- 100 500-mg tetracycline capsules
- 40 Demerol tablets
- 50 Bonine seasickness tablets
- large tube, zinc oxide
- large bottle calamine lotion
- large tube Aureomycin salve (for saltwater ulcers)
- 36 Lomotil tablets
- 36 laxative tablets
- 12 Dexedrine
- 12 Valium (5-mg)
- USAF surplus first-aid manual
- Mycostatin antifungal vaginal suppositories
- 100 Wash 'n' Dri towelettes

SPECIAL REPAIR GEAR

- small kit, 5-minute underwater epoxy
- bosun knife with screwdriver and marlin spike

- 1 roll waxed whipping twine and three sail needles
- 3 packs waterproof matches
- 3 small cans Sterno Canned Heat with asbestos hot pad
- stainless steel hose clamps and spare rubber for raft hand pump

FISHING KIT

- 12 large offshore lures with 6-foot steel leaders and swivels attached (4 each of yellow feather, plastic mackerel, plastic squid)
- 100 assorted hooks (large, medium, small)
- 40 assorted lightweight steel leaders and swivels
- 50 assorted lead sinkers
- 300 feet 40-pound test line
- 300 feet 25-pound test line
- 250 feet parachute shroud line for floating multihook rig
- assorted artificial worms and spawn sacks for small-bait fish
- fine cheesecloth for shrimp straining rig
- small hand gaff with rubber tip for point
- scaling tool

FOOD AND WATER

- 2 1/2-gallon plastic picnic dispenser, sealed with waterproof duct tape and tethered to flotation fender and raft painter
- 3 1-gallon plastic antifreeze jugs, steam-cleaned and sealed with duct tape; stored in main duffle
- 12-inch garage funnel with 6-foot soft plastic tube for rain collection from top of raft canopy
- 6 heavy-ply plastic trash bags for dew condensation
- heavy-duty 16″ × 24″ plastic waste basket for rain collection and bailing, plus 4 sponges
- 4 graduated plastic measuring cups
- 16 small cans assorted fruit in unsweetened juice
- 8 cans date-and-nut brown bread
- 20 Carnation breakfast bars, foil-wrapped
- 40 Pillsbury food sticks, foil-wrapped
- 14 M&M candy packages, foil-wrapped
- 300 malted milk tablets, foil-wrapped
- 60 multivitamin with iron tablets
- 2 plastic squeeze bottles pure lemon juice
- separate: C-rations, one case (12 meals)

TOOLS

- fisherman's sheath knife and small whetstone
- 3 small pocket knives with can openers
- 2 small "G.I." blunt-edge can openers
- plywood cutting board, 12″ × 18″ × 1/2″
- 2 pair heavy rubber work gloves (for handling fish and line—raft paddle is heavy enough for a killing club)
- needle-nosed pliers with wire cutter
- small screwdriver kit for radio gear
- small combination pliers and adjustable wrench

- large roll 2-inch waterproof duct tape
- raft repair kit with extra patches and rubber stoppers

BOOKS, ETC.

- *Survival Afloat,* by Don Biggs (David McKay Co., New York)
- paperback anthology
- plastic-coated deck of cards

The foregoing is a partial list of equipment included in dufflebag flotation kit.

2. EMERGENCY REPAIRS AFLOAT: HOW TO PLAN FOR THE WORST

Any skipper who takes his family and friends to sea, either on a summer cruise or an ocean crossing, has the implicit responsibility of providing a seaworthy vessel. This is an axiom with which few will argue, but how many skippers feel truly prepared to carry out major emergency repairs afloat, making a damaged boat seaworthy again?

Everyone with a cruising boat keeps *some* tools, spare parts, and repair materials on board. Not many captains I've talked to, however, feel adequately equipped to rig an emergency rudder, effectively patch collision leaks or hull ruptures, replace a stove-in hatch, or repair serious damage to the standing rigging. Most coastwise cruising sailors and also a lot of bluewater people rely on good luck with the weather and on the proximity of boatyards. Sooner or later, though, some skippers run out of luck, either hundreds of miles offshore or in a secluded gunk-hole. Effecting emergency repairs under these conditions becomes the test of a person's seamanship.

In my opinion, the most important preparation for an emergency lies not in amassing tons of expensive, complicated tools and gadgetry but in developing a repair plan: a logical sequence of actions you will undertake in the event of this or that damage. Such logical thought is at the heart of all naval or merchant marine damage-control training. Although I'm not suggesting such elaborate preparation, I fully agree with the philosophy behind professional damage control: imagine every worst-case situation, and then work out a *practical* repair plan. Vague and optimistic statements such as, "I'll jury rig something or other" simply avoid reality.

Boats do suffer damage, and thinking about the worst case ahead of time and then putting together the proper combination of tools and repair materials can save you a lot of expense and worry during your cruise. Whenever you start planning for *any* emergency repair, you must compromise between having too few tools and having too many. In short, you don't want as much repair equipment as possible; you want the *right* selection.

For this discussion, I've made an arbitrary division between tools and repair materials and between the needs of coastwise cruises and extended offshore passages. Above all, I've tried to be practical and to exercise the judgment of compromise I cited above.

I have a thirty-foot fiber glass sloop, and when I'm provisioning and equipping it for a long offshore passage, space and weight considerations (not to mention money!) limit the amount of emergency repair equipment I can carry on board. So I select my equipment by walking through actual emergency-repair situations. This keeps my inventory to a practical minimum to meet the actual needs I perceive.

For example, before embarking on our first Atlantic crossing, Carol and I began developing repair plans for two potential serious situations: hatch failure and hull fracture from a collision with heavy flotsam.

Our planning led us to an important discovery. Although we had an adequate inventory of tools on board, we had almost none of the *materials* we'd need to make such repairs. How *do* you repair a collision split in the fiber glass hull that is located below the waterline, underneath the deck sole and bunk frames when the surface is wet and greasy, and salt water is seeping in at a steady rate?

Thinking this hypothetical problem through led to our solution. Get a good supply of underwater epoxy such as Sea Goin' Poxy Putty. It cures underwater in temperatures as low as 10° F.; it sets firmly in about half an hour, and it cures completely in twenty-four hours. To keep the epoxy in place inside the actual fracture, we acquired a supply of soft rubber (1/32-inch neoprene) sheeting that we could tack down quickly with either heavy-duty staples or small bronze boat nails and battens.

We did not have to use this material offshore, but in the Azores I made good use of the underwater epoxy and sheeting. In Horta Harbor I discovered that the bronze cap that seals the cutlass bearing on my propeller shaft had come adrift and the threads on both the cap and the shaft tube were stripped. The shaft and bearing were wobbling badly, and I was faced with a dilemma. Don't use the engine, or hoist the boat onto the seawall so the bronze cap could be brazed into place.

Instead, however, I dove with a mask and snorkel and securely fixed the bearing cap in place with underwater epoxy. This repair held up for several months and several hundred hours of engine time until I could have the boat hauled in Greece and carry out more permanent repairs.

When we considered the potential problem of a stove-in hatch or hatches during our damage-control planning, we quickly realized just how important this type of planning is. Like most sailors, we took our hatch integrity for granted, and we had no real idea how to replace one that had been smashed by a heavy sea, or how to reinforce one before it could be smashed. You might argue that such occurrences are too rare to worry about. But if you sail either the Atlantic or Pacific in the summer you run the risk of encountering a hurricane, and only a fool doubts the power of a hurricane sea to damage a small sailboat.

By walking through our repair procedure we saw that 1/2-inch marine ply, precut to the exact size of the inner hatch well, could be fixed in place from *inside* the cabin using 2-inch lag screws with plastic anchoring sleeves. For additional security, the entire plywood patch could be cemented to the coachroof ceiling (in our case, the

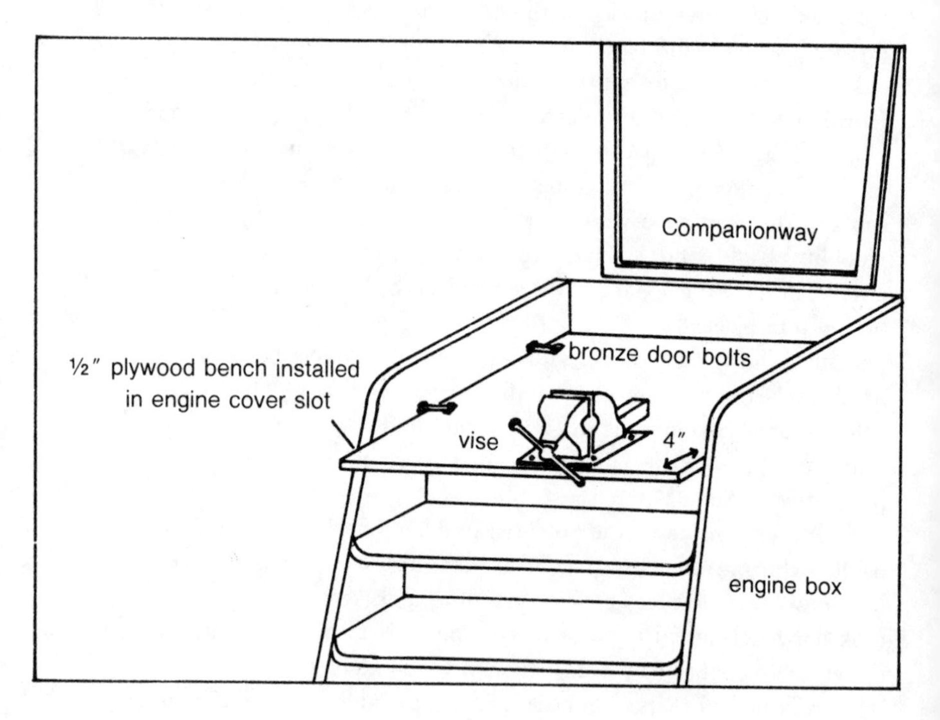

Figure 3: Diagram of the author's emergency vise/workbench arrangement installed over the engine. Extending the board from the forward end of the box permits the vise to operate freely. The same principle can be used for other areas such as bunk frames and storage bins.

hull liner) with underwater epoxy before being anchored with the lag screws. It was during the dry run that we decided to include a cordless electric drill in our special tool inventory. We tried to imagine what it would be like, in hurricane conditions, to drill holes through plywood and coachroof ceiling with an old-fashioned brace and bit. A 3/8-inch cordless electric drill, with batteries fully charged, is a relatively inexpensive and extremely versatile tool.

When we considered practical repairs to damaged hardware, we saw we had no practical place to anchor our heavy 7-inch vise and no proper workbench surface where we could pound and bend metal. Again, our damage-control walkthrough helped us solve the problem. We developed a portable plywood workbench for our vise and for working on jury-rigged hardware.

Our 1/2-inch plywood sheet slides into the slot in the fiber glass engine box that is normally occupied by the varnished teak engine cover (Fig. 3). By extending the plywood workbench front out four inches, the vise base is well supported and the vise is free of obstacles. The plywood sheet is held in place by the engine-box slots on each side, and by four bronze slide bolts that anchor into small holes drilled in the fiber glass housing. To round out our portable blacksmith shop, we included a 1/4-inch scrap steel plate (8-inch oval shape) and a small propane gas torch for heating metal.

This year, I bought a small, inexpensive solid oxygen gas welding and brazing set. It's compact, lightweight, and easy to use. With a stainless steel and bronze welding rod, I can repair or replace almost any piece of hardware on the boat.

For rigging and hardware repairs, we included several pieces of 1/8-inch and 1/16-inch stainless steel plate, precut and with bolt holes drilled, to be used as mounting plates on the mast, the boom, or the hull chainplates. We also acquired a variety of galvanized cable clamps (known in some chandleries as wire rope clips). These are the U-shaped type with two locking nuts. We purchased enough extra stainless cable to replace one stay and one shroud and also got extra 3/8-inch anchor chain in 10-foot sections that could be used for rigging wire in a pinch. We also had a variety of long bronze and steel carriage bolts, shackles, and galvanized lap links to use in fixing any emergency rigging.

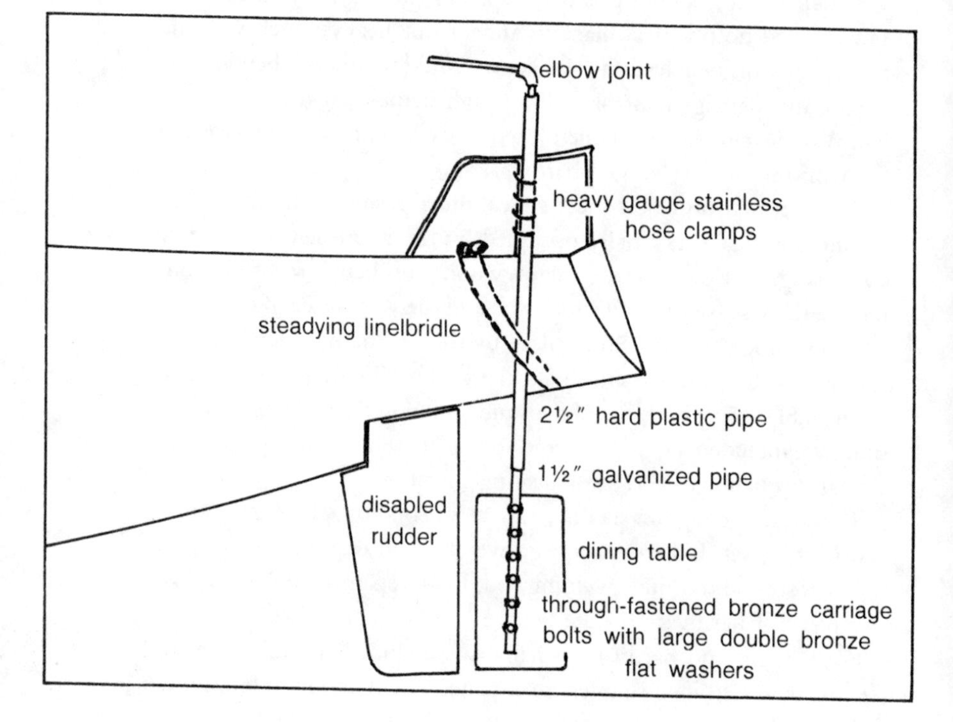

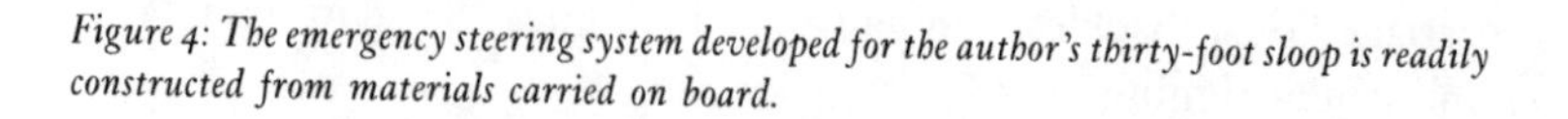
Figure 4: The emergency steering system developed for the author's thirty-foot sloop is readily constructed from materials carried on board.

The final big repair problem for our damage-control plan was jury rigging an emergency rudder. There are a lot of good ideas on this subject, but we modified one offered by Richard Henderson in his excellent cruising manual, *East to the Azores.* For our emergency rudder blade, we decided to use our dining table, stripped, naturally, of its trim and hardware. It's high-quality marine plywood approximately 42 inches by 30 inches. The rudder shaft is a 7-foot section of 1 1/2-inch galvanized pipe joined by an elbow to a 4-foot section of the same pipe. To make a practical tube for the new rudder shaft, we chose 2 1/2-inch hard plastic plumbing pipe secured by heavy-duty hose clamps to the stern pulpit stanchion (Fig. 4).

This emergency rudder would be simple to assemble and mount, and it would be easy to use. Above all it would be durable and quite capable of steering the boat across an ocean. As with all our major emergency preparations, we accounted for physical exhaustion and injury to one of us when we planned the assembly and mounting of this rudder.

Emergency repair tool and equipment inventory

BASIC TOOLS

- 94-piece standard and metric wrench and auto tool set. This set includes: 42 sockets with reversible ratchet and extension bars; 12 box-open-end wrenches; an 18-piece hex key set; an 8-piece ignition wrench set; 3 screwdrivers and a hacksaw with 3 blades. This type of set comes in a rust-free hard plastic tool box and is available for around $100 from the large catalogue department stores.
- Power driver-type ratchet screwdriver set with 8 separate blades
- 2 pipe wrenches (1 large, 1 small)
- Small tap and die set
- Grommet tool kit with 50 #3 grommets
- 2 wood and two cold chisels
- 6-piece metal and wood file kit
- Standard brace and bit drill with 5 bits
- 3/8-inch cable or bolt cutter
- 7-inch jaws vise (mounted on plywood bench)
- Keyhole saw, with spare blade
- Wire brushes, large and small
- Yachtsman's knife with pliers/wrench and lid in a sheath for going aloft
- 30-inch wrecking bar with claw
- Standard hammer with claw; hard rubber mallet; 2-pound smith's hammer

- Large and small Vise-Grip pliers
- Large and small Channel Lock pliers
- Electrician's pliers, with wire cutter blades
- Large and small needle-nosed pliers
- Yachtsman's variety set of marine fasteners (nonferrous nuts, bolts, screws, etc.), available through most marine supply houses
- Extra-heavy-duty staple gun with 1250 9/16-inch rustproof Monel staples
- 12-volt work lamp with battery clips
- Small set: pins, punches, and awls
- 6 6-inch C-clamps

OFFSHORE PASSAGE TOOLS

- 3/8-inch cordless electric drill (fully charged), with case-hardened bits
- Saw blade and wire brush wheel for drill
- 3 rolls waterproof duct tape (2 inches by 40 feet)
- 2 quarts Sea Goin' Putty Poxy Underwater Epoxy
- 2 quarts (4 pint cans) standard fiber glass epoxy resin, with a good variety mat, roving, and glass fiber tapes
- Variety of 2-inch lag screws with plastic anchoring sleeves
- Variety of long heavy-duty bronze carriage bolts and nuts
- Variety of 3/8-inch galvanized U-shaped cable clamps
- Variety of 1/8- and 1/16-inch stainless steel plate, some precut and drilled for use as emergency chainplates
- Propane gas torch
- Solid oxygen welding-brazing rig, with bronze and stainless rod, welding goggles, and asbestos welder's gloves
- Sheets of Neoprene rubber matting
- Silicon bronze nails; large variety 1 3/4-inch and 3/4-inch tacks
- Rip-stop waterproof sail repair tape
- Standard bosun's kit
- Variety solderless wiring connectors with 100 feet of replacement wire, plus brass lamp, fuse, and switch fittings
- One sheet 1/2-inch marine plywood precut into hatch "strong boys" and porthole covers. Approximately 2 by 3 feet left uncut for emergency hull repairs
- Large variety stainless steel hose clamps
- Universal-type chain wrench
- Large selection of stainless cotter keys, pins, clevis pins, shackles, etc.
- Precut 1 1/2-inch galvanized pipe for emergency rudder shaft and tiller (with elbow joints prethreaded)
- Small mechanic's wheel puller
- Variety of cutting blades, knives and scrapers

Inventory of the emergency repair equipment carried on board the author's boat includes a basic set of tools for everyday use as well as a special inventory of items that are carried whenever the boat goes offshore.

Our tool inventory in the accompanying list is self-explanatory, but here are some comments on a few of the items:

- The drill saw bits for our cordless electric drill allow you to rip through both plywood and fiber glass hull laminations with relative speed and ease.
- Make sure your cable cutter is rated capable to cut your size rigging.
- We include a 12-volt work light with battery clips because working in a confined area using a small flashlight is often impossible.
- Take along a good variety of solderless electrical connectors and clamps.
- A good whetstone for knives and chisels is an item many sailors overlook.

Think about what your own worst case situations will be, and walk through the solutions to those situations; when you are finished you will have a set of procedures and tools with which you can live.

3. THE OVERDUE NOTICE: EXPANDING THE FLOAT PLAN CONCEPT

Although solid figures are difficult to obtain, it's safe to say that there are substantially more American sailors voyaging offshore today than there were ten years ago. West Coast sailors are practically commuting to and from the Hawaiian Islands and the South Pacific; cruising families from the East Coast regularly ply the summer Atlantic, and many make the direct passage from New England to the Caribbean early each winter. When one considers cruising sailors from Europe, Australia, and New Zealand—not to mention the Japanese—the number of offshore passagemakers increases greatly: on any given day of the year, there are probably several hundred small-boat crews far out on the empty reaches of the world's oceans.

It's fair to ask, therefore, how many of these new ocean-voyaging skippers have done everything practical to assure the safety of their crews. In Ric Martini's thoughtful article, "Going Against the

Grain" (*Sail*, September 1981), he directly addresses the issue of offshore safety: "Careful planning, adequate preparation, and experience are the primary ingredients that insure a safe passage." To which any conscientious skipper can only add, "Amen." But what happens to a crew if, despite planning, preparation, and experience, a boat *is* sunk or disabled far offshore, well away from the air routes and shipping lanes?

Many experienced sailors I've met discount this possibility, countering any such speculation with glib assurances that modern boats are built " . . . stronger than jetliners," or that " . . . it's not the sea that hurts a boat, it's the land."

Almost everyone would agree, however, that Angus Primrose and Alain Colas were seamen who combined planning, preparation, and experience in their offshore passagemaking, yet they died at sea in separate accidents within the past three years. The offshore ketch *Spirit* was described as being "extremely well-found," but it was holed and sunk by submerged flotsam during a delivery from Hawaii to California in 1976. According to the testimony at the well-publicized subsequent damage-suit trial, *Spirit* sank quickly after striking the flotsam during a gale. The five crew members did not have time to take with them the boat's comprehensive survival pack or EPIRB before boarding two rafts that quickly blew away from each other in the gale. Twenty-one days later, one of the rafts was rescued by a freighter, the Coast Guard was alerted, and a massive air-sea rescue search was begun for the other raft, which was located seven days later. During the total of twenty-seven days adrift, two crew members died. The fact that the castaways did not have an EPIRB or a comprehensive survival pack undoubtedly had some bearing on the long time spent in the rafts. But the question still remains: what else could have been done to prevent this and similar tragedies?

I do not presume to have an unassailable answer to this important question, but I do feel that I've found at least a partial solution in what I call the Overdue Notice. Simply stated, the Overdue Notice is a brief departure-date-ETA-route plan—modified "Float Plan"—which the offshore skipper completes in several copies and distributes to the proper authorities and interested parties at the time he departs on his passage.

The original Notice is sent by air mail to the harbor master (U.S. Coast Guard Boating Safety Officer for American ports) in the first scheduled port of call. Other copies should be sent to close relatives or associates who can be counted on to activate overdue search procedures if necessary. The Notice should be kept to one neat, typewritten page; rambling or hand-scrawled documents tend to get lost in the bureaucratic shuffle (see Sample Overdue Notice). It should clearly list all the boat's vital statistics and distinguishing characteristics: rig, hull color, LOA, displacement, sail number, number of crew members; the intended course from departure port to arrival port—that is, rhumb-line course (95 degrees true, and so on) *and* possible variance from that course; the exact departure date; a list of survival equipment; the best estimate of the arrival date (ETA) at the first scheduled port of call; and the date after which the vessel should be considered Overdue.

The function of the Overdue Notice is this: if the boat has not checked in with the harbor master or Coast Guard by the Overdue Date, it should be considered to be in difficulty and a search should be considered. Likewise, if the other recipients of the Overdue Notice have not received a safe-arrival telegram from the captain by the Overdue Date, they should contact the Coast Guard to determine whether or not a search is warranted. In this manner, shipping and aircraft along the intended route can be alerted that the boat is Overdue and presumed in difficulty and the chances of rescue greatly improved.

I have used this system on several offshore passages, and I can attest that it has worked well for me. When I checked in with the Horta, Faial harbor master after a twenty-eight-day passage from New York, I found my Overdue Notice, stuck with a pin to the careful Portuguese translation of the document that he had made, on top of the papers in his Action-Pending box. He assured me that a search would have been initiated if we had not arrived by our Overdue Date, or if we had not contacted his office of our safe arrival elsewhere.

Sitting there in the harbor master's office, I couldn't help thinking of the Dougal Robertson family *(Survive the Savage Sea)*. The Robertsons spent thirty-seven agonizing days in their liferaft in the Pacific, drifting relatively near the shipping lanes converging on the

Panama Canal; no one knew they were overdue, so no search was made for their vessel.

I am not suggesting that the Overdue Notice is a foolproof panacea that will miraculously prevent all human casualties offshore. However, the prudent skipper should undertake every practical measure he can to minimize danger to himself and his crew. In his informative article, "Report Me to Lloyd's" (*Sail*, September 1981), Frank Mulville offers an interesting position-reporting procedure that would work well in conjunction with the Overdue Notice described here. Of course, a reliable Single Side Band radio telephone and a regular radio-contact schedule is another safety measure many skippers might wish to consider. I'd like to point out, though, that the Lloyd's ship-reporting procedure depends on making contact with a cooperative merchant vessel. Also, an SSB radio schedule with the folks back home depends on electrical power and a working transceiver on board the boat: both conditions that are, alas, subject to change at a moment's notice.

The Overdue Notice, however, is not without its own potentially serious problems, including the following:

Reliably estimating passage duration and Overdue Date: This is not easy, especially for the inexperienced passagemaker. On my first long offshore voyage (New York to Gibraltar, via the Azores), I consulted the Pilot Chart and *Ocean Passages for the World*, then decided that my two-handed passage from New York to Faial, Azores would take no more than twenty-five days—a 2,550-mile rhumb-line course of 95 degrees true at 100 miles a day. The wind roses on the Pilot Chart for July all showed prevailing favorable westerlies along the route, and the average percentage of calms was only 3 percent all the way to Faial. Further, the percentage of predicted easterly headwinds was less than 5 percent; gale percentages were minimal. Therefore, I figured daily runs of 100 miles would be a relatively simple goal; after all, that's only an average sustained speed of 4.1 knots: no big deal for a fast thirty-foot sloop with two experienced sailors on board.

So much for ignorant optimism. It took us 28 1/2 days to make Faial; we had *six* days of dead calm, and force six plus easterly headwinds during five full days. Instead of sailing a nice, steady 2,550-mile rhumb-line over the ground, we logged an irregular 3,160-mile tract back and forth across the parallel of latitude 39 North.

My error in estimating the ETA and course area lay in my mistaking the statistical averages of the Pilot Chart and *Ocean Passages* for the "real-world" probability of an actual passage. Therefore, my ETA of twenty-five elapsed days and my Overdue Date of thirty-five elapsed days were both unrealistic. Ric Martini suggests adding 30 percent to an upwind passage's duration. In my Overdue Notices, I now go even further than that for any passage and calculate my ETA at 25 percent beyond the optimal speed on rhumb-line voyage and my Overdue Date of 40 percent beyond this optimum.

The danger of false alarms: No reasonable sailor wants to be the cause of an unwarranted international air-sea rescue search. These rescue efforts are costly and bring risk to the seamen and airmen involved. For this reason, anyone sending an Overdue Notice must recognize his personal responsibility in using this procedure. If, for example, he states in his Notice that he is sailing from New York to Horta, Faial, Azores, and actually bypasses Faial and lands in São Miguel, he is morally—and probably legally—obliged to notify the Horta harbor master and the stateside recipients of the Notice in writing (by cable) that he has altered route and arrived safely elsewhere.

Also, when informing relatives back home of your safe arrival at your scheduled destination, do not rely on a telephone call or an air-mail letter; both can be unreliable from some overseas ports. Use a full-rate international telegram (not a low-priority night letter "LT" rate) and send a clear, previously agreed-on message, such as "Boat and crew arrived safely in Faial on August 4. No problems." I've lived in some of the more remote parts of the Third World and always found that telegrams were the surest means of international communication.

Reliably estimating intended course area: This can also be difficult. As shown above, the rhumb-line course is often hard to follow. Therefore, the skipper should sit down with his offshore charts before completing his Overdue Notice and plot his possible variance from the rhumb-line course. For example, on a passage from New York to Faial in the summer, optimally along the 39th parallel, on a rhumb line of 95 degrees true, he might actually be pushed as far north as Latitude 42 or choose to go down as far south as Latitude 36 if it's a bad year for continental depressions on the Atlantic. In short, he must carefully study not only the statistically predicted winds but the currents and all possible weather patterns that might affect his route and course area sailed. In the Notice he should then clearly state his intended course, and also the latitudes between which he *might* be sailing. Armed with this information from the Overdue Notice, the coordinator of a search can study the weather that has affected the intended course area for the period of the passage and select the most promising search areas.

I've discussed both the theory and practice of the Overdue Notice with U.S. and European Coast Guard officers and with professional seamen of the Merchant Marine. While most agree that the procedure could definitely help prevent casualties if used correctly, almost all had reservations about the Notice being abused by inexperienced yachtsmen who do not realistically estimate their passage duration and Overdue Date or who capriciously decide to change destination and do not cancel their Notices. There was also fear that the procedure would be needlessly used for short-haul voyages in well-traveled cruising grounds. Some yacht sailors with whom I've discussed the idea felt it was a needless constraint placed on the freedom that offshore cruising offers regulation-bound twentieth-century mankind.

Ultimately, of course, the decision whether or not to use the system rests with the individual captain. Before reaching this decision, though, he or she should carefully compare the procedure's possible advantages with its specific responsibilities.

Sample Overdue Notice

Sailing Yacht ETA and Overdue Notice

Date: June 1, 1982

TO: Harbor Master, Horta, Faial, Azores (Portugal)

FROM: John A. Jones, Captain/Owner U.S. Sailing Yacht *Sea Rose*, U.S. Document Number 547689

SUBJECT: Passage from New York to Horta, Faial

1. The U.S. sailing yacht *Sea Rose* departed New York on *June 1, 1982*, en route directly to Horta, Faial, Azores.
2. Estimated time of arrival (ETA): *Sea Rose* should arrive in Horta by July 1, 1982.
3. OVERDUE DATE: If *Sea Rose does not arrive* in Horta or contact the Horta harbor master by *July 13, 1982*, this yacht should be considered OVERDUE and experiencing difficulty.
4. Distinguishing marks and characteristics, *Sea Rose:*
   a. Glass Reinforced Plastic (GRP) sloop (single mast), 30 feet (8.23 meters) long, 4-ton displacement, 25 HD diesel auxiliary engine with power range of 500 miles.
   b. Hull: white; cabin: white; sails: dark red; sail number: U.S. 11234.
   c. VHF 6-channel radiotelephone, 25-watt; call sign: WZ 103B.
5. 40-cm radar reflector: mounted on backstays.
6. Survival equipment:
   a. Avon 4-man automatic canopy life raft with offshore survival pack.
   b. Narco EPIRB mayday radio beacon with one extra battery: 121.5 and 243 MHz.
   c. White strobe light, red parachute and hand flares, signal mirrors, air horn, and whistles.
   d. Emergency food and water for two persons for 25 days.
7. Crew: John A. Jones and Helen C. Jones
   123 3rd Avenue
   New York, NY 10011 USA
   Telephone: (212) 555-1100
8. Intended Course Area:
   95 degrees true rhumb line from New York to Horta, Faial.
   Depending on weather conditions, I may sail as far north as Latitude 42 North or as far south as Latitude 36 North.

I certify that the above information is true and correct:

signature

John A. Jones, Captain

4. THE OFFSHORE SAFETY PLAN

Before a sailor ventures offshore for the first time—especially shorthanded in a small boat—he is bound to worry some about accidents. Most of us suffer this predictable anxiety late at night; we toss on damp sheets with visions of pitchpoling halfway to Bermuda or of sheared keel bolts a thousand miles outbound from San Diego. Beyond these highly improbable dangers, though, there are other, more common accidents that can be just as frightening to contemplate: boiling water burns in mid-Atlantic; a man overboard at 3:00 A.M.—with the other crew member sound asleep below; your spouse or child impaled by that damn tuna gaff *somebody* insisted on lashing to the rail . . . and all the scary rest of it.

But how many of us actually do something to alleviate our more valid fears? How many sailors squarely face the legitimate offshore seamanship problems of accident prevention and crew safety? By this I mean the development of a practical crew safety plan that, when followed, will go a long way toward protecting the safety of both boat and crew. Such a plan should directly address potentially dangerous areas and situations, such as nighttime watchkeeping, man-overboard emergencies, deck safety and sail handling in rough weather, fire and burn hazards, and preparation for severe weather.

Before our own first ocean crossing in *Matata,* Carol and I sat down and worked out a practical crew safety plan, using the same approach that we'd developed for our survival and emergency repair plans (see parts 1 and 2 of this Appendix). We first considered the "worst-case" scenario for each potential hazard, then carried out a practical, step-by-step walkthrough solution for the specific accident-prevention problem each hazard raised.

In developing our plan, we found that we had to rethink some of our previously held notions of good seamanship. Round-the-clock watchkeeping, for example, was too onerous and time-consuming for a two-person crew on a long passage. Equally, we decided that changing headsails up or down at night to achieve marginal speed increases was not worth the risk of accident or worth disturbing the person off watch who was trying to sleep below. After a period of similar careful deliberations, we came up with our Offshore Safety Plan: a set of self-imposed rules and procedures which we tried to follow to the letter throughout our first crossing, and which we still follow today whenever we make an offshore passage.

The reason for these procedures is the prevention of personal injury through accident or the loss of the boat due to a collision or fire. In following this plan on our first crossing, we both noticed a general reduction in the level of diffuse anxiety that often afflicts neophyte passagemakers; we found it a lot easier to sleep off watch, knowing that the person in the cockpit would not end up in the drink and that the boat itself wouldn't likely be crushed under the bow of some supertanker.

Following are the important elements of our Offshore Safety Plan:

Watchkeeping: The formality, sequence, and duration of watches will obviously vary from crew to crew, but it should be remembered that watchkeeping procedures on a shorthanded passage have a direct bearing on collision prevention, on navigational accuracy and subsequent landfalls, and on preparing for severe weather. We decided to keep formal, three-hour watches in a fixed sequence during the hours of darkness only. Daytime, whomever happened to be in the cockpit was responsible for sail trim and for keeping up the running log. But at night, when there was increased potential of collision and when sea conditions were difficult to judge, the rotation of regular watches gave us a sense of structured control. This produced the psychological security necessary for the off-watch person to sleep well below decks.

The navigational benefits of formal watchkeeping were obvious; we had no problem keeping up the DR because the watchkeeper carefully logged each course change and tack, any wind shift, and the hourly speed average. To these hourly watchkeeper's log entries we added a bilge sounding every three hours, as well as regular barometer, sky-cover, and swell condition reports. Finally, we always logged ship sightings: speed, direction, and—when possible—vessel type, so that we would know when we were in the shipping lanes. Also, we would know what types of vessels were in our vicinity to call on for help in the event of a serious emergency.

Deck safety and sail handling: Because we knew that each of us would be in the cockpit or on deck alone during part of every night, we gave special consideration to the watchkeeper's equipment and to deck safety. We went through a worst-case scenario: the watchkeeper falling overboard while the other person slept below, ignorant of the tragedy. First, we developed procedures to prevent the watchkeeper from falling overboard, and then we planned for his rescue in the event such an accident actually did occur.

Depending on how cold it was, the watchkeeper wore either a hooded float coat or a light foam flotation vest, with a two-snap safety harness over it. He also carried the following emergency equipment: a sharp bosun's knife and a whistle on a lanyard; a waterproof pocket strobe; a red-lensed pen light (to protect night vision in the cockpit); an orange dye-marker packet; a kit of six red aerial miniflares; and a long-life collar light on his vest or float coat. We each wore this *Star Wars* rig on every night watch, religiously, storm or calm. Since the equipment stayed with the vest or coat, getting into the watchkeeper's outfit required about a minute's time, but this slight inconvenience was more than offset by the sense of security the gear engendered.

Once dressed for his watch and in the cockpit, the watchkeeper automatically snapped his safety harness onto either the port or starboard jackline. These lines were composed of a single length of 1/2-inch braided line that ran from a deck ring outside the cockpit coaming, flush with the deck, all the way forward, then through the heavy bow cleats and back down the other side to the opposite coaming ring. With his safety harness snapped into the jacklines, the watchkeeper could move forward with both hands free, without the hassle of snapping into and out of shrouds or lifelines, or onto stanchions.

It was unusual for the watchkeeper to go all the way forward alone at night, however. We had a policy of effecting sail changes when both crew members were awake at the end of a watch. Generally, we tried to anticipate sail reduction, and to reef or go down to a smaller headsail before dark. Obviously, one can't always have such foresight, so, once in the Med, we rigged our headsail halyard with a downhaul and led both halyard and downhaul back through blocks to the cockpit. Thus rigged, it was a relatively easy matter for one person in the cockpit to douse the jib and secure it on the foredeck, using the sheet and downhaul. The person going forward never had a dangerously flogging headsail with which to contend: no small safety consideration, especially shorthanded, far offshore.

We also made a careful survey of our deck equipment: whisker poles, boat hook, fish gaff and blocks, and so on; and we moved or replaced any piece of gear presenting an obstacle to our feet—especially our bare feet, particularly at night. Those sharp-pointed items we couldn't conveniently move (such as large cleats or the spinnaker pole), we padded with waterproof duct tape. To make sure the decks were as clear as possible, we practiced going from bow to stern at night blindfolded; no smashed toes or gouged ankles meant success. We also added a larger midmast seal-beam light to illuminate the foredeck. This installation was well worth the bother, as it not only provided ample working light, even on the foulest night, but also lit up both the main and headsails quite effectively whenever we wanted to show ourselves to an approaching ship.

I had planned to install alloy steps on the mast before sailing, but that modification had to wait. I did make the time to rig two extra halyards before we sailed, so that we had a total of five: two internal, three external. Now that I've got my mast steps, I wonder how I ever sailed without them. Using a safety harness, I can quickly climb up to the spreaders in perfect security, without going through the whole bosun's chair drill, thus increasing my range of visibility severalfold. If I have to go up the mast to work, I can do so without Carol manning the halyard winch; she is therefore free to take the helm and keep the boat on the steadiest point of sailing while I'm aloft. In my opinion, extra halyards and mast steps are two pieces of inexpensive security every shorthanded passagemaker should consider installing.

Our deck safety planning also included singlehanded reefing practice. At first, this exercise seemed more trouble than it was worth. After all, we were used to reefing as a team, usually with Carol on the tiller and mainsheet, and me up at the main halyard winch and reefing pendant. But by carrying out the worst-case scenario planning, we soon realized that neither of us was adept at reefing alone, especially not at night in bad weather—the conditions when quick reefing might well be most important. We learned, however; we doggedly practiced climbing from cockpit to the halyard winch and back. After a few trials, we wised up and consulted some recent seamanship publications about the most efficient and direct method of reefing. This, of course, involves lowering the boom with the topping lift to the lee rail and sitting on the deck within an easy reach of the halyard winch and the reefing pendant. After we applied these techniques, single-handed reefing was no longer such a frustrating—and dangerous—feat.

We would not have made this progress, however, if we had not first squarely faced the possible need for mastering these techniques. In short, our safety plan was definitely working.

Man-overboard routine: This is one of the ultimate emergencies at sea, a calamity few of us like to think about. A man-overboard situation becomes even more threatening when you're shorthanded on a long passage offshore and you are also battling rough seas.

We frankly discussed this potential hazard before sailing, and we had to admit just as frankly that our previous man-overboard preparations—those we'd made for short, coastwise cruises—had been slipshod and downright Pollyannish. In the past, we had simply hoped that nobody would fall off the boat, especially on a stormy night. But in developing our safety plan, we decided we had to prepare ourselves for this actual emergency situation.

First, we decided that our inventory of watchkeeper's rescue equipment—the flotation vest, strobe, whistle, and so on—was adequate for the purpose of locating the person who has fallen overboard in darkness, steep seas, fog, or rain. Next, we determined that, should a person's safety harness or the jacklines fail and he were cast overboard, it would be best if he could somehow remain attached to the boat, especially if the other crew member was asleep below. Therefore, we rigged up a 100-foot floating polyester water-ski line, with a bowline at the end and knots tied in it every three feet. This line we secured in a coil to the stern pulpit on the port quarter. In rough conditions at night, we simply trailed this floating line astern; it was light and floated high, causing very little drag and seldom snaring sargasso weed. With the line trailing, we knew that if one of us found himself in the water, he could stay connected to the boat. It was a simple trick to grab the floating line once we had practiced this procedure a couple of times during our shakedown cruise. Even with the boat moving at hull speed—around 8 knots—the person at the end of the line could keep his head above water by putting his arms through the bowline and floating on his back. We also tested how audible the whistle was with the off-watch crew member down in his bunk and the main cabin door closed; it could be heard easily.

Given this arrangement, we next chose what type of maneuver to employ when rescuing the person in the water. After two or three practice runs, we discovered that no turn whatsoever was needed if the person overboard were floating well and secured by the water-ski line, 100 feet astern. All the person on board had to do was stop the boat in the water, either by turning the bow through the wind and backing the jib, or, if sailing downwind, by simply letting the sheets fly. Once the way was off the boat, the victim at the end of the floating line could be pulled back to the stern quickly and easily. To get back on board in this situation, we kept a 5-foot length of thick, braided line with two bowline footholds in it attached to a stern cleat.

To rescue a person drifting free when sailing to windward, we finally settled on a slight modification of standard man-overboard procedure: the emergency jibe—reversing course by turning the bow dead downwind, rather than tacking through the wind—as our easiest course of action with only one person in the cockpit. Once the turn is made, the helmsman lets the jib sheet fly and controls the boat speed with the mainsheet. He also throws out the coiled water-ski line (if not already deployed), and rounds up on the mainsail once he's reached a point slightly to windward of the victim's position; the boat then slips slowly downwind, and the floating line is dragged in a closing loop across the victim. The helmsman stops the boat, and the victim is pulled on board.

To carry out this maneuver when sailing downwind, the helmsman first beats up to windward on the same tack (to prevent having his view blocked by the sails), reaches a point a couple of boat lengths upwind of the victim, then tacks. Once through the tack, the helmsman lets the jib sheet fly and controls the boat speed in the same method described above (Figs. 5 and 6).

These maneuvers might seem complicated, but, after proper practice, we found them practical—maybe the only efficient and dependable methods a person in a boat alone can use to rescue his crew mate who has gone overboard on a dark and stormy night.

Fire and burn hazards below decks: A lot has already been written on this subject, and prudent cruising sailors are well aware of the dangers posed by leaking stove and engine fuel or by boiling liquids.

Many first-time passagemakers, however, do not consider the problem of safely preparing hot food and drink in extremely rough seas. Gimbaled galley stoves with pot lids are fine under most conditions, but, as most offshore sailors eventually learn, there are times when it's almost impossible to safely keep a pot on a stove. As most galleys are located aft and to one side of the boat's center of gravity, the movement can be so bad that even making a mug of instant soup is a dangerous procedure.

We solved this problem by mounting a gimbaled Sea Swing canned heat stove on a midship bulkhead, where the motion was least severe. After a little hunting around, we located a small pressure cooker and a small tea kettle with a spring-loaded spout lid, both of which fit snugly into the gimbaled aluminum cup of the stove. Thus equipped, we could boil and pour water, or heat canned food and serve it, without having to remove either the tea kettle or the pressure cooker from its secure bulkhead mounting. In reality, the tea kettle-Sea Swing combination was a kind of gimbaled samovar; I've seen it merrily—and safely—humming away as the boat swooped and pounded through a vicious autumnal equinox gale off Sardinia.

Galley stove fires present another problem, one that most sailors don't always consider. In our safety plan, we eliminated most of the fuel hazards by using a two-burner, unpressurized alcohol stove. Alcohol is the only stove fuel that can be easily extinguished with water. Naturally, we kept a dry-powder chemical extinguisher near the galley, but we also had a gardener's spray-mist bottle of water in a box above the stove: a tool that could be used to quickly squelch small fuel flare-ups without resorting to the overkill of the fire extinguisher. To put out grease fires, we kept a plastic canister of baking soda in the galley spice rack.

We decided to store our alcohol stove fuel in a heavy-duty plastic jerry can, which was, in turn, stowed inside a large plastic bucket in the lazaret, well protected from punctures or tip-spills. How you choose to store your flammable liquids or stove fuel is a matter best settled by you and your crew. It is important, however, that you do give this potential hazard the consideration it merits.

Weather anticipation and offshore forecasts: Too many sailors I've encountered in cruising rendezvous ports such as Horta, Gibraltar, and Malta are not only unable to anticipate weather from sky signs, barometer readings, and so forth, but they're also unaware of and unconcerned about their ignorance. Obviously, the safety of a boat and its crew depends in part on how well the vessel weathers storms, and this, in turn, is dependent on how well the crew has prepared for bad weather. In short, weather anticipation should be part of any serious offshore safety plan.

We rode out a total of six gales on our first long passage from New York to Greece—one of them so severe we lay ahull for eighteen hours. And before each storm, we were reefed, battened down, and psychologically prepared to face the difficult conditions. Our ability to anticipate bad weather was a skill—in my opinion a vital part of good seamanship—which we acquired by reading several of the excellent books that are currently available on this subject, by trying to formalize our years of practical weather observation, and by keeping careful log entries on such weather indicators as barometer tendency, progression of cloud cover, wind progression (backing or veering), and swell direction. Nothing about this system is mysterious or even very complicated, and we found that keeping abreast of the weather conditions gave us a comforting sense of involvement with our marine environment.

For storm warnings, we relied on the WWV short-wave frequencies (2.5, 5, 10, 15, 25 MHz) and on the voice broadcasts of the British Ministry of Trade; these latter frequencies may change somewhat during the year, but they can be obtained from the *British Admiralty List of Radio Signals,* volume 5.

In conclusion, I'd like to comment on the relative formality and complexity of a safety plan for offshore cruising. Some readers may feel that the plan Carol and I developed would be better suited for a bicentennial anniversary cruise of the Bounty with Captain Bligh replaced by a Teutonic efficiency expert. Indeed, I'm aware that many sailors go offshore expressly to *escape* the constraints of regulation-bound life ashore. To them I would simply say this: ocean passagemaking is analagous to Himalayan mountaineering or polar exploration; following the skilled discipline that has been handed down to us by generations of professional seamen does not erode enjoyment or freedom. In fact, one definition of freedom is having control over one's own destiny. To me, good seamanship—as exemplified by a solid offshore safety plan—epitomizes this control.